# Chance's Children

*By Frank Perry*

# Prologue

Taulgir stood in the failing light. One foot was poised on the bottom step of the temple, the other, planted in the dusty village street. He stared up at the doors leading into the sanctuary. Through the opening, golden candle light illuminated the face of the god in the niche against the backwall. Peace. The god's image invited him into the temple. A cool breeze cut through his threadbare tunic, hinting at a colder wind, later tonight. Around him were the lights of homes that weren't his. On the wind was the smell of suppers he couldn't share.

He turned his gaze down to his feet. It would be so simple to lift up a foot, simple and irreversible. He could step up and into the temple, and the life of a priest. Or, he could step back into the street and make his own way in the world. Either way he would not return to his old life. That was a path that was now closed to him. After a lifetime of being passed from cousins to uncles, he'd found himself with a second-cousin who took him as a apprentice glass-blower. Now that too was over.

It ended like the rest, driven out because of the accidents and misfortunes that followed him like a stray dog. This time it had been the roof of the furnace collapsing. It was all so stupid. It wasn't his fault that the furnace was old, and the bricks crumbling. Even if he had wanted to go to the Quarter Fair that day instead of working at the furnace, he couldn't be blamed. But it always happened: a sick cow, a drought or a fallen roof, and everyone was quick to say "It's Taulgir's fault" or "He has the Evil Eye."

Now he was done with them all. As he peered into the temple, before him, the pull to enter was strong. Once inside the bronze doors, he could surrender to Peace and let the past fade away. Inside was the home he'd never had.

But the pull of the deepening night, at his back, was waxing. It called to something deep within him, something that answered back. He had survived the evils that plagued him because his pride would not let him give up. Now that pride woke and called out to the darkness. His pride would not let him yield to a god. Why should he be the one to bend when others rejected him? Let them look out for themselves. Why should he put his hope in the hands of the god? His hopes and dreams were his own. Let the gods, too, look out for themselves.

Sneering up into temple, he lifted his foot from the step and, turning, stepped out into the street, into the night.

A soft scraping sound woke Thord. The boy raised his head from his bedroll, brushing the long, blond hair back from his eyes, to catch a glimpse of a red fox dragging his new sword, scabbard and all, down a hole in the rocks, just twenty feet from his camp.

"Gods!" he shouted. "Drop that!"

But by the time he had gotten to the hole, the sword was gone. He stuck his arm into the hole as far as it would reach and got a nip on his hand.

"You damned thief!" He sucked on his bitten finger as he cursed. From the hole came a yipping and barking that sounded close to laughing. He tried shifting the boulders that formed the mouth of the hole but they were too heavy for even his broad shoulders and strong arms to budge. The only result of kicking, cursing, and throwing stones down the hole was more of what he was now sure was laughter. When he finally gave up on recovering his sword, he sat on his bedroll and brooded.

He had started his Passage with the sword, given to him by his uncle. A sword and three silver pieces were the normal gifts when a sixteen year old boy made the Passage into manhood. That was when he had started the lone, three-day trek across the mountain pass named The Brow of Fate. When he began he had hoped for a vision or an omen. But instead of meeting a dragon or dreaming of ships and crowns, he had woken up to see his sword disappear into a hole in the rocks. Now at sixteen, his life was already over. His sword was lost and his hopes with it.

Now if that was an omen, Thord thought, it was not one his father would be pleased with. Even if it was just a hungry fox looking for something to chew on, he knew it would be seen as an omen. The result would still be the same. There was no sword in his future. He was not destined to find glory or treasure. Nor would he serve as a mercenary guard to a great eastern king. When his father heard this, Thord would be stuck on the farmstead for the rest of his life. Without a sword, there was no chance for adventure out beyond the cold islands of his homeland.

After another, more desperate, try at moving the rocks from around the hole, he gave up. He ate a cold sausage and tied his bedroll back on his pack. Throwing one last stone down the hole, accompanied with a curse on all thieves four-footed and two-footed, he hauled the pack onto his shoulders. With his hand he swept back his blond hair from his face and started down the mountain.

The early summer sunlight flooded the trail in front of him. Snow sparkled from the peaks above him as he walked. Under his feet, the trail descended from the rocky heights into the dark pine woods below. The only sounds were of his boots crunching on the bare trail beneath him, his cloak snapping in the light breeze, and the rattle of the contents in the pack on his broad back shifting as he walked. Beyond the forests lay the blue sea, dotted with ice floes breaking off the great rivers of ice that pushed their way down from the mountains. His destination lay a day's walk ahead. He had climbed from the east into these mountains three days ago as a child. He had crossed over the Brow of Fate, the saddle between the two white-peaked mountains that rose like horns above the pass. Now he was walking out of the mountains into the west as a man.

Below him, the trail turned and he saw the first sign of habitation since he had started his Passage. At the edge of the forest, half way into the dark pines stood a small thatch-roofed house and a smithy. Its big doors on both sides of a corner stood open, letting in light and a view of mountains at Thord's back. The trail brought Thord to a few yards from where the anvil stood on a heavy block of wood just inside. On the anvil lay two pieces of curved iron beside a heavy hammer, and nearby sat a wooden bucket full of water with the handle of an iron ladle sticking out of it. As Thord approached, he could hear the creak and whoosh of a bellows inside the smithy. In the shadows inside, he saw a bearded face lit from below with a red light from the coals of the hearth. Just as he was about to pass, the smith came out with a white-hot iron bolt held in a long pair of tongs.

The smith was a big man with thick arms and hands. Despite the cool mountain air, he wore only wool trousers and a leather apron. His thick, black hair and beard were matched by thick patches of black hair that stuck out from his chest and arms.

"Hello lad," the smith called out when he caught sight of Thord. He walked to the anvil and dropped the bolt into the metal pieces to form a hinge. "You must be thirsty. Have a drink," he said, pointing with the tongs at the water bucket.

Thord saw the smith flip the metal over and begin beating on the end of the cooling bolt to flare it and keep it in place. When Thord had finished drinking half of the ladle, the smith stopped pounding on the iron and looked up at him.

"Pour the rest of that over this for me. If you would."

Pouring the remaining water in the ladle onto the iron, Thord realized that the smith was making a wide, heavy slave collar. When the hissing stopped, the smith took the collar in his hands and pulled on the two pieces until the muscles in his shoulders bulged with the strain.

"Yes," he said peering at the collar. "That will hold the two together."

The smith looked at Thord and then back up the trail from the mountains. "You must be done with your Passage. I hope the Gods have given a sign that pleases you."

"If the gods have given me a sign, I'm not sure I like it," Thord replied. "The only thing that has happened is a fox stole my sword."

"That's bad news, lad, and not just for the reason you think. You're off the trail and will need to backtrack a ways to the main path, and there's an outlaw in these hills between here and the town. Without a sword, your life's not worth the pack on your back. Or perhaps it's worth just that. We can't let you travel down to the town without something to protect yourself." The smith turned back toward the forge. "'Prentice!" he yelled.

A small lad of about ten came from the inside. His bright red hair stood out against the dirty white of his tunic. "Yes, sir!"

"Have we any swords in the back? This young man has lost his and needs something to replace it."

Thord perked up at the term "young man." He was a man now that he had finished the Passage of the mountain. Whether or not the sword was an omen, he was still a man. The thought brought his broad shoulders a little squarer and he straightened up to his full six feet.

"Well, we don't have any swords. You've been making plows and scythes for a long time now. We do have that axe you made. But will that do?"

"It'll have to do. Go and fetch it."

He turned back to Thord. "It's not a sword, but it should convince any robbers that you're more trouble than you're worth. I made it some time back but it seemed nobody wanted it. Axes are out of fashion these days. Until lately it's been so peaceful here that I've not made any weapons for a long while. That will be changing, I fear."

The apprentice staggered out of the smithy, barely able to carry the axe. It was of an old style. The broad head flared from less than a palm's width at the haft to a full foot at the curved cutting edge. The pole stuck out the back of the head in the form of a heavy, square-pointed spur, about four inches long and slightly curved to form a hook. The haft was three feet of hard wood reinforced with iron bands spaced the full length. The smith took the axe and held it up to the light.

"Yes," he said, more to himself than to anyone else. "This will do."

He turned and extended the haft to Thord. "Try this. You look like you've the arms and shoulders to make use of it."

Thord was surprised to heft the axe so easily. When he had seen the apprentice lug it into the yard, it seemed like it was all the boy could do to lift it, but now that it was in his hands it felt light, almost nimble. He shrugged off his pack and, stepping back from the smith, took a few practice swings. While he had used an axe to cut down trees, Thord had never practiced with a war axe before. As the smith had said, axes were old-fashioned and few of those who called themselves warriors would use them. The only man Thord knew who had used an axe was his great-uncle Thurstein. Forty years ago he had been unusual in carrying one. Even so, Thord liked the balance. While it moved with a deliberate arc, a pull or push of his arm could change the speed and direction as easily as any sword he had practiced with. The blade looked able to remove an arm or leg without slowing down. The spur could punch through any armor a man could wear and still remain standing. Brushing the dust from the head, Thord saw the steel was marked with the faint pattern left by the hammer . There was no trace of rust on the blade, the edge looking as if it had just been whetted.

"You're wondering how much I'll charge you," the smith said as Thord handed back the axe. "Well, I wouldn't sell it for less than six silver pieces but that it has a flaw in the head."

Thord gazed at the axe. He hadn't seen anything but the smooth steel.

"Oh, it's nothing you could see by just looking." The smith must have caught Thord's glance. "But it's there in the metal. I can maybe fix it in a day or two but I'd have to charge for it. Or you can have it now, as it is, for two silvers. Don't worry. The one who sees the flaw will fix it. But it will keep you safe well enough until then. Fair?"

Thord couldn't see any problem with the axe. He needed something and the price was in his pouch with a silver piece to spare. His uncle was waiting for him at the end of the trail for the return home and he couldn't wait even if he'd had the other three silvers.

"Yes, I'll take it, as is."

"Good lad!" And the deal was done.

Thord slipped the axe haft through his belt and handed the smith the silver. As he turned and began walking back up the path, the smith winked at his apprentice and the boy flashed back a wide grin. If Thord had glanced over his shoulder just then, he would have noticed that the apprentice wasn't built as heavily as he had thought and that his ears were quite hairy, a bit pointed and rather high on his head for a boy. As he walked, Thord could not hear the roars of laughter that flowed down from the empty clearing where the forge had been. While he was deaf, others, far off, heard the laugh.

\*\*\*

Later that day, when Thord reached the town at bottom of the mountain, he met the priest who took the omens of those who made the Passage.

"Smith? What smith? There's no one that lives in those hills." The priest looked worried when Thord told him of his trek. "You say the smith had black hair and his apprentice had red hair?" When Thord nodded, the priest said more to himself than to Thord, "Gods, what is going to happen now? Vorkki and Nikki!"

Thord's neck hairs prickled at the name of the god who was also called "The Joker," "The Trickster" or "Chance," and the name of his companion, a red fox, sometimes called "Luck".

"You must be mistaken," Thord put in. "The fox stole my sword. Wouldn't that mean Chance has given me a peaceful life?"

"Oh, it would have if it had ended there. But Vorkki met you and you bought an axe from him. An axe with a flaw did he say?" The priest shied away as he looked at the axe thrust through Thord's belt. "It can at best mean war and at worst… Only the Gods can tell. He left you with one silver piece, though. That leaves some hope that you will prosper. May you have good fortune," the Priest gave the blessing. But as he spoke, he seemed doubtful that his words would have any effect.

At that, there was more laughter on the mountain. Only this time, Thord heard it echoing in his head.

***

From across the table, an eight-year-old boy watched a troop of entertainers perform in the palace hall. Gaudily dressed clowns scampered after each other swinging huge paddles, while tumblers did somersaults and stood on one another's shoulders. The young prince sat beside his father at the center of the high table. The king's outstretched hand held a goblet, one finger extending to point at a young woman sliding a thin sword blade down her throat. "Look at that, Nicki. There's how to eat skewered lamb without a napkin."

But the boy only had eyes for the juggler. The man was a blur of motion in the center of hall. He stood in the center of the room, where the ceiling was highest. In his red and white piebald costume, the juggler's feet danced under an umbrella of whirling arms and flying objects. The only part of the man that Nicki could see clearly was the red hair and the laughing face. The young man was weaving a pattern in the air with five rings. All Nicki could do was watch. Five? No, now a sixth ring was in the air. The new one seemed different, less a ring than a band, and shiny iron grey where the others were of different, bright colors. The new ring caught the light from the candles and threw it back in tiny sparks that grabbed at Nicki's attention.

Nicki slid from his chair and popped up on the other side of the table. Looking up, the smiling face of the juggler was framed by the whirling rings. Nicki was drawn to the juggler's dancing and began to dance, himself. With each step he took, the juggler's face grew bigger and brighter, until it and the rings filled the hall. Red, blue, green, yellow, white and grey, the rings flew. Soon, all that remained was the face of the juggler and the grey ring. The boy watched the ring sail up into the air. The band floated up three times. The last time, it drifted up and was lost in the ceiling, never to come down. Then there were only five rings again. Nicki looked at the juggler, who winked at him and laughed all the harder. To the young prince, the laugh echoed loud in his head until it spilled out of him and his own laughter joined the Juggler's. Together, they danced.

## *Chapter 1*

Prince Nicolio sat at a table in the palace library. The shelves of books filled the walls on three sides. The room was bathed in light from the tall, narrow windows making up the fourth side. In front of him was a thick manuscript on the practice of kingship. Looking across the table he could see his tutor, the court wizard Ganian, pacing in front of him, lecturing on the duties of a king. Facing Nicolio at the opposite end of the room, a middle-aged scribe was working at a copy stand. The scribe's face bore a grimace, clearly showing what he thought of the wizard's voluble lecture style in the sanctity of his library.

Ganian stopped in front of Nicolio. He placed his hands on the table and leaned forward. "Tell me, what is a king's role in his kingdom?"

Nicolio was bored. It hadn't always been this way. This old man had taken over his education two years ago, when he was fifteen. At first the prince was thrilled with the things that Ganian taught him. The wizard's knowledge of the stars and weather, of plants and animals, was beyond anything Nicolio had imagined. His knowledge of foreign countries and peoples was even more interesting. But six months ago, his tutoring changed. He could point to the exact moment. Nicolio had been learning court dancing with the Master of Protocol when Ganian had stormed into the room and ordered them to stop. Ganian insisted that there were more important things for a prince to learn and there would be no more dance lessons. Since then, his life had become a grind of study followed by more study. The freedom that had been his as third prince was gone. Now there was only a numbing routine of classes and more classes. "A king's role is to govern the kingdom," he answered, the question too obvious for a second thought.

"Wrong! A king has to serve the people of his kingdom," Ganian almost shouted. "A king is more a servant than is the lowest slave. A slave has one master, a king is the slave to all his people. Before a king can govern wisely, he has to know what it is to be a slave. Only then can he can understand what it is to be a king." His eyes bore into Nicolio from under his thick white eyebrows. "How could you rule well if you don't understand the lives of all your subjects from the highest to the lowest?"

If only he could see the lives of the people in slums, Nicolio thought. With that, a vision of walking at night through the slums of the city sprang into his mind. Now that would be an adventure! Until six months ago, he had been able to make other forays into the worlds of the merchants and craftsmen in disguise. He had slept in a merchant's tent at a

1

caravansary. Dressed as a merchant's son, he had walked the streets in the craft quarters watching how swords were made, and had haggled over the price of barrels. But he had never gotten to the wharves or to the slums that separated them from the better parts of the capital. That would be a new area full of new people and new sights. If he could view the city from bottom he would be able to see how real people lived. He would find out what they talked about and how they thought about their lives.

"How can I know about their lives if I am kept cooped up in the palace like some prize parrot?" Nicolio retorted. "If you want me to know about the common people, I need to get out more and see them. Let me visit the slums and the docks, where the real people live."

Ganian's eyes lit up. "You want to see how the lowest people live? There is a way you can do that. Not as a prince or even as a merchant's son, but dressed as a slave you would see the city as it really is and feel a part of it. Do you think you can carry that off? It would be risky, but as a slave you would be invisible, and being invisible, nothing would be hidden from you."

"Yes, I can do that. I'll go with Sergeant Borodo as his slave. I'll be safe with him."

"Are you sure you can do this?" the wizard asked. "To carry this off, you will need to act as a slave down to the smallest detail. You will need to become Borodo's slave for the evening."

"I can do it." Nicolio nodded. How hard could it be? The palace slaves did it every day, and he was a prince.

"Then we are finished for this morning." The prince thought Ganian sounded too happy, like a man who just got the better of a bargain Nicolio didn't know was being struck. "I want you to think about how you will play at being a slave and come back before dark this evening. Dress for the role you will play and bring the sergeant with you. Ask him to think of a place to take you. It should be someplace where you can see the underside of the city and still come back in one piece."

***

Late that afternoon Nicolio and Sergeant Borodo walked toward the wizard's study. In his role of Borodo's slave boy, the prince had dressed in a short, black tunic with a yellow belt, hair band, and matching yellow sandals. The bottom of the short tunic left most of his bare legs showing. At seventeen, he was slight and didn't have a beard worth growing. He looked more like he was fifteen. His hair was short and black, matching his tunic.

They found Ganian talking with King Merigo. The two were gazing out the window at the city beneath them. The wizard was dressed in the same blue robe he had worn that morning. The prince's father was dressed for dinner in a white tunic and hose. Both men were tall and lean. They were a lot alike, thought Nicolio. When the king turned to say something to Ganian, the prince was struck by the similarity of their profiles. From this angle, the wizard looked more like the king than did Duke Marcalo, the king's brother. Their faces shared a nobility that was not present in Nicolio's uncle.

"Are you certain this is a good idea?" his father was asking the wizard.

"He has many things to learn and this is one of them. Don't worry for his safety. He will be safer than you think."

His father turned when Nicolio and Borodo entered.

"Nicki, I am not sure I like this. Are you sure you want to do this? Ganian says it is important for your education, but there are risks." Nicolio's father looked him up and down. "You know what the queen will say when she sees you."

"Yes, father. Borodo will be there to protect me and as a slave, no one will notice me."

His father looked from his son to Borodo. Nicolio saw him glance down. He must have seen Borodo's sword because he nodded. "I will let you go, but I want you to keep your eyes open. You are there to learn, so pay attention to everything. When you return, I will want to hear everything you've seen and heard."

"Father, Ganian says that a king has to be a slave to his people. Is that true?"

Merigo glanced toward Ganian. "While I agree with Wizard Ganian in most things, in this case I must say there is more he left unsaid. Nicki, to be a king is not just to be a slave to the people but also to be a slave to Fortune. The king that pretends to be neither does so at the risk of his kingdom and his life."

He turned to Borodo, who bowed. "I know I don't have to remind you to keep him safe. You've done just that for the past ten years. Just keep him out of too much mischief. I don't want to explain Nicki's behavior to the captain of the watch tomorrow."

"Yes, Your Majesty."

Turning back to Nicolio the king continued, "Now I have to speak to the guard captain. Stop by the private dining room before you go out."

"Yes, father."

With that the king took his leave of Ganian and left the three of

3

them alone.

The wizard strode up to Nicolio. "Let me look at you." He put his hands on the prince's shoulders and turned him slowly around. "Not bad. But to play the part of a slave you need one more thing."

The wizard turned and picked his way across the floor, through piles of books, back to a carved wooden cabinet. Opening the door, he pulled out a wide, heavy iron collar. "With this on, no one will suspect you are anything more than what you pretend to be. Hold your chin up."

As Nicolio raised his head, Ganian placed the collar around his throat. The collar closed with a loud snap. The cold iron on Nicolio's neck sent a shiver down his back.

"You do have the key?" Nicolio asked.

"Yes, certainly. It's right here." Ganian went back to the cabinet, but came back empty-handed. "Oh. I must have misplaced it. Don't worry, I'll find it before you come back to the palace. Now I want you to tell me what you expect to learn tonight."

An hour later, the prince and Borodo approached the royal dining room. As they reached the door, they met Nicolio's second brother, Dario. First Dario's eyes passed over Nicolio to Borodo. When he opened his mouth to speak to the sergeant, his eyes snapped back to Nicolio.

"Well, what have we have we here?" Dario walked around Nicolio as he spoke. "Well Nicki, it looks like you've finally found where your talents lie. So, you've gotten so many pages and slave boys into your bed you've decided to join them. Very pretty."

The jab hit home and Nicolio flushed red. But he had always stood up to his less favorite bother in the past and this was not to be an exception. "Say what you will, Dario, but my bedmates don't have to be packed off after four months, with a fine dowry, to some country baron's youngest son,."

Nicolio's response touched an old sore that would have started a fight if Sergeant Borodo hadn't stepped between them with a quick, "Princes, is this the place for brawling? Wouldn't this be better settled on the practice grounds tomorrow?" The thought of a bout with single sticks, and the welts and bruises that even the winner would carry away as a trophy, cooled both princes down. The two turned and passed between the two impassive blond giants who stood on either side of the door. If the guards had understood what had passed in front of them, they gave no sign. The guards stood stolid, just as generations of their forbearers had stood. The only difference between these two and the two that stood before this door three hundred years earlier was the depth that the tips of their bare sword blades had worn where they rested, in the hard stones of the floor.

The two princes and Borodo entered a dark wood paneled room with a massive, marble topped table surrounded by carved wooden chairs. Dario stepped to the side and, mimicking the majordomo, proclaimed, "Your Highnesses, your son."

With that, everyone in the room looked at Nicolio as he entered behind Dario. Nicolio had expected something like this from his brother, so he was prepared. Instead of feeling embarrassed, he used the time to study the faces in front of him. His father had the face of a man who knew this was coming and was preparing himself for an assault from his wife. His oldest brother, Danalo, wore the same expression, an affable bafflement, that marked his face at any change in a well worn routine. Danalo's young bride was easier to read but more mercurial. Several expressions seemed to shift in and out of her eyes. Nicolio thought at one moment, she was amused by the antics of this, to her, foreign royal family. At another moment she looked peeved at not having gotten an invitation to the costume ball. In the end, her good nature took over and she settled into a demure smile while she waited for the whole thing to be explained.

Nicolio's mother had a very different face. She turned on her husband and demanded, "What is going on? Why is your son dressed like some cheap boy from the docks?" The stress she placed on the 'your son' implied that she held her husband completely responsible for this outrage.

"I told you earlier that Nicki was going to the lower city tonight and that he was going in disguise. Nicki and Ganian came up with this as a way for him to attract less attention."

She turned to face Nicolio. When their eyes met, he could see the fire she was about to set loose. He was waiting for the blast when her eyes lost focus for a moment. He had seen his mother's eyes shift like this once before. That was when he was twelve and she announced at breakfast that her father had just died. It took a week for the news to arrive by ship. When her eyes cleared, the fire had changed to something else. Her gaze passed around the room, at the other faces, and when she came back to Nicolio the fire was gone. It had been replaced by something new to Nicolio. Where there had been anger, there was a sadness he had not seen before. "It's all right, Nicki. You must go. But before you leave, a toast." When everyone had a goblet in their hand, she raised hers, "To Family." When the toast was done, she looked at him and quietly said, "Go now."

***

Later that night, Sergeant Borodo walked down the back streets near the waterfront. Two paces behind him Prince Nicolio followed. But no, Borodo thought, it wasn't Prince Nicolio who followed, but Nicki, his slave. And he wasn't Sergeant Borodo, but Merchant Borodo, and Merchant Borodo was out looking for an evening of entertainment in the low parts of the capital.

Borodo was dressed in green. His short coat and hose were in a style favored by the people of the Wameer forests where he grew up. Saying that if he needed to look the part of a traveling merchant, he should wear something from his travels, he had topped his outfit with a red feathered cap from the far western shores of the Home Sea. On the right side of his belt he wore a small money pouch. On the left he carried a short, heavy-bladed sword.

Squish!

"The Mother's Arse!" Borodo cursed as his boot landed in a pool of dark muck hidden in an even blacker pool of shadow. "Watch your step, Nicki."

Borodo caught the sound of a barely stifled laugh coming from behind him.

The streets they were passing through were some of the oldest in the city. If there had ever been a design to them, newer buildings and older boundary quarrels had long since given the street plan over to chaos. Buildings in this part of the city were mostly of brick or stone. Given the night mist and the half-rotted state of the few wooden structures they passed, Borodo thought only masonry must last more than a score of years this close to the harbor. But even the brick and stone buildings showed signs of neglect with loose shutters and sagging eaves.

For the most part, the streets were lined with two-story shops and warehouses. This late at night, all of these were closed and heavily shuttered. Some of the buildings were obviously mansions left over from times when this part of town was more fashionable. Most of these were now inns and brothels serving the seamen and stevedores. These were definitely wide open. Their doors spilled light, sound, and the occasional drunken patron onto the streets.

As they were approaching one of the inns, two sailors staggered out, arms over each other's shoulders giving some stability to their progress. When they passed, they lurched closer to Nicolio. The closer one belched something into his friend's ear and laughed. Borodo heard a yelp from behind him.

This time it was Borodo's turn to stifle a laugh. He could sense what had happened by the way the footsteps behind him converged and by the sudden intake of the prince's breath. A quick look behind him confirmed what he thought. The two sailors were still laughing and staggering down the street while the prince was rubbing his backside. What better proof of how good the prince's disguise was than to be pinched by a drunken sailor?

Borodo hoped that exposure to the real world might dampen his charge's taste for "adventures" but he doubted it. The prince was always looking for something new. Borodo thought the prince must feel insignificant when compared to his brothers. There hadn't been a third royal prince in several hundred years. First sons became king. Second sons led the armies. As the third son, no one knew just what was expected of the boy. The prince was smart and inquisitive. He soaked up everything that his tutors gave him. He had a positive gift for languages and already could speak several spoken in nearby lands, and he was fluent in the common trade tongue. The simple fact was that the prince had everything but a purpose.

When they came closer to the waterfront Borodo found the place he was looking for. He had made some discreet inquiries and been given the name of The Green Lady as a bar where sailors and stevedores hung out. His source suggested that smugglers might be a better term to describe the patrons. The advantage of such a place for his purpose was that a bar where illegal deals were made would not want to attract the attention of the city watch. Such places had an incentive for running a peaceful, orderly establishment.

Borodo pushed aside the heavy leather curtain that served as a door and entered.

***

Nicolio slipped into bar behind Borodo as the curtain fell back to block out the night.

The inside was dark, the only light coming from some smoky lamps hanging in the rafters and a few candles on some of the tables. The room smelled of smoke, sour ale, sausages and sweat. There was a bar running down the right side of the room where several clumps of men stood drinking from wooden mugs and speaking in low voices. Tables were scattered around the other walls. Nicolio followed Borodo as he moved to occupy the last empty table near the back. Nicolio could see a large man sitting at the next table as Borodo sat down. From the long blond hair falling down his back and a thick, drooping mustache, Nicolio could tell he was a Floelander, like his father's guards.

Nicolio moved to stand against the wall between Borodo and the

Floelander. As he stood there, he felt the presence of the man beside him. There was something about him that attracted Nicolio, a raw power that he hadn't felt from the other men he knew.

Shortly, a middle-aged woman came over and demanded what Borodo wanted.

"I am a merchant from Wameer and don't know the local beers. What have you got that's not bitter?" Borodo asked.

"You'll want the lager, then," she replied.

"Good enough. I'll have a mug," Borodo said. "And a cup for the boy," he added hooking a thumb at Nicolio.

"Will you be wanting more?" The barmaid turned and asked the Floelander.

"Not just yet," he replied. His voice was low and softer than Nicolio expected. His speech was slow as if he were working out the words one at a time. The accent was not as heavy as the new arrived palace guards and marked him as someone who had spent some time away from the islands that made up the Floelands.

Nicolio was beginning to feel warm as he stood near the Floelander. He watched out of the corner of his eye, while the man stared into the bottom of his mug for a few moments. The Floelander seemed to come to a decision for he smiled, took a long drink and turned to face Borodo.

"Good evening to you. I am Thord Thurgoodson," he said. "I heard you say you are a traveling merchant. I am thinking to take a position as a guard. Will you be hiring guards soon?" The Floelander spoke in the slow formal speech of all of that people.

As Borodo turned toward the Floelander, he glanced at Nicolio, who winked with the eye toward Borodo. "Well, I might need someone for the return trip. Are you good with that?" Borodo pointed behind the Floelander's table.

For the first time, Nicolio noticed that leaning against the wall was a great-axe. The haft was three feet of dark wood, reinforced with iron bands, the head resting on the floor. The edge was a foot of steel, while the back of the head ended in a heavy, slightly curved spur.

The Floelander's eyes seemed to focus on the distance.

"I am alive," he said softly, with a slight emphasis on the word I.

The Floelander was a young man, twenty-five maybe. Nicolio saw he had huge shoulders that filled what should have been a loose fitting tunic. His golden hair spilled down over those shoulders. He had a mustache that drooped below the corners of his mouth. He looked toward Nicolio, who found himself staring into the bluest eyes he had ever seen.

8

The blue was set with glints of gold from the candle on the table. He felt himself being pulled into those eyes. It was as if the blue ocean was sucking him into its depths. If the barmaid hadn't shown up with the ale, Nicolio thought he would never be able to look away.

Nicolio took a quick drink of his ale to clear his head. As Borodo took a pull on his mug, the Floelander turned his chair to face him.

"This is not a night to be drinking alone. In my country this night is sacred to Vorkki, the god of chance. Here you sometimes call him Fortune. Please join me. We will have some drink from my homeland and maybe play Vorkki's Bones."

Borodo shifted his chair to the Floelander's table.

"I'm called Borodo and this is my slave, Nicki."

The Floelander's eyes lit up. He reached behind him to pull a heavy sea chest and drag it between himself and Borodo.

"Sit down, little Nikki. This does call for drink, I am thinking. In my homeland, Nikki is 'the little fox' and is Vorkki's companion."

# Chance's Children

## *Chapter 2*

Borodo's head felt as though someone had put an iron bucket over it and was beating out a reveille drum roll. He opened his eyes and saw the scarred wood of a table top and, beyond its edge, a room full of people. All shouting and gesturing. Gods, what a night! Whatever the Floelander had ordered had tasted vile but had a kick that was still making his head reel. They had drunk and diced for hours. Thord had been full of stories about the lands to the north and west. Borodo had watched Nicolio drink up the stories and drink up whatever had been placed in his cup. He couldn't complain about that, as he had matched the Floelander drink for drink himself. That was a mistake. After a few hours, Nicolio had been so drunk all the lad could do was moon at the Floelander, nod his head and giggle. The last thing Borodo could remember was losing Nikki at dice. That would be a funny... Losing Prince Nicolio to a Floelander at a game of dice! Gods, no!

Borodo looked around but there was no trace of either the prince or the Floelander. He lurched to his feet and charged through a loud, jostling crowd to the bar.

"The boy and the Floelander I was drinking with last night, where are they?" Borodo demanded of the red-eyed barman.

"Gone," came the reply. "He settled the tab and left you these," the barman said. The man reached under the bar and handed Borodo a pair of dice.

Borodo clutched the dice and demanded again, "Where are they?"

"Gone, I said. The Floelander paid up and gave me the dice to give to you. He said you would want to see them. Said you could try winning the slave back, next time you meet."

Pointing to a man at the back of the crowd, the barman said, "He hired Elgar and his barrow there, to carry the lad, his winnings he called him, down to the docks. He hoisted his sea chest on his shoulder and that was the last I saw of either of them."

Borodo stood there dumb. Gods, the king would have him flayed alive. As he thought of what would happen, he started to make sense of the hubbub around him. He heard the words palace and traitors over and over.

Turning to one of the men, he asked, "What happened at the palace?"

"Haven't you heard? The king's Floelander guard killed the king and his three sons. They killed the whole family. Gods give them peace.

The Grand Duke Marcalo stormed the palace and killed all the Floelanders but couldn't save the royal family."

Borodo stumbled back to his table. He needed to think. Dead, all dead. No. Nicolio was alive. What should he do? Duty said he should return to the palace and report that the prince was alive. The problem with duty was that the duke would either have him flayed for losing the prince or have him murdered for knowing the prince was alive. The more he thought about it, the more the latter possibility looked the more likely. Borodo knew the Royal Guards and he trusted them a lot further than he trusted the king's brother. The only choice was to find the prince and rescue him. No, not the prince, but now the rightful king! But where was he to start?

Six. Borodo absently tossed the dice while he thought. Nine. At the same time he made the decision to follow the Floelander he realized why the Floelander had left the dice. Four. He wanted Borodo to know the dice were not crooked. The prince had been lost – and saved! – by a fair throw of the dice.

* * *

Thord sat on the sea chest in the small cabin and looked at the young man sleeping in front of him. Let him sleep, he thought. There was no need to rush into this day.

Thord smiled as he looked at his prize. He knew this was the stupidest thing he had ever done. It was likely that this would get him killed. But the Little Fox was so beautiful, the risk was worth it. He had been attracted to him the morning before, when he had caught a glimpse of him from across a courtyard in front of the palace. Striding past the guards into the palace, he was beautiful but out of reach. But when he had seen him walking into the tavern wearing that collar, it was more than just a physical attraction; the desire was immediate, attainable. It was a long time since he had felt something this strong for anyone. He knew then that he had to have him.

He reached out to lift one of the black locks. The curl of soft hair slid off his finger to lie with the others. As he reached out again with a callused hand, a knuckle touched the iron collar under those locks. The cold metal sent a shiver up his arm. But instead of pulling his hand away, he left it against the iron. Rather than cool him, the metal had the opposite effect. The cabin suddenly became closer and warmer. The desire in him grew. The feeling surprised Thord. He had indulged his attraction for other men many times before, but this was stronger than he had felt for anyone for years. Now, having this Little Fox, if only for a few weeks, was worth any risk, at least for now, and the thought that he had won him at dice, on Vorkki's Night, was the finest jest he had ever heard. Vorkki, the god of chance, was sometimes called The Joker, and this was a joke to end all jokes. Thord began to chuckle when he thought about it. Then the thought came to him that he didn't have the slightest idea whom the joke was really on. With that thought, the chuckle turned into a quiet laugh and then into a roar.

\*\*\*

Nicolio felt awful. He couldn't bear to open his eyes. If the pounding ache in his head was any indication of what it was like beyond his eyelids, he didn't want to have anything to do with what was out there. His neck was sore. His arms were stiff and cramped. The bed was moving in slow circles. And to top it all, his tongue tasted like a lump of old leather. What had he been drinking? The air was full of creaks and groans and filled too, with a maniacal laughter that he couldn't place either inside or outside of his head.

He decided to risk one eye. What met that eye was not the sheer curtain of his bed and the carved and varnished panels of his bedroom, but instead, rough, tarred wood. He tried to roll from his stomach to his back but his elbow wouldn't get out of the way. His wrists were clamped together behind his back by some sort of cold hard band. He started to panic and tried to scream for help but found his mouth was stuffed with leather and he couldn't spit it out, his cry turning into a choked groan. He turned his head to face the other side and found he was looking straight into a pair of familiar blue eyes. He knew those eyes. They were the eyes of the Floelander from the bar. There were tears running down the Floelander's face as he laughed.

"Well, my Little Fox is awake," His hand reached over and tussled Nicolio's hair. "How is your head? Not too good, I am thinking," he grinned.

The Floelander got up from the chest he was sitting on to stoop under the low beams. "Don't worry, my little Nikki. Some sea air will help clear things up."

Sea air! They were on a ship! Gods. Last night came flooding back. Nicolio remembered drinking with the big Floelander and Borodo. And he remembered the game of dice and... Oh, gods no! He remembered nodding yes to Borodo, when the Floelander had suggested Borodo put him up for a stake. They had all laughed when a pair of twos,

"Lover's Eyes," had come up and the Floelander pulled him to his side. Nicolio tried to tell the Floelander it was a mistake, that it was all a prank, but all that came past the leather stuffed in his mouth was a series of grunts and groans. As he struggled to get up, a heavy hand on his back showed him how futile it was to try.

*  *  *

Thord lifted Nikki's chin and looked into his dark brown eyes. Those eyes were filled with fear now, but he hoped that would change before they reached their destination. Gods, he is beautiful! Thord thought. Whether he was worth the trouble Thord had gotten into was a question he never bothered to ask. How many times had he had risked his life for a small bag of gold? How could gold be compared to owning these brown eyes?

But to keep those eyes safe would require something from Nikki as well as the threat of Thord's axe. He needed this Little Fox to behave and try no tricks until they reached land. If his Little Fox's real name or the name of his father reached the captain or crew, it could be the death of them both. The chance for a prince's ransom would be too strong to resist.

"We must talk. Truthfully, I must talk and you must listen," he said rubbing his thumb over the leather gag and smiling at his own joke.

Thord seated himself back on the chest.

"I am your new master. I won you last night. You and your master were very drunk and I forgive you for being afraid of me. But I will not harm you."

With the back of his finger Thord brushed a hair from the face before him. The brown eyes that met his were wide with fear, but did not turn away. Beyond the fear Thord saw courage backed by intelligence. Good, Thord thought; he will need them both.

"Little Fox, I want to see how clever you are. You have not seen this ship, but it is not a large ship. The crew is very large, too many men for a ship like this. Why so many men on a ship this size? Not to sail it. I come from a country of sailors and I know how many men it takes to sail a ship. No, Little Fox, they must do something else. What trade can pay for so many men?"

When he saw Nikki's eyes go wide he continued, "Yes, I see my Little Fox is clever. Now we are safe. I am here on some business the captain would not want to go wrong. But even with that, there are some things you have to do for both of us to stay safe."

Thord looked hard at him and continued, "Never mention pirates or anything to do with them on this ship. The less they think you know, the safer you are." Thord leaned over and whispered directly into Nikki's ear. "And never say the name Welgon."

Thord saw the name sink in, the brown eyes widen and dart to the door behind where Thord sat. Welgon was the name of the son of Duke Lolgon, taken by pirates four years earlier. The story was told all over the Home Sea of how pieces of the duke's son, packed in salt, had been sent to the duke for months. Both ears, his nose, every other finger, and his tongue were all delivered to the duke before the ransom was raised. Thord saw the fear in Nikki replaced by real terror.

"Good. I see you will be good and not talk over much. We have a long voyage. While we are at sea you must behave. When we reach port and are off this ship, we can then talk and you can tell me anything you like, I promise I will listen. Do you accept this?"

Nikki nodded.

*** 

Nicolio watched as Thord took a key laying beside him on the chest and stooped over him. The Floelander grasped his wrists in one hand and the prince felt a snap as the band around them came apart. He tried to move his arms, but found the grip that held them was as strong as the iron had been.

"There, Little Fox, don't try to move too fast. Your arms will be stiff for a while." At this, Thord reached behind Nicolio and removed the leather gag. "Now, you will obey me and not cause trouble?"

Prince Nicolio thought back to a ceremony in the Temple of Mercy, two years ago. He remembered the hooded, shuffling figure in the black robe behind the row of priests. After the ceremony, he had joked about who that person could have been. His father glared at him and told him in a soft voice, that the person in the robe had been Welgon, but no longer answered to that or any name.

Nicolio looked at Thord with lowered eyelids and nodded his assent.

The Floelander reached up to a ring over Nicolio's head and untied the end of a rope. Thord gave it a few turns around his left wrist and, taking him by the shoulders, pulled him from the bunk. Nicolio struggled to pull away, but found that the rope wrapped around Thord's wrist was tied to his collar.

"There – easy, Little Fox. It is all right. I am your master now." A callused hand took Nicolio's chin and turned his face to where he was looking into those blue eyes. "Do not worry. I tell you, you are safe with me."

Safe?! Nicolio thought. How could he be safe, chained on a ship full of pirates, bound for who knows where, and in the hands of an outlander who thought he owned him?

Thord turned and pulled Nicolio through the cabin door.

The sun was high when they stepped out on deck. When Nicolio's eyes adjusted to the bright light, he flushed red as he was led by the rope into the view of a deck full of sailors.

"Hey, Floelander? Where did you get the boy?"

"If I had him, he wouldn't need to be kept on a line. I'd keep him on his back!"

As he was led across the deck at the end of the rope, Nicolio wanted to sink through the broad planks. The sailors' obvious intent made him even more aware of how helpless he was to protect himself. Nicolio found himself moving closer to the Floelander, seeking some security behind the bulk of the man's body.

Thord brought him toward the bow of the ship where a large man in a leather apron sat beside a small glowing hearth.

"Are you ready for him?" Thord asked the man.

"Aye. Sit him with his back to that," the man answered and pointed to a small anvil bolted to the deck.

Nicolio was pulled to the anvil and pushed down to sit on the deck. When his back was against the cold metal, Thord took the iron collar and turned it around to where the ring was at the back of Nicolio's neck.

Thord squatted in front of Nicolio and took hold of the collar in both hands. "Hold still, little Nikki."

"Here, put this over the boy's head," the smith came up to Thord holding out a wet cloth. "It will keep his hair from burning."

It was stifling under the sodden cloth. After some pushing, Nicolio felt something being pushed into the collar, followed by eight or ten blows from the smith's hammer. When his head was engulfed by a bucket of cold seawater, he tried to jerk free, but the Floelander's grip was unbreakable. He smelled seawater, steam, and the sharp tang of quenched iron. The cloth was pulled from his head. As Thord turned the collar around Nicolio felt cold metal drag across his shoulder.

"There, that is better. Now you have something of mine on you." He lifted a heavy, fist-sized ring from Nicolio's chest. A foot of chain ran from it to the ring on the collar.

Gripping the end of the chain on Nicolio's collar, Thord hauled him to his feet and led him back across the deck. Nicolio's face flushed as the sailors whistled and hooted. He was pulled into the low cabin and pushed onto the berth. The Floelander took the padlock and locked the chain on his collar to another chain hanging from a ring on the bulkhead.

"There now, you are not going anywhere for a while. You must be hungry and thirsty. We will have something to eat later. But before we do, we will get to know each other better."

Nicolio knew what was coming. He had done much the same with his father's slaves. But knowing what to expect and having it happen were different things. He wanted to say no, that it was all a game. But the image of the hooded figure in the Temple of Mercy stopped him. That and something else held him motionless, like a bird watching the approach of a snake. He sat, unable to move, waiting, looking into eyes filled with a blue fire that burned into him.

Thord gripped his shoulders. Twisting him, Thord shoved him down to his stomach on the coarse ticking, and pulled up the back of Nicolio's tunic. No longer held by the blue eyes, Nicolio tried to resist, but with his hands cuffed behind his back and the heavy hand pressing on his back, he was only ground further into the bedding. He was helpless.

When it was over, Thord had left the chain locked to the bulkhead. Nicolio was pushed onto the bunk with his face against the hull and Thord had climbed beside him. The Floelander now lay with an arm thrown over him and was breathing softly into his ear. Nicolio lay buried, chained and helpless, under the weight of that arm. His senses were buried too under a dull pain and the taste of tears. His face burned. Partially it was from his cheeks being rubbed into the coarse cloth but more it was from the humiliation. His shoulders ached with the strain on his arms from being cuffed behind him. Forcing the rest to the background was the pain of being used.

Over all was the smell of sweat, of sex, and of fear. He wished he could sleep and forget this had ever happened. But sleep didn't come. He wouldn't wake up and find it was all just a nightmare.

Nothing like this had happened to him before. He had never imagined that it could happen to him. Before, he had always been in control and had never given a second thought to the feelings of the pages and slaves he had pulled into his bed. The pages were his for the asking. They would tell him all the right things; they would make all the right noises for their station. He didn't flatter himself. He knew they were in his bed to advance their status. That's why he never stayed with one for more than a week. After the first few times, he realized that there were too many tangled threads left hanging from a long relationship between a prince and a page. The slaves were simpler. They didn't expect anything in return.

Now that he was no longer setting the rules, it was different. He, Prince Nicolio, had been taken and used by someone. He had never considered the pain of others. Now the pain was his and he was afraid. But what he feared was more than just the pain and humiliation that he felt. Now that it was over, the pain was subsiding. But as it receded into his memory, it was replaced by a sense of emptiness. Outside of what he knew he should feel, there was something else that he was afraid to look at. Deep inside, he had enjoyed it.

He had always seen himself as Prince Nicolio, born to a long line of kings. Waking this morning, he had become the property of an outlander. Now he had been used for the pleasure of a common warrior, no better than plunder from some sacked village. If this could happen in the space of one night, what was he? His eyes were wet with tears, but he no longer knew if their source was the pain of what he had gone through or for the image of himself that was now lost forever.

*** 

Thord lay with his arm over Nikki. He tried to use its weight to still the shivers that were racking Nikki's body. He held him to his chest, hoping to prevent those brown eyes from slipping into themselves and becoming lost.

Now that it was over, Thord was released from the need that had driven him since he had first seen his Little Fox. He thought that love was a strange thing, if love this was. Yes, this was love. He had known lust before and knew the signs, the act driven by a need that vanished like smoke when the fire is spent. But here, there was no lessening of the feeling, now that the needs of the flesh were gone. If anything, it was stronger, the fierce need changed to a fierce tenderness. He had felt this for someone before, but that seemed a lifetime ago. Indeed, it was a lifetime ago.

As he lay there, breathing softly into the black, curly hair, he thought back to another time. He had loved then with all his soul. That had begun with a tender caress and ended in blood. How would this end, after beginning in violence?

*** 

During the past week, Nicolio had settled into the rhythm of their life on the ship. Not so much a rhythm as a grind, the prince thought to himself. Every day was the same, moving over an endless sea without a hint of land. When they were on deck, their time was spent in watching the waves or in their tiny cabin. The only break in the monotony was when Thord pulled him by the collar to the narrow bed they shared. That, at least, was never boring.

Thord was on deck early every day practicing with a shield and heavy club. When he finished, Nicolio would go to the ship's cook for a hot sausage and barley gruel for their breakfast. When they were not in bed, Thord would tell stories of his homeland or ask about Nicolio's life as Borodo's slave. Nicolio found it harder and harder to keep his story straight and Thord seemed to take a great deal of pleasure from going back over the details. He was almost never allowed out of Thord's sight. He was told that Thord trusted him, but not the crew of the ship. Nicolio was just as happy with that. His tunic had been put away for the voyage and was replaced with a short loincloth. Whenever he was on deck, the prince could feel the eyes of some of the crew lusting for him. With Thord near, he felt both protected and vulnerable.

The sun was warm this morning and Nicolio stood beside Thord with his back to the rail. He was watching an old seaman at work with a mallet and chisels. He was carving a large block of wood. As the prince watched, the shape of a horse began to emerge from the block, its front hooves rearing upward and the back, disappearing into a wooden wave. The day before, the figurehead of a mermaid had been removed from the bow, split up and added to the ship's stack of firewood. The name *Sea Sprite* was painted over and *Foam's Mare* was now in its stead. He could only guess that *Sea Sprite* was unwelcome in their next port.

Looking up, Nicolio watched the main mast trace great slow circles in the sky. There was a light wind on his back and it filled the great triangle of the lateen main sail and the smaller one of the topsail. Despite its sinister trade, the ship was beautiful under sail. Or maybe it was because it was a pirate ship, and the needs of that trade, that gave it the grace it showed as it glided over the water. Grace seemed to be a trait that too often wrapped the tools of violence and death.

In the light wind, the ship slipped through the sea, leaving a foaming wake on the water to mark its passing. Nicolio peered forward to the two square sails of the foremast and could just catch a glimpse of the leeward top corner of the small square sail riding under the bowsprit, where it rose above the forecastle. Aft was the tight-sheeted triangle of the mizzen. The brilliant red and white striped sails against the blue sky made a stark contrast to the squalid scene on the deck. It was early in the day and most of the crew were drunk.

The captain stood on the quarter deck with the two men who worked the whipstaff. The part of the crew whom Nicolio now recognized as the current watch were gathered on the forecastle. The rest of the crew were either on the main deck or below. Those on deck were divided roughly into thirds, some gambling, some passed out in the leeward scuppers and some enjoying the pleasures of three slaves. The two women, lying among the bales and coils of rope, and the youth, pushed over the rail. seemed to accept their suitors with dull, mindless resignation.

Occasionally, one of the pirates would peer to where Thord and he stood. The intensity of those stares reminded the prince of his vulnerability and drove him closer to Thord's side.

Nicolio jumped when Thord put his hand on Nicolio's shoulder. He tried to step away from Thord's touch and what it implied but Thord grabbed the chain on his collar and pulled him closer. Helpless, Nicolio was pulled until his face was staring up into Thord's. Thord held him for a moment, looking down at him. Nicolio was only aware of the blue eyes and a slight smirk, framed by the drooping blonde moustache.

"Still trying to pull away, Little Fox?" For emphasis, he pulled Nicolio even closer before letting go of the chain.

The pull on his neck suddenly gone, Nicolio nearly fell before he regained his footing on the rolling deck. He stood wanting to say something back to Thord but couldn't find any words. He was powerless and hated himself because of it. His face was burning with rage and humiliation, and something more he didn't want to think about. But if Thord saw, he ignored it.

"Time, I am thinking, for breakfast." The Floelander dismissed him and turned back to watching the horizon.

Nicolio could only turn and obey. Now he was reduced to the role of servant, fetching breakfast. But even the slaves and servants in the palace carried roast meats and wine on silver platters. Here, it was made worse by carrying the rough wooden bowls of greasy porridge and sausages that made up breakfast on the ship. In the palace, the servant who brought Prince Nicolio a dish like that would be wearing it. Here, Nicolio would eat it or go hungry.

As Nicolio made his way across the deck towards the companionway that led below to the galley, he passed by a group of the gamblers. Before he reached the steps a shout from behind him spun him around. Two of the pirates had jumped up from their game. Steel flashed in the morning light. With a gurgling cry, one of the men collapsed on the deck. Nicolio stood frozen watching a stream of red blood run down the to the leeward side. The second man stooped over body and with a jerk of his dagger, cut the a heavy gold ring from the dead man's ear. Blood dripped from the gold.

A voice from above, caused Nicolio to drag his eyes from the deck to look up. The captain was leaning over the rail.

"You men, get that body over the side and wash that blood off the deck!" With that, he was gone again.

Two men came aft from the forecastle and dragged the body to the rail. The splash from the body hitting the water was matched by several buckets of water hitting the deck. Sea water streaked with red blood ran down the deck.

Stumbling, Nicolio turned away. A hairy arm shot in front of him and grabbed the chain hanging from his collar. In front of him was pirate from the fight.

"Where might you be going?" Nicolio was yanked to the side and pushed against the bulkhead. The hand gripping the chain pulled upward, the edge of the iron collar forcing him to look up into the leering face of the man. The collar cut off his breathing and he was forced onto his toes to keep from choking. He tried to pull down on the collar, but the man was too strong.

"Why don't you stay here and keep me company?"

The collar cut into Nicolio's throat choking him. What air he managed to inhale was rank with the pirate's ale-sour breath. He felt a hand moving down his side. His eye caught motion behind the pirate. A large hand appeared on his assailant's shoulder.

"Let him go." Thord's voice rang loud in Nicolio's ears.

The iron collar was no longer cutting into his throat. The face in front of him spun to the side. In front of him, Thord and the pirate faced each other.

"Hey, Floelander! How about sharing your little plaything?"

For the first time, Nicolio could see the pirate clearly. Though leaner, the man was taller than Thord. He had a long scar on his cheek and more scars on his bare chest and arms. There was a long, thin knife in a leather sheath on his belt.

"No, friend. The lad belongs to me and I am not thinking to share him."

Thord had pulled Nicolio to him with his left arm and put his right hand on the hilt of his own dagger.

"Come on, mate," the sailor drawled. "I'm called Tel Throat Slitter and I would take it as real unfriendly of you if you won't share."

Thord held Nicolio against the bulkhead as he stepped forward

21

between him and the pirate. But as the man reached for his knife, a small, one-eared man sprang between them.

"Hold on a bit, Slitter," he said and turned to Thord. Pointing to his one ear he continued, "I heard the captain call you Thord. Might it be that you are called Thord Vorkki's Child?"

"There are some who call me that."

At that, the man called Slitter gave Thord an anxious look. While he kept his hand on the hilt of his knife, he took a step back.

The small man looked at Thord and then at Slitter. "I call for Ship's Peace. Are you willing to swear to it? There's to be no fighting on board. Agreed?"

"Aye. Ship's Peace," Slitter muttered.

Nicolio peeked from behind Thord at the two pirates. Though Slitter's face put a on a brave show, an anxious hope was written in his eyes.

"Ship's Peace," grunted Thord.

The pirate let out a soft breath.

"Come along, Slitter. I'll get you a drink." One-Ear led his crewmate below and Thord took his hand off the hilt of his dagger.

When the two men had disappeared down the forward hatch, Thord drew Nicolio from behind him. Nicolio's head was pulled into the Floelander's shoulder.

"Easy, Nikki. Why do you shiver? I told you, you are safe with me. I'll see that you come to no harm. Other people pay me to keep their things safe. You don't think I would not protect my own? Don't fear."

Until Thord spoke, Nicolio was too shaken to feel himself tremble. Earlier, he had wanted nothing more than to get away from Thord, now fear drove him to push harder into Thord's side. But beyond the fear of being in the hands of the pirate there was something more. He had seen the change come over Slitter. One moment, the man had been ready to fight to the death and the next he was backing away with fear written in his eyes. Who was this man who held his arm around Nicolio's waist? Why did the name Vorkki's Child cause Slitter to back down? Vorkki was the Floelander's god of chance. Chance's Child probably meant bastard. But though Slitter didn't know Thord, the man did know the name and was afraid of Thord Vorkki's Child.

In the past week, Nicolio had started to think he knew this man who thought he owned him. And while Thord was certainly immensely strong, and he had no doubt that the Floelander was good with his axe or with the heavy dagger he carried, Slitter didn't look like a man to cringe from another's strength or his skill with a weapon. What shone in the man's eyes was closer to the fear of ghosts or demons than the fear of a man. In bed for the past week, Thord had given Nicolio ample proof that he was no ghost. Nicolio knew little of demons, but if Thord was one, he was no demon Nicolio had heard about. No, Thord was clearly a man. So who was this Thord Vorkki's Child, that his name could cause a cutthroat to back down?

Thord reached down and gripped the chain on Nicolio's collar. He pulled up until Nicolio's face was turned up, fixed on the blue of Thord's eyes. "Unless my pretty Little Fox wants to see if our friend Slitter comes back, I am thinking we should go to the cabin for a while." As Thord said this, he wrapped his other hand around Nicolio's waist and gave a little tug that briefly lifted him off his feet. "He is cool enough now, but more drink, maybe, will change that."

*** 

Later Nicolio lay beside Thord, in the cabin. The air was hot and stuffy so they had shed their clothes when they climbed onto the berth. Thord was stretched out with his back against the hull. Nicolio lay beside him. Nicolio watched him in the dim light as the Floelander slept with one arm as a pillow and his blond hair spilling on to the ticking. He snored softly.

The question came again. Who was this man next to him?

Nicolio looked over the massive shoulders and arms. There, even in sleep, the muscles stood out like cables under his tan skin. Partially blocked by one arm, the muscles of Thord's chest were slowly rising and falling. His gaze followed on down to the narrow waist and hips and he felt more than an aesthetic interest stirring in himself. He had felt drawn to the Floelander when he had first seen him in the bar. Now, he was even more unsure of what was happening. How drunk had he been that night he nodded yes to Borodo, when Thord proposed putting him up as the stake in that dice game? Nicolio remembered feeling attracted to the Floelander when their eyes first met. He had wanted him in his bed. Gods knew he had gotten what he wanted but wishes don't always come true the way you imagine. Now he was trapped. His only options were to either stay with his role as a slave or declare that he was a royal prince. And Thord's mention of the name Welgon had convinced him that he was better off in one piece as a slave than being carved up for ransom tokens.

He looked at the man beside him and thought, "If, until we reach a civilized port, I'm to play the role of catamite, I may as well play it well." With that, he rolled into Thord and buried his head in the chest that lay in

23

front of him. Thord woke just enough to bring an arm over him and pull him closer.

*** 

Marcalo closed the heavy door behind him. He was glad to be done with the stench and the screams. After putting up with it for the better part of the evening, it was good to be finished. It was troublesome that he couldn't trust this to some underling. But he didn't want word to spread that there could be a son of his dead brother still alive. Employing a deaf torturer kept any secrets in the dungeon, but it meant he had to personally oversee the questioning.

In the end, he knew little more now than when he started. After hours of questioning with the help of a hot fire, all he had learned from Nicolio's slaves was that his nephew had left the palace, dressed as a slave, in the company of the prince's body guard. Marcalo was certain the two slaves knew nothing more. Nicolio's manner with slaves was not such that he would create any loyalty. Not that any amount of loyalty would have stood long against hot irons. No, they could tell him nothing about where the prince was now. They couldn't tell anyone, anything now. Having them killed was a waste, but Marcalo couldn't allow anyone else to question them. They wouldn't have been worth much now anyway.

Marcalo knew he had to find some other way to locate his nephew. As long as Nicolio was alive, the boy was a threat. Marcalo would have to rely on his wizards. He didn't trust them, but they had been able to keep his brother's wizard, Ganian, from discovering the plot. Now he would have to deal with them again to find Nicolio.

It was too bad that Nicolio had to die. Marcalo would have preferred not to have to kill him, but that was not an option now. If only he had been able to get closer to the prince, he might have been able to convince the prince to join with him. After all, they both had suffered from the chances of birth. Marcalo should have been king but his less competent brother was born first and Nicolio was doomed by the chances of birth to be beneath his older brothers. With Marcalo's own infant daughter lost to sorcery and his wife to grief, Marcalo needed an heir. But the wizard, Ganian, had always managed to come between Marcalo and Nicolio, poisoning the prince's mind against Marcalo. It was too late now to go back on his course. Nicolio would have to die.

# Chance's Children

## *Chapter 3*

As the ship approached the city, Thord sat Nicolio on their berth. He took his chin and turned his face up so Nicolio found himself looking into Thord's eyes.

"Little Fox, I am going to trust you. But I want you to trust me. I have not harmed you and I am thinking that you started to like our time on the ship. Well, trust me for a little longer. I have business on the dock and I don't want you to cause any problem. I have something for you tomorrow that you will like. This has not been so bad, has it, my Little Fox?"

Nicolio didn't know what to do. What was Thord talking about? He had planned to sneak away at the first chance that came on shore and run to the Tronmar Embassy. But then, Nicolio had decided that he liked the Floelander. He had been put through a lot, but Thord had been more gentle than he had expected and this had, in fact, been the kind of adventure he'd dreamed of and never expected to have. Thord was certainly more fun in bed than any of the pageboys he'd had before now. This time the sex had been different because of his position as Nikki the slave. With the pageboys or slaves, there had been no chance of any sex going both ways. They had always done what he asked, but despite what they said in bed, he guessed there was little enthusiasm on their part. But Thord did more than Nicolio had expected. Thord hadn't been too rough and had shared his food and drink equally with him. Of course, he couldn't really blame Thord for any of it. As far as Thord knew, the Floelander had won him at dice and so had the right to use his property, just as, when he wanted, Nicolio had used the palace slaves. As he thought of returning to the palace and the endless routine of tutors and state dinners, Nicolio began to feel that there, he was more confined than he was with the Floelander.

It couldn't be helped. He was a prince and had to remember his station. He knew that half the army of Tronmar and all of the fleet must be out looking for him by now. But he could hold off running back for a day or two more, he told himself. He had to wait until he was sure that the local authorities knew Prince Nicolio was missing, before he would be believed. Besides, when they had settled into a routine on shore, it would be easier to escape.

He realized that Thord was looking at him. The Floelander was waiting for an answer.

"Yes, sir. I trust you." And the truth was, beyond all reason, he did.

***

From the deck, Nicolio had watched sailors in the ship's boat row a cable to the shore. Now he watched their backs straining at the capstan to warp the ship to the quay. Thord stood, wearing a chain mail hauberk, with a foot on the sea chest Thord had hauled from the cabin. One hand rested on the head of his axe, its haft grounded on the deck in front of him. Thord's other arm rested on Nicolio's shoulder, the hand lightly holding the ring on Nicolio's chain.

Nicolio gazed at the groups of people who waited on the dock as the ship tied up. A merchant waited on the quay with a wagon and a half dozen or more armed men. A line of stevedores stood at one end, waiting for work. On the street at the end of the dock a collection of slaves holding large, fringed parasols over whores in bright dresses beside even brighter dressed pimps waved and called out to the sailors.

The first up the gangplank was the merchant with half a dozen men that Nicolio thought he wouldn't like to meet on a dark street. Their hands stayed on the hilts of their swords and they had the air of people who liked using them. The merchant strode up to Thord.

"You did well," he said, looking down at the chest.

He passed Thord a pouch. Nicolio could hear the jingle of heavy coins as Thord slipped it in his belt.

"I will send the rest to you this evening when I've checked the chest. You will be at the Green Perch?"

"I will be there for a while," Thord answered.

"Good. Very good. It is always good to do business with a man who can deliver without a lot of questions."

With that, Thord tugged on the chain. Nicolio shouldered Thord's sea bag and followed the Floelander down the gangplank. They passed between the bales and jars stacked on the wharf. Glad as he was to be on solid ground, after the weeks at sea, he felt that the street was rolling under him more than the ship had been.

From the wharf, Nicolio followed Thord through streets crowded with sailors, stevedores and merchants. Fronting the narrow streets were chandlers, alehouses, and all of the other shops that made a port. They climbed up crooked streets lined with two-storied timber-frame buildings, the dark wood outlining whitewashed plaster. When he looked back, he caught glimpses of the sea between the brown tile roofs. One white sail was coming into port, a warship. Thord kept leading him further into the

28

city and away from the sea and his home beyond it.

After the sharp tang of tar and salt, the smells of the city were overpowering. Thord must have seen his nose flare as they passed the open door of a bakery because he stopped and bought them a sweet roll still hot from the oven.

"Here. This should hold us until we can get dinner," he said as he pulled the roll apart and handed Nicolio half. The hot roll melted in Nicolio's mouth as he chewed.

After walking through more streets filled with donkey carts, beggars, and gangs of ragged children, they came to the doors of a large building. The sign above the door read "The Green Perch." But instead of the fish Nicolio had expected to find hanging above the door, there was a green beam sticking out over the street. On the beam stood a young man dressed in an iron collar and a short tunic of yellow feathers.

"Thord! Good to see you back. Who's the toy?" He called down.

"This is my Little Fox. Nikki, this is Yellow."

"Nice. Very nice," the young man said looking down. "But Blue will be jealous. He always thinks of you as his own."

"He will find someone else," Thord said as he led Nicolio into the inn.

When they entered, behind them they could hear Yellow call down to a passerby. "Hey! Mato! Why not stop in for an hour? White misses you more than your wife does."

"Thord! Welcome!" A small, middle-aged woman in a dress made of multicolored pieces of silk, hurried to meet them. "You are staying, of course. And what is this?" Reaching over, she lifted Nicolio's chin. "The boys will not be happy, you know, unless you are planning to sell him. I might make you a good deal," she said turning his chin from side to side to get a better look.

"No, Katina. He is mine. I won't be selling him, I am thinking. But we will be staying."

When Nicolio's chin was released, he shook his head to free himself of the touch. He had become use to being handled by Thord and had even started secretly to enjoy it. But this was someone else. The talk of selling him left him feeling like he was some sort of livestock.

"Green! Take Thord's belongings up to his usual room and see that a bath is ready." Katina said this to a young man standing behind her.

Green was about twenty, with brown hair and soft brown eyes. He wore a dark green tunic and green sandals. He reached for Nicolio's chain.

"No. I will keep him," Thord said, and Green took the sea bag from Nicolio.

\*\*\*

They followed the innkeeper into the common room. Across the room stood a bar backed with shelves of glasses and mugs. To the left was a fireplace and to the right, the double doors opened up on to a gallery surrounding a courtyard. Unlit brass lamps hung under a high beamed ceiling. At this hour, the sunlight poured in through the doorway and a row of windows. Several men sat at tables scattered through the room, one or two young men or boys with each. All of the staff were dressed in a different color and none dressed in much. Some wore collars, clearly slaves owned by the house. Others did not have collars and must be hired boys. Nicolio wondered if they worked on a commission or were paid by the day.

"If you would care for a drink while your room is readied," Katina said, pointing to an empty table, well away from the other customers, "we can talk about some business that has come in while you were gone."

"Wine would be good now, I am thinking," Thord replied.

Katina went to the bar while Thord led Nicolio to the table. Thord leaned his axe, head down, against the table. He pulled back one of the high-backed chairs and sat down pulling Nicolio to his side with an arm around his waist. While they waited for Katina to come back, Nicolio rested an arm on Thord's broad shoulders and watched the other occupants of the room. At one table was a well dressed man, probably a merchant, of about fifty. A brown-haired young man dressed in a short pink kilt stood behind him with a flagon. On the man's lap sat a younger blond slave in a white tunic who was holding a goblet to the man's mouth. At another table, two young men watched a boy in brown dancing to the melody of a grey-clad flute player.

When Katina came back, she set two goblets on the table and poured wine from a pewter ewer. "To your safe return." She raised her glass in a toast.

Thord took a long drink and passed the goblet to Nicolio. "Drink up. It's better than the beer that was rolling around in the ship's bilge."

That it was. Nicolio took a drink and followed it with a second before handing it back to Thord. The wine was half sweet and a match for any at his father's table.

After refilling the goblets, Katina hooked a thumb at Nicolio. "Should we talk in front of him?"

"It is all right. He is a smart lad and knows when it is good to speak and when to keep his teeth locked."

"Well then, I guess there were no problems with this last trip. Your client was happy with his delivery?"

"I delivered his box," Thord said, handing the goblet back to Nicolio. "What is in it and what he thinks of it is not for me to know, I am thinking. If he wants to deal with hobgoblins, that is for him. Dealing with hobgoblins is not to my liking. I am happier when it is men or elves or even dwarves and just gold or jewelry that have to be delivered. But his gold is as good as any, and there should be more of that coming this evening."

In the days they were at sea, it never occurred to Nicolio to wonder what was in the chest or why Thord never opened it. The chest had been just a piece of furniture. They had sat on it and eaten off it but nothing more. He realized that probably Thord didn't have the key and had only the vaguest idea what might have been in the box.

Nicolio handed Thord back the empty goblet. Thord looked into the goblet and up at Nicolio. "Not so fast, my Little Fox. It is not good to drink too fast when sitting to business." He pushed the still empty goblet to the far side of the table. "But now, Katina, is there anything new?"

She leaned over and spoke quietly. "An agent from the Grey Lady was here three weeks ago. He said there is a packet waiting to go east this spring. He offered your usual price and said there would be a bonus if it arrived before mid-summer. It would be the same as the trip last year. You can pick it up at the head of the caravan road in Weskala and drop it at the other end in Dorisan." Nicolio caught her giving him an appraising look. "If you take the job and need a place for your fox here, I can put him to work until you get back. He can work for the same rate as the free boys, two thirds for the house, his third would go to you and tips can go to you or he can keep them. He's a pretty one and would make good money."

Nicolio stiffened. The arm around his waist pulled him closer to Thord's side. Thord smiled up at him.

"The Grey Lady has something going east? I did not like the last trip. Too many knew of it. I will think on it. But now I am thinking only of a hot bath." Saying this, Thord pushed his chair back and stood up with his axe in one hand and took the chain on Nicolio's collar in the other.

Nicolio followed the now familiar tug on his neck through the common room and up a flight of stairs to an upper gallery that wrapped around the courtyard. A young man about Nicolio's age, and dressed only in a blue loincloth and an iron collar, ran up to Thord. "Thord! I'm so glad to see you back." He gave a hard look at Nicolio and how Thord held his chain, and then beamed at Thord. "I missed you," he purred. "Did your business go well? Will we have you with us for a while?"

"Nikki, this is Blue. Business did go well, but I am not knowing how long I will be here."

Green was coming out of the room as they approached. "Blue, help Red fill the bath. They are going to be in room twelve."

"Right away. It's good to have you back, Thord," he said. With one more sour look at Nicolio, he ran off down the gallery.

As Green handed Thord the key to the room, Thord asked him to have wine and dinner sent up after their bath.

They entered a broad room with a low ceiling. Two diamond-paned windows in the far wall let in a bit of light. A large wooden bed covered with a soft blue quilt was against one wall. A table with two chairs and a carved chest, all of a dark wood, completed the furnishings. Thord leaned his axe against the bed and said, "Good! I am thinking that a hot bath would be as close to heaven as man can get right now."

They could both hear the sounds of someone pouring water in the room next door. When Thord opened the connecting door, they saw Blue and a boy about the same age, emptying buckets of hot water into a wide shallow copper tub sitting on the tiled floor.

"Give us a bit of time to get more water, Sir," said the second boy. He was dressed in red, the same color as his hair. Nicolio saw he did not wear a collar.

With that, both Red and Blue took the empty buckets and went out a door to the gallery. True to his word, they were both back with more buckets by the time Thord had hung up his mail shirt and stripped. Looking at the water steaming in the tub set Nicolio to strip off his sandals and tunic as well. When Thord climbed into the tub and waved him in, Nicolio didn't need a second invitation.

Hot water and soap and someone to splash with were indeed heaven.

After their bath, Blue and Red returned with a large jug of wine and a tray of dishes.

Nicolio poured two cups of wine as Thord started pulling a roast pheasant apart. Blue gave Nicolio one last look as he left. As Nicolio looked at the hot meat and warm bread his mouth watered. This had never happened before the long voyage eating hard bread, hard cheese and harder sausages. He had settled into a chair next to Thord with a steaming bowl of onion soup in front of him when Red came back from the door.

"Sir, what is the news?" Red asked. "I have heard that you are back from Tronmar and may have more news."

Thord looked up from his plate.

"There is naught much to tell. The king builds new temples and pirates raid the coast. That is not news," he said around a leg of pheasant.

"Not that, sir. What about the news that came today about the murder of the king and his family by the royal guards? And of the king's brother taking the throne and killing all the guards? Sir. What about that?"

Nicolio started to choke. Dead? His family killed! It couldn't be. He was about to shout that it was wrong, but before he could get the first word out, a fist came crashing into the side of his head. The last thing he remembered was the floor rushing at him through the descending darkness.

\*\*\*

When Nicolio woke up, he was lying on the bed with Thord standing over him.

Thord had a look on his face that Nicolio hadn't seen on the Floelander before. He looked worried and embarrassed at the same time.

"Nikki, are you alright? Forgive me for hitting you, but I had to stop you. Something is wrong and you were about to say something that maybe no one should hear."

He continued, "Red told me all the news. It is not good news. They are saying that the Floelanders of the guard killed the king and all the royal family."

Nicolio started to sit up but felt dizzy and fell back.

"Oh, what have I done?" the Floelander wailed. "Little Nikki, I must be honest now. I have not been honest before."

He went to the door and looked out. He shut the door and came back.

"Nikki, you must listen to me. When I am done it is my turn to listen to you." He said the last part of this with resignation in his voice. "I know more than I have told you," he said, taking Nicolio's hand. "I must be honest now. When we met in the bar in Tronmar, it was not the first time I had seen you. No, I saw you and Borodo earlier in a courtyard of the palace. I visited my cousin Oladd and saw you pass across the courtyard. You were so cute I asked who you were and my cousin told me about you. When we met again in the bar I knew I had to have you, if only for a little while. I got you both drunk and when I won you, I took you. Now, I am sorry for all of this. I planned to tell you tomorrow of the little joke that I had played and send you back to Tronmar. But now I see that I have not been very clever and the joke was not so very funny. Now I must try to make things right."

He stopped and Nicolio looked up into those blue eyes. "What can I do to set things right?"

Nicolio's head hurt and it was hard to think. But he had to know more. It couldn't be true, but by the emptiness in his heart he knew that it was. "Tell me all you know of … of my family."

"I have heard that a ship arrived an hour after we did. It was a navy ship from Tronmar and an officer went to the embassy here. Then it was announced that the king and his whole family were dead. It happened the night we met. They say the Guard seized the king. Late in the night, the army stormed the palace to rescue the king. There was a fire at the palace. They say the Floelander Guard killed the king, queen and all three princes." At this a look of disgust hardened Thord's face. "I do not think the Guard did this. The men of my country are honorable men and would not do this thing. The king's brother has taken the throne and all the guard killed."

*No! It can't be true.* Nicolio thought, but somehow he knew that it was. He wanted to give in to what he felt but couldn't, wouldn't. No, he had to think about something else, about the future. He knew his uncle too well to believe that he was not at the bottom of this. His uncle had always thought he should have been king. Now he was.

"… will try. I owe you a debt. I will take you to the embassy and do what I can do to set this right," Thord ended.

Nicolio looked at Thord and could see the anguish that drove him. "No. Anything to do with Tronmar is my death. You were right that the guards were not the cause. My uncle is behind this. And if I live, he is not king," Nicolio said this with a forcefulness that surprised himself. "No, I cannot go to the embassy."

He had to think about something else, not his family but about now. He was alive because of Thord's "joke." He knew this for certain. If he had been in the palace instead of passed out on Thord's berth, he would have been murdered with his father and mother and … *No! Don't think of that yet.* He knew that it was only chance that saved him. Or maybe it was Fortune! If Fortune had caused him to be "lost" to Thord then maybe there was more going on than he knew or could know. "A slave of Fortune" was what his father had said. Now that seemed to be all too true.

"No, I can't go to the embassy or return to Tronmar. Fortune has brought us together. I owe you my life. You won me and by doing so, you saved my life," he said taking Thord's hand. "I know my uncle killed my father and…" *No, not yet.* "If I go back he will kill me too."

*If Fortune gave me this then I must play it.* "No. I can't go to the embassy, but I should leave here. It's not ... I'm not safe. I can't be a prince or a king. Not now. At least not yet. Fortune has made me your slave. So be it."

A shadow carrying an empty bucket left the next room and crept down the gallery.

\*\*\*

"Sire, we can't find him. There is enough of his energy to be sure he's alive but we can't say where he is. All we can tell is that he's not nearby." The speaker looked up from a low table in the center of a windowless room. Five torches lit the five corners of the room. At the midpoint of each wall was a chair. In four of the chairs sat mages. The fifth chair was empty. Its prior occupant stood beside the table in the center of the room. All four seated mages and the speaker looked exhausted. In the flickering light, dark shadows lined their eyes. On the table was a silver dish with a lock of black hair in it. Around the dish were instruments of metal and glass and words written in blood.

The sixth person in the room was a tall powerfully built man. His short black hair was shot with gray and his beard more so. He stood by the one door. Two liveried soldiers were just visible standing outside on either side. When he spoke, there was steel in his voice. "How did you let him get out of the palace without you knowing about it? Why can't you find him? He is just a boy and I need him found."

"Sire, either he is being protected by some power, or he is surrounded by some barrier of cold-iron, or both. But we cannot see him. We will keep looking but it may take time to pierce whatever or whoever protects him."

"Do it! I want him found and I want him dead."

When the king had left, Morik returned to his chair and looked around at the other wizards. Of the two women, one was slumped in her chair staring at the floor. The other woman was unconscious, her head lolling on her shoulder. Of the two men, old Kirr's breath came out in great gasps. Only one of the four was looking up.

\*\*\*

Taulgir sat with his eyes moving from chair to chair. In his mind, he was appraising each of the other wizards in the room. He had only been promoted to this group when his master had gone into the planes between worlds, looking for Ganian, and had not returned. When his gaze turned to Morik, he was met with an equally appraising pair of eyes. *Let him look.* He thought. *I wonder what would be in his eyes if he knew the true reason my master did not return from his last spell.*

"You did well, Taulgir. You carried out the part required of you better than I hoped."

"I thank you, sir."

"No need to call me sir anymore. You have shown yourself to be more than an apprentice."

"Again, thank you. I hope my skills in Demonology helped."

"Yes your skill with the demon was very good."

Taulgir feigned an exhausted sigh and returned the gaze. *Yes, you wonder about me, don't you? As long as you are worried about my ability to control demons you won't notice my real research. Demonology is for children. Wait until I have finished mastering Theology. When I can manipulate the very gods, it won't matter what you think, old fool.*

\*\*\*

A soft tapping woke Thord.

"Sir!" Came a whispered voice at the door. "Wake up, sir!"

Thord slid from where he had lain next to Nikki. The boy was asleep now. His head rested on the damp pillow.

Thord drew his dagger and pulled the door open a crack. In the moonlight from the courtyard he could see Red beside the door.

"Sir, I have come to warn you. You are in danger. There are two men from Tronmar in the street with knives. I heard them from my window. I think they are coming to kill your slave. I saw that Blue is with them."

"Is there anyone else about?" Thord asked.

"No sir. The house has all gone to bed."

"Are there any horses in the stable?"

"Yes sir."

"Red, will you saddle two for us? I will leave enough money to pay for them."

"I know just the two. I'll saddle them and wait for you. Luck with you sir." Red crept down the gallery.

A quarter of an hour later, the door from the bath opened slowly. There was enough light from the half-shuttered windows to see the two forms in the bed. First one shadow entered, then another. The creak of a floorboard sounded a warning but it came too late for the second assassin.

36

A hand was clamped over his mouth and Thord's dagger was in his back before he could turn. The first whirled around to be tangled in a blanket thrown from the shadows. Before he could shake loose the thick cloth that covered his head and fouled his arms, Thord was on him and he joined his comrade on the floor. There had been no sound louder than the thud of the two bodies hitting the floor.

Moments later, Thord and Nikki were mounting at the gate of the inn. Red held the reins for Nikki as he climbed into the saddle.

"I would offer you luck, but I know you already ride with it, Nikki," Red said, tossing his head in Thord's direction.

A cock crowed from a coop near by. Red looked up at Thord.

"You need to get going and I have something to do." As he said it, Red turned his head towards the sound of the rooster.

"Thank you, Red." Thord tossed Red a small bag. "Here is enough to pay for the horses."

Red snatched the bag out of the air, tossed it and caught it with a hefty chink. "I'll see that it gets where it belongs."

"This is for you with our thanks," Thord said as he flipped him a large Owanian gold crosis. Red caught the thick, palm-sized gold piece and grinned as he bit into the soft metal.

When they rode out the gate, Thord was not surprised to see Blue lying in the shadows nearby with a dark pool of blood under him. There had already been blood on the dagger of one of the assassins when the man entered their room.

* * *

When Thord and Nikki had left the courtyard, Red flipped the crosis in the air. He caught it and hurled it over the back roof of the brothel. When he threw it, he knew it would be found by the ragged brown-haired boy who he had seen picking over the garbage heap. He wondered just what the boy would do with it, with enough money to buy an apprenticeship or to feast for months. If he remembered, he would come by someday and see how a child of the streets would use that much money.

The bag of gold was a different matter. He couldn't use it to pay for horses that had never been in the stable in the first place. Red tossed the bag into the air and it vanished. For the last week, he had shared a room with Yellow and had grown to like the mortal for his good humor and open smile. He knew of the loose board where Yellow kept his tips hidden. Yellow hoped to buy his freedom in a few more years and now he wouldn't need to wait.

The bodies and the mess also disappeared. A runaway slave was not unusual. Whether or not anyone at the embassy would miss the new king's agents was of less concern to Red than the crowing of the rooster in the next yard.

\*\*\*

In the growing light, Thord and Nikki rode through the streets toward the south gate. Behind them the cock began to crow again but the sound was cut short. They picked up the pace as a chorus of squawks and yips erupted behind them.

\*\*\*

"Vorkki? What are you up to?"

"Sister! It's so good to see you here. You spend too much of your time reading your scrolls and don't come out into the world enough these days."

They stood on a high stony place overlooking the sea and a city of men that huddled on the coast beneath them. The wind on their faces blew their long black hair in streamers as they looked out. Their cloaks, his of gold and hers black lined with silver, were caught by the wind and whipped out snapping behind them. The sun was just beginning to rise over the mountains to the east. From this wind-swept height, the city lay dark beneath scattered pink clouds.

"Why should I come out to see the world when everything is already written? But when you and that fox of yours are up to something I find it safer if I know what it is," she responded. "It wouldn't have to do with Arjel's recent mood shifts? Would it?"

"I can assure you, I am not responsible for any changes in the humors of War. Though I must admit to some pleasure when your husband's plans don't work quite the way he wants," Vorkki said with a slight grin curling the corner of his mouth. "But your husband is not my concern. This morning, I was merely watching the Children."

Having seen what he had come to see, he turned to his sister and pulled her to his side.

"If your dear but excitable Arjel is going to be occupied for a while, why don't we forget about your husband and go back to my hall? I'm sure we can find something amusing to do to pass the morning."

As Chance and Fate turned and left the high place, a large, red fox appeared from the bushes and followed them. The fox looked pleased with the world and even more pleased with himself. There was blood on his fur and a few chicken feathers clinging to his muzzle.

\*\*\*

The chant died away into the echoing domes and vaults of the temple. The last of the incense rose from the altar as the priests of the God of War withdrew from the Holy of Holies to return to the inner rooms of the temple. The old priest in the side chapel watched them march out and turned to leave himself. As he too turned to leave, he saw again the young man who had been standing in the back of the temple during the ceremony. The priest had noticed him intently watching throughout the ritual and had wondered what brought him to the temple. Most of the laity who visited the temple to War did so for a reason. They were either women who prayed for the safe return of sons or lovers, fighting far from home, or they were young men, who came to ask for courage or glory. But this man didn't fit the mold of the young men who prayed here. The man was well dressed in the latest style, though all-black was not the usual color chosen by the youths that went looking for war. The priest thought he was too slight of build to be a warrior by choice and too well dressed to be a conscript. And the priest had been struck by intensity of the man's eyes as he had watched the ritual.

The young man saw him and gave a short bow. "Good day to you, Your Holiness."

"And to you as well, good sir," the priest replied. "Are you here to ask for a blessing?"

"No, not today. I am new in the city and thought I would come to the temple precinct to pay my respects to the gods."

"Ah, I am warmed by your piety. Then you have visited some of the other temples?"

"Yes, I have been to several. But tell me if you would, do all the gods have temples here?"

"Most. Though there are two gods who have no temples on the Holy Mount."

"Two? Why would any gods be excluded from the High Place? And where may I find their temples and their priests?"

The old priest looked at him with some surprise. "You must know that of all the gods, Fortune and Fate alone are not found here. No ritual or offering touches them so they have no priests or priestesses. As for their temples, go to the docks and ask for the nearest temple to Fortune. Any

39

tout will give you directions if you have an offering to make. There, you may make your offering on any number of altars. If the dice or the cards or the wheel go your way you may even come back with more than you offered. If you want to find the temples of Fate, look outside of the city. There are a thousand altars to Fate standing in the cemeteries."

Hearing that, the man bowed again to the old priest and left. As he walked away, the priest felt a shift in the aura around him. He asked himself, *What would a wizard be doing at the temple to War?*

Chance's Children

## *Chapter 4*

They had ridden hard, south toward the city of Weskala. The attempt on Nikki's life had failed but they could be sure there would be others. Nikki had wanted to flee as fast and as far as possible but Thord knew that speed would not bring safety. They had halted the first night in a grove of trees to the side of the road. Over their campfire that night Thord spoke against a dash in any direction.

"Is there no one that you can go to who would be willing to help against your uncle?"

Nikki sat hugging his knees, looking into the fire. "Oh, there are several kings and princes who would be more than willing to help me. They would take me in and provide me with a castle and troops. But the troops would be loyal to them and not to me, and the castle would be more a prison than a fortress. After some posturing on the border and a great deal of negotiations that I knew nothing about, a deal would be struck for the 'peace of the realms' and I would quietly lose my head, declared a pretender." He stared into the fire. "No, without any troops loyal to me, there will be no help from any of the kings around the Home Sea. It is better to run far and fast than to look for help. No one will help."

Thord used a stick to poke the fire, causing sparks to shoot up into the night. He didn't stir the embers because the fire was low, but to break the trail of Nikki's thoughts before he followed them too far down into despair. "Your uncle will learn of the men I killed at the Perch. It is not as bad as it might be. He will know they are dead, but nothing more. Men who go to do murder in the night do not leave word where they go. But the fact his men are dead will draw his spies this way."

He poked the fire again. "We need to be away from here but we cannot run away. 'All eyes see a running man.' To run will attract attention and word of this will reach your uncle. Already, we have ridden too fast to go without notice. We need to become invisible where everyone can see us. I have done this before. When something must not be found the best thing is to make it so common everyone sees it and no one notices it."

Thord stood up and walked around the fire to stand beside Nikki. He rested his hand on Nikki's shoulder. "Come. We will sleep on this. In the morning we will see with clear eyes."

Red had only tied one bedroll on the saddles. When they climbed into the bedding, Thord pulled Nikki's head against his chest. Thord listened to Nikki's soft breathing and thought long into the night. Before the moon set he had made his decision.

In the morning Thord roasted a sausage for their breakfast. When he had cut it in half and given a piece to Nikki, he looked him in the eye and said, "When we spoke at the Perch, you said that you could not go back to Tronmar. And you said that since Chance would not let you be a king you would accept being a slave. What is in the mind of the Gods is not for mortals to know. But, I do not think that Chance saved you for no reason. I am thinking, you may someday be a king, but not yet. For now, you must hide. If you will still be a slave, we may yet keep you out of your uncle's sight."

Thord reached across and rested his hand on Nikki's shoulder. "Will you do this? Will you trust me? It means you must not play at this but live it. Anything less and the spies of your uncle will see through it."

Nikki looked up the length of Thord's arm until his brown eyes were looking directly into Thord's. "I trust you. I have to. You have hope and I have none. Yes, I will do this."

Thord gripped Nikki's shoulder. "Good, Little Fox. We will ride to Weskala. I will do some business and we will go on to Dorisan. From there, we will find someplace to go to ground while we think of what to do."

It was a week's ride to Weskala. During the ride, Thord began teaching Nikki some of the hand signals used by seal hunters in his homeland. "We may need to talk and not be heard," he explained. To the hunting signals for caution, danger, look, and quiet, they added new ones for guard, spy, and some others that were theirs alone.

When they arrived in Weskala, Thord got them a small room in a shabby inn near the east gate to the city. Rather than go out they ate dinner in their room. Afterwards, Thord checked the door and windows. He had done this many times over the last years. But this time he was more careful than usual. Finally, with the door and shutters bolted and his axe leaning against a stool beside the bed, they slept.

The next morning Thord woke to a room full of sunlight. He sat up to see Nikki wrapped in a blanket, sitting on the stool looking out the open shutter. The window faced the rising sun and the pink light outlined him as he sat. He was holding a corner of the blanket to his eyes. Thord was about to stand when he saw the axe was leaning against the wall beside the bed. Wide awake now, he stopped and stared first at the axe then at Nikki and back to the axe.

"Did you move my axe?" This was said with more strain showing than he'd intended. But Thord was having a hard time controlling his voice as he looked at the axe.

Nikki turned and looked surprised. "Yes. I woke and couldn't get back to sleep. I wanted to sit and watch the dawn. I'm sorry if it bothers you. I'll put if back if you want."

Regaining some of his control, Thord looked into Nikki's face. The eyes that looked back at him were red, tears ran from them down his cheeks. Thord wanted to pull him to his chest but he had to know something first. "It was just that I didn't expect to see it moved. I need to see you put it back the way it was. Can you do that?"

A confused-looking Nikki rose and rubbed the back of his hand across his face. He carried the stool back to beside the bed. He stepped to the axe and with both hands on the haft, lifted the axe from the floor and set it down beside the stool. He stood back and took in a deep breath. "I really am sorry if it bothers you. I won't touch it again."

"No. It's alright. I expected it to be where I left it. Don't worry about it." Thord reached down and picked up the axe.

"It's so heavy," said Nikki, looking at the axe in Thord's hand. "I don't see how you can carry it all day, let alone fight with it."

"Yes, it is heavy." Thord looked at the axe. He was barely able to hide his shock. In the years he had carried the axe, no one had ever been able to pick it up before. His father had tried to move it and when he couldn't, would never touch it again. His uncle had tried and wouldn't give up until he hurt his back. Both were strong men and now this young prince had done what they could not. Until he saw it, he hadn't believed it possible. There was much more going on here than he thought. He pulled Nikki to him and wrapped his arm around Nikki's shoulders. He held the dark head against his chest. "It is heavy," he repeated, thinking of the weight of the steel, the wood, and the dead that were part of the axe. "But if you need to move it, do it. It is alright. I trust you."

***

After breakfast Thord left Nikki locked in the room while he went out and did business. When he returned, he had sold the two horses and bought two oxen and a large traveling cart. He also carried hidden in his tunic a new pouch of gold pieces and a small canvas packet sealed in wax.

After eating supper in the common room, they returned to their own room. Thord checked to see the hallway was empty before closing the door and explaining his plan. "I have found a train of wagons leaving for Dorisan in six days. We will join it. I have paid for our trip with some gold and by agreeing to act as a guard. You will go to tend the oxen. We have five days to outfit the cart and buy supplies for a hundred-day journey. To pass for merchants we will also need to buy a cargo."

"Little Fox, I know how to buy supplies for a long journey but I am not a merchant. What do you know about buying and selling?"

"I've been taught some of what makes trade profitable. The best I can do is try."

***

The next few days were spent frantically getting ready to leave. Thord found a merchant who would sell them the gear they needed, and he laid in provisions: smoked bacon, dried beans and flour. Nikki began to think better of the meals they had eaten on the pirate ship.

Thord and Nikki poked through the markets looking for a cargo that would give them the appearance of being honest merchants. In the end, Nikki found a load of iron pots covered with enamel. The secret of this was new at this end of the Home Sea and Nikki knew that further inland, they would be able to sell them for a good price. There was still some space to fill and Nikki remembered being told that wherever foreign merchants stayed, there was a market for simple things from their home. When Nikki found a shop selling preserved fish he dragged Thord in and looked over the jars and boxes. He settled on forty small glazed jars, sealed with wax, of pickled eels, and as many of smoked oysters.

"Why would we want to carry this to Dorisan?" Thord's look was one of bewilderment and disgust. "This is foul enough here. Why would someone who lives four hundred leagues from the sea and has never seen an oyster buy it?"

"Dorisan is a large trade center, Master." Even after weeks on the ship and on the road, Nikki had a hard time with that last word. "There will be merchants from all over the Home Sea who have not had food from their native country for years. To them these will be a taste of home." In the end, Thord agreed.

As hard as it was calling Thord "master," it was less of a blow than the first time they yoked the oxen to the large two-wheeled cart they would take to Dorisan. Gone now was Nikki's fine black tunic, replaced with coarse brown homespun that was little more than a sack with holes cut in it for his head and arms. The sandals had been replaced with heavy boots. But the worst came when Thord took a padlock and locked Nikki's collar to a chain bolted to the yoke. In a few weeks he had gone from being a prince to being part of a team of dray animals.

Nikki felt tears forming as he looked up into Thord's eyes.

"No, Little Fox. This is hard but it must be done. Even if you had a magic cloak that made you invisible, people would see your footprints in the dust or your breath on a cold morning and you would be found. Like this, everyone will see you and no one will look at you."

\*\*\*

The night before the caravan was going to leave, Nikki and Thord were eating in the inn's common room. They were enjoying a last meal before weeks of camp cooking. Nikki was standing at the bar trying to get the barman's attention when he caught a conversation at a nearby table. He tensed when he discovered they were speaking in his native language.

"... doubt he's here," came a low voice. "No one at the palace seems to know anything."

"Well, we weren't told he was going to be here, just to watch out for anyone who might claim to be royalty." The second man's voice barely carried over the general noise.

"... stuck up princeling ... hard to hide ... airs ..."

Nikki couldn't catch all of the third voice. He was too afraid to turn his head to hear better.

"What do you want?" Nikki nearly jumped out of his skin when the barman's voice broke in on him.

"I'm sorry, sir. My master asks for another jug of ale, please sir." Nikki put all the servility he could muster into his voice.

Nikki kept his head lowered when he carried the jug past the table with the three men. The last thing he heard was: "...If he's here, we'll find the little..."

As he sat with Thord, he couldn't help thinking about the men. His thoughts were edged with fear of being found. But there was another side to what he'd heard. If these men were talking about him, what did it say about Prince Nicolio? Thord was right when he'd said Nikki would have to live the role of slave. If he had spoken to the barman with his old tone, those men would have known something was wrong, collar or no collar. At the palace, Nicolio always got what he wanted and let everyone around him know that. Maybe he'd been a "stuck up princeling." But he couldn't stay one, at least not and stay alive.

\*\*\*

The next day they left. As they moved out with the caravan, no one gave any attention to the last cart and the dirty slave leading the oxen. Nor did any take notice of the large man with an axe walking with three other armed men as rear guard. But as the end of the caravan passed a thatched mill near the city, three men watched the gate from under a pine tree. They stood by their saddled horses. The last cart had passed when a young man riding a fine chestnut horse rode out of the gate, turned left, and galloped away, north, from the city. The three men mounted and rode north, one loosening a long dagger in its sheath.

\*\*\*

The train of some thirty carts and wagons moved slowly, the pace held to that of the slowest team of oxen. Nikki trudged beside the pair that pulled their cart. Every day was the same. He watered his team and hitched the yoke to the heavy cart. Thord came and locked his collar to a chain on the right-hand side of the yoke, and he spent the rest of the day keeping the flies off of the team and himself. The chain allowed him enough freedom to move from one side of the team to the other and no more. He would walk with the team until the caravan halted for the day and the team was unhitched to graze. Nikki would lead them to water and pasture and lead them back to the cart at dusk. Only when they had been bedded down for the night would Thord unlock him from the yoke. They would sit by the fire and roll into blankets under the cart to sleep on the hard ground.

When the journey first started, Nikki had been ready to cry by the end of the day. He spent every day chained to a pair of oxen as if he were as dumb as they were. But there was no choice. If they were to escape from the spies of his uncle, then they must be what they said they were. People would be less likely to take notice of a caravan guard and an ox-boy than of an lone warrior with a slave-boy as a bedmate. A spy might see a prince in a young boy riding fast beside a Floelander. But no one would look for the heir to a throne chained to an ox cart.

The ruse seemed to work. No one paid any attention to Nikki. The other members of the caravan walked past him as if he wasn't there. And in fact to them he wasn't. He was just a part of a team of oxen, of less importance than the oxen themselves. The only person whom Nikki caught glancing at him was the passenger of the cart in front of him. The man was a diplomat returning to the Dragon Emperor's court. He traveled with a young guard, a serving girl, and, of course, an ox-boy.

At first Nikki had hated the team he was chained to. They were stupid and stubborn. When he tried to turn them they would pull straight and when he wanted them to pull straight they would turn. But after the third day on the trail he realized that they were "chained" to the yoke even more than he. While he at least would sleep under the cart with Thord, the oxen would never go far from the yoke. It would wait for them every day until they could no longer pull. Beyond that there was nothing. He felt sorry for them and started to try to make up for their loss of freedom by brushing them every afternoon as they grazed and making sure they got the best fodder he could find.

Once when they were pulling up a steep hill, he went in front of the yoke and pulled with them.

"Pull, Flick Ear. Pull, Rattle Hoof," he said. The three then threw all they had into the yoke and the cart began to move smoothly up the hill. Nikki didn't know where the two names came from. They had just popped into his head as he looked at the pair. He could see where Flick Ear would fit because he noticed for the first time that the left ox would flick his right ear whether or not there was a fly on it. But Rattle Hoof? In his mind he saw a young calf with a copper milk pail caught on his hoof running around a farmyard, being chased by a scolding milkmaid. After that he always called them by those names and they always responded.

***

Nikki lay still for a long time. He lay still but his thoughts raced. Beside him, Thord snored softly. How Nikki wanted sleep, but it wouldn't come.

An hour ago, he had been sitting across the fire from Thord. He was watching the play of light on Thord's face, the shadows reversed, coming from below. He stared at the way the fire turned Thord's blond hair from sun-gold to red-gold. They had finished eating and were sitting quietly. Thord's eyes flashed in the firelight. Thord stood, came around the fire, and seized the chain on Nikki's collar. Nikki was pulled to his feet and more drug than led, pulled to the bed they shared under the cart.

Neither one had spoken. There wasn't anything that needed to be said. Nikki wouldn't resist. Thord didn't need to ask.

In the moonlight, the long wisp of Thord's hair laying across Nikki's arm now looked silver. The broad chest, a hand's span from Nikki's face, rose and fell with the rhythms of sleep.

He should be angry, outraged. He had just been pushed to the ground and used in a way he never dreamed could happen to a prince. But he wasn't a prince. He had traded a prince's gold coronet for a slave's iron collar. This was what he had accepted. He could no longer decide who would share his bed. Decision had been taken out of his hands. The world where he could decide had ended when his family was murdered. It

49

vanished in a single night of blood and death. Could he unwind the skein of time? No. To live, he needed hope and he had none. By tying himself to Thord, he bound himself to Thord's hope. He belonged to Thord. He needed to belong to Thord.

Laying on the ground, he felt Thord's lust in the air around them. Nikki could still feel it clinging to his body. No, Nikki thought, it wasn't lust. It was passion. That was the difference, that's why he felt calm looking at the man next to him. Never in his life had someone felt passion for him. Any number of bedmates had told him they loved him but Nikki knew they lied. Love was just a game that courtiers played with each other as they jockeyed for position.

Thord was different. Thord didn't hide what he felt. He didn't talk about love. To Thord, love was something done. Nikki was sore from the act of love. But he was happy too. He rubbed at his ear and wondered if the bite mark would show tomorrow. That was something he never had to worry about in the past and, now that it happened, he still didn't worry about it.

***

One morning at the edge of line of hills, Thord changed the routine. The caravan had gradually left the settled lands and they were now in an open country of grass and small stands of trees. Here there were few signs of people. The road had drawn steadily closer to a range of mountains. Three days ago, it had turned to follow the range south. As they moved, the mountains on their left shrank to hills, dark with pine forests. Ahead now there was a gap in the hills that promised a pass leading to the east.

Thord looked at the hills for a long time as Nikki yoked the team and cleared the camp. This morning, although he still snapped the lock to the chain running from the yoke, he left Nikki's collar lead out of the lock. Instead he tied the lead to the lock with twisted grass.

"I don't like the look of the trail ahead. There are bandits in those hills, I am thinking," he said.

He took one of the spare wheel spokes and loosely tied it to rest on the top of the yoke.

"A slave can't have a sword or knife, so this is the best I can do for you. Do you think that you can protect yourself with this?"

"My father's arms teachers taught me to use a sword by first using a stick. So I can try, Master."

"Good. I'm going to range along the side of the trail and will be

50

close by if a fight starts. But you must remember not to even pick up a sword or dagger that falls on the ground. You know the law about slaves using swords."

With that Thord slipped away into a ravine that led west toward the trees.

***

The day dragged on. About noon, the caravan was passing between two groves of trees when the attack came. It started with a howl of pain from the trees to the right. A shout and a chorus of cries followed from both the left and right sides of the trail.

Hard-faced men with swords and short spears came running from the trees on both sides of the trail. Nikki seized his chain near where it was tied with one hand and the end of the wheel spoke with the other. The closest two bandits ran for the back of the wagon in front of Nikki. There, they were met by the guard, his feet planted and his curved sword held high. The first bandit went down at the first swing. The man's insides spilled onto the ground. The second bandit became wary and a slow dance followed as the two men shifted back and forth, each looking for an opening, the bandit edging to the left and right as the guard kept between him and the cart.

Nikki looked towards the edge of the trees and saw Thord in the center of dozen men. His great axe was a blur as it spun in a wheel around him. He made no sound as his attackers darted in and out, trying to get through the ring of silver that he wove between them and him.

One man charged from the side only to find that Thord had used the weight of the spinning axe as a pivot to spin to the left. Instead of Thord, the bandit found the moving axe head and his death. Thord was already weaving a new pattern when the ruin that remained of his attacker's skull hit the ground.

Nikki saw two more bandits running to join the fight at the cart in front of him. The guard fell back to stand before the rear of the cart. He stood with his sword ready while the old man who was traveling in the cart stayed still, standing at the back with his hands in his sleeves.

The three bandits began to move in. Nikki yanked on his chain and broke the grass that held it to the yoke. He ran up to the three and smashed the skull of the first with his wheel spoke before they knew he was behind them.

The second turned and swung his sword at Nikki. The blow carried through empty air as Nikki ducked low and brought his club under the man's shield to strike his knee. As the bandit put his hand out to catch himself before he hit the ground, Nikki finished him with a quick swing to the head.

Nikki turned to see the third man down in front of the guard. He caught a glimpse of the old man jerk his hand out of his sleeve and point behind Nikki. Nikki turned and was staring in the face of another bandit with a sword raised to cut him down. Before Nikki could react, the man toppled over. He lay on the ground with a small silver hilt sticking out from beneath his chin. When Nikki turned back to the old man, he saw him standing where he had been with his hands in his sleeves. This time, Nikki could see the glint of steel from inside those sleeves. The two exchanged smiles and Nikki turned back to the fight.

But the fight was over. He felt the hard wood of the club biting into his hands. Looking down, his fingers were white from clutching the oak. Blood had run down from the end to soak his hands. At his feet were the two men he had killed. The face of one was turned up, now surrounded by a ring of blood-covered grass. The face centered in the circle of blood reminded Nikki of a picture of a god he had seen on the wall of his mother's sitting room, the god of the harvest with a bright apple behind him. But this was an ill harvest.

The end of the spoke was shaking in his hands; Nikki realized he was trembling. He eased his grip on the spoke and tried to stand still. He wanted to throw the club away from him, but knew that would not change what had happened. Instead, he shifted his hold and looked around him. On one side of the caravan, the surviving bandits were running back to the trees. On the other, stood Thord. He slowly turned round and round, standing in a circle of bodies and pieces of bodies. His shield was gone, along with his helmet. He was covered in blood. More gore formed red pools between and under the bodies.

Nikki shouted. "Master? Master, are you hurt?"

Thord made no answer. He just kept turning in slow circles staring around him. His axe was raised over his head.

The guard at the back of the cart started to move toward Thord but the old man stayed him and shook his head.

"No, my young friend. You would only join the dead and I need you alive," was all he said.

Nikki ran to the cart and filled a bucket from the water barrel on the side. He started slowly walking toward where Thord stood.

"Master, it's me, Nikki. Master, it's over. They're all dead. Master," he said as he stepped over the bodies that strew the ground towards where Thord stood. Coming closer, he started to tremble again and stopped to gain control of himself. Thord had stopped turning and stood still with his axe in his hands and a far away look in his eyes.

"Thord, it's me, the Little Fox. It's me, Nikki. Master?"

As Nikki came closer, a shudder went through Thord and he looked at the bodies in front of him. He took in a deep breath and let it out.

"I see you are alright, Little Fox. I knew you could handle yourself."

"Are you hurt, Master?" Nikki asked, handing him the bucket.

Thord took the bucket and poured water over his head and some into his mouth.

"Me?" He looked down at his hands. "No, I am not hurt. A scratch, two maybe. Here," he said handing the bucket back. "Drink, Little Fox."

Thord stripped off his clothes and washed more of the blood from his body. Afterwards they passed between the bodies, back to the cart. As Thord slipped on his spare tunic, the guard from the other cart came up and addressed Thord.

"Sir, my lord wishes the company of yourself and your slave at dinner tonight. He wishes to thank you for what you did, and to thank your slave for helping beat off the attack on his person."

Thord turned to look at Nikki. His eyes widened when he saw the blood-covered wheel spoke beside the cart.

"Tell your lord that we will be happy to eat with him."

\*\*\*

The caravan moved another league into an open area and made camp. Nikki watered and groomed the oxen as Thord spread their sleeping mat under the cart. When they were both washed up, the guard came up and they followed him to the old man's cart. A pot was hanging over a campfire tended by the young girl. The old man sat cross-legged on a carpet. Two other carpets were spread on the ground, one on either side and all facing in on the fire. The guard led Thord and Nikki to the carpet on the old man's right and then seated himself on the left.

"Thank you for coming to our poor camp. I am Prefect Fan Go in the service of the Dragon Emperor. This is Lii, my body guard, and Agate, my niece," the old man made the introductions.

"I am Thord Thurgoodson."

"Ah," said Fan Go. Turning to Nikki, he continued, "And may I have your slave's name as well? I would thank him properly for his defense of myself and my niece."

"He is Nikki."

"Ah. Good. My thanks to you both for your brave fight." With this he nodded his head to Thord and then to Nikki.

Lii placed his sword on the ground in front of him and bowed until his forehead touched the scabbard.

"You have my gratitude as well," Lii said.

The old man turned to where Agate was stirring a pot and said. "Agate, please pour wine for these young men. And if you have a moment, please join us."

Despite Fan Go's protests at having so poor a meal to serve, the dinner was the best that Thord and Nikki had eaten since joining the caravan. During dinner the old man questioned Thord about his travels.

Fan Go explained, "I am an ambassador for my emperor. He is interested in knowing what lies in those parts of the world of which we know nothing but rumors. Are you called Vorkki's Child?" Fan Go asked Thord.

"Men call me that."

"That is very interesting. I have heard people speak of this but have never seen it. But perhaps it is something you do not like to talk about."

Thord looked toward the rising moon. "No. This is not for telling in the night. There is too little light and too much blood nearby."

When the last of the dried fruit was served, Fan Go asked if they would allow his niece to entertain them with a dance. Agate retrieved a stringed intrument from the cart and, after tuning it, Fan Go began to play. The music filled the night and Agate began to dance.

Nikki had never seen dancing like this. Agate moved with a grace that was beyond the best that he had seen in the palace. She flowed over the ground, keeping time with a tambourine. He found his fingers following the rhythm on his thigh as she moved. Without knowing why, Nikki saw tall thin trees against the sea in the darkness behind her. He could smell the salt on the air. He felt himself being carried away with her as she danced. She danced and, in his mind, he danced with her.

When she stopped, the world stopped. Nikki sat staring at where she stood. Not looking at her as much as trying to hold in his mind what he had seen.

"You enjoyed her dance. Good," said Fan Go.

"She dances like nothing I have seen," said Thord.

"Perhaps, if you like, I can ask her to teach your Nikki to dance. It would be a way of repaying you for your courage against the bandits and, also, of passing time on this journey."

\*\*\*

Later that night, Thord and Nikki lay wrapped in their bedroll, Thord turned over to face Nikki.

"You wonder about what happened today. I have not told you this. I was not sure how I could tell you. Now, I am thinking, I must. Do you know what it means to be Vorkki's Child?"

At this question, Nikki looked down. "I thought it meant that… I thought it meant you were a child of chance – a bastard."

Thord rolled onto his back, convulsing with laughter. When he got control of himself again, he took a playful swat at Nikki's head. "A bastard? No, not that. If my mother heard you say that it would be all I could do to keep her from breaking your head. No, Vorkki's Child means that I have a gift from the god Vorkki. A gift or a curse. They are hard to tell apart. When I became a man, I received my axe from Vorkki. When I use in battle, I lose myself in the killing."

Thord raised himself up on one elbow and looked into Nikki's eyes. "When I am fighting, you must never come near me. I will not know you. I have killed many men and not all were my enemies. My axe knows neither friend nor foe. It only knows blood and I do not want to find your blood beneath my feet."

"But if the axe is so terrible, why not get rid of it?"

"When the gods give a man something, it cannot be discarded lightly. There is purpose to this axe. I am thinking, it carries some doom that cannot or should not be turned. Good or evil, I do not know. What I know is that to give it up would be to surrender and to lose the right to say, 'I am a man.'"

Thord reached across and pulled Nikki to him, the links of the chain cold against his arm. He held him against his chest and vowed to himself that he would never let it happen again. He would keep Nikki safe. Somehow he would do this; he had to do this.

Holding Nikki against him, Thord felt the tension in Nikki's body. "What are you thinking, Little Fox?"

Nikki sighed. "I am remembering the men I killed today. I see them in front of me and wonder who they were. I want to know what led them to be there and if I could have avoided killing them." Here he paused. "Do the men you've killed trouble you?"

As Thord heard this last, he felt a shiver pass through the body in his arms. "I was told years ago by someone, that he never thought of those he killed. That to think of them would make a man mad and it is better to forget them. I think he was right." He squeezed Nikki to his chest. "But I have to tell you that I can never forget them. I have also to say, I never liked the man who told me that."

*\*\*\**

Nikki tried to match the girl's movements as she spun upward. But when he was three quarters around, the chain on his collar swung and hit him in the shoulder. He lost his concentration and landed on his back. In the past ten days, he had practiced every night but still found himself floundering when he tried to repeat the motions that Agate made so effortlessly.

"I can't do it. Every time I try to move, this chain gets in the way."

Agate came up and helped him to his feet.

"Are you sure the chain is in the way? Or is it that you place your body in the way of the chain? The chain does not move except when you move. Use the chain as a center and move around it," she said. "Now, try again."

It did work! When he thought about where the chain was and where it needed to be, he found he could move. It came slow at first, but the more he tried the more his motions flowed around the center. The chain ceased to be outside the motion but became part of the dance. The chain was part of him, and together, he and it moved through the motions of the dance.

There had always been eyes at the edge of the firelight when Agate danced. But after the third week, Nikki noticed that not all of the eyes were fixed on her and that more were beginning to watch him.

*\*\*\**

One evening when the caravan was eight days from its destination, Nikki was dancing while Fan played. As Fan ran the bow across the strings, Nikki turned and swayed to the steps of the dance. Nikki began to feel the music move into his body. The dance was growing into the music and the music was blending into the dance. Both were merging into him. He poured his concentration into the dance. The dance, the music and he began to swirl into a tighter and tighter ball. He began to lose contact with the world outside. The fire dimmed. The night sky faded. Everything became focused on the knot formed by the joining of the three parts that made up the dance. Then he felt a shifting. The knot became smaller and smaller. It formed a single point with nothing outside of it. He passed through that point and on the other side, the world opened up. From above, he saw himself dancing in the firelight. But he saw more. He saw the fire and saw the flames rising from the wood. The coals glowed red and yellow and shimmered in the heat. The stars shone bright and hard in the night sky. The wind was making patterns in the grass and those patterns were part of the dance. He saw Fan playing beneath him, not looking at the dance but looking at where Nikki floated above the dance.

Fan stopped.

Nikki collapsed into himself and fell to his knees.

"Please, please play. I…I …"

"No Nikki. That is enough for tonight."

"No! You must play. I felt… I felt something. You must!"

"No. Tomorrow I will play. Rest now," the old man said as he got to his feet and walked back to his wagon.

Nikki knelt beside the fire. He wanted to dance. He needed to dance. Nothing was more important than to return to where he had been. Then his strength gave out and he toppled to the grass.

\*\*\*

Thord looked from the boy to the back of the old man. He knew Nikki must be all right or Fan would not have left him there. He felt something he didn't understand had passed between the old man and the boy. They had shared something that was beyond what he knew or could know. Something stirred in him. It wasn't jealousy of what Nikki and the old man shared but more of a sense of loss that for the first time he could not share something in Nikki's life. He walked over and lifting Nikki up and carried him back to their blanket.

\*\*\*

Fan put the erhu back into its case.

A non-voice came to him as he sat.

*Do you understand why I think he is so important?*

*You were right, Ganian, my old friend.*

*I thought you would agree. The first time he danced like that, it echoed all across the palace. It was trapped inside the wards I had placed to protect the king. If I hadn't put a stop to it, it would have broken the wards and maybe me as well.*

*But so much power! If I hadn't stopped him this time there is no knowing what he could have done.*

*Yes, he needs direction. His power will be needed but it must be trained first. At the palace, all I could do was prepare him. You are to be his first tutor.*

*How far should I take him, Ganian? There are only a few days left before we must separate. He has years more to learn. To power like his, I can only offer so much.*

*I know. No one of us can teach what he can learn. If you can give him a sense of direction, he will find his next teacher himself.*

*You also must know he is a threat to you. As his power grows, the blood-bond between you will draw more power from you.*

*I know. I feel it even now. But I'm old and I don't have much time left on this plane. My power was already waning. Even a hundred years ago, I would have seen the usurper and his wizards preparing to strike. As it was, only a god's intervention saved the boy.*

*But why do the gods care? They seldom meddle in the affairs of men.*

*There is something going on that I don't understand. Something about the usurper's wizards is drawing the gods into this.*

*I will do what I can now. But when he is ready to learn more we will meet again. The veils are thinning. You must leave before we are seen.*

*Good be with you.*

*And with you.*

***

Borodo sat in an inn in the Floelands.

"Thord, you say? There are a lot of Thords. 'Tis a common enough name. But which Thord do you mean?"

The landlord was a big, redheaded man with a short beard, close-cropped hair, and a broken nose. He was taking away the wooden platter from Borodo's dinner when Borodo asked him where he could find Thord.

"There are quite a few Thords. Now there's Thord Grey Beard that has a farm on Skarg. And there is Thord Long Spear from The Breakers. Can you tell me more about this man? Is he a big man?"

Borodo almost had to laugh. A big man? Thord was taller and broader than Borodo but here he would be about average height. Though Thord's shoulders were a match even for the giant that loomed over Borodo's table.

58

"Not tall," he answered. "But broad through the shoulders. He's a young man and he carries an axe."

"An axe, you say." The innkeeper's expression changed from open and helpful to closed and cautious. "If he carries an axe, that would be Thord Vorkki's Child, and you'll not be finding him here or any place in the Floelands, I am thinking. At least, you won't find him here for a couple more years. You should talk to Bragdar the Law Speaker if you want to know more."

With that, the man turned and disappeared back into the kitchen.

Borodo found out nothing more that night. Everyone he talked to clammed up when he asked about Thord Vorkki's Child. Vorkki's Child. Berserker.

In the morning, Borodo went looking for the Law Speaker. He found him sitting on a stool under a tree with his dark blue robe pulled up around his feet. On the grass in front of him sat a group of children.

Despite the man's long white hair and beard, he spoke with a firm tenor voice. "Braegi's sons were Braegar, Braegun and Margi."

The children replied. "Halgar's son was Boldar and Boldar's sons were Halfdan and Boldan. Boldan's son was Braegi. Braegi's sons were Braegar, Braegun, and Margi."

Looking up, the Law Speaker saw Borodo watching them.

"Children. We have a visitor from the eastern lands. Welcome him."

"Be welcome guest," came from the dozen children.

"How may we help you?"

"Well, sir. I was told that you could tell me about a man I wish to find. He is named Thord and I am told he is called Vorkki's Child."

"Why are you looking for Thord Vorkki's Child?" Bragdar asked, his voice steady but intense. "Is this about a killing?"

"No. It's about a game of dice. He won something from me and I would like to buy it back."

"You won't find him here." Bragdar turned to a child of about ten. "Why was Thord Vorkki's Child outlawed? Wangar?"

The boy stood and recited. "Waldgood's sons were Wengood the Green and Thurstein. Wengood's son was Thurgood. Thurgood's sons were Wengood Iron Hand and Thord. Thord received an axe from Vorkki during his Passage."

"Felrod's son was Halrod Long Sword. Halrod's sons were Halgood and Felrod the Fair."

"Thord and Felrod both had the bright eye and they fell in love at the summer fair in The Breakers. Halrod's wife was Gudrun Gilrun's daughter.   Gudrun planned to marry Felrod to her sister Halrun's husband's sister Balrun's daughter Walmar."

"When Gudrun heard that Felrod the Fair loved Thord Thurgoodson, she said to her husband. "Halrod, if you will not put a stop to this, you are not the man I thought I married. I will divorce you and take my lands back to my family.""

"Halrod Long Sword called on Thurgood to stop Thord from seeing Felrod. But Thurgood would not support Gudrun's wishes because of a feud over some cattle that had belonged to his cousin Forstien that had strayed onto Gudrun's father's land."

"Gudrun would not let the matter drop.   To appease Gudrun, Halrod called Thord out."

"Halrod, Halgood, and four of Halrod's carls met Thord and three of Thurgood's carls on the beach near Forgald's Stead. After the carls finished marking out the square, Felrod the Fair rode up. But too late he came, for the blood harvest had begun. Thord stood with wide eyes as Halrod ran at him with his long sword and shield. Thord took Halrod's sword on his shield and swung at Halrod. Halrod blocked the swing and caught the axe on the edge of his shield. But Thord pushed the axe toward Halrod and the tip of Vorkki's axe head took Halrod in the shoulder and drew first blood."

"Halrod jumped back. Thord stood still and looked at the blood on the axe. When Halrod came forward again, Thord raised the axe and split Halrod's shield. Halrod fell to the axe with his skull cloven."

"Doomed, the two brothers Halgood and Felrod ran into the square to the side of their father. But the god-gifted axe had been bloodied. Thord, now Vorkki's Child, turned on the brothers and first slew Halgood as he came running. Felrod the Fair stood staring at the bodies of his father and brother and at the man he loved, as the god's axe took his blood also. Thord ran down and killed all but one of the carls, Snorr Steel Fist, who was still on his horse. That day, nine men journeyed to their fathers."

"When the matter was brought before the Law Speakers, Thord kept his teeth locked. The Law Speakers held that the deaths were from the god's axe and that Thord Vorkki's Child was blameless.   But it was agreed that Thurgood's son could not stay in the Floelands and he was declared outlaw and had to go out of the Floelands for ten years."

\*\*\*

Borodo sat and stared into his mug. What could he do? He was sitting in a Floeland tavern while his king was gods knew where in the hands of a mad killer.

He sat idly rolling the dice the Floelander had left him. He knew he didn't have much of a chance of finding Nicolio. He had searched for months and not found a trace of him. The trail was cold now and the chance of finding Nicki, whichever way he took from here, was no better in one direction than in any other. The dice clicked on the table as he rolled them. A four and a two.

"Six brave men." A tall man stood in the door in a white surcoat over chain mail. The surcoat bore a red bear rampant. "I am Captain Paelee and I need six men to join my company bound for Killar. King Menori of Killar is offering mercenaries good pay to hold the peace with King Marcalo of Tronmar, and better pay and plunder if the peace fails. Who's a man who remembers the Floeland Guard and would pay back Marcalo for his treachery?"

This brought a chorus shouting.

"I am Walgood Archer. I am in." A lean man in his thirties at the bar stepped out into the middle of the room.

"Osgood and Osman Wandorsons are in." This came from a pair of young men with an enthusiasm that told Borodo they were fresh off the farm and new to war.

Borodo rolled a pair of threes.

A man in the back stood. He looked to be a veteran of more than his share of fights. "I, Hrapp Sharp Sword, am in."

"I remember Vandor Haldorson, whose death is not avenged. I, Halmar Haldorson, am in."

The dice clicked on the table as Borodo rolled again, a five and a one.

"Five brave men have joined. I need six."

Borodo pocketed the dice and stood up. "I, Borodo of Tronmar, also remember the man Vandor Bright Helm. I am in."

***

The air shimmered. Where before there had been a taproom on a northern island, now there was a stone balustrade looking out at pinnacles of ice and rock thrusting through the tops of white clouds. Chance stood, looking at the sun setting beyond the edge of the world.

"Don't you ever tire of meddling in the business of others?" A deep voice boomed behind him.

"No. It seems I don't. But that's why we were called to this place, isn't it? To watch over the Children below? But what brings you,

Brother-in-law?" Vorkki asked turning to face the red-haired God of War.

"I am here to warn you to stay out of my affairs. Paelee's Company was meant to go east for a rebellion I have in Widmar."

"Oh, I'm sure you will find other warriors willing to murder and rape in the sacred cause of Prince Wilrod," Chance said. "And I really did need someone for a game of dice and there they were."

"Oh, I will find someone else. You can count on it. But you can't count on my being as forgiving next time you interfere," Arjel threatened. The God of War cocked his head slightly and frowned. "I will never understand how you continue to find betting interesting when you cheat."

"But my dear cousin, the excitement in the bet isn't in winning or losing. It's what the players are willing to place on the table."

# Chance's Children

## *Chapter 5*

The air was full of sounds and smells. Some of each were delicious and others were less appealing. The sounds of singing and laughter and the smells of grilled meat and fresh bread, mixed with the sounds of braying animals and the smells they left scattered on the ground. But at the end of a long trek, the open-air bazaar was heaven.

Nikki squatted under an awning by the cart. On a cloth in front of him were the last items of the cart's cargo. The pots and pans had sold quickly and for a good price, as he knew they would. The art of putting enamel on iron was new and Nikki had made sure to get good pieces. He had seen in the markets of Tronmar that items that were novel and useful sold better than things that were only either useful or novel. These last items though were harder to sell.

"Pickled eels! Smoked oyster paste!"

Nikki looked up to see two men standing in front of him. One was in his forties with black hair, and by his speech was a man from Tronmar, though dressed in the local style with a long colorfully-striped robe. The other was some years younger, a local man and clearly a servant.

The first man reached down and picked up a jar.

"Wirgo's! By the gods, it's been two years since I had pickled eels, not to mention Wirgo's Eels!"

He looked up from the jar and saw Nikki. The pleasant surprise on his face melted into something else. Surprise, shock, calculation and then a false calm that hid all the rest.

"It has been a long time since I had these. I remember having them at a dinner at the palace in Tronmar where I was seated next to a young prince," he said casually. "I told him that such things from home were sorely missed by those of us who traded in far places. He was a smart lad and I am sure he remembered our conversation."

He bent down to look at another jar and quietly said. "You are in trouble. How can I help you?"

Now Nikki recognized the man. He had been at a dinner and that is where the idea of buying these very items had come to Nikki.

"By telling no one," he whispered. Louder he said. "Yes, these are the finest eels and oyster paste, Sir. Clearly a man of your senses would appreciate such delicacies."

They haggled over the price. It was hard for Nikki to keep the merchant from jumping to a suspiciously high price from the start. But finally, a price was agreed on.

When the deal was done, the merchant asked when Nikki's master would be back. Nikki told him that Thord would be back in an hour.

"Your master has a fine cart and team," said the merchant. "I will take a jar of each with me. If you would deliver the rest of the jars to the house of Baelo this evening, I would like to discuss a business arrangement with your master over dinner. I will send a man to guide you there.

\*\*\*

Thord returned as Nikki was finishing packing the jars back in the cart.

"So Little Fox, giving up so soon? Is there no market for eels, a hundred leagues from the sea?" Thord laughed.

"Just the opposite, master. They are all sold. A merchant from Tronmar saw them and bought them all." Nikki gave a hand sign that Thord had taught him that said *be alert*. "He has invited you to dinner after we deliver these. He has an offer to discuss with you."

"How much did he pay for the eels?" *Danger?*

"Forty silvers." *I don't think so.*

"Half a silver each for jars worth three coppers? My Little Fox is a fox." *We go. Careful.*

\*\*\*

Before sundown, Baelo's man returned to guide them. The cart lumbered into the corral behind a large house where several men were waiting. As they came in, Thord's hand shifted casually from his belt to rest on the head of his axe. But his caution was unnecessary as one of the men directed the others to begin unloading the jars.

"Be careful with those jars! Break one and the master will have your hide for a saddle." Turning to Thord he continued, "Sir, I am Gogin the head steward. Merchant Baelo wishes to offer you the use of the bathhouse before dinner. He says your slave will be serving you so he too may use the bath." Nikki caught a look that passed over Gogin's face that said *and you need a bath*.

They were led to a low building and shown the bath with a large tank of hot water. Thord had stripped and was about to climb in when a young boy came in.

"No!" He cried. "Not until after you have washed!"

He led Thord to the middle of the room and doused him with

66

water. Taking a small brush and soap, he lathered Thord up and then doused him again.

"There you go, sir," he said pointing to the waiting tank. "Now you, boy. Come here. You stink." The boy wrinkled his nose. He took a coarse brush from a shelf. "I can't imagine why they want a dirty slave like you to wait at the table, but I'll try to clean you up."

After soaking, Thord was dressed for dinner in a borrowed robe of thin, green cotton. No amount of adjustment would close the robe around his shoulders so the front had to be left scandalously open. Nikki was given a clean white tunic and they were led to the table.

Dinner was set up in a small garden. A low table surrounded by cushions was placed under a vine trellis. In the cool night air the smell of night-blooming flowers mixed with the aromas coming from the kitchen. Thord took a position with the wall of the house behind him, with Nikki kneeling beside and just behind. Baelo and his wife Marga sat across the table. On one side was Baelo and Marga's son, a young man of twenty named Baedano, and on the other side were their two younger daughters, Marga and Marta.

"Perhaps you would have your slave pour us wine," Baelo suggested when they were all seated.

In the center of the table were goblets and a wine pitcher. Thord watched as Nikki took the goblet closest to him and filled it. He then presented it to Baelo. He filled the goblet from in front of Baelo's son and offered it to Baelo's wife. Only after shuffling all the goblets did he fill the last goblet and place it before Thord.

Baelo smiled through all this and when the goblets were filled he looked at Thord and offered a toast: "To Trust. Something that must be earned," and drank the entire goblet.

When everyone had drunk, Thord returned the toast. "To Trust."

During the meal, the conversation turned to Baelo's family home in Tronmar."

"We do miss life in the capital. Of course Baelo was there not long ago, but it's been five years since I was there," Marga was saying. "It is so beautiful there in the spring. The Festival of the First Flowers is such a wonderful time. I remember seeing the queen dressed in a green and yellow gown, standing beside her husband and throwing the First Flower from the balcony of the palace. They were surrounded by their three sons wearing crowns of flowers. We stood in the garden among the crowd of cheering people, looking up at them. It's hard to think of them as dead."

"I hear the new king is..." She broke off speaking and stared over Thord's shoulder.

Thord could hear the sound of Nikki's soft choking behind him. He reached back and brought him down to his side and pulled Nikki's head onto his lap. "You will have to pardon him," he said to Marga. "He is from Tronmar and grows homesick at times. I am thinking he misses his own mother and father."

Thord stroked the head on his thigh and thought how hard Nikki must fight to hold back so much. When Thord looked up, he saw the look of disdain on the face of Baedano.

"It's disgusting to see slaves putting on airs, as if anyone should care that a slave is homesick."

"Baedi! I won't have that tone at my table," Baelo almost shouted at his son.

Baedano looked shocked at the force behind his father's response.

Nikki sat up, wiped his face and murmured something Thord didn't catch. He got to his feet and moved to stand behind Thord again.

When the last course was cleared away, Baelo turned to his wife. "Dear Wife, now we men must talk business. Please take the children."

When Baelo, Thord and Nikki were alone, Baelo leaned over the table. "Is the new king looking for you?"

Thord answered. "We can't be sure, but I am thinking he must be."

"Then you need to vanish for a time." Baelo looked at the vines above them and continued, "I have thought on this and may know just the place. You can go there and be lost to the world, at least until spring comes. There is an inn in the north called The Snow Rose. I know the man who runs it. Let's just say that I had dealings with him some years back in Tronmar and he took his profits to the far north when he retired. His name is Janlo."

"Janlo, you say?" Thord's eyes lit up at the name. "It wouldn't be that he retired about ten years ago would it?"

"You know him then?"

"No. I don't know him," said Thord. "But I know of him. A lot of people who sail The Home Sea have wondered where Black Janlo was. Some of them were more than passing curious."

"Ah. Well, he runs an inn now and would prefer to remain ... unfound. We have an agreement. I send him a cartload of spices and fine wine for his kitchen before winter sets in and he sends back a cartload of furs in the spring. He gets what he wants and I get what I want and both of us make a good profit." He looked at Nikki. "If you would be interested in disappearing for a while, you could take your cart and spend the winter at The Snow Rose. I can't think of anyplace further from Tronmar."

Thord thought about it. Yes, that would cover their tracks for a while. "When would we leave?"

"I was about to send the cart. If you agree to make the trip, I'll have your cart loaded instead. The cargo is in my warehouse now and you can go up river by boat for the much of the way. You could spend the night here and leave tomorrow."

Thord looked at Nikki. He saw in his face the longing to sleep in a real bed under a roof. "The day after will do."

Chance's Children

## *Chapter 6*

Thord and Nikki had left the river and turned east into the flat grasslands. After three days they passed the last of the villages and turned north. At this point the road turned into a mere track and then disappeared all together in the featureless grass between the river to the west and the distant mountains in the east. With the caravan, they traveled in a moving village. Now they were alone, the team and cart a ship on a green ocean.

Before they left, Baelo had told them not to worry about finding their way.

"Just keep going north. The valley will narrow before you reach the forests. When you get there, find where the river leaves the forest. There you'll find the first goblin village. A road from there leads on to The Snow Rose. Be careful of the goblins, though. If you are low on supplies don't try to deal with them. If they know you need something, they'll haggle with you until you've traded the cart and all for a bag of dried beans."

Once they turned north, they left the villages of men and entered a land of short grass and tall clouds. The land was for the most part empty. Several times they saw herds or flocks in the distance but they never passed close enough to tell whether there were herders tending them or if they were wild. By the time they reached the northern end of the valley, they had been traveling forty days.

The first sign the land ahead was inhabited was the sight of smoke rising from the edge of the forest. Just inside the trees they came to the first goblin village. The road ran between two rows of stone houses with low, thick sod roofs. They were watched from behind trees and over fences by small goblin children with bright eyes and long ears pointing straight up. As they approached, they were met by a dozen goblins with long spears. One stood before the others, resting the butt of his spear on the ground at his feet.

"Strangers, what do you bring to the lands of the Earth Folk?"

"We come bringing peace and trust." Baelo had told Thord about the challenge and the response. Even though Baelo had assured them the goblins were friendly, Thord kept his hand on his belt near where the haft of his axe was thrust through it.

"Then, be welcome," the goblin answered. At that, the other goblins sloped their spears on their shoulders and turned back into the town.

The first goblins stood looking at Thord and Nikki. "Are you carrying supplies for The Snow Rose?"

Thord nodded.

"I am Mannnki and I hope you're carrying cinnamon. My cousin's youngest daughter is getting married at The Rose next month and I am looking forward to a piece of Janlo's spice cake." This last was accompanied by a broad grin full of pointed teeth. Like the other goblins, Mannnki stood some five feet tall. He had a low brow and large hooked nose. His ears were long and pointed, and jutted straight out from the sides of his head. "The day is still young so you will want to keep going, I suspect. Just follow the road behind me. There will be a good camp site about four hours along."

From there, it took a further five days travel on a rutted dirt track to reach The Snow Rose. The road ran through dense forests of old trees. The only breaks in the trees were the fields around the two more goblin villages that straddled the road.

The inn stood in a wide clearing. On either side of the road were small fields between low stone walls, dotted with hay ricks. It was large and built around three sides of a courtyard. An eight-foot wall with a wide, roofless gate made the fourth side, the wall showing irregular stones where the white plaster had broken away. As Nikki brought the cart to the inn he could see two other tracks that left from the gate, leading to either side and disappearing into the dense forest. Through the trees behind the inn, he caught the sparkle of water from what must be a lake or wide river. When they entered the courtyard, a goblin came from a stable door on the left. He was young, with his long pointed ears just starting to fall. He was dressed in a brown leather tunic and high green boots and was holding two empty wooden buckets at his sides.

"Good sir, may I help you?" He asked to Thord in a high musical voice.

Thord walked up to him.

"Yes. I have a cargo for Janlo and The Snow Rose."

Nikki had halted the team just inside the courtyard and was looking around. In the center of the courtyard was a stone curb enclosing a small, round garden. In the garden was a single rose bush with several white roses blooming. There was a small detached building to one side with a trough beside it. A well house, thought Nikki. The main door to the inn was in the central block, facing the gate. The door was a good six feet wide and ten feet tall. The wing on the right had another door the same size. There were two rows of windows on that side. The lower row was made of large windows with the sills six feet from the ground. The upper row was smaller, just under the eaves of the thatch roof. The windows turned the corner and marched across the first half of the central block. On the other half were three rows of windows of average height. On the third side was the stable. Chimneys poked up through the roof at various places. At the left end of the central block, a cone-shaped section of roof was topped by a larger chimney. Smoke rose from that one and the two in the center.

The goblin boy had disappeared into the main door and reappeared with a tall, gray-haired man. The man wore wool trousers and shirt and a long white apron. He was wiping his hands on his apron as he came up to Thord.

"I'm Janlo. Sammmi says you have a cargo for the inn." His voice was low and had a rumble in it. He spoke the common trade tongue, but his accent was from the west end of the Home Sea.

"We came from Baelo," Thord said.

At this, Sammmi clapped his hands. "Finally! Your cooking, Janlo, has been getting dull these few weeks. It will be good to have some spice added to dinner again." He turned to Nikki. "Come. Bring the cart, boy." And he started walking toward a small door in the left corner of the courtyard near the well.

When the cart was unloaded and the oxen bedded down in the stable, Nikki walked across the courtyard to the inn's main door. As he passed the small garden in the center, he was struck by the rose planted in its center. It had been getting colder as the weeks had passed and they had traveled north. Now there was frost each morning and the trees were either shedding their last leaves or were bare. The rose was still green and the three blossoms were perfect, white against green.

He came to the main door. The wood was heavy and plain with no decoration beyond the iron hinges worked in the shapes of branches. The door was almost twice his height and half that wide. He opened the small door cut into a corner of it and stepped through. Once inside with the door closed behind him, he turned to find himself in a vestibule. He walked past a few coats and hats hanging on pegs to reach the main room. To one side was a set of steps leading down into a gloomy room. He could just make out the shapes of oversized tables and chairs in the sunken room. He turned to the sound of voices on his left. The room in front of him was large with tables and chairs scattered about a central fire. The walls were paneled in dark wood with no tapestries or hangings. At one table sat three goblins, drinking from mugs. Nikki thought they must be old by the way their long ears stuck out and down to almost rest their tips on the goblins' shoulders. He was aware of them studying him. When he walked forward and the chain from his collar swung free, they turned back to their conversation. Their reaction reassured him. Though uncommon in the north lands, slaves were of little note.

Nikki kept walking to where Thord sat at the far end of the room with Janlo. An elf maid leaned against the bar directly behind Janlo's chair. As Nikki passed the hearth, he could feel the heat from the stack of burning logs. Wisps of smoke escaped from the hood over the fire to leave the room smelling of oak. He walked between the fire and a table occupied by a large orange cat, taking in the heat.

When he got to Thord, he saw on the table were a plate with a large wedge of pale yellow cheese and two mugs. Thord was slicing a piece from the wedge as Nikki walked up.

"Here Little Fox, have some of this cheese." Thord held up the cheese on the end of his knife. When Nikki had taken it, Thord pointed to the mug in front of him. "The beer is good too." He turned back to Janlo. "Baelo said we would be able to work to pay for our keep over the winter."

The cheese was sharp and salty, not Nikki's favorite but better than the hard cheese they had carried coming north. When he reached for the mug, Thord wrapped an arm around his waist and pulled him to his side. Feeling the warmth from Thord's body, he took a long drink. The beer was full and rich, the bitter taste balanced against the smoky taste from the malt. He took another sip and set the mug down in front of Thord.

Janlo swept his arm around at the common room. "If you cut and haul wood to keep the fires going, you are more than welcome to room and board and enough drink to ease the long nights. It's not as bad as it sounds. Most of the inn is empty during the winter, so it takes less wood than you would think. Do you agree?"

When Nikki caught Thord's hand signal asking if he agreed, he responded with a "*yes.*" But Janlo must have caught the sign, as he gave Nikki a hard look when Thord voiced, "Agreed."

Nikki kept watching Janlo. The elven woman stood behind Janlo and ran her long fingers through his gray hair. She nodded to Nikki. "I'm called Sil and we'll be getting to know each other through the long winter."

"Ah, don't you be worrying about the work," she said to Thord. "It's not hard. The forest is close and the inn takes only a log or two a day most of the winter. There'll be plenty of time to have to yourself and your little friend here. And if you've a mind for it, you and I can do some hunting when the snow sets in for good. The deer in the forest are most obliging and will help look for your arrow, if you should miss your shot."

\*\*\*

"I thought that elves and goblins hated each other." Nikki looked around the common room at the mixed crowd of elves, goblins, and a few men. He sat on the bar, his feet swinging from the edge, with Sil on a stool to one side and the large orange cat that called The Rose home, stretched out on the bar beside him.

Sil looked over the crowd as if for the first time. "Well, true it is, that in the past we did not see eye to eye. There were wars in plenty here in the north. But that was before The Snow Rose."

She took a drink from the mug in front of her. "Oh, that was a thousand years or so back. Then there was always fighting. The goblins wanted to cut down the trees and turn the forests into fields, and we wanted the forests left alone for the deer and the boar hunting. We spilt a lot of blood in those days. One of our bards named Bel and a goblin witch named Bolllna got together to bring peace. They planted a rose and laid a spell on it. There could be no fighting between an elf and a goblin within a long bow shot of the rose. A magical truce, you might say. As no elf would trust a goblin and the goblins wouldn't trust elves, a man named Waylo was found who would see to the peace. He was a trapper, as I remember, good looking but for a scar down one side of his face. Once we all got used to the idea, we started to meet here to settle problems. Waylo built a small inn and that was the first Snow Rose. Since then The Rose has burned down and been rebuilt three times, but it's always been run by a man or a woman. It was hard getting used to dealing with men. They come and go so fast. Thirty years or less and you need to learn how to deal with a new one. The beer changes. The food changes. Even how the beds are made changes. I suppose it would be simpler to have a dwarf at The Rose. Then it would only change hands every few hundred years. But then we would be eating dwarf cooking, and it is more than worth putting up with a new man every twenty or thirty years to avoid that."

She drank from her mug.

"Janlo took The Rose ten years ago. A fine man he is, too. In all the years the Rose has been here, I can't think of a better man." At this, she gave Nikki a sideways look. "That master of yours is a fine man too, mind you. But when you've lived a few thousand years, you want something a little more mature. Oh, Janlo is a fine man indeed. My friends think I'm mad to bed someone who will be gone in twenty or thirty years and grow old before that. Maybe they're right and maybe not. But they haven't spent the night in bed with him. I'll take my thirty years and savor them."

***

It was the day before the solstice. Snow lay thick on the ground. It clung to the crotches of the birches and maples and piled thick in the pine boughs. During the short day, Thord and Nikki had cut firewood in the forest. Thord used the inn's double-headed axe to fell the trees and lop off the branches while Nikki and the team dragged the logs back through the snow to the inn. Each time he brought a green log from the forest, he pulled it to a pile outside the inn. When the log was in place, he hitched the team to a log from last year's pile and dragged it to the door of the kitchen. The sun was sinking as Nikki led the team into the courtyard with the fourth and last log. Nikki had brought the team wide when they came to the gate so he could get a straight pull to drag the long log through the gate. Before dragging it to the side, he kept the team moving straight in until the end of the log would clear the gate post. This brought him right up to the central garden. As he turned the team, he couldn't take his eyes off the rose. It always filled him with joy to see it. Outside the gates, the world was frozen. Snow and ice covered the fields and trees. Even though the courtyard was swept of snow, there was no getting away from the numbing cold that seeped into boots and gloves and bit at nose and ears. But even now, with the snow drifting across the fields, the white rose stood in its patch of green grass. One new bud, as white as the snow beyond the gate, was ready to open and join the other two blossoms.

Later, when the team was rubbed down and in the stable, Nikki and Thord came tracking snow into the common room. There, they found Sil talking to another elf. She waved them to come over and join them. Nikki had gotten used to seeing the varied peoples that came to the inn for an evening or for a week. He had become familiar with goblins from the nearby villages and even seen trolls down from their mountains. And though he had met many of the Woodland People that drank in the common room of The Rose, he had not seen the elf beside Sil before.

He was not dressed in the usual browns and greens the Woodland People wore but in bright colors. He wore a tunic of scarlet over yellow trousers. A blue and violet cloak hung on the wall behind him. If he didn't know better, Nikki would have said this elf looked old. His long hair was white and there were wrinkles around his eyes. But the signs of age ended there. He flowed to his feet when Thord and Nikki entered and the voice that called out to them was vibrant with life.

"Come. Join us." While his voice was smooth and light, still it filled the whole room. "Sil has been telling me about you. I am Bel and you must be Thord Vorkki's Child. Come sit. You must give me the songs and tales of your homeland. The ones I know are from half a thousand years ago. There must be new ones." He turned to Nikki. "And you must be the Little Fox."

Sil stood up. "You two look more than half frozen. Why don't you be sitting by the fire while I get something hot from the kitchen. Janlo's got some venison sausage and bean stew over the fire that will put the life back in you."

As she left, Bel waved them to seats facing the fire.

By the time the two had pulled off their outer boots and had shed their cloaks and coats, Sil was back with two steaming wooden bowls of stew. Setting the bowls in front of them, she said, "Eat. You look more like blocks of ice than men. I'll fetch you some mugs; but you'll get no ale until I see more of the stew in you than in the bowl."

When she returned with the mugs, Sil took up the conversation that Thord and Nikki's arrival must have interrupted. "Still, I didn't think to see you here this winter, Bel. I thought that it would be Malllmi again this year that was to bless the Rose."

"No. Malllmi is getting older now. She doesn't get around as easily as she did, even fifty years ago. Besides, I have business in the area this winter and so I will be doing the blessing."

"Well, it's fine with me. You'll never be wanting for a meal or a drink in the Rose. Not that we would short Malllmi either, but I do dearly love to hear you sing. And the smell of that potion she cooks up is enough to make me turn as white as the rose."

*\*\**

Boom bom-bom boom bom-bom boom boom.

Boom bom-bom. Nikki sat up. The sound echoed all around him. Moonlight was flooding through the window that looked out onto the courtyard. In the cold light, he could see Thord in the bed next to him, sound asleep.

Boom bom-bom boom. The sound was loud enough that it should have rattled the bed frame. But nothing moved. Thord slept.

Nikki slid from bed and went to the window. In the moonlight, he could see the robed figure of the bard, Bel. He stood with his back to the inn, facing the center of the courtyard and the garden with the white rose. He held a frame drum in his left hand. With his right hand he struck the drum.

Boom bom bom Boom. Waves of sound rolled from the drum. In the pauses between the thunderclaps of the drum, Nikki could hear Thord's soft snoring.

The bard stopped. He turned to the inn and, looking straight at the window where Nikki stood, beckoned with his hand. Nikki glanced at where Thord lay sleeping and then pulled on his trousers and boots. He wrapped a spare blanket around his shoulders and quietly left the room.

Nikki stepped out the door of the inn into a world of pale grey and jet black. The moon shone full in the sky and black shadows filled the corners of the yard and pooled under the eves of the inn. The frost-covered stone flags of the courtyard sparkled in the moonlight. His breath came like white clouds lit from above by the moon. Once Nikki was in the courtyard, Bel waved him to the side and turned back to the garden.

Boom bom bom boom. The drum again sounded. This time, Bel began to sing. Nikki tried to follow the words, but the song made no sense. At least, the words in it made no sense. But Nikki began to feel a thread spinning out from them. They were filled with a harmony that was not from the world that Nikki knew but was from some place else. It was from some other time when the world was young and the moon shone new on the land. The song grew and swelled. The bard's voice remained as clear as ever but the volume rose to match the drum. It grew beyond the thunder of the drum to fill the courtyard and to spill out into the sky.

As the song reached up, the moon flared bright. It dazzled Nikki to look at it. But though blinding, the only place where the light struck the courtyard was the small garden. The rose was bathed in light. In the clear night, the moon radiated brighter than the sun on midsummer's day. The light beat down on the rose until the rose looked white hot.

Nikki felt warmth radiating out from the rose, a warmth that struck his side facing it and passed through to warm his heart. It was the warmth of Life. The song continued.

The stars nearest to the moon began to flash brighter. A wave of light spread in an ever growing ring through the sky, igniting each star it passed. When the ripple reached the horizon, the night sky was ablaze with moonlight and star-fire. The garden shone with a white light.

Boom bom-bom boom. The song ended. The silence collapsed out of the sky. The moon and stars winked back to the normal night sky. But the garden held the light. Rather than blink out, the light slowly dimmed. It was as if the light was sinking into the garden and not shining from it. The light in the garden faded until it was again just moonlight and inky pools of shadow.

When the light was gone, Bel turned to Nikki.

"I think that calls for some ale. Don't you?" He winked, turned and walked back to the inn.

\*\*\*

"I hear you dance," Bel said.

They were sitting at a table near the hearth. The warmth coming from the banked coals began to take away some of the chill. Nikki had raided the kitchen and found them half of an apple tart and filled a pitcher of beer.

"Yes, sir. I dance a little, when I can."

"Would you do so now?"

Nikki couldn't refuse. He pulled off his boots and slipped the blanket from his shoulders. He walked in front of the hearth with its dull coals to where the stone floor was kept clear of rushes. The stone was cold under his feet as was the chain that hung down his bare chest.

"What kind of dance would you like?"

Bel glanced from Nikki to the hearth and said. "You look cold. Give me a dance about fire."

Nikki turned to where the coals lay under their ash and began.

"Become what you dance," Fan Go had said. He could see the coals with his eyes. He drew the image into his mind until he could picture the embers with his eyes closed. They glowed dimly with a slight, shimmering pattern. Where the coals glowed brightest were sparkles of light. A faint smell of smoke seeped into the room. The pattern took shape in his feet and his arms. He began to move with the shifts of heat above the coals. His upraised fingers took the patterns of flame. He moved and slowly turned. As he turned, his awareness spread, like the light of the flames, around the room. He became the warmth of the coals. Nikki turned and flowed with the warmth. As he turned, he saw Bel watching him. After a number of slow circles, he began to drift into the coals. As he swung past, he saw Bel glance from him to the hearth behind him.

"That's enough. Come sit with me."

Nikki snapped out of the dance. He could feel warmth on his back and could see the glint of a fire in the bard's eyes. He turned to see a flicker of flame rising from the heap of ashes. He was suddenly tired. He half stumbled to his chair and pulled his mug to him.

"You didn't know you were doing that, did you?" Bel pointed at the small flame that still rose from the coals.

Nikki was looking at the solitary flame in the hearth. His beer mug was forgotten halfway from the table to his mouth.

"I thought not. Drink up. You deserve it." Saying this, Bel picked up his own mug and took a long pull on it.

That seemed to break the spell that lay on Nikki. He let out a breath he had not known he was holding and gulped his beer.

"You have a great deal of inborn talent, lad. You feel it move in you. But you don't know what to do with it, now, do you? If you are willing to work hard, I am willing to teach you how to gain control of your dancing. It is a rare gift you have, and one not to be left only for your own amusement. Are you willing to learn? Are you willing to work?"

*  *  *

The torch made the attic glow with a flickering red light. The ceiling sloped in from the floor on both sides to meet twenty feet up in the middle of the room. The thick wooden beams forming the truss of the roof marched down the roof line ten feet above Nikki's and Bel's heads. The far wall curved away on either side and sloped back to meet the ridgepole ten feet beyond the floor. Nikki recognized it as the plastered stone cone that formed ceiling of the kitchen. Set high in the roof were small dormers with windows to let in some light.

While the center of the room was now clear, the sides under the eaves were choked with boxes and trunks. This held the cast-offs of hundreds of years. Janlo had called it "left luggage." The room contained centuries of things left by travelers. Under the thick dust were labels that proclaimed "Fadddic will return for this" and "Hold for Uk." That morning as Nikki had cleared the center of the room, he had come across a small casket. When he tried to lift it, the rusted hinge broke and the lid had come off. Inside, the casket was filled to the top with gold pieces. Resting on top of the gold was a small cameo of a woman and a lock of brown hair. Nikki had put the lid back on and pushed the chest into a corner.

"This is a fine place to practice. A bit cold, mind you, but that will make you practice the harder." As Bel spoke, his breath came through clouds of steam.

He walked to the far end of the room and stuck the torch in a bracket in the stone. Moving to the side he sat on a box facing the torch. He pointed to the floor a few feet in front of the torch and told Nikki to sit on the blanket he carried.

"Now we know you can dance, so that's out of the way. But can you see? There are many blind people in this world. Some are born blind but most are people who never bother to see."

He pointed at the torch and said. "Look at the flame. Just look at it. Try to see everything there is to see about it. See its where, its when, and its how. After that, you can look for its why."

Nikki focused his mind on the flame. He tried to think of everything he knew about it and tried to see things in it he didn't know. He stared and time crawled by as the cold crept into his arms and legs. He exhausted everything he knew about fire and torches. He saw everything he could see that connected with what he knew and still he looked. His mind was beginning to blank out as he stared. Then it hit him like a blow. Fire! He was inside it looking out through it at himself and the room. He sat up.

"There you go! You see it, don't you?," Bel spoke, calling Nikki back to the room. "But it took you a long time to see it. Why?"

"I'm not sure. There was so much to ..." But before Nikki could explain further, Bel interrupted him.

"Right you are! You were going to say there was so much to think about and that's what took you so long to see. If you had just looked at the fire in front of you and not thought about other fires and other torches you would have seen into it without wasting your time with things that don't matter."

That was what Nikki was going to say but not what he meant. He meant that he didn't know everything about fire but he realized that was the problem. His tutors at the palace had insisted he look at each thing as a reflection of a universal type. Now he was being told to see each thing as something unique.

"Yes! When you looked at this fire, you focused on fire. What is important is not the *fire* but the *this*," Bel continued. "If you focus on the this, it doesn't matter what word follows it."

"Now for a dance," Bel said. He took up his drum and began a slow, soft beat. "Look into the fire again and this time don't waste time with other fires. When you see into the fire, let it warm you and then start to dance. Keep it slow. Janlo would be rightly mad at us if we were to be burning The Snow Rose down."

This time, Nikki just looked into the fire. He let his mind see only this fire. After a bit, he pulled it into himself and poured himself into the fire. The cold was banished. He rose and began to move with the fire. He felt the beat of the drum and found it was a mirror of the pulse of the fire. He kept his steps small and his hands close to his body. He knew, without knowing how, that the fire would now follow him just as he would follow it. If he swung his arms wide the flames would widen. If he jumped it was because the fire rose up. The beat, the light and the dance filled him, and from him they filled the room.

\*\*\*

Marcalo sat in the private audience room.

When the guards opened the door, Morik hurried in to bow in front of the king. "Sire, we have found him!"

"Where is he? Is he dead yet?"

"Sire, while we do not know precisely where he is, we know he is in a valley to the east and far north. His life is still protected by something but we were able to locate him. Some power broke out of his protection and revealed him to us."

"Good. I will have some trusted men meet with you. Tell them where to look and they will handle this."

"Sire, he is too far away for your men. It would take months of travel to reach the area and by then Nicolio may have left. We have a plan that will bring faster results."

"Do it. But I will send my own people in case you fail."

\*\*\*

Thord and Nikki were sitting at breakfast with Bel when Sil and Sammmi came into the common room from the kitchen.

Sammmi was carrying his own breakfast and set it on the table beside Bel. He looked at Thord over a mug of steaming cider. "Janlo says there's plenty of wood for today and tomorrow so you don't have to go out into the cold for more. Only fools and elves go out in this cold." The last was spoken with a nod toward Bel.

Bel pulled himself up into a haughty pose and with mock gravity responded, "Are you suggesting that the Woodland People are fools?"

"No, just that any who can't sit warm in a snowdrift all day is a fool to be out in this weather."

"You may have a point there."

Sil pulled up a fifth chair and squeezed in between Thord and Bel. She nudged Thord in the ribs. "Fool or no, if you've a mind for it, we could do with more meat. Are you up for some hunting? Oh, but I know where there is a fat boar waiting for the pot. And beside, too much work and no sport makes you slow and dull. What say you? Are you the fool I think you are?"

Bel looked at Nikki and then to Thord. "Go ahead. I've been wanting to teach Nikki to reach into his audience and that is best done when we've all day to do it."

Thord turned to Sil. "Why not? Sure, I will come."

"Then dress warm but easy. We'll be climbing through the woods and be out in the snow until the sun is long down. A couple of my kinsmen will be hunting with us."

When Thord came out the main door of the inn, Sil was waiting with three elves he hadn't met before. She tossed him a boar spear and a white cloak, and introduced the others.

"Thord, this is Ban, and this is En and her niece En. Don't go mixing them up. En is the taller of the two." As she spoke, one of the Ens straightened up while the other slouched down making one taller. Then they reversed until the other was the taller. At this all four of the elves broke into gales of laughter. The truth was that there wasn't any difference between the two elves that Thord could see at all. He started to laugh.

Ban stopped abruptly. "Don't go encouraging them, man, or they'll be pulling this joke for yet another thousand years."

The thought of the same joke lasting for centuries sent Thord laughing until cold tears ran down his cheeks.

When they stopped laughing, Thord took a closer look at Ban. He was tall with a wide grin on his face that said he was either very happy to be standing in the cold or had already fortified himself against it. The Ens carried bows and a boar net wrapped around a stout pole.

At the gate was an empty sledge. "Would you be so good as to drag that along, Ban?" Sil asked. "I for one don't want to be carrying a gutted boar all the way back to the inn."

Ban picked up the rope on the front of the sledge and they turned to trudge through the snow on the road east and into the forest. Sil and Thord walked in front, breaking a path in the deep blanket of snow that covered the land.

Thord looked back at the other three elves and over at Sil.

"Tell me, I can see why you're out hunting for The Rose. But why are the others here?"

"Well, like all the Woodland Folk, they have a tab with Janlo. No matter what the goblins say, we don't have big piles of gold hidden in the woods. Why, at best, it's hard to come by more than a gold piece every few years. It hardly lets you save more than a few hundred in a thousand years. So instead of coin, when one of us drinks or eats, it goes on the tab. Well, when the larder gets to be empty, Janlo brings out the tabs and someone goes out hunting. We'll get our boar today and maybe a deer or two tomorrow and they will be on the good side of the tab."

After just over a league, they halted beside the road.

One of the Ens pointed into the forest. "He is in there."

"You're sure this is where you saw him?" Sil said, looking south into the deep forest.

"I'm sure it was here. Not five hundred yards in. I saw his run ten days back. He'll not have moved since then."

"Leave the sledge and let's get to it." Sil turned south and headed into the heart of the forest.

They made their way into the forest through foot-deep snow. The elves slipped through the snow and undergrowth without a sound. Thord tried to match their moves but was not as successful. After one brush with a low branch that sent a small avalanche down his back, Ban turned to him with a sour look.

"How do you expect to find a boar?" he whispered. His pale, almond eyes flashed as he turned to Sil, "He makes more noise than a troop of goblin tinkers returning from a wedding party."

"Don't worry. He brings as much Luck with him as he does noise," Sil replied in the same low tone. She turned back to Thord. "And you, you great ox, remember what I was telling you last time we hunted. Flow over the ground, don't stomp on it like it's the very dirt what you came to kill. And don't you lift your foot until all your weight is balanced on the other foot. When you put your foot down, don't put your weight on it until it is on the ground nice and settled. Have you been doing it the way I showed you?"

"I've been practicing."

"Practicing!" Her whisper was more of a rasp. "That's where you're going wrong. You can't practice it. You have to live it every time you pick up one foot and put down the other. It's the amateurs that practice. And don't walk with your knees locked, you walk like a troll. Let's go, but be quiet, man, or the beast will hear us for sure, Luck or no."

They came over a rise to look down into a winding draw with a clear game trail running along the bottom. The snow on the trail was freshly trampled.

"Let's set the net around that bend." Ban pointed down to the right, where the trail rounded an arm of rock that jutted out from the ridge they were on.

One of the Ens loosened the arrows in her quiver and moved to a position behind an evergreen bush at the top of the ridge while the rest moved along it and descended to the bottom on the far side of the bend.

When they were at the bottom, the other En continued across and up the other side of the draw to disappear over the ridge. Ban unrolled the net and handed a section to Thord.

"If you would just stand there in the middle of the trail and hold this up, we will tie the ends to the trees up the sides, then we can make ourselves comfortable."

When the net was tied and staked across the trail, the three of them pulled back twenty feet down the trail. They each made a nest in the snow and waited with their white cloaks about them. As they sat below the net, Thord kept looking behind them.

"And what do you think you're at?" came Sil's soft whisper.

"What if he comes from the other way?" Thord looked again down the trail.

"Daft! The wind's blowing that way. If he is behind us, he'll smell us for sure. If he's back there we'll be sitting in the snow all afternoon and evening for nothing. I can't say if he is in front or in back, but I can say that if he comes, it won't be from that direction."

They settled in the snow at the bottom of the ravine to wait. The cold that seeped into Thord's feet and hands seemed not to affect the elves. Above their heads, the sky could be seen as patches of blue between the black and white of snow-covered pines. In places the blue was cracked like the surface of a frozen pond with the fine lines of leafless branches. Thord's breath drifted away in the light breeze that carried the sparks of snow falling from the branches overhead. Occasionally, a pine bough would spring up, having loosed a cascade of snow onto the forest below.

Time moved slowly as Thord sat and waited. In his mind, he looked back at the past. He thought of those dead at his hand. Most had been pirates or highwaymen or assassins and he wasted no time on them. The fate that overtook them had been set in motion long before their deaths. But some had been good men or more than that. Those had died for being too close to him. Their deaths were the result of him. Was he cursed to kill those around him? To kill those he loved? He looked down at his hand. What met his eye was more of a claw than a hand, white as it squeezed the shaft of his boar spear. He eased his grip and let the blood flow back into his fingers. Never again! But he knew as he made that pledge that it was in vain. He could not control the axe any more than he could give it up. His fate was tied to it. He would carry the axe and the axe would kill. His only hope was the promise of Vorkki that someone would free the axe and free him.

Turning away from thoughts of things he couldn't change, he went back over the previous hunts Sil had taken him on. He tried to remember everything she had taught him about hunting. There were few large animals to hunt in the Floelands, so he had never learned how to stalk game. His life since he left his homeland revolved around how to stalk or evade men, and he was finding those skills were not always useful when the dealing with creatures that lived by smell and hearing more than by sight and reason. Fooling a deer was far more difficult than fooling a man. He wondered how much more difficult it would be when the opponent was as cunning and dangerous as a boar.

After a time that was lost in the quiet of the snow and the forest, Sil turned to Thord and whispered softly, "While we're here you may as well get some good from the wait. It'll come in handy for the next time we go hunting. Now would you tell me what you hear?"

Thord sat and listened to the stillness around him. "Nothing."

"Nothing? Are you deaf, man? The air is full of sound. First there is you. Listen and hear your breathing. That is always the loudest. You sound like a great bellows. In and out, in and out. Listen for it and then get rid of the sound. Listen past it. What do you hear?"

Thord listened. Yes, there was his breath, soft at the edges of his nose and down his throat. He tried to listen to what lay between those breaths.

Thump thump, thump thump.

"I hear my heart."

"Yes. Now close your eyes and listen beyond that. Listen for me."

Thord closed his eyes and in his head he let the sound of his heart join the sound of his breathing and listened.

"Yes, I hear you now, and Ban as well. Your breath is faster than mine but your heart beats slow."

"Good. I knew you had the makings of an elf, even with those blunt lumps you call your ears. Now reach out further. Can you hear the breeze? But don't just listen to it, find it. Find where the sound of the breeze comes from. Listen. It will tell you where the rocks and trees are, if you only listen to it talking."

Thord sat and listened for a time that felt like hours. There it was, a sound beyond the breathing and the slight movements made by himself and the elves. There it was. The sound made by a leaf that rattled against its branch on a bush above and behind him. The wind made a soft whistle as it wrapped around an outcrop of rock where the trail narrowed in front of him. He was about to speak when a finger was placed against his lips. He kept his eyes closed. A faint sound far up the trail. Hooves sounding a tattoo on buried rocks and frozen ground. Hooves coming closer. The sound of leaves shaking slightly as something passed by. Closer.

There was a soft, creaking sound from the top of the ridge further up the trail. Then came the twang of a bow string. The narrow ravine burst with sound, yelling from the ridges on either side and the mingled sounds of an arrow hitting flesh and the loud squeal of the boar. Thord's eyes popped open to see a huge boar charging around the bend in the trail, his white tusks flashing and red blood flying from an arrow deep in his shoulder. The boar was heading straight into the net. He took it with his head low to the ground and with a heave of his snout, ripped the bottom up from the stakes and charged under it. His long tusks caught for a moment in the net and he was spun around with his right side in front of Thord and the elves. Ban was the first to reach him. He charged with the spear forward and managed to take the boar in the side. But the blade must have missed the heart. The boar shook and sent Ban flying. He landed with a thump against the boll of a tree and slumped to the snow. Sil got in the next blow, but by then the boar had freed his tusks and turned to charge. Sil's spear took him high in the scars and gristle of his shoulder. She held on to the end of the spear, but the force of the beast's charge lifted her off the ground and sent her up into the snow on the bank.

Now Thord was alone with the boar hurtling down the trail like a black and ivory avalanche. He stayed crouching in the snow with his left knee bent and his right leg braced behind him, grounding the butt of his spear in the frozen earth. The spear stretched out in front of him, blade almost flat on the ground. As the boar's snout passed over the spear blade, Thord jerked the spear up until the tip caught the beast in the throat. The boar charged and Thord felt the butt slide over the frozen ground until it caught and held. Now with the tusks flashing little more than a foot from Thord's face, the blade went in deep until the cross piece jammed against bone and flesh. The force of the boar's charge lifted the boar from the ground and bent the spear shaft until it snapped in Thord's hands. The beast fell to the earth with his legs kicking and then lay still. Thord closed his eyes and after listening through the ragged heaves of his breath and the pounding of his heart, he heard the last breath flow out of the boar.

When he opened his eyes he saw the two Ens running lightly down the sides of the ravine with notched arrows. Ban was standing beside the tree where he had landed with one hand against the trunk, supporting himself. Sil was covered in snow and laughing as she slid down the bank to the trail.

As Sil came up she took the broken spear shaft from Thord's numb fingers and tossed it to Ban. "See? I told you he carried Luck. Now let's be getting the brute cut open before it gets stiff on us."

With the boar bending the pole that had carried the net, and with Thord and Sil on one end and the other three elves on the other, they managed to get the boar up the ravine and to the sledge. As they pulled the heavy carcass back to the inn, Ban kept staring at it.

"Ah, but that's the biggest boar I've seen in this forest in a good five hundred years. After this, I don't think that we'll be owing Janlo but maybe one deer." He pulled a flask from his cloak, inspected it to be sure it was whole, and handed it to Thord. "You can hunt with us any day you've a mind. Luck, she said. I saw that spear break under the beast. It was more than common luck that stopped that brute."

It was full dark with the moon rising into a dome of hard, cold stars when they reached the light and fires of The Rose.

***

The room was dark. The closed door and shuttered windows kept out both the cold night air and moonlight flooding down from the sky outside. The few candles that stood on the bar served only to heighten the darkness that filled the far corners of the wine shop. In one of those corners, four men sat at an uneven table. All four were foreign to this city, but the youngest had lived here most of his life.

"I can help you," the young man was saying. "I know who you are looking for, and I can guide you to him."

"How do you know what we want?" This came from the lean man across the table. As he spoke, his left hand spun his wine goblet while his right hand was invisible under the table.

"I know a lot about what goes on in this city. When strangers start asking for word of a countryman of mine, my friends think I should know." The young man's voice was low and intense. "I can help you. But I want something in return."

The older man glanced at his two companions and then back. His right hand came up from under the table to rub at a long scar on his cheek. "Maybe we can use you. What was your name again?"

"Baedano, son of Baelo of Tronmar."

"And what is the price of your help, Baedano? For the right help, we can pay in gold."

"What I want is to return to Tronmar with a place at court."

"Why do you think we can offer something only the king can grant?" The man's right hand slipped back under the table again. At the same time, the man on Baedano's left shifted his chair back from the table.

"I have good ears and heard part of a conversation between some travelers. I only understood it when I heard you were offering gold for information about one of them. I know who you work for and what you want. You won't find them without my help. For what I offer, an introduction to the court is a small reward."

"Perhaps," was all the other man said. He brought his hand up again to pick up his goblet. He took a drink of the sweet dark wine. "Yes, I'm sure our employer could find uses for a young man with your ... sensibilities."

Baedano smiled and held up his own goblet. "To the king and those who serve him."

\*\*\*

The taproom faded into darkness. Chance looked up at the sound of his sister's footsteps.

"Vorkki, I can't see why you allow yourself to get close to these mortals. Don't their base desires and weaknesses bother you?"

"Oh, I agree with what you say about some of them. There are others, but they too have faults. But who are we to speak of them? We may be immortal, but are we free of the same weaknesses? Greed, power, lust – don't we have these? If there is a difference between us and the mortals, it is that our passions are stronger than theirs. And when those are played upon, we can work even greater evil. When the Elder People called us here, it was to watch over the Children. They were dying and called us to act as guides, when they were gone.

"Is it a wonder how mortals behave, with us as their gods? When I look at what can be found in the hearts of mortals, I see only a faint echo of what we find in ourselves. Evil and Good.

"But this is an argument we've had many times. Let's find something that is more pleasant than the failings of men and gods to pass the time." He stood up and took her hand in his.

\*\*\*

It was mid-day when Nikki and Thord entered the inn, stomping the blood back into their cold feet. Only when they had settled at a table with steaming bowls of onion soup in front of them did they begin to warm up. As they ate, Thord watched Nikki. He had been mostly quiet during the day. Thord thought he knew Nikki's moods but this was a new one. When Nikki was quiet, it usually meant he was thinking of his family. At those times, the sorrow for the dead would show through in his wet eyes. Other times Thord knew Nikki was thinking about Tronmar in the hands of his uncle. Then the eyes Thord saw would hold a conflict between the determination to take the throne away from the usurper and the knowledge he was helpless to do it. But this was different. Thord could see the sadness, but it looked not like the old grief but more wistful, something misplaced, maybe, and not something lost.

"What are you thinking, Little Fox?"

Nikki looked up from his soup and into Thord's eyes. "It's stupid. But, it's twenty-three days since the solstice and today I am eighteen. If I were home, my family would hold a feast for my birthday. And this year, I would be a man. But now..." He looked back down into the bowl in front of him.

As he spoke, Sil had come up silently behind him. Thord looked up and saw her wink at him and again silently retreat to where Janlo was polishing the bar. As he and Nikki ate their soup, looking past Nikki, Thord saw Sil talking as Janlo looked back across the room at them. When she finished, Janlo nodded and disappeared back into the kitchen. Shortly, he came back out. He looked at Thord and held up his arm, hand flat and fingers together, in the sign Thord knew as "no bottom, end of shoal water."

Sil came up as they finished their soup. "Off you go now. The trees won't walk to the woodpile by themselves. We've a wedding tonight and I need to see the house ready. Nikki, you'll be serving the guests so when you get back be sure to clean up and dress nice. Now out with you both."

When the two returned late in the day, they entered an inn that was transformed. The usual evening smells of meat and cabbage were buried in the smell of Janlo's spice cake. The common room was rearranged with a table across one end in a place of honor. A handful of the local goblins had arrived and were nursing ales. Some of the Woodland Folk had cleared room for the dart board. Thord and Nikki were intercepted by Sil and sent off to the inn's bath-house and told they had an hour before the wedding started.

As they soaked the cold out of them, Thord thought he could see some lightening in Nikki. In the tub across from him, Thord saw a brief smile as he slid into the hot water. It didn't last long. It was followed by a sigh and the corners of his mouth turned down. Thord guessed that, feast or no feast, the thought of serving others on his birthday was not going to lift his spirits. Well, they would see about that.

When they finally came down, Nikki in his black tunic from Tronmar and Thord in his best hose, shirt, and leather jerkin, the common room was full. The only empty table was for the wedding party. Sil grabbed Nikki and Thord by the arms and pulled them to the kitchen to where a large spice cake covered in honey-butter was on a tray. She faced Nikki with a dead serious look.

"Now I want you to take this in and set it on the table for the guests of honor. I want you to look as grave as you can, as this is to be as fine a feast as The Rose has seen in many a long year."

When Nikki entered carrying the cake in front of him, the crowd went silent. With Thord behind him, he walked the length of the room to stand before the empty table and set the cake down. When the tray was out of his hands, Thord reached under his arms and lifted the surprised Nikki off his feet. As he turned and began carrying his sputtering burden around the table, the room behind him burst into whoops of laughter and the banging of hands on tables. Though he couldn't see Nikki's face himself, Thord could see in the faces of the others what that face must look like. He sat Nikki down in one of the chairs to a chorus of "To your birthday!" shouted over raised mugs and glasses. Thord sat next to Nikki and got a look at his face. Surprise, joy, bafflement, all were there to see.

Sil came up with glass of wine. Offering it to Nikki, she said, "You don't think we would be forgetting your birthday, do you?"

"Forget it? How did you know it?"

"Well, I haven't lived the past couple thousand years without knowing what I need to know, when I need to know it." She winked as she said this. "Now drink up so the party can begin in earnest."

As the night progressed, Thord began to fear for Nikki. Thord was sure that tomorrow his back would be sore from the thumping it was taking from thick goblin hands, and he wondered if the number of times his face was crushed into the chest of an elf would leave the lad's nose bruised. But Thord could see the glow spreading though him. Later, when someone called for a dance, Sil objected.

"It's his birthday. Would you be having him working on the day he becomes a man?"

The chorus came back. "Right!" "Just so!" "Dance! Dance!"

Nikki got to his feet. "It isn't work to show how much I appreciate all this."

Thord watched as Nikki moved to the center of the room. He turned to where some goblins and Bel had set up a band. "Play a dance tune everyone knows."

After a bit of muttered discussion to choose the right song, they began. And so too did Nikki, stamping and clapping out point and counterpoint to the rhythm. The tune was lively and, as Thord watched Nikki, he began to feel Nikki's dance seep into him. His own feet started to move to the music. He wasn't alone. After a bit, some of the goblins got to their feet and began to dance as well. Soon, tables were being pushed to the side to make more room. Thord found himself in front of Nikki and realized that the only people in the inn who weren't dancing were the ones playing the music, and their feet were moving where they sat. He didn't remember much after that. The last thing he could recall about that night was laying on his back in bed and Nikki leaping to straddle his chest. He remembered the shivers from the contrast between the hot body on his stomach and, as Nikki leaned down to kiss him, the cold chain resting on his chest. He didn't remember anything after that but in the morning they both were smiling.

***

The common room was crowded. There was a group of eight goblins from the north stopping on their way to a wedding. Half a dozen of the woodland people were exchanging drinks and boasts in a corner near the fire. Two elves and two goblins had started a game of darts. Though each side swore the other was cheating, they kept playing and buying drinks, hopeful that if they could not win by their own skill, their opponents could be vanquished by the ale. A couple of men at the bar had come in from the forest to sell furs to Janlo. And last, there were three trolls in the lower room with a jeroboam of mead.

Nikki was setting a tray of empty mugs on the bar when the call came.

"Give us a dance!" came a voice from near the door.

It was followed by a similar call from the bar. Soon, a chorus of voices was calling for a dance.

Under Bel's pushing and with Thord's agreement, Nikki had begun to dance more often in the common room on busy nights. At first, he was hesitant to dance in front of the crowd. But as time went on he could read into the individuals that made up the custom and found he could lift their spirits. Feeling their pleasure at watching him fueled his own pleasure in the dance. Now, he looked forward to being called to dance.

"Dance for us a clear spring under the moon," came from an elf near the fire.

"Give us an autumn field." This was from a goblin in the corner.

"Want stars. You do dance sky," came a low rumbling voice. This last was from the wide doorway into the lower room where three trolls were drinking.

"The sky it is," said Nikki. He pulled off his shirt and laid it across a chair.

When he stood in the open, he began to stamp his foot to a slow beat. The other feet in the room picked it up and after a handful of beats, Nikki could feel the vibrations from the floor and began to dance.

As he danced, his mind traveled back to the south where his tutor, the wizard Ganian, had shown him the night sky. That night flowed into him and out into the dance. They had stood on one of the towers in the south wall and looked into the black vault of the heavens. Ganian had pointed to the constellations and named them. The old man had talked about emptiness and vast distances. Nikki had watched the stars wheel around in the night sky and felt the wonder of the night.

In his mind he saw those constellations again and began to move through them. He took the stars from his memory and held them in his hands. As he danced, he flung the stars from his fingertips to hang among the smoke-blackened beams above his head. He danced The Hunter and The Dragon. He followed the moon as it passed through The Weaver. His dance flowed from constellation to constellation and from star to star. He reached out into the beat the crowd made, to pull them along with him. Nikki swung them around in the great arc of The Scythe. He cupped his hands and made a ball of light, like the goblin children making balls of snow. With one hand he pulled a streamer of light from it and tossed the white ball up, the great comet he had seen riding in the far south. With a wave of his open hand, he spilled its tail out across the sky he wove. The dance slowed and the dawn crept in and extinguished the stars and stopped.

When he stopped, the goblins thumped the table with the palms of their hands. The elves called for another dance. Nikki would have been flattered more, but he expected the elves would have called even louder if he had tripped over a chair leg. He was more pleased with the way the two men at the bar had exchanged looks. He had given them a vision of a sky they remembered together. The real surprise was the voice from the lower room.

"You see good. You see and you dance. You come drink with us."

When he pulled his head through the neck of his shirt, he was face to face with Janlo behind the bar. Janlo was holding out a cup.

"Join them. You don't get a chance to drink with trolls every night, you know."

Nikki took the cup and walked down the steps into the lower room. When the inn was built, this room was intended for trolls. The high ceiling of the common room extended into the room. This, and the four feet of steps leading down from the floor of the main room, gave fourteen feet for the trolls to stand upright. The room was big but still only held two massive tables and eight chairs. What light there was came from the door and two candles in sconces. The room was cold and dark and just what trolls wanted for a pleasant evening.

Nikki climbed up into a chair and was brought up short by a childhood memory of eating at the table with his parents. His eyes looked out even with the table top. It wasn't a perfect match with the memory. Instead of his family, he sat looking up into the faces of three trolls. He smiled, thinking there was some resemblance between his oldest brother and the tall faces, small eyes, and broad, flat noses of the trolls.

"Lin," said the troll across from Nikki. "You no got manners. Clear table. He sit up where we talk."

The troll on the right slid a large platter of grilled onions on sticks from the end of the table in front of Nikki and put it on the far side of the table. Nikki climbed up on the table and sat cross-legged. Now he could see the trolls better. His eyes were almost on the same level as theirs and he could see into their faces. A huge hand picked up the jeroboam and carefully poured mead into Nikki's cup.

"You call Fox," said the troll on the left. "Me call Kol. This Vil. This Lin." He indicated the troll across from Nikki and then the one on Nikki's right.

"We like you dance," said Vil.

"Yes, we like. You see stars," Lin said, and held up the small bucket of mead from in front of him.

The four of them then drank. The mead was sweet and strong and helped to drive off some of the chill. Nikki took a second, quick gulp.

Now fortified, Nikki waited for a conversation about gods knew what. He half expected to be told the endless stories about their lives that elves were full of, or of the weather and family that dominated the conversation of goblins. What came next was neither of these.

"You dance stars in south," said Lin. "When you see stars? Three years mid summer?"

Nikki was shocked. It was mid summer's eve three years ago, when he and Ganian had stood on the turret and looked out into the night. His mind tried to get around how the troll knew so much about what Prince Nicolio had done and where he had been. Could they have seen his dance so clearly that they could tell apart stars they had never seen?

Finally he nodded his head. At that, Vil pointed a blunt finger at Kol.

"I tell you. I tell you hundred years that not Bin's Visitor but Kil's. You say it come in 47 years and I say it come three years back in south. I tell you."

"I say you wrong," Kol retorted. "That not Kil's. That Bin's. Fox see other visitor. One point hard guess. But maybe Vol's Visitor. Vol not tell full path."

"Vol's far south. Not Vol's," came from Lin. He was refilling the drinks. When he got to filling Nikki's cup, he winked and repeated. "Not Vol's."

This brought a fresh round of arguing between Vil and Kol over what the paths were for half a dozen comets, or "visitors", as they called them. As they argued back and forth, Lin sat back with a light in his eyes and a look that must pass for satisfaction on a troll.

"Bin's Visitor not stable. Bin's shift. Bin's touch that star."

"What star?"

"Star Fox see. Three eighths below Rol 17. No name. Call Fox 1."

On it went. Nikki was lost in a maze of stars with names he didn't know in skies that no books remembered. After several rounds of mead, he blurted out that he didn't understand how they could know all this.

"How can you see and remember the movement of stars a hundred years ago?"

Vil looked at him across the table.

"We shepherds. Nights alone on mountain with sheep. See stars not much else."

Kol looked up to the ceiling, or maybe to something beyond the wooden beams. "Sheep fine when young. After 500 years sheep dull. Stars always change. Stars not dull. 500 years or 2000 years, stars not dull."

At that, they took up the argument again. Before the trolls had finished a second jeroboam of mead and another platter of onions, "Fox" had a further six stars named after him and Thord had come and half-led, half-carried him to bed.

***

It was in the deepest of winter when the word came from the north. A group of ogres had come over the mountains from the northern ice. They had raided a goblin village and moved south to the edge of the forest. The news was brought by a goblin named Warrrgit, who had trekked through the snow eight days looking for help to defend his village. The ogres had not attacked it when he left, but it was only a matter of time before they would be looking for fresh meat.

The call for help did not fall on deaf ears. The petty rivalries between the Forest People and the goblins were nothing when compared to the mutual fear and hatred both felt towards the ogres. The council was called in the common room of The Snow Rose. Thord was sitting on a stool with Nikki sitting on the bar beside him.

A goblin stood up to speak for the three closest villages. He was old. The tips of his long ears drooped down to touch his shoulders. Even so, when he spoke his voice was strong and firm.

"This is not the first time ogres have crossed the mountains to attack our people," he said. "It will not be easy to beat them back. But we all know what will happen if we don't. Sixty years ago, I was too old to join in the fight, but I remember the battle forty years before that. I would not ask for this if I hadn't seen the butchered bones that were all that was left of the villages they overwhelmed."

Hin spoke for the elves.

"We have all seen the evil of these monsters. We will fight."

Sil leaned over the bar and whispered to Thord. "Besides, Vorkki's Child, it'll be a glorious fight." She had a gleam in her eye that made Nikki glad he was not an ogre just then.

"How many ogres are on this side of the mountains?" asked an elf.

"You will think fear counts every foe twice. But there are at least sixty ogres," Warrrgit replied.

That brought a chorus of shouts. "Sixty! Are you sure?" "Sixty ogres? I've never heard of more than twenty together." "What is their sign?"

Warrrgit had an answer for the last question. "They follow a snow cat."

In the end, the elders of the nearest goblin villages pledged to send two hundred spearmen to the north. The Forest People offered to send another hundred bows. All agreed to meet at the inn in two days.

The next day, Nikki and Thord were in the kitchen getting ready for the march north. When Thord had volunteered to go, Nikki would not be left behind. Nikki was packing food while Thord was oiling his mail shirt. Sil came in and Nikki asked her about ogres.

"Well, ogres are one of the cold tribes."

When she saw the blank look on Nikki's face, she continued, "Their blood is cold. Elves are of the hot-blooded tribe. Men, dwarves and goblins are warm-blooded. Ogres and trolls are cold-blooded. Have you touched a troll?"

Yes, Nikki had been shocked the first time he had touched the skin of a troll. It was cold. It was as if he had put his hand on rock that lay in the shadows of a mountain.

"Like trolls, ogres don't feel cold. And like trolls, they're hard to kill, as well. Their hide is tougher than any leather. Swords and spears bounce off unless you hit them where the skin bends. The neck under the jaw is best, but under the arm will work if your blade is long enough."

"Why haven't we heard of them in Tronmar?" Nikki asked.

"That's because they can't hunt that far south. Their eyes only see heat. If the air is warm, it's as if they are in a fog. It leaves them blind. They only cross the mountains into the south in winter. And fortunately, they don't often cross even then," she said.

"What were they talking about when they spoke of the ogres following a sign?"

"Ogres don't have speech as we do. They are solitary and seldom come together in groups of more than three or four," she explained. "But they will follow something that they see as not normal. They can sense anything magical and a group of them will follow it. They seldom cross the mountains unless something leads them. But to draw together sixty ogres means the sign must be very powerful."

She turned from Nikki and looked at Thord. "Thord, I would be forgetting the armor. It won't be doing you any good at all. Ogres don't have swords or spears. They only use bone clubs. Speed is better than armor."

As Nikki packed, Sil and Thord talked about the best ways to kill ogres.

***

In the morning, the goblins met in front of The Snow Rose. When Thord and Nikki stepped through the gate they came face to face with an argument.

"He's too young," a goblin was saying.

97

"Let Sammmi come, Malllki," another goblin was saying.

Sammmi stood in the center of the group. He had a spear, a shield, and a look of determination in his eyes.

"I say his ears are too high. In his face you can see the strain of holding them low."

"And which of us didn't lie about his age when we first went to battle? I remember a certain young snip who pulled the same thing a hundred years ago. And I'm looking at him now!"

"I don't like it." But it was clear by the laughs around him that Malllki had just lost the argument.

Sammmi turned to Thord and Nikki and gave them a wink.

***

This night the troop camped in a large glade. The surrounding snow-filled trees turned the clearing into an amphitheater. The goblins had swept out the center and piled the snow to the outside and dug burrows into the mounds. A cook fire was built in the center. The goblins formed groups around their stacked arms and talked. The next night they would reach the village of Kliill Waters. After three nights of sleeping in the snow, everyone was ready for something with a roof.

The elves had come in from scouting to eat from the communal pot. When the stew pot was empty, the forest people withdrew into the trees to find shelter in the branches.

A goblin produced a flute and began to play. This brought out several more flutes and a drum and soon a group of goblins were shoulder to shoulder in a circle singing drinking songs.

Sammmi stopped playing his flute and came up to Thord. "Have Nikki dance for us. Have him dance something to take our minds off the wind and the cold."

Nikki caught Thord's wink as he turned to him. "Little Fox, we can all use some cheering up, I am thinking."

Nikki shrugged off his coat and hat and walked to the drummer.

"Sir, may I give you a beat?" he asked. And when the drummer held out the drum he began tapping the drum.

Thump tap, tap, tap Thump tap, tap. Thump tap, tap, tap Thump tap, tap.

As the drummer took up the beat, Nikki walked to near the fire and began to dance. It was hard at first to forget the cold and the ring of faces. He had to fight his awareness of the cold ground under his feet to be able to turn into himself. As he began to reach into the rhythm, the flute players began to pick up the beat and work their own melody around

98

it. Nikki started to sense the feeling of the players and then the feelings of the whole group. As he danced, he reached out to the flames at his back and wove them into the dance. The crowd around him began to take on the heat from the fire. The frowns and hunched shoulders gave way to relaxed smiles. He managed to spread the heat to the minds around him in an ever widening circle. When he reached the edge of the glade, he could sense the Woodland Folk in their trees and spun the warmth out into the night.

Now the dance had him. He felt as if he could turn back winter if he could just reach far enough. He spun and wove to each new piece the flutes introduced. He reached further and further into the fire and into the night. The night was cold. His reaching found a knot of cold that would not warm. First there was one, then another, and still more ice cold pieces of the night. He tried harder to break the ice but it wouldn't give. The cold was getting closer and clearer. It was a cold, hungry hate.

He froze. "Ogres! The ogres are surrounding the camp!" he yelled.

The quiet in the trees beyond the camp was broken by the shouts of the elves. The goblins turned and ran to their spears.

Nikki stood with his back to the fire. He stooped and took a flaming pine branch in his hand. The camp was full of noise and blurs of motion.

All around him were knots of goblins. Though the ogres had come unexpectedly, the goblins knew what needed to be done. Each group would take a single ogre. Some would use their spears to hold it at bay while the others would jab for the throat or under the arms.

An ogre came charging from the forest. But before it reached the goblins, an elf had leaped from a tree onto its back. A flash of steel in the firelight marked a blade from behind ripping the ogre's throat.

The rest of the ogres charged into the clearing. The battle began in earnest with knots of goblins and elves trying to take each ogre.

Nikki was in the center of the battle. His burning brand would do little to stop an ogre but he had to find a way to help. He remembered what Sil had said in The Snow Rose. *Their eyes see only heat. If the air is warm, it's as if they are in a fog.*

He concentrated on the fire. His feet began to move with the fire. The crackling sound of the fire became music and he danced. He moved in a slow circle around the fire. The flaming branch in his hand took a life of its own. The heat from the flame spun out into the night when he swung the brand. He could see the fire grow all around him. It filled the night. He whirled and spun the heat out into the air around and around. It filled the glade. The bonfire became a column of flame lighting up the night. He spun faster and faster. The air in the clearing glowed with the heat from the fire. Still he danced.

\*\*\*

Thord fought at one end of the glade. His axe brought death as it moved. Around him the bodies lay where his axe had left them. The axe made no distinction between the softer or harder parts of ogres. Thord was lost in the battle.

\*\*\*

The air grew first warm then hot. The ogres were confused. Their blows missed and they failed to see death coming for them. The goblins and elves began to gain the upper hand. All but a handful of ogres were down now.

Then the cat came into the clearing in a single leap. She landed facing Nikki. Her fur was the color of new snow. Her teeth were two great, ivory daggers. Her eyes glowed red with a fire that burned in some other place. Those eyes were fixed on Nikki where he danced in front of a tower of flame.

The great cat crouched. The muscles in her back bunched and rippled as she readied the leap. Where the ogres were brutish, she was beautiful. She was elegant death.

Caught in the dance, Nikki was only aware of the two red fires of the cat's eyes. When they shot towards him, he flung himself backward towards the flames he called upon. The blow that should have killed him only helped to carry them both into the flames. They rolled free of the fire.

The fire that Nikki had called up seemed to be unable to touch him. He rolled to his hands and knees. His face came up to look into the eyes of the great cat as she crouched inches from him. He smelled the singed fur. He felt the hot breath on his face. All he saw were two eyes, now amber. And then, in a great bound, the eyes were gone back into the night.

\*\*\*

The smell of burned hair filled the room.

Taulgir sat like the others. His eyes were heavy and he breathed in short gasps. But it was a charade. He was barely winded. The other four wizards were not feigning exhaustion.

Wila, who had controlled the great cat, was slumped in her chair. The ends of her hair curled where the fire had touched it and broken her spell. Taulgir knew she had tried too hard. The distance was too great for the spell she had initiated. Still, it might have worked if all four of the others had given all their strength to her. He knew this, and knew that she knew it as well. And, he knew she was aware of who had held back. Taulgir reached out with a touch. It was just a hint of a touch on her mind, just the very slightest of contacts. Yet, as she teetered on the edge of life, it was just enough to push her over the edge and into oblivion.

Two minds had known that touch. One had no reason to tell anyone, and now the other never would.

***

In the light of the dying fire, the goblins and woodland people began to count the cost of their victory. The battle was over. When the spell that held the snow cat was broken in the fire, the great cat had left. The remaining ogres had turned and followed her into the forest.

Thord stood alone, staring into the night, within a ring of dead. His axe was still in his hands. The night around him was returning to black and white and gray. The red was washing from his sight. It was seeping into the snow along with the blood.

The past and present flooded into him as he stood. There was a familiar voice calling his name from some vast distance. Closer at hand were the memories of the past quarter hour.

He had run, axe in hand, to the edge of the glade. As he ran, he felt the terror welling up in him. Views of himself dying filled his mind. He saw himself smashed by great clubs and eaten while he still screamed. He saw parts of his body dragged through the snow by huge, clawed hands. He felt a spear thrust through his chest. He saw bone crush his skull. Over and over he died. As he ran to his death, the world was filled with a grey haze, the haze of death. But that haze began to take on color. It flushed red and he knew the Rage was on him.

An ogre had come crashing out of the trees in front of him. Its face was all teeth and eyes. In its hands was the four foot long leg bone of some great beast. As it raised its club, Thord stepped toward it and to the side. Before the club could come down, Thord swung his axe. The blade bit into the ogre's neck and collar bone. Without the framework to support

101

the arms, the blow collapsed with the ogre. Thord ripped the axe from the falling body and turned to find more to kill.

A second ogre charged, only to fall as a downstroke of the axe opened it from shoulder to knee. A third came and then a fourth. Each came bearing Thord's death. But the terror of those deaths fed the axe, and each who came died.

***

Barrrki was backing up. The ogre in front of him kept coming at him. The rest of his team was trying to pin it but it kept coming. Barrrki's spear jabs only slowed it to a walk as it came forward. The goblin knew it was only a matter of time before he slipped backing up in the snow and the ogre would have him.

A thrust from the side took the ogre's attention for an instant. Barrrki turned with his spear to run. When he turned he saw the man. He stopped, rooted with the spear pointed at the man's chest. Barrrki saw only the wild eyes and the axe that knocked his spear away and came for his life. He never saw the second blow that took both legs off the ogre behind him.

***

Thord relived each moment of the fight. One by one, the deaths he had seen were played out. And one by one, the Rage in the axe turned his deaths into the deaths of others. He had seen nineteen deaths. Now there were eighteen dead ogres at his feet. Eighteen ogres and one goblin. He stood looking at the bodies as the voice came closer.

"Thord. It's alright. It's the Little Fox. We're alright."

"Is it? Is it alright?" asked Thord staring at the goblin's body in the snow. He allowed Nikki to lead him to the fire and settle him on a log.

Twenty-six goblins had died in the attack. Nineteen elves had also been killed. There were not many wounded. The blows from ogre clubs either missed or they didn't.

Nikki watched as the elves carried their fallen comrades into the forest. Sil walked with them. Nikki started to follow when a heavy hand on his shoulder stopped him.

"Let them go, Lad."

It was Malllki.

"Let them go. Where they are going, you and I can't follow," the goblin said. "They will not want anyone else there when they say goodbye to their friends. Elves can live forever. So when they die it is a wound they all share. I think their bravado is because of that. They can't bear to see their own death so they hide it from us and from themselves.

"Come," he said. "We have to take care of our own."

He led Nikki to where a goblin lay in the mud. There was no way to recognize the face. The head had been horribly smashed by a bone club. Nikki gasped when he saw the flute stuck in the belt. It was Sammmi.

"Yes," said the goblin. "We were trying to hold an ogre. Warrrin had already fallen. Sammmi charged in to distract it so we could get a clear shot at its throat. When it turned to hit him, I thrust as hard as I could, as fast as I could. I wasn't fast enough. I wasn't."

Malllki reached down and pulled the flute from Sammmi's belt. "Here, take this to Janlo. Tell him that... Tell him..." He turned away.

When Malllki turned back, his eyes were wet.

"Give me a hand with him. He's not heavy."

They laid Sammmi with the other goblins on a pyre of pine branches. A torch was placed in Nikki's hand.

"You would honor us and our dead if you would send them on."

Nikki thrust the torch into the wood and stood back. As the flames spread, the goblins formed a circle around the pyre and began a low song. From somewhere in the trees Nikki could hear another fainter song. He walked back to sit with Thord. Thord took Nikki and pulled him to his chest and held him as fire again lit the glade.

As the flames of the pyre lit the night, Nikki was aware of the eyes of the goblins being concentrated on Thord. After a time, Malllki walked over and stood before Thord.

"Thord, we know how Barrrki was killed. We don't understand it, but we know. We don't hold you responsible for his death. But neither can we forget how he died. If we seem cold, forgive us."

Nikki stood. Anger burned in his eyes. "How can ..."

Thord grabbed him, pulling him down to his side.

"I understand, Malllki," he said quietly. "Things are as they are and neither of us can bring the dead back."

***

In the morning, the goblins left for Kliill Waters. They didn't know what they would find there. But whatever it was, they wouldn't need help now that the ogres were dead. Sil and some of the elves came and began to skin the ogres that had fallen where Thord fought.

Sil came over to where Thord and Nikki were readying their packs

103

for the long trek back.

"I told you it would be a grand fight, didn't I?" She said. "This valley hasn't seen anything like it that I can remember since the dragons left. Five hundred years is too long without a tale worth a song."

"These will be our gift to you," she told Thord, pointing to the pile of ogre hides.

"I can't see why I would want them, whether or not I killed them," he said.

"Oh, you will. Give us some time. You will." And with a wink, she turned back to the task.

***

One morning as winter was loosening its grip, Thord was in the common room of the inn. Sil came in and dropped a bundle on the table in front of him.

"Remember what you said about ogre hides? Well, here they are again."

She unwrapped the bundle and in it was a hauberk of blue-white scale armor. Each scale was made of ogre leather with a branching spine of polished bronze down the center like the veins of a leaf. The scales didn't have the look of leather. Instead of a flat color or even the color of polished leather, the scales shone with a depth that drew the eye into it. Looking at it was closer to looking at old ice. Thord thought of the icebergs that drifted around his homeland. While the color was white, deep in each scale was a pale blue that looked to be a foot or more under the surface.

"It's lighter than those iron rings you wear, and won't clink like a merchant's purse when you walk in the forest."

It sounded like leaves in the wind when Thord held it up and shook it out. He slipped it over his head. It fell to his knees and the sleeves reached to just below his elbows. On the table were greaves and arm guards. All with the pattern of leaves on ice.

# Chance's Children

## *Chapter 7*

"Spring will be here soon," Thord said as he rested on a new felled tree. "I am thinking we will need to decide what to do before we leave here. We told Baelo that we would bring back the furs but beyond that what?"

Nikki stood beside the oxen, scratching Flick Ear between the eyes. "We can't come back here, as much as I would like to. That snow cat did not guide the ogres here to hunt deer. My uncle knows I'm here and has wizards working to find me. He'll be certain to try again if I stay in one place."

"Well if you think you can't go back to the Home Sea until you have men willing to fight for you, that only leaves east over the mountains to the northern elf kingdom or south through the high pass to the Golden Empire. Old Fan said we should head that way. He may be right, I am thinking."

"Then when do we leave?"

"We will either have to go soon, while we can make it to the grasslands when the road is still frozen; or, if we wait for the thaw, it will be weeks for the mud to dry enough for the cart."

"Then we need to go now."

Thord heard the heavy sigh that escaped Nikki. Thord felt the same way. They had both made good friends here. Thinking of what he knew of Nikki's growing up in a palace, he thought maybe Nikki had made better friends the past months than in his whole life before.

"Then we need to get ready. I'll tell Janlo we'll be leaving in two days. No, three. I am thinking that we'll want to enjoy The Rose and say our goodbyes slow."

***

The evening before they were to leave, they were in the common room. The cart was loaded with supplies and the goods they were to carry for Janl;, that and some things they had picked up themselves to fill the empty space. They planned to leave with the rising sun in the morning. But that night they were going to enjoy one last evening in The Snow Rose.

While Thord sat at a table near the hearth, Bel came into The Rose. Setting his pack on the floor and leaning his drum against the wall,

107

he took a seat with Thord.

"Oh, I was just in the forest hereabout and thought I might stop in for some music and an ale or five."

Nikki came by carrying a tray full of mugs. He dropped three off at their table. "I'll be back as soon as I take these to the corner table."

Bel looked across to the bar. "Janlo! What are you doing, working the lad on his last night?"

Janlo stopped polishing a silver goblet. "It wasn't my idea. I tried to talk him into taking his ease but he said he would be happier if he carried drinks one last time. The Rose is full tonight so I couldn't argue too much."

Sil came over, carrying a large flask and some small cups. "Thord, you remember telling me about how your kinsmen use heat and cold to turn barley wine into something special? Well, I was hoping to let this set a bit longer, but we tried doing it ourselves. Have some and tell me what you think of it."

She poured some into one of the cups and passed it to Thord.

He took a sniff from the top of the cup. "Well, it smells right. But it's how it goes down the throat that tells you if it's good or not." He held the cup to his mouth and took a gulp. He shook his head from side to side and started choking. When he stopped coughing he looked at the cup and then at Sil. "You've got the right of it, I am thinking. It's a bit green still, but I'm not saying that's a fault."

Just then Nikki came up with his empty tray. He pulled a stool next to Thord and sat down to his ale.

"Little Fox, see what you think of this." Thord pushed the cup across the table.

Nikki took a sip. He sucked in his breath and looked Thord in the eye. "Gods, that takes me back to the night we met. You kept passing the bottle around until old Borodo bet me on the dice and you won." Looking at Sil he went on, "If he offers to gamble with you don't take him up on it."

"With his Luck, that would be the last thing I'd be doing."

Nikki took another sip and followed it with some ale. He set the cup down in front of Thord and leaned his head into the large chest. Thord lifted his arm and laid it on Nikki's shoulder. "The taste does bring back memories." They sat in silence for awhile.

"A dance!" "A dance and some music!" The company took up the cry. "You'll not get away without one more dance." "No! One more dance."

Bel took up his drum. "One more. Show me what you've

learned." He began to sound out a rhythm.

Nikki stood and moved to the center of the room. Thord watched him as he began to take in the beat from the drum. Thord had seen him dance fifty times and every time it was different, and yet always the same. When he watched Nikki, he could feel himself being pulled into Nikki's dance. Nikki drew him in as a candle pulls on a moth. He was drawn into the wonder of the dance along with everyone else in the inn. With them, he felt the joy that Nikki found in the room. A joy that somehow Nikki could take into himself and release tenfold back to those who watched. The dance spun on and it was good just to be there as Nikki took his memories of The Snow Rose and whirled them out to the goblins and elves and men that made The Rose special. When he stopped, there was a tear in even the crustiest goblin farmer's eye. No one asked him to dance again. They wanted to keep that one dance fresh in their hearts.

\*\*\*

They had crossed out into the open plain the day before. Now the tree-covered hills were twelve leagues behind them and in front was a seemingly endless stretch of rolling grass land. Since dawn, the only signs of life in their world were the distant herds of wild cattle and the tiny dot that was their cart. That was changing. Moving out of the south was a line of riders, men on horseback, coming fast. Not trusting any strangers in this deserted country, Thord pulled his hauberk and helmet from the wagon and waited for them in front of the cart.

As the men approached, Thord began to feel the Fear seeping into his hand where it rested on the axe, thrust through his belt. Nine men.

"Little Fox, this is trouble. When it starts, hide and don't come near me until it's over. Defend yourself but keep away."

Now the Fear was gripping him. He felt a sword through his throat. He lost his right arm to another one. Death came and told him all she had in store for him. Swords, a knife and a club. Ten times Death taunted him. But this time there was a difference. This time, he saw a face. Nikki's face was above the club that smashed his skull and splintered the teeth in a jaw that tried to scream. Now, for the first time since the axe had come into his hands, there was more than just Fear. When he saw Nikki looming over the oaken wheel spoke, he also found courage. A courage driven by love. This time he would accept the blow. He would not fight the club. His love would let him face his death. Not even his own death was stronger than his love.

\*\*\*

In the end, it was over quickly. The first rider to reach swung a sword only to have his target step aside. The horse screamed and bolted as the tip of the axe scratched its side. Thord saw its rider unable to control the horse and stay upright with only one leg braced in the saddle. The other leg hung down beneath the horse, the foot still caught in the stirrup but cut off at the thigh. Another rider left with his side opened to the spine. Some of the men dismounted and came in on foot. They tried to attack from several directions but the axe was everywhere. Thord darted in and away and each time there was a body on the ground. He yanked his axe from the skull of the last man in front of him when he heard two sets of feet racing toward his back. He turned with the axe sweeping around to see a knife fall from the hand of a man. Behind him, Nikki was pulling his wheel spoke from the ruins of the attacker's head. Thord kept the axe swinging and let it go. It left his hand in a lazy spin, sailing through the air, only to stop in the chest of the last rider. The rider's sword fell from his dead hand before it could come down to take Nikki's life.

Thord fell to his knees. He put his face in his hands as great sobs broke from his chest. As he knelt in the grass, surrounded by blood, he felt two hands on his shoulders. Looking up his eyes met soft brown eyes, as Nikki squatted in front of him.

"It's alright, Master. I couldn't stand back when I saw him come at you from behind. I had to stop him. It's alright, Thord."

Thord took the hands from his face. Gripping Nikki's wrists, he kept looking into those eyes.

"Yes, it's alright. It is better than you can know, Little Fox."

They searched the bodies. There was little to mark them except they all carried gold, new minted with the face of Nikki's uncle.

Looking at the dent left by his teeth, Thord nodded his approval and dropped the gold piece back into the pouch. "Assassins. They must have been on the road for months to be this far from Tronmar. Your uncle didn't put all his trust in the ogres and the cat. How did they know where to look?"

Nikki looked up from one of the bodies.

"I can tell you that. Isn't this Baedano, Baelo's son?"

Distorted by death and a skull crushed by Nikki's club, the face was still recognizable.

"Yes, it's Baelo's son. Do you think Baelo is working for your uncle?"

"I doubt it. The only thing he seemed to be hiding was us. And, I don't think he would have sent his son with the assassins. He could have told them where to find us without risking his own son. Besides, Baedano was carrying some of my uncle's gold. If Baelo was behind it, he would be the one with the money." Nikki continued to look down on the body of the man he'd killed. "No, I think this was his own act. I remember him saying he wanted to be back in Tronmar. He must have met the others in Dorisan. They would have been asking for someone who looked like me. He seemed smart and must have guessed I was the one they wanted. They probably offered to take him back with them and give him a place in my uncle's favor."

"Then we will keep on our way. When we see Baelo, we will not tell him about this. If he asks, we didn't meet anyone on the way." Thord looked around at the bodies, scattered in the grass and up at the sky. Black birds were already circling. "The birds can have these others, but we will bury Baedano. We owe at least that to his father."

They kept the gold but unsaddled the horses and drove them off. The gold would raise little interest, whereas someone might recognize the horses as belonging to a passing group of strangers. There was no need to give people a reason to ask questions. They would stick to their plan. Once they dealt with Baelo, they would join up with a caravan and keep heading south.

## *Chapter 8*

The caravan had left the arid plains four weeks back. At first the donkeys had made good time in the foothills, but for the past eighteen days they had been climbing steadily into the heart of the mountains. The air here was thin and cold. On either side of the pass the mountains rose, peak beyond hard peak. Even now, in midsummer, the first peaks they passed had been topped with snow. But here, far into the mountains, the snow spilled down the slopes and turned the pass ahead into deepest winter. The caravan would cross the top of the pass today and by nightfall be descending the other side. The weather looked bad. Clouds had been gathering in the early morning, veiling the mountains before them. But there was no chance to wait them out. The last groves of stunted trees ended three days back down the trail, and to wait for even a day would leave the caravan without enough firewood to cross the pass and reach the lower forests on the other side. To wait meant to retrace their path for more wood. It would be a week lost with no guarantee that the pass would be open when they returned to assail the mountain again.

Theirs was the last string of donkeys in the caravan. Nikki was checking the pack lashings on the fifth and last donkey when Thord walked back from talking to the caravan leader. Thord looked hard at the clouds.

"I am thinking it looks bad ahead, Little Fox. Tie a line to yourself and tie it to the first donkey. I'll tie on to the last one. If the snow gets thick, keep the donkey in front of you in sight and follow it."

Nikki looked at the narrow pass ahead and wondered how they could get lost in the hundred yards or less that made the cleft in the mountains, the only possible path. Still, he tied the line around his waist.

At a shout from the guide, the caravan began to move up the pass. An hour later, the snow began. At first it came down light and was no more than enough to dust the tops of the donkey's packs. But soon the snow was falling thick and fast, drifting into the tracks of the donkeys ahead. Nikki had to pull hard on the lead donkey to keep in sight the dark blur of the donkey ahead of him. The caravan pushed through the deepening snow for hours. The cold and wind bit his hands and face. In the thin air, it was difficult to drag himself up the slope. His feet, in their snow-encrusted boots, felt like lead. When he was not sure how much further he could go, Nikki, at last, felt the trail at his feet begin to descend. A blast of windblown snow blotted out the form of the donkey ahead of him and Nikki pulled harder to make the donkeys catch up to the rest of the caravan. After a minute of stumbling forward, he could again see the dark blur in front. He fought the snow, and his own weakness to keep up as they moved into the blizzard. Another hour of trudging through into the falling snow, and the track entered a narrow defile between two sheer rock faces. The shadow he was following vanished in an instant and Nikki almost ran into a stone wall that blocked his path.

"What is the matter?" Thord called over the wind to Nikki. "Why do we stop?"

Nikki looked around and could see nothing but bare rock. "I've lost the trail," he shouted back. "I don't know how, but it vanished and left us in a blind canyon."

Thord forced his way up through the snow and looked at the stone walls. They both turned and looked back along the path they had come. Already, the wind off the heights was filling their tracks with drifting snow.

"Well, we can't go looking for the trail until the snow stops. I am thinking we will have to take what shelter is here and wait out the storm."

At that, there was a click followed by the groan of hinges from behind them.

"Do not just stand there like a couple of fool mountain goats! Get your donkeys in out of the snow. I cannot hold the door open all day."

They turned around to see a large doorway filled with yellow light. Silhouetted against the light was a man-shaped figure about four feet high.

"Get in. Get in," the figure shouted into the wind and waved an arm. "Or would you rather stay out there and freeze?"

Given the choices, Thord nodded to Nikki and they led the donkeys into the room beyond the door.

As the last of the donkeys came through, the dwarf heaved at the door and slammed it shut. The thick stone door sent out a boom that Nikki felt, even through his thick boots and numbed feet.

"That is better," the dwarf said turning to Thord and Nikki. "Do not worry about the donkeys. My lads will take care of them. There is a warm fire and a hot meal for you inside."

Looking at the way Thord's hand rested on his belt next to where his axe was thrust through it, the dwarf pointed and said. "You will not need that just now. But keep it handy if it makes you feel better."

Thord smiled sheepishly but kept his hand near the axe. "Our thanks. I am called Thord and this is my slave, Nikki."

"I am Kronnar. And if I did not know who you were, I would not have opened the door."

Kronnar was typical of the dwarves that Thord and Nikki had met at The Snow Rose. At a bit over four feet, he was slightly taller than most they had met before. He was thick-set with shoulders nearly as broad as Thord's. His dark brown beard spilled down the front of his green and silver tunic in a torrent of curls to end just above his belt. Below his tunic were a few inches of green hose covering his knees before disappearing into worn brown boots.

He pointed to a door in the wall to the left. "Come along. We have a room for you. It has a fire, food and a bed. By the look of you, you could use all three."

He led them to a small room with a fireplace and a low table with a platter that held cold roast meat, bread, and a flagon of wine. There was a bed in the corner, piled high with blankets. "Tomorrow when you have rested, we will go further into the mountain and there we will talk. We always keep a guard on the outside door, so if you need anything just ask him. I will leave you until tomorrow."

The next morning, or at least Kronnar said it was morning, they were brought a breakfast of grilled sausages and honeyed oat porridge. Afterwards, they were told to get what they needed from their packs.

"Do not worry about the rest," Kronnar had said. "The donkeys and the packs will be waiting at the lower door when it is time to leave. Just bring what you would need for a long stay in an inn. We will supply the rest."

They followed the dwarf down into the stone for hours. The tunnel ran straight into the heart of the mountain. The few openings they passed led, for the most part, down or level. The tunnel was lit by a line of torches that came to life as they approached and winked out when they passed. Their path went from darkness into darkness.

Thord asked where they were going, but was only told to wait.

"When we get to the Spring Hall, we will talk."

After the better part of a day steadily walking, the passage entered the inhabited parts of the mountain. Here there were more side tunnels and they started to pass dwarves, alone or in groups.

They turned down a short corridor off the main tunnel and entered a hall. The space was a forest of stone columns rising thirty feet from the floor to fan out forming a maze of interlocked vaults. Scattered about under the columns were tables. In the center was a pool of water, filled from a spring spilling down from the ceiling.

Kronnar led them to a table near the center, where a dwarf woman sat.

"Mornanie, this is Thord and this is Nikki. This is Mornanie," Kronnar said, making the introductions.

Mornanie rose to her full three and a half foot height and bowed. She was dressed much like Kronnar, with a tunic of blue with gold threads. Instead of a leather belt, she had a red silk girdle, and where Kronnar wore heavy brown leather boots, she wore heavy black boots. "Welcome. Please sit. You must be hungry after walking here from the High Gate. I will have food brought."

"Let me see to it," said Kronnar, turning and walking toward a door across the hall.

"Sit, sit," continued Mornanie. When they were seated on the low, heavy chairs, she went on, "You must be wondering why you are here. Now, it could be that it is because of the dwarves' legendary hospitality. Or it could be because we saw you in the snow and felt pity stir in our hearts." At this, she winked. "But I see you are not buying that. Alas, you are right. We brought you in from the snow for reasons of our own."

At that Nikki had to smile. He had dealt with a number of dwarves at The Snow Rose and, while they never shorted the bill, there was never a copper extra on the table when they left.

"A friend of mine whom you know, Bel, said you would be coming this way. He suggested that I might want to meet you. He thinks that there are things you both should learn. If you are willing to spend some time here, we are willing to put you up and show you some of what we know."

The mention of Bel brought Nikki instantly to alert. What was the connection between the elven bard and this dwarf? What did the dwarves know that Thord and he should learn?

Thord looked hard at her. "What is the price?"

"The price?" said Kronnar as he walked up. "Not gold. What you can learn here can't be bought with gold. What we offer can not be sold, only given. If we think giving it to you will do us the most good, forgive us that bit of selfishness. And besides, the choice is either staying here and sharing our board," (and at that a dwarf came up and placed a large platter of meat, cheese, and bread on the table) "or going back out and watching the snow drift over your heads."

Thord must have caught the shiver that ran through Nikki as the dwarf spoke of the snow outside. "I am thinking that we will take up your offer if, that is, there is ale to go with that meat."

Kronnar pointed past Thord. "It is coming now."

***

Nikki missed the beat. In the middle of a spin, one foot caught the other and he fell onto his hands and knees.

"No, no!" Mornanie shouted. She put the palm of her hand on the silver strings of the harp and the sound died. "You need to move into the structure. You grasp the whole of what you see. That is good, but only a start. Now you need to go beyond the whole to what makes it part of everything else. You see into the point. Now you must step through it."

Nikki collapsed on the floor. He was so tired he could barely follow the dwarf's words. For the last week he had tried to "step through the point" and failed. He was too big and there wasn't enough force behind him to push himself through. How could he force himself through a single point? He *knew* it couldn't be done.

Between Nikki and Mornanie stood a gold tripod. Where the three legs met rested a single, perfect diamond. For the last week, Nikki had danced with that stone, trying to see what Mornanie saw in it. And for a week he had failed to grasp the structure in the stone. When they started, Mornanie had told him that the flawless diamond was the simplest structure of all the stones. The simplest of stones and he was failing even that. He wanted to kick the thing across the room, but knew that would only make him feel worse for failing not just to master the stone but also to master himself. He started to pull himself to his feet when Mornanie stopped him.

"Sit and listen."

The dwarf began to play again and now Nikki sat and poured his attention into the music, letting the stone fade from his mind. He followed the music as it rose and fell. As it spun around slowly, he could feel it begin to center around the stone in the middle of room. He could feel the dwarf in the music. As he listened, Nikki found that Mornanie was not spinning the music smaller and smaller but was pulling herself in and the music was only following her. Then Nikki felt the dwarf enter the stone and could hear the music coming from within the diamond.

Then he knew why he failed. No force was great enough to force him into the stone. He needed to bring himself to a point and then enter. He stood and began to dance to the music that still came from the diamond in the center of the room. He danced and pulled himself into a smaller and smaller space. Now the dance was following him and not him following the dance.

He pulled the last of "Nikki" into the space beside the stone and slipped into it. There he found a perfect order. Each part of the stone was connected to its four neighbors and each one hummed the same note when struck by the waves of the music. There, too, was the source of the music. And there inside the stone, Nikki danced and Mornanie played.

\*\*\*

Thord brought the axe from the side in a killing blow. But Kronnar just stepped in under the swing. Bringing his shield up, the dwarf hit the haft of the axe and sent the blow wide to pass over his head. With a quick spin, he sent Thord's shield the way of the axe and hit Thord's behind with the flat of his practice sword, hard enough to knock him to his knees.

"What kind of a swing was that? You great oaf! Is that more from that plowman uncle of yours?" Kronnar taunted. "The God of War must be getting senile if that is the best there is on the field."

Thord climbed to his feet and wiped the sweat from his forehead with the back of his hand. He had spent the last hour swinging a blunt practice axe under the eye of Kronnar. He felt like he was practicing back in the Floelands at his great-uncle Thurstein's farm. Only the old man had never been as exacting as Kronnar was. The dwarf would stop him in mid swing and correct the slightest misplacement of his foot or elbow. When they sparred, Thord had some success but, more often than not, the bout ended with him sitting on the ground rubbing a fresh bruise and looking up at the dwarf.

He sat with his eyes on the dwarf, but his mind was looking ahead to a pint of beer.

"Stop your wool gathering. I know what you're thinking. You think, Why do I need to practice? The axe knows what needs to be done. But there you're wrong. You can't always trust to magic; sometimes you need to fight your own battles. So get up. That beer will still be there when we're done."

As Thord got to his feet, he wondered if the old dwarf really could read his mind.

"Come on and try that again. But don't swing round wide like you are some kind of windmill. How would you fight in a forest or a narrow hallway? Snap the axe forward with as little arc as you can. Try again."

A few minutes later, Thord again found himself on the floor. "Enough for now." Kronnar said as he sheathed his sword and extended a hand to Thord. Pulling him to his feet, Kronnar suggested that an ale was called for to restore their strength.

With the blunt axe put away, and having shed the padded practice armor and shield, Thord limped to a table flanked by two chairs against the far wall of the room. He pushed the back of one chair to the wall and eased himself down with his feet sticking out in front of him. He sat slightly twisted to favor his latest bruise.

Kronnar sat at the opposite side of the table and pushed the pitcher of ale towards Thord. "You lost. You pour."

When the ale was poured, they began again swapping old stories. This time, Thord was talking about a pirate attack.

"I knew I had to get onto the pirate ship or risk killing my ship mates. So I jumped up onto the rail and down onto the deck of the other ship."

"How did you say you got down to the deck?" the dwarf interrupted.

"I jumped up onto the rail and swung on the main sheet down into the waist of the ship to land feet first sending two of the pirates flying," Thord elaborated.

"Oh. Now I understand." Kronnar nodded. "That is better."

And Thord went on with the tale he was telling.

At first, Thord was happier working under Kronnar than he thought he would be under Nikki's tutor. Each evening, Nikki came to dinner looking worn down from a day of study. At least, Kronnar would only work Thord for a couple of hours a day. The rest of the day was spent swapping stories with the old dwarf. Kronnar would talk of old wars and battles, and Thord would tell of his various fights and travels. Early on, Thord began to think the dwarf was losing his memory, for he would ask Thord to retell a story he had heard just the day before or to repeat something Thord had just said. Whenever this happened, Thord would tell the story with a little more detail, if just to keep it interesting for himself. Only after the first week of telling the same stories a third or fourth time did Thord realize that the dwarf's memory was perfectly clear. The reason for asking to hear something again was to get Thord to tell the storybetter . At that point, Thord began to take more care in the telling of each story and to listen closer to Kronnar as he told his tales. Now, Thord found that telling tales left him as tired as the arms practice, and he was as exhausted as Nikki at the end of each day.

\*\*\*

They sat at dinner in the great hall. Kronnar sat on one side of Thord and Nikki knelt between Thord and Mornanie on the other side. There were few other occupied tables in the hall this evening, and those were across the hall towards the far wall.

Thord and Nikki would be leaving in the morning and this was their last dinner with the dwarves. After the roast had been polished off and the sweet rolls and cheeses were finished, they sat and talked. As the ale passed back and forth, Nikki looked down the long hall. He had come to see the grace in the great curved columns and the spider-web of high arched ribs that crisscrossed the ceiling. He felt the flow of power that pushed down through the vaults and the stone columns from the weight of the mountain above their heads. And he knew the path of the spring that seeped through the cold rock and spilled from the ceiling to fall into the pool in the center of the room with the sound of silver chimes.

Mornanie leaned over to Nikki and said, "You feel the strength of the mountain."

And it was true. He could feel it. He felt it welling up in him. He rose and walked to the front of the table. The hall was alive all around him. He could see the flow of lights in the stone and hear the music of the columns and walls. He began to dance with that music. A slow dance formed in his mind and he danced to the rhythm of the mountain. He rose and fell with the peaks and valleys. He let himself sway with the streams that flowed down the lower slopes and the clouds that glided across the flanks of the mountains. He saw all the colors locked up in the stone. He could follow the patterns of crystals that made up the rock and knew their kind. The walls shimmered with light as Nikki pulled first one way then another on the veins in the stone. He knew the veins of metal in the rock and shifted the gold to the surface, only to put it back and bring out the light of silver. He let the silver flow back through the crystals like sand flowing between his fingers. He danced into the mountain.

As he danced he became aware of a different light. A different music was present in the hall. He turned toward the table and saw the great axe that Thord carried. It was leaning against his chair, its head on the stone of the floor. The stone of the floor groaned under the preternatural weight as this god-forged axe rested on the flags. But maybe resting wasn't the right word. It was waiting.

The axe glowed with its own set of colors and its own private music. The music was strident, brassy. It was the sound of battles won and lost long ago and of battles yet to be fought. The music was of bravery and strength and of skill. The music carried themes of death and sorrow and also of hope born of courage. But there was a different sound underneath those.

From the axe also came the clamor of discord, wild and always threatening to drown out the song placed there by the smith. But the sound didn't come from the steel of the axe. It came from something else, something that had crept into the metal before the axe was forged. As Nikki moved toward the axe, he could see the grain of the steel. There was a pattern in that metal that did not show itself to the casual eye. The very crystals in the steel formed runes. Nikki could not read the language in the steel but he could sense the runes and what they said. He knew what was there. The word "Cleaver" was written in the steel. But there was something else. There was a set of runes that didn't make sense. There was a word before "Cleaver" that he couldn't make out. It might have said "All" but the runes were twisted and distorted by something under the surface of the steel.

Never skipping a beat, the dance drew him to where the axe stood on the stone. He took the axe from the floor and moved to the center of the room. There, as he slowly circled, he saw into the axe. There in the metal, he found some of the story of the axe and there also the problem. The Smith had caught a piece of star, white hot, as it fell, and worked it. But something had been in the steel when it was forged, an impurity that had not come out under the smith's hammer. A piece of something evil from outside this world was embedded in the metal.

Now, as he danced, Nikki willed himself into the steel. The bonds holding the crystals loosened until his hands could work the metal like clay. He pressed the flaw with his thumbs and felt the metal yield under his pressure. The metal flowed from his push and the splinter of evil, buried in the steel, came to the surface. Nikki pried it from the axe and flung it into the fire blazing on the hearth. As it touched the flames, it flashed into nothing. He began to knead the steel back to the smith's original form. When he was done, he could read the lost runes. There in the steel were the words "Fear Cleaver."

Later, Nikki did a dance only for Thord. They were in their room. Nikki threw off his tunic and began to dance. This dance was for and of Thord. The music came from within Nikki, from the love between them. The power of the dance filled the room until it became hard to breathe. It welled up until the very walls seemed to glow with it. Finally, Nikki knelt in front of Thord. He took the iron collar in his hands and turned it until the lock was beneath his fingers. Nikki began to work the cold iron with his hands. When he was done, there was no trace of the lock or hinge. All that remained was a single smooth band of iron with a chain attached.

"I am yours, Thord," he said as he knelt at Thord's feet. "Now and always. I never wish to be free of you."

Thord stood up from the edge of the bed they shared, towering over Nikki. With his hands under Nikki's arms, he lifted him up off the floor until Nikki's toes left stone. Their eyes met. Thord kissed him. Then, with a laugh he fell back onto the bed, dragging Nikki down on top of him.

***

Far away on another mountain, two figures stood under the stars.

"Well brother, I see the young one missed the trick you played on him when you forged that collar."

"Missed? No, he felt it the moment he took the collar in his hands. He knew and didn't mind."

"He didn't care? How can you be so sure?"

"He didn't break the spell I put on the collar when I tricked his lover into using water he had drunk from to quenched the hot hinge pin. He took the magic and let it flow through the iron until it formed a full circle within the collar." He looked up at the stars. "It's what he wanted. And besides, if I hadn't contrived their meeting, you would have."

"Perhaps."

***

In the morning a bleary eyed Thord and Nikki were roused out of bed by Kronnar. "I do not recall seeing any two looking so much like last week's death and carrying such big grins as you two have." After a quick breakfast they headed down the tunnels to a lower door. There they said their goodbyes.

"Our thanks to you for you hospitality." Thord bowed to Kronnar and Mornanie.

"And thank you for all you taught me," Nikki said bowing from where he held the lead on the first donkey.

"We did what we wanted. Our thanks will be if you use what we taught you well. Now off with you." She pointed to where the door stood open with green and yellow daylight streaming in from the glade before the door. "And when you go down the trail, remember that for the past few weeks you have been inside the mountain."

A short walk led them to the main trail. The sun had disappeared behind the mountains above, and dark was settling in, when they saw the lights of campfires from a caravan ahead. On reaching the camp they were hailed as they approached.

Out of the gloom a man approached.

"Thord? Is that you?" The man was the guide for their caravan. "When we didn't find you after crossing the pass we thought you must have frozen to death. How did you survive these last three days?"

Three days? A confused Nikki was about to speak when Thord

cut him off. "We found shelter in the rocks."

After they unpacked the donkeys and crawled into their bedroll, Thord answered Nikki's unvoiced question.

"In the mountain time moves differently than it does on it. Any child who listens to the old tales knows this."

*** 

Taulgir stood facing the south in a small courtyard. He squinted in the glare of the sunlight bouncing off the bone-white plaster walls and off the shards of marble that stretched beneath his feet. The courtyard was open to the blue sky. All of the trees that might have overlooked the interior and shown a view of life had been cut down. On the cardinal compass points, four tall basalt panels stood out from the blank walls, each concealing a doorway. Deeply graven into the dull black slabs were symbols sacred to Arjel, the god of war. On the west was Victory, on the east Strength, on the north Valor, and on the south Cunning. All focused inward to the center where Taulgir waited for the sun to reach its zenith. At his back was a glowing brazier, the fire kindled from roof beams pried from a sacked temple to Peace. Resting in coals lay the blade of a sword, its steel forged from plow shares and fishhooks. In front of him lay a stone altar made from a merlon wrenched from the highest battlement of the palace. On the altar waited a silver hammer. To his left stood a blindfolded charger. The stallion's white coat was covered in the sweat of fear. Chanting a hymn to Victory, he waited. When the sun reached the top of the southern panel he turned and pulled the blade from the fire. Placing it on the altar he took up the hammer and, calling the name of the god, smote the red hot steel three times. Turning, he strode to the war-horse and thrust the glowing sword into the animal's heart. With a deafening bray, the horse reared up toward the sky and fell to the earth. Before leaving that place, standing with the horse dead at his feet, its red blood staining the gravel, he raised the newly quenched blade to the god's symbol of Victory.

With the doorway behind him and the roof of his villa between him and the sky, he took in and let out a deep breath. Whirling around, he swung the blade at a tall, bronze candle holder, standing in the corridor. The thick bronze shaft parted like the stalk of a sunflower cut by a farmer's sickle, sending the candelabra crashing on to the stone floor. Holding the blade in front of him, he began to laugh.

Fool priests, he thought. With this much power right under their noses, they spent their time reciting prayers with no knowledge of what the prayers could do. For days he had watched the priests of Arjel go through this same prayer. Only he had the wit to see where it fit with the ancient records of the rites. Only he had seen where over time the priests had corrupted the prayer from the original. And only he had found the flaw in that original prayer. It was he and not the priests or even the ancients who could do more than beg the god's help. For him the unwitting god had no choice. A blade was a small thing but it showed the way to greater possibilities.

\*\*\*

Vorkki watched the scene from far off. He had seen the preparations for casting this spell. He had looked on as the wizard wrought the sword. He knew the planned result. But only he had noticed the errant gust of wind that lifted a leaf from a felled tree outside the villa.

The wizard had been intent on his spell. He had not felt the Chance breeze that brought the leaf over the courtyard wall. At the moment the sword was plunged into the horse, that breeze had set the leaf on a groove in the symbol of Victory, partially obscuring the carving. It had fallen to the ground a moment later and another gust swept it around the stone to leave it lying just beyond the door behind.

Vorkki left. A god couldn't spend all his time with the affairs of one mortal. Chance knew where a youth was betting with his fellows. The boy had wagered he could sneak into the bedroom of the most beautiful girl in the city without alarming her father. Leaving that high place, the Joker was followed by a red fox. Or perhaps it was one of those small lapdogs with the loud annoying bark that trotted behind him.

\*\*\*

Three days latter, Taulgir entered the privy audience hall carrying a long bundle wrapped in red silk. As he walked down the wood-paneled hall, he was aware of the guard who followed at his back, ready to cut him down at the first misstep. Before the throne was a uniformed soldier, on his knees with his hands bound behind his back. In the room, Taulgir could smell the sour odor of the dungeon. The prisoner knelt between two guards. The king stood grim, looking down from the dais. Taulgir had no doubt that the king had timed his own audience to overlap the scene in front of him. It was a reminder of the king's power and of the need for loyalty.

"To speak of my dead brother's son as if he were alive is treason!

Take him out and execute the sentence."

Taulgir came up and bowed low to the king. "Sire, if I may be so bold as to ask that you wait but a moment, I have a gift that you will find useful in dealing with traitors."

"And what is that, wizard?"

Taulgir did not miss the edge in the king's voice. Despite himself, he feared he may have pushed too far by interrupting the king. But the risk was worth taking if he wanted to be more than just one of the king's wizards. He unwrapped the end of the bundle and, on one knee, held the exposed hilt of a sword out to the king.

"A gift, sire. Perhaps you would like to try it out on this traitor."

The king's harsh look turned softer as he took the sword and drew it from the offered scabbard. As the king's hand touched the grip, Taulgir let out his breath.

"If I may suggest sire, test the blade on the man's mail."

The king looked from the sword to Taulgir and then to the man at his feet. Stepping off the dais, he brought the blade up and swung it down to strike the trembling prisoner's mailed shoulder. The hall was filled with the sounds of parting steel links and a death cry, cut short when the edge of the sword swept through mail and bone to find the heart.

Taulgir stood and bowed to the king, in his outstretched hand he held the cloth wrapping from the sword. Stepping back from the widening pool of blood, the king took the offered silk. As he wiped the blood from the blade, king looked at the sword in his hand.

"Yes, I am pleased. Dine with me tonight."

"As you command, sire."

## *Chapter 9*

The caravan passed down valleys that seemed to have been ripped through the stone of the mountains. The ragged, snow-covered heights stared down on the narrow track that wound between the great cliff faces. Occasionally, as the caravan descended the narrow path, they would hear the deep rumble of a distant mountain freeing itself of a burden of ice and rock. Once, they were forced to stop for half a day while they made a new path on the edge of a recent landslide. The valleys here were empty of any kind of peoples: dwarf, goblin or man.

Four days' travel down the mountain, they entered a broad valley, the mountains at their back, settling into rounded hills on either side. Here the track became a wide road leading to a place of men. A squat fortress stood across their path, its crenelated walls and towers dotted with guards and flying long, yellow banners. The road ran up to a three-story tower in the center of the wall, where it disappeared into a wide gate. Before the gate, the land was barren with no sign of man beyond the road.

As the caravan entered the first city in the lands of the Dragon Emperor, Thord and Nikki were confronted by one of the guards in the courtyard behind the gate.

"Hold a moment. I have been told to look for a tall golden haired man and a slave. Are you called To Waa Da and your slave called Little Fox?" The guard spoke the trade tongue well but mangled the first name so badly that it took Thord a moment to realize it was his name.

"I am Thord and this is The Little Fox." As Thord said this, his left hand strayed to hook a thumb in his belt, next to his axe.

"Prefect Fan instructed me to keep a watch for you. He left me some letters of introduction to give you." Reaching into his sleeve he produced three scrolls. "I have been told to give you these and to say that if, after you finish your business, you are interested in employment, you should proceed to the capital and present the scrolls to the office of the minister of the army."

"Thank you," Thord said as he took the scrolls.

"It is my honor. I am always pleased to server Prefect Fan in any way."

Through the final gate, they entered a world of shops and street hawkers.

\*\*\*

For the next twenty days, the caravan moved toward the heart of the empire. As they traveled, the villages turned into towns and the towns into cities. It was midday when they arrived at a great walled city, the capital. The caravan had shrunk as merchants turned off the main road at one fork or another. Approaching the capital, they became a small part of the thronging commerce on the road. Now, the remaining few who had crossed with Thord and Nikki entered a walled market just outside the city gates.

Nikki rented them a stall in one of the side aisles, and that afternoon Nikki walked around the market to find the local range of prices. The next day, Nikki set out their cargo of furs and one of the twelve earthenware bottles of vinegar he bought from the goblin village near the Snow Rose. When buyers stopped to look at the furs, Nikki would haggle over the price in a mix of the trade tongue and what local language Nikki had picked up from the members of the caravan and urchins hired along the road.

Each time someone came to look at the furs, Nikki would accidentally brush the bottle and knock it off the counter, onto the flagstones. The bottle would bounce several times with an almost metallic ring. He would pick it up off the ground, brush the dust from it and place it back on the counter. The third person to witness this performance stopped and picked up the bottle. Nikki watched as the man's eyes were drawn into the soft brown glaze on the bottle. It was a glaze so rich that the color appeared to come, not from the surface, but from the far side of the bottle.

"Slave, what is this?"

"Sir, that is a bottle of a rare seasoning from the goblin lands in the far north. Some say it is the secret to their longevity. But my master has never allowed me to try it."

"Longevity?"

"Why yes sir. You must know that no goblin is considered to be old who has not seen four hundred years. They all serve this at their tables once every ten days."

"And how much does your master ask for a bottle of this?"

At that a round of bargaining began that ended with the buyer walking off with the bottle and Nikki pocketing two silver pieces and four coppers.

Thord came out from the back of the booth. "Little Fox, you are a liar. That was just a bottle of vinegar and nothing more."

128

"There you are wrong, Master." Nikki waited until the man was out of sight in the crowd before pulling a second bottle from beneath the counter. "Both of us were lying. I lied when I told him it was the source of the goblin's long life, and he lied when he said he was interested in the properties of the vinegar. What he was interested in was not what was in the bottle but the bottle itself. You remember the mugs and bottles at the Rose? I have never seen such pottery. It was thin and light and yet almost unbreakable. Do you also remember Fan Go's niece serving us wine in small crude looking cups? I asked him why a man of his position would use such and he told me the cups were valued for their simplicity and grace. When I saw the goblin-ware, it had the same qualities as Fan's cup, and the firing was superior to anything I have ever seen." He picked up the bottle and looked into the deep, soft browns of the glaze. "We both lied and knew we both lied and, lying, both got what we wanted."

A small man in a blue robe came up and asked about the furs. Nikki set the bottle he was holding on the edge of the counter and it fell to the ground.

Nikki bent down to pick up the bottle and winked at Thord.

"Stupid slave! If you had broken that, I would have beaten you." Having said that in response to Nikki's wink, Thord shoock his fist at Nikki and walked back into the booth. A few minutes later, the man walked away with two beaver pelts and a bottle of goblin elixir for his mother's rheumatism.

***

That evening, after closing the stall, Thord and Nikki walked in the market looking for dinner. Around a corner from their stall Thord stepped over a small patch of wet earth and started to laugh. From the ground came the strong smell of goblin vinegar.

On their third day in the capital they locked up the stall and entered the city, looking for the ministry of the army. Finding it, they presented the scrolls to an official in the front hall. They were quickly ushered into an ornate office where a small, balding man sat behind a heavy, carved rosewood desk reading one of the scrolls. The man took in Thord and Nikki with an appraising eye and looked down at the scroll again. When he looked up again his face bore a look that could only be the resignation of a long-suffering, lower bureaucrat. His eyes traveled from Nikki's face to the collar and chain and then to Thord again.

"Prefect Fan Go speaks highly of both of you," he said, holding open one of the scrolls. "It is most irregular, but Prefect Fan suggests you be given a commission as a lieutenant in the emperor's service. I can only offer you command of a small unit of irregular troops. They are currently here in the capital, but will be transferred to the east in the next few months. If that is not acceptable, I'm afraid you will have to wait until another unit becomes available." He trailed off giving the impression that the wait could be a long one.

"Pardon, please." While Thord and Nikki had been practicing the local language during the time it took to go from the border to the capital, Thord had not managed to catch more than Prefect Fan, commission, command of some sort of troops, and east. He looked at Nikki and raised his eyebrows.

Nikki was always good with languages and was able to fill Thord in on the main points.

"So, a commission no one wants?" Thord must have filled in on his own the gaps of what had not been said. Nikki knew that in most armies, irregular troops meant an odd assortment of foreign mercenaries and conscripts from the local jails. Not what a noble would prefer if he wanted to rise in rank, but a posting to an obscure outpost in the east would buy Thord and himself time to work out their next step.

Thord turned to the man behind the desk and nodded. "Yes. I will take it."

It was agreed that they would return the next afternoon to take up the commission.

*** 

Borodo sat alone, nursing his ale and listening to the talk around him. The ale house was packed with locals and people in town for the quarter market. The room was full of talk with a dozen conversations echoing from the high beamed ceiling and paneled walls. He sat at a scarred and stained table near the long bar and listened to as many people as he could. This wasn't the first time he had ventured into Tronmar to gather what news there was. But with forty leagues between him and the border of Killar, it was the furthest he had ventured into a country now full of informers and spies. He was always careful where and how he used his ears because, while he had acted the spy in Tronmar several other times, each time could always be the last.

"...sister married a tinker out in..." "...a good price for a..." "...So I says to him, let's take this outside and see who..." "...this new wizard's tax will be the ruin..."

There it was.

"...old Ganian never asked for a palace when he was court wizard."

"No, but he never had anything that needed to be done quiet, if you know what I'm saying." This last was said low enough that Borodo had to cock his head to catch it. He lost the rest when a mug banged down on his table from the other side.

"Cousin! Good to see you. How's the wife?"

Borodo's right hand was under the table and on the hilt of his dagger even as he turned to face the voice. Uniform! He was about to rise when he saw the face, Lieutenant Tigo, his commander from fifteen years ago. He eased his weight back onto the chair but left the hand where it was. Tigo's glance showed him that the position of that hand was not lost on his old commander.

"We should catch up on old times, cousin." Tigo had sat down in the chair beside Borodo. "Yes, I haven't seen you in years, I've hardly laid eyes on you since you started working at that fancy house up north. I'd heard you left there."

Borodo picked up his mug in his left hand and held it up. "I see you've come up in the world, captain." As he drank, he turned his head so he could still watch Tigo around the side of the tankard. "Yes, up indeed. Can you stay and talk or do you have duties to attend to?"

Tigo looked around and nodded toward the door where three soldiers stood at the end of the bar. "No, this isn't the place to talk. It's too busy and my men can't be left for long. But we have a lot of catching up to do. There's a place by the bridge called The Red Cape. It's run by a friend of mine. The food's bad and the wine is worse, but it's quiet. If you meet me there tonight, I'm sure there are a lot of stories we can trade. Maybe you'll tell me about that young wife of yours." He looked Borodo in the eyes.

"The Red Cape. Alright, I'll be there."

He watched Tigo walk across the room to his men. Tigo was a small man. His hair was black, shot with grey, and cut short for the crested helmet he carried under his arm. After more than thirty years of soldiering, he still carried himself well. There was an edge in his voice, though, that sounded like a man who had troubles. Tigo had used the word 'cousin' instead of saying Borodo. Could that mean the name Borodo was dangerous? And why did he ask about Borodo's 'young wife'? Tigo knew that he wasn't married. In fact, Tigo always said that Borodo was married to the crown. Could he be asking about the prince? Did he know or guess something about Nicolio?

Borodo forgot all about the 'wizard tax.' He finished his beer and left, in case anyone else should show up and want to have a less congenial talk.

That night Borodo sat in the back corner of a dark low taproom looking at a plate with most of his dinner still on it. Tigo had been a man of his word. The food was bad and the wine worse. Borodo had managed some of what the barman called rabbit, but the beans in grease were as bad as they looked. Not that he would have eaten them in any case. A man who needed to stay unnoticed in the dark couldn't afford to eat beans. He reached down and brushed something that crawled up his leg from the straw-covered dirt floor and wished Tigo would come soon.

As if conjured, a hand brushed away the leather curtain over the doorway, and Tigo walked in. He looked around the room and at the barman, who nodded twice, before walking across to Borodo.

Gone was the uniform and anything that might hint of one. He wore a dark grey tunic and soft-soled boots. As he sat down next to Borodo, the proprietor came up and leaned over to put a wooden cup on the table.

"It's quiet. No one's nosing around." The voice was low and meant not to carry.

When they were alone, Tigo lifted his glass. "To the king, Good keep him safe."

Even with the sour wine, Borodo had no trouble drinking to that. He stared at Tigo.

"So cousin, how are you faring?"

"Better now that I found an old friend. Though I didn't expect to see you here." Tigo leaned closer. "Did you know you're wanted by the palace?"

"The king wants me?" Borodo casually looked around the room.

"I didn't say the king; I said the palace. These days the king has little to do with whom the palace is interested in finding. You're pretty high on the list, if the size of the reward they offer means something."

One of the customers chose that moment to lurch past them toward the back door.

In a louder voice, Tigo went on, "Tell me about that pretty young wife of yours. She is well, I hope?"

The sound of water came from behind them.

"Well that's a long story. But the short of it is I don't know. You see, as luck would have it, she ran off with a traveling man. I've been looking for them but she and this new man of hers seem to have vanished.

I think I would know if she was in trouble, but for now I can just wait for her to come back."

"She's gone? That's bad news." Tigo's face grew grave, his eyes narrowing in the shadows. "That's very bad news. I would dearly like to see her in her home again. But you think she's alright?"

"I have a feeling she is. If she wasn't, I think her uncle would have stopped looking for her. Don't ask me why, but I think she'll return. I keep waiting and searching."

"Yes, there is her uncle. He's always looking for news."

The sound from the back ended and the man staggered back past them to the far end of the bar.

"When your wife comes back, the family will be more than happy to take her back. I can't speak for everyone, but I think I speak for most of us. Am I right that you've taken a job with her uncle's rival?"

"It was the only job that was offered. I'd rather work here, but…"

"True, cousin. We all do what we can but with her uncle's butler running things, there isn't much we can do. We should be off. I would say keep in touch but that will have to wait until your wife is back and safe in her own home."

Tigo nodded toward the barman who stepped out the door. They could see him framed in the doorway as he stretched and looked about. He came back in and shook his head in Tigo's direction.

"Maybe we should go out the back."

They made their way through the maze of alleys behind the bar to a point some fifty paces up the street from the where they started. When Tigo was about to step into the street, Borodo blocked him with his arm. Looking around the corner of a building, Borodo was just in time to see a dozen men rush from the shadows and into the Red Cape. He pushed Tigo back into the alley where they split up and both disappeared into the night.

*** 

The narrow brick street was lined with two-story shops. The shutters on the second story windows were thrown back to let in the late morning light. Soon they would be closed to keep back the worst of the afternoon heat. The ground floor façades were recessed to provide shelter for tables piled high with goods. On this block the shops mostly sold shoes and boots, with some cloth sellers and a tin smith. The smell of rancid animal fat and urine that clung to the new leather made sure these shops wouldn't share the street with grocers or butchers.

Nikki was enjoying the walk. The life of the city was familiar, not in the details but in the patterns. Here, a thousand of leagues from his home, were the same merchants selling nearly the same goods. Dirty children ran through the dusty side streets and alleys, playing the games that children played everywhere. He could be walking in the streets of Tronmar. But he wasn't. Instead of strolling with his faithful Borodo two step behind him, he was following two steps behind Thord Vorkki's Child. Behind them was a hired man pushing a hand cart, with all they owned piled on it. They could have carried it themselves, but Nikki had convinced Thord that he needed to look the part of an officer.

In front of Nikki, Thord strode down the middle of the street. Instead of his usual subdued colors, he was dressed in the bright yellow and black of the Imperial Army. A yellow cape hung from his shoulders. In back, it was thrust to the side where the haft of his axe stuck through his belt. He wore the scale hauberk of ogre hide. On his head was an iron and leather cap with a single, long pheasant feather dyed jade green, the symbol of a lieutenant of the Imperial Irregulars.

The street opened into a plaza. The far side was bounded by the city wall. To the left were more shops, mostly wine shops for the garrison. On the right stood a long two story building. The plain façade and small windows said 'barracks' as much as the imperial banner over the door. In front of it were several groups of men, either asleep in the sunshine or dicing on the steps.

As Nikki and Thord approached the barracks, one of the gamblers rose up.

"You must be the new officer. We was told they were sending some green lieutenant."

Nikki had a chance to look at the man as Thord strode up to him. A head shorter than Thord, he was a thickset man with the jet black hair of the Empire. There was a thin scar on his cheek that looked more like the work of knife than a sword. Nikki was coming to know the type. A man who thought a few years in the army preferable to the gallows.

"I am your commander, To Waa Da. Where is your sergeant?"

The man hooked a thumb at a bench near the wall. Stretched out on it was a man snoring loudly. Near to hand was a bottle. His stained yellow shirt was pulled away from his trousers to reveal a strip of hairy paunch. Nikki watched as Thord walked up to the sleeping man. With a shove of his booted foot, he sent the bench and its occupant crashing to the pavement. The man didn't even wake up.

The men standing around started laughing. Thord came back to stand before the man who had spoken.

"What's your name?"

"I'm To'a."

Without warning, Thord sent a fist smashing into To'a's face. The force of the blow lifted the man off his heels and he landed on his back. Spitting blood and rubbing his jaw, he looked up at Thord. He started to rise but settled back with a groan.

"What was that for?"

Thord stood over him. "What was that for? Sir!"

"What was that for? Sir!"

"That was to let you know how it felt so we wouldn't need to do it again, Sergeant To'a. Get someone to show me to my quarters. While I settle in, you will get the men ready for me to inspect." Nodding toward the overturned bench and the still snoring drunk behind him, Thord continued, "And sober up the private, if you can."

Still rubbing at his jaw, To'a climbed back to his feet. "Did you say sergeant? Sir."

"Yes, Sergeant. Did I make a mistake?"

The man looked at the other men behind him and turned back to face Thord. "No, Sir! You! Lu. Show Lieutenant ..." Nikki could see the man working his sore jaw around the unfamiliar name and finally coming out with "To Waa Da to his quarters."

"Good. You have an hour to find your men and get them lined up. Sergeant To'a."

As Nikki followed Thord into the barracks. He could hear the new sergeant behind him.

"Kiu! Go to The Yellow Sun. Find Mu A and tell him to get back here with everyone there. Run! Fa, get to ..."

With that, Nikki passed into the gloom of the barracks and into the life of The 123rd Imperial Light Horse.

*** 

After a month, The 123rd was beginning to look like soldiers. It hadn't been easy. Still Thord was surprised at how fast it happened. He had gambled and won. It was a gamble to hit To'a. But he knew that he had to set himself at the top from the beginning. It was a gamble to make To'a sergeant. But that paid off as well. When To'a had been the first to speak, Thord guessed he was the man the others listened to. It certainly hadn't been the old sergeant. He'd been right. To'a didn't need much from Thord to get things done.

Though Thord had never been a leader, leading men seemed to be familiar. In a fight, all the people around him tended to become dead. So he didn't have any experience as either a leader or a follower. But he seemed to know what had to be done. It didn't occur to him until after the first few days that what he was doing and saying was coming, not from his own experience, but from the experience of others. He'd listened to the dwarf Kronnar's tales of wars and armies, and only now did he understand what the old dwarf was talking about. In those stories, he saw his own past. In those other soldiers, he saw his own men. In the beginning, when he didn't know what to do, he would remember what the heroes in old stories had done and use that to guide him. More and more now, he found that what was needed came from himself. But however it happened, it was working.

The men were looking like soldiers now and not like gutter sweepings. That had taken a couple of meetings behind the barracks. But after each one, there were fewer interested in challenging him. He had watched the change in the men. At first they grumbled sullenly when forced to do things like clean the barracks or polish their armor. Now they still grumbled, but they smiled as they complained of the injustice of army life.

It was the horses that took the most effort. When he and Nikki had first seen them, he was shocked that animals could be reduced to such a state. Nikki ran to them alternately sobbing and cursing. Thin, worn, and spiritless, they looked less like horses than the ghosts of horses. Thord had made several men eat manure for that. Now under Nikki's direction, and with good fodder and exercise, they were gaining both flesh and spirit. Both the men and the horses were becoming a troop.

Tomorrow the true work would start. After a month, he was ready to start drilling the men to fight. Teaching the men to care for themselves and their horses was one thing. But to teach them how to kill was something else. Thord was sure that some of them knew how to kill in an alley or a lonely stretch of road, but that wouldn't help them in a battle. He knew it even if they didn't. But he had already started by giving them something they hadn't known they lacked. In the last month, they had begun to trust each other, and that was the first step to winning a battle. He had approved when some of the men had taken to sparring with each other when they had free time. Tomorrow he would give them javelins and set them to charge and throw. Then they would see the power of having a hundred comrades at your side. That's when they would learn to be soldiers.

But that was for tomorrow. Tonight was different. Instead of rice, beans, and cabbage, Thord provided an ox and several pigs roasting on spits in the courtyard behind the barracks. Clay jars, each holding a duck, onions, and spices, lined the fire pits. He had barrels of rice wine set out. The wine, the talk, and the men flowed freely around the fires. He sat on the ground with a plate of pork in his hand and a cup of wine at his feet. He and his men traded stories as the moon rose over the walls.

One of the men asked about Thord's axe.

"Do your countrymen use an axe on horseback? Sir."

"No 'sirs' tonight. Save that for tomorrow. Tonight I'm To Waa Da. But no, we don't use an axe for horse back. In my country we don't fight on horses at all." Continuing over the man's shocked look, "If you knew my country you would understand. At home I'm a man of average size. My country is cold and the grass poor. The largest horse on our islands is a pony against the horses here. The sight of my father or uncle riding to battle with his feet dragging the ground beside the horse's hooves would have our enemies dying with laughter long before they could come within sword's reach. My people fight on foot." The man's eyes focused on something in the distance for a moment. The grin that spread over his face told Thord what the man thought of the sight.

As they ate and drank, Nikki sat beside him. Thord pulled him to him with an arm over his shoulder. Beneath his arm, he felt the warmth of Nikki's body against his. He leaned over the top of Nikki's head. He could smell the dark locks mixed with the smoke and the aroma of roast meat that filled the air. When a group started to dance, he could feel the music's tug on Nikki.

"Go on, Little Fox. Join them. I haven't seen you dance since we came here and I am thinking it's about time."

In the red glow of the fire, Nikki's eyes lit up. He stood and walked over and said something to the ring of men. One turned toward Thord.

"If it's alright with your master."

Thord nodded and leaned back on both elbows. He wouldn't need to talk for a while. Nikki would say all that needed to be said. As he watched, Nikki joined into the circle. At first it seemed that he was merging into the dance as it was. But soon, Thord saw the change take over as Nikki pulled the dance and the dancers into his own dance. The steps were all simple with a lot of stomping, arm waving, and clapping. None of the men seemed to notice the changes when they began. But soon they were matching Nikki, their feet rising higher and their arms moving more like flowing water than a market hawker waving in customers. The

137

ring flowed round and round, and Thord caught glimpses of Nikki as the turning brought him past where Thord watched. Nikki's black hair flowed out behind him or swirled around his face as he spun to the rhythm of the dance. His bare legs and arms moved ever faster dragging the beat with him. Thord lost sight of him for a time when more men joined to form a second, outer circle. For an hour Nikki danced. Men began to drift in and out of the dance. After watching for awhile, Thord put down his plate and joined for a time. He danced with the others. He danced with Nikki, sharing something that they all felt but only Nikki understood. When Thord finally stumbled out of the ring to find his cup, he was happy and exhausted. He sat and drank and watched the dance with the others. There were few who could stay in the dance for long and fewer who could sit for long without going back into it. When Nikki finally left the ring, he sat beside Thord and fell asleep leaning his head against Thord's side. With fingers entwined in the Little Fox's black locks, Thord looked at the men still dancing. He saw that, somehow, Nikki had managed to leave something of his magic in the ring. Somehow, the dance carried on, drawing from the men themselves while the source of the magic slept against Thord's shoulder.

When the fire had died and the first hint of dawn touched the eastern sky, Thord lifted Nikki and carried him to bed.

***

Thord watched his men charge. The enemy was a group of straw-covered posts planted in the ground with cross pieces tied to them where a man's arms would be. The men charged into them and hacked at the first "enemy" they met. Some of the men pushed their horses on through but more became bogged down, attempting to hit as many of the posts as they could.

Galloping his horse up to the mêlée, he cursed them. "Fools! Idiots! Dead men!" He jumped to the ground and seized a fallen cross piece. "Never stop! To stop is to die!"

He strode in among a knot of riders. "You think being on a horse makes you stronger than a man on foot because you're higher up? Fools! If that were so then men would fight on stilts. Once you stop, any fool can cut you down from your saddle."

To prove his point, he turned to the nearest rider and struck the man's exposed leg. He waded into them, striking left and right. A leg here, a push with the end of his stick to send a man toppling over, a lighter swat on a horse's rump causing it to bolt with its rider barely hanging on.

When he finished, the field was a disaster. "Never stop." He raised his voice to carry across the field. "Better to hit your first man and ride on than to hit a second and die. A man on horse is like a scythe, useless if not moving. Now form up and charge again."

Watching his men, he thought back to long winter's nights listening to his father and uncle spin tales about their time in the wars. They had gone east as young men and joined a mercenary company. Their tales were full of the battles they had fought. Sprinkled in those stories were the tricks cavalry would use against infantry and what his father and the others would do to stop them. It came to him that when he spoke of a scythe, it was an echo of what his father had told him years ago.

He smiled as he watched the men, his men, charge through the ranks of straw soldiers. They were learning. He was learning.

***

During the next few months, Nikki watched as both the 123$^{rd}$ Imperial Light Horse and Thord gained in experience and confidence. Thord drilled his men until they could respond instantly to any command, the men and horses moving in harmony. He could lead a charge over rough ground with the men still in line at the end. Thord could take them in a fast column that transformed instantly to a charge to the left or right. Nikki's father's best troops couldn't do better.

For Nikki, the past months had been busy as well. He had taken charge of the stable when he saw the poor condition the horses were in. His father had insisted that he and his brothers care for their own horses. That and the skill he had gained tending his oxen and donkeys had come in handy in understanding what was needed to help the horses. Because of their intelligence, the horses were more demanding than the oxen. But once they learned to trust Nikki, that same intelligence meant that they could communicate their problems better.

Nikki had also been kept busy with the paperwork involved in running the 123$^{rd}$. He managed to get control of the scattered mass of forms and requests left by the previous commander. Sorting out the maze of imperial bureaucracy proved to be an even harder task. He found his lessons in the government of Tronmar gave him the basics, but that was all. For every bureaucrat in Tronmar, there were three in the empire, each with an office in a different building and each with a different colored stamp that was needed for any request to be approved. Nikki wasn't certain if the reason for the complexity was to employ as many scribes as possible or to keep the army commanders too busy filling out paperwork to be able to plot a rebellion. In the end, he guessed it was partly both.

It was a relief to receive orders sending the 123$^{rd}$ to the eastern frontier. It meant a frantic round of requisitions for the rations and the travel documents needed for the move, but it also meant that they would no longer be penned up in the capital, under the eye of every mid-level bureaucrat looking for advancement.

Finally there was something real for the men to do. Their orders were to move the unit to the border and make contact with the elves of the plains to the east. Then they would form part of an ambassadorial mission to the king of the elves. After the mission, they were to escort the ambassador back to the capital. Simple and safe.

It was good to be changing location. Nikki had begun to worry about staying in one location too long. His uncle's reach was long and Nikki had no doubt that eventually, he and Thord would be found. They needed to be on the move and this looked like a perfect mission.

# Chance's Children

## *Chapter 10*

They were twenty days into the plains. Ahead of them, the grass stretched on to the horizon in the east. They followed a river on their left. In the flat country, the reeds and dwarf willows that lined its banks hid all but occasional glimpses of water. Two leagues to the south marched a line of hills and beyond them stood a wall of purple mountains, half veiled by distance. The hills were covered in dark pines; white stone broke through the ridgeline like bleached bones. The blue sky above held a few dark birds, wheeling in the distance.

The wind had been at their backs all day, but now it veered around to sweep out of those brooding hills. Under him, Thord could tell his horse was restive. There were no clouds and the air was hot but not oppressive. Still, Thord felt that there was something coming. He sniffed the air but found only the smell of grass crushed beneath hundreds of hooves and the smell of the horses and men around him. He turned to where Nikki rode beside him. "Do you smell something on the wind? Not a storm, I am thinking, but something. The horses smell it."

Nikki shook his head. "I don't smell anything unusual. But my horse is shying away from the wind as well."

The breeze continued to swing around until it was in their faces as they rode eastward. After that the horses settled down again, Thord still felt uneasy about what it was that the wind had borne out of the hills.

The column moved on, two hundred and fifty men. In the front rode Major Mei Ka, alongside the wagon carrying His Excellency, Ambassador Lu Go. Behind them came the hundred men of Red Company, 91$^{st}$ Imperial Infantry, now ill at ease on horses, to allow the embassy the speed to reach the Wagon People, negotiate the treaty, and return before winter. Following them came the baggage train, with the bulk of Thord's men in the rear. In front and on either side rode more of Thord's men as scouts. Thord had sent them out, even though nothing more threatening than a rabbit could hide in the leagues of flat land covered with short grass that stretched in all directions.

As the sun was setting behind the column, they drew near a low hill. At the front of the column, Thord could see the brightly-colored cloak of their elven guide, Kil, as he spoke to Major Mei. Sergeant Lii rode back with the order to halt and camp on the top of the hill.

Lii and Thord sat on their horses beside the column. Lii turned to the south. "The elf is worried about something. The major is all bluster and says he's confident that 'nothing would dare' attack a column of the emperor's men. He wanted to push on, but Ambassador Lu had eaten enough dust for today and was looking for any excuse to stop early."

When the camp was pitched, the wagons unhitched, and the men's mounts unsaddled, one of the men riding sentry around the camp galloped up to where Thord stood watching his men lay out their bedding.

"Sir! There's a group approaching on foot. They are coming at the run out of the hills about a league to the south. I didn't get close enough to tell what they are but they are not men and they are carrying weapons."

Thord turned toward the line of hills that sprawled along the horizon. "Where?"

"There," the man said, pointing to where the nearest hills jutted out into the plain.

Thord could make out a smudge against the bottom of the hills. From it he could see the spark of steel in the light of the lowering sun.

"How many?"

"At least a hundred."

Thord looked again. Yes, at least that many, likely more. "Ride back out and watch them. Don't get too close, but see if you can tell what they are, and try to get a better count of them. I'll alert the major."

As the man galloped back across the grass Thord turned to his men. "Pile up your bed rolls and stand ready for a fight. Pull back to where the wagons can act as part of the line." With that, he ran across the camp to where Major Mei and Ambassador Lu were sitting in camp chairs.

"Sir! An armed party is coming fast from the south. They are a league away but will be here in less than an hour."

As Thord was speaking, Kil their elven guide came up fast on his horse. He reined the horse to a stop, the horse's hooves throwing up lumps of earth and grass. "Ghouls coming from the north! Two hundred or more."

The ambassador turned pale. "Ghouls? There can't be ghouls here!"

Major Mei puffed up his chest. "Don't worry. They won't be foolish enough to attack." He stood in the pose of a fearless warrior, anxious for battle, but the eyes that kept darting toward the south spoke differently. Turning to Thord and the lieutenant in command of the regulars he gave orders to form a defensive line. "Just in case."

***

Thord strode out to stand a dozen yards in front of the line of his men. He stood alone, where his axe wouldn't find the blood of his own men. The scales of his armor glinted like ice in the faint light of the moon. The bright hard edge of his axe was the match of the silver crescent that hung low in the western sky. He could smell the stench of death that clung to the ghouls where they gathered in the gloom in front of him. In the faint light, he made out their tall, thin shapes, their white flesh contrasting with night black armor. As the ghouls crept forward, he waited, dreading the waves of Fear that would pour from the axe to engulf him, dreading the scenes of his death that would bring on the Rage. But even knowing the Fear would come, he stood his ground, grimly determined to fight.

A ghoul charged out of the dark, its tall, white face broken by two yellow eyes and an open mouth full of long, pointed teeth. Raised in its two claws was a great blade, more square-tipped cleaver than sword. The creature ran straight at Thord. As the blade came down, Thord stepped in with his shield to block the ghoul's blow and send him spinning to the side. The force of the descending sword drove the tip into Thord's shield. Thord felt a sharp pain in his forearm. As the momentum of the ghoul's charge carried him past, Thord turned and brought his axe down to rip through its back, the axe making no distinction between leather sewn with steel rings or bone knit with muscle and sinew.

Thord gritted his teeth and winced at the pain in his arm and felt the warm blood run down to where his hand gripped the shield. He stood staring at the dark mass of the ghoul where it lay, twitching, on the grass in a widening pool of black, steaming blood.

He stared for only a moment and then lifted his axe to the stars and laughed. He was free! There was no Fear! Death did not haunt him. The Rage was gone. Free! He was no longer a soulless killer driven by a terror beyond his control. Now he could fight, feel pain, and maybe die, but he would fight and die like a man. He laughed again and the laugh was picked up by the wind and carried across the field. The men on the hill heard it and, hearing the joy that welled up from within that laugh, drew courage from it. Thord could hear his own laugh riding back out on the waves of light that swirled in slow spirals from where he had left Nikki holding a torch. Ghouls, who know nothing of laughter and not seeing the peril it bore, pressed forward.

The ghouls surged up the hill to where Thord stood. The next to reach him thrust with a heavy spear. But Thord's shield deflected the barbed head and his axe lashed out to sever the thick shaft and the clawed hand that gripped it. More came on as Thord settled down to the work before him. Block, parry, kill. Parry, kill. Duck, block, kill. The ghouls were on three sides of him now. In the dark, Thord could hear their breath on the wind and the rattle of their armor. He let his ears reach out into the night. There with the wind and the noise from the camp he could hear the ghouls and count them. Three score and two were on this side of the hill. Parry, kill. Three score and one. Behind him he could he could hear his men as they waited for the onslaught. But one wasn't waiting. Thord heard the steps of a man running the few yards to take a stand on his left. The dull sound of steel halted by flesh told him now there were three score. More feet ran down the hill. Soon Thord was the head of a wedge of men. Thord's laughter turned to song. With a great surge, his men scattered the ghouls into the night.

He stood with the bodies strewn around him and picked some thirty men. "You men come with me. The rest of you take any wounded back up and reform the line."

With that, he led his men around the hill to take the rest of the ghouls in the flank. Half way around the hill he heard shouts and hooves from the camp. In the darkness in front of him, four horses with riders galloped out of the camp and into the night. The silhouette of one of the riders bore the helmet with three tall feathers that marked Major Mei. The flapping of silk told him that one of the others was the ambassador.

"They are riding for help!" he shouted back to his men. He knew that the better men would know the truth. But they would pretend it was true and come on anyway. For the ones with less experience, who would believe the lie, it might keep them from despair.

In front of him, Thord could see that the Imperial Regulars were hard pressed by the ghouls. Their line was bending back under the pressure and would break if nothing happened. He was about to make something happen.

Thord had led his men around the hill so they would take the ghouls on the right, the side away from their shields. When his men crashed into their flank, the first line of ghouls went down before they knew where the attack came from. Confused, the ghouls began to turn to face Thord's men, only to expose their sides to the men on the hill. Thord's men kept fighting and rolling up the line in front of them as they were joined by more regulars, now freed, as the ghoul line crumbled back onto itself.

By now, Thord's shield had long been tossed away as useless kindling. His armor had taken a several hits that should have killed him, but bounced off the ogre hide. Dodging, ducking, and hacking, he cut a path of death and ruin through the line in front of him. His men pushed in close behind to give protection to his sides and to widen the hole he made.

When Thord's men had pushed deep into the main body of the ghouls, the enemy broke and ran from the field. Thord called back the men who would have pursued them into the dark.

"Back to the line, boys! There are still too many of them to chase in the dark. I am thinking they won't want to come back any time soon, but form up anyway."

Back in the camp Thord stood beside a fire and with him was Sergeant Lii. Now with the lieutenant killed at the start of the battle, Lii was the highest ranking of the regular troops. There too were Kil and Nikki. He looked at the men manning the perimeter, and at the wounded in the grass around him.

"Well, we beat them back. Of the hundred who were under me, there are sixty-two ready to fight and eighteen wounded. Lii?"

"Sir, I have forty-nine on their feet with sixteen wounded. The rest are dead, sir."

*Sir?* Thord thought. He glanced around. Lii, Kil, and Nikki were looking at him. He was about to protest when Lii stopped him.

"Sir. As the only officer left, you are in command. You are now captain."

Thord turned an imploring face to Nikki.

"Master, he is right. The men need a commander. They've seen you fight and even the regulars now respect you. You're in command and that's final."

Kil placed his closed fist over his heart. "You are in command."

With a sigh, Thord turned back to Lii. "Sergeant, if they see we are on guard, the ghouls won't attack again tonight unless they get reinforcements. Break the able-bodied men into three watches and let two at a time sleep in their armor, if they can. In the morning I will decide what to do. Nikki, go to the ambassador's wagon and watch it to make sure nothing happens to anything the ambassador left. Ghouls or no, there may be temptations that are too much for some of the men."

Thord lay a long time looking up at the stars. He had barely a hundred men who could fight and a third as many wounded. He knew the ghouls hadn't gone far and that there might be more nearby. If he marched back, he could expect no help for at least a hundred leagues. For days they had marched with a wide shallow river on their left. Though nowhere was it more than a foot deep, the river bottom was mostly quicksand with no ford for horses, let alone wagons. They would have to pass alongside the hills. He couldn't outrun the ghouls with the wagons and he wouldn't leave the wounded behind. The only hope was to keep moving forward. But that meant at least one more pitched battle. The elf Kil had said that the ghouls traveled on foot, as there was no animal that would carry them. The ghouls looked to be solid fighters. Their surprise at the resistance was what had turned the fight against them. That wouldn't work a second time. He needed a way to fight heavy infantry and win. How could his outnumbered hundred break their line?

It was cold on the hill top. As he thought, Thord sat up and looked at the dying fire beside his bed roll. The ashes were dimming and only one larger block of wood gave any hint it could still burn. He reached over with a stick and poked the ashes until sparks rose and ripples of pink and yellow flowed across the coals. He then brought his stick down hard and hit the last log where the cracked and charred surface looked thinnest. The blow broke it in half. He watched the flame rise from the inner sides of the two pieces. He stared first at the flame and then at the stick in his hands. With a smile he leaned back and fell asleep.

When the dawn came, the field was quiet. Beyond the line of weary men, the grass was covered in blood, some red and some black, but nothing more. There were no bodies. Neither ghoul nor man lay in the blood-soaked grass. As Thord looked out, Kil came up.

"Don't look for your dead, Captain. The ghouls took them. If it is any comfort, they eat their own as well."

From the hills to the south rose thin columns of smoke.

In the growing light, Thord took stock of what was left of the column. He sent Nikki to see what supplies and animals were left while Lii and To'a gathered the men together. When the men had formed up into lines, Thord walked in front of them. The ranks looked tired. The older veterans stood straight enough but some of the younger men showed more than a little fear in the way they stood with hunched backs and shifting eyes.

"Men, you fought well. You stood your ground and taught a lesson that won't soon be forgotten." At this a thin cheer rose from the ranks. "But, we're not out of the plains yet. They're still out there and they won't give up after one blooding. They are going to dog us until we break them or they eat us. And since I, for one, will not be eaten without a good horseradish sauce, we'll just have to kill them."

That got a laugh from the older men who Thord guessed were thinking much the same thoughts. He could see the effect of the laughter on the younger men. They had fought well last night, and now being reminded of that, the men stood with a little more of the courage they had found in the dark and the death.

"Now men, we're not going to go looking for a fight but we are going to be ready when one comes. These ghouls fight as heavily armored infantry. When attacked, they fight close together with shields overlapped. The way to fight them is to stir them up so their shield-wall loosens, and then smash them hard. Sergeant Lii, I want your forty best riders to form up in two groups with their pikes to act as lancers. To'a, you're now in command of my company. I want the best forty men you've got on horses with bows and javelins. Split them into two groups. When we go to fight, the rest will stay and guard the wounded. Now this is what we're going to do…"

When every man knew his role, they broke camp. The wounded were loaded on top of the supply wagons. Thord and Nikki rode in front of the column. The troops formed a cross with twenty of Lii's men in front and twenty more behind. To'a's men rode on either side. Kil rode out ahead of the column.

They were an hour on the move when Kil came riding back. He stopped in front of Thord. "I found something you should see."

The two of them rode out ahead and to the south of the line of march to a spot marked by a column of circling birds. There on the ground lay parts of four bodies. To one side was a head resting on its side. A helmet with three feathers was still in place with the strap under the chin. There were no arms or legs and all four of the torsos had been cut open. Thord guessed that, if he looked, he would find the hearts and livers missing.

Kil rode on ahead while Thord rode back to fall in beside Nikki. He answered Nikki's unvoiced question. "If I am the commander, now you are the ambassador."

The column pushed on for another two hours before Kil came racing back. Thord didn't need to wait for the news. He could see the dark line breaking away from the hills to intercept them. Thord stood up in the stirrups.

"Take it slow, men. Let them tire themselves out rushing to meet us." His voice carried across the plains. "Remember what I told you and we'll make them wish they liked eating turnips."

The column continued on as the black line drew closer. When it was half a league in front of them, Thord halted. Rising in his stirrups, he shouted out his orders.

"They're close enough, men. Form up and let's finish this."

The four units formed a line in front of the wagons. The two groups of lances were in the center with light horsemen on each side. As they moved forward, the groups pulled apart until there was a gap of some fifty yards between each group. The light horse moved ahead of the rest and approached the line of ghouls from the right and the left.

When the men began to move, the ghouls pulled their own line tighter until they formed a wall some sixty wide and three deep. Thord marked two ghouls who looked to be in command. At this distance, he could make out one with a tall spike on his helmet and the other with long yellow streamers hanging on his shield. They were in front, directing the others as they fell into line. As To'a's men approached, the ghoul commanders moved back and took up positions in the shield-wall, disappearing among the bristling ranks of spears.

To'a stopped his men and began sending arrows into the ghouls at sixty yards. The archers loosed their arrows in volleys, first from the left, then from the right, and then the left again. Back and forth, a hail of steel came down on the ghouls. When a group on the left broke from the ghoul ranks to charge the archers, To'a's men just rode further away and sent more arrows at their pursuers. This cost the ghouls some dead before they fell back into the main body. The archers moved back into position and continued to shoot more arrows. As the arrows came in, the ghouls turned first left, then right, then left again, trying to block the rain of steel. Right, left, right. It was then that Thord ordered the charge.

The armor of ogre hide flashed like ice in the bright sun as he led the first twenty in from the right to smash the center of the wavering line. They came in a tight mass at the gallop, leaning over their lances. Thord led his charge straight for the ghoul with the spiked helmet. Looking down the length of his lance, Thord got his first look at a ghoul in daylight. Glaring over the top of its shield, the ghoul's face was moon white, fractured with the lines of black veins, just under the skin. If there was any hair it was hidden under its helmet. The eyes were jet black, shaded by low brows. Thord aimed his lance for the ghoul's face. As the ghoul brought its shield up to cover its face, Thord dropped the lance and took the ghoul in the hip, just below the bottom edge of its shield. The lance head tore in until it hit bone, when the force spun the ghoul's body to the side while Thord passed by, ripping the lance out as he thundered on.

Caught between blocking the arrows from the sides and the line of lances rushing down on them from in front, the ghoul line broke. Thord's men rode through the ghouls and passed on. Behind them they left a dozen dead or wounded ghouls and five of their comrades. Thord's men were through the other side and wheeling around when Lii's men hit the ghouls from the left. This time the line was already broken. Lii's men thundered through leaving a trail of dead and dying ghouls. With waves of arrows pouring in from the sides, Thord's men hit the line from behind as Lii's were beginning to turn for a second charge. Again and again, they charged. With lances broken, it was work for saber or axe.

When Thord saw a group of his men unhorsed, surrounded by ghouls, he charged into the melee and dismounted to stand beside them. The shield he had marked earlier appeared in front of him. Now he was able to see that what he had taken for streamers were a dozen long braids of golden elf hair. The ghoul raised its sword, but Thord didn't wait for it to fall. Stepping forward, his axe clove the shield and the arm that held it. The ghoul stared blankly at the black blood gushing from the stump of its arm and never saw the second blow that sent it into the darkness.

Thord stood with his men, a storm of ice and steel. At his feet the hot, black blood steamed where it covered the ground. The enemy that ringed the unhorsed men were hit again and again as they turned from the men on foot to the mounted men still charging through them.

Finally the last of the ghouls broke and began running for the hills, to be pursued by the archers until they ran out of arrows.

When it was over, they counted the dead. Twelve of the regulars had died in the charges. Four of To'a's men were killed when they were caught closing in to throw javelins. A hundred ghouls lay where they fell, with another thirty bodies marking the way to the hills.

When Thord's men rode on, they took their dead away to bury where they wouldn't be easily found. The bodies of the ghouls they left for the flies and the birds, and for any ghouls that dared to return.

\*\*\*

They traveled late into the evening that day to put as much distance between themselves and the ghouls as possible. When they finally camped, Nikki had time to go through any papers left by the ambassador. As he walked to the wagon, he could hear Thord at one of the camp fires, praising the men's courage and skill and joking about the battle.

Among the silk cushions and boxes of provisions, Nikki found a box of documents. He couldn't read all of it, but he was able to puzzle out most of what was there. They seemed to be written instructions relating to what the emperor hoped from the treaty with the elf kingdom of the Wagon People. In the bottom of the box was an imperial purchase authorization for gifts related to the mission.

In the treaty, the emperor wanted two things above all. First, he wanted one or more trade fairs to be held on imperial ground or on the border. The other thing the emperor was looking for was cooperation in patrolling the east. There were disturbances in the lands to the south and

151

east of the empire and the elf lands. The trouble was now spilling across the border into the empire itself.

A second chest contained the items to be used as gifts and bribes. But where the documents specified a dragon brooch of first quality emeralds, the brooch Nikki found didn't match the description. The palm-sized brooch was of a dragon, coiled into a disk. The gold was pure, but the gems were badly flawed and their cut didn't match the setting. Nikki could only believe that the stones had been switched and he guessed the ambassador had pocketed the good emeralds. The rest of the chest was a similar collection of second rate baubles that would hardly impress the mayor of a farm hamlet. Nikki knew that if these had been presented as gifts to his father, there would have been no chance of a treaty ever being signed. He needed to do something before they reached the elven king.

\*\*\*

A further two days riding bought another blur of movement on the plains ahead of them. Initial anxiety turned to relief as they watched. For, this time the distant motion marked the coming of riders and, here in the plains, riders meant elves. Thord, with Nikki riding beside him, called Lii and To'a to him. Thord stared ahead at the fast moving column. As it drew closer, the blur of movement resolved to a riot of color -- reds, blues, greens, and yellows set off with flashes of silver from bridles and saddles.

"I want the men to look sharp. We still have a job to do, and I want the elves to know that we can not only fight but do it with style." To'a and Lii spun their horses around and rode back to their troops.

Kil rode ahead to meet his kinsmen. Thord could see him fall in with the elves to ride beside the leader. After a few minutes, an elf at the head of the column waved an arm in the air and half of the elves broke from the main group to ride towards the hills to the south, while the rest continued on toward Thord's column. When they came abreast of Thord's men, the elves wheeled to pace the column while the leader and Kil cantered to where Thord and Nikki rode at the head.

Kil extended his hand toward Thord. "Captain Thord, I wish you to meet Ven, the leader of Wolf Troop. They will escort you the rest of the way. Ven, I present Captain Thord Thurgoodson."

Ven looked to be of average height and slight build, like most elves Thord had met. Long, blond hair flowed from under a crested helmet. Ven's voice was high and light.

"Welcome to our land, Thord Thurgoodson."

Reaching up, Ven pulled the helmet off. As the blond hair spilled loose from the helmet, Thord realized with a shock that Ven's ears were not pointed. Ven was human! She was a woman and only a couple of years younger than himself. His confusion must have been clear to read on his face because she spoke at once.

"I am Ven, called the Changeling. For Wolf Troop, I say that after what Kil told us of your fight against the ghouls, you and your men are most welcome."

Kil placed his fist on his chest. "Here I must take my leave and return to the western border. You have five more days before you reach the camp of the king. But between your men and Ven's troop, you should have no trouble. Ride with the Sun." He turned his horse and galloped back along the line of men and beyond.

Ven pointed ahead. "There is a good campsite in front of you. It has a sweet stream and you can get firewood from the trees along the banks near the ford. You should reach it in four or five hours of march. One of my people will make sure you don't miss it. I'll go ahead of you and scout the area. When you've made camp we will talk about the rest of the journey."

"That will be good." Even as Thord replied, Ven was turning her horse toward the column of elves. At a word from her, the horse sprang away.

***

Ven rode into the camp of men with the dusk. Across her saddle was one of the antelope she and the hunting party had killed. Stopping before the cook fire she dropped the carcass to the grass in front of the cook. "This is for your men."

The cook looked at the antelope and grinned up at her. "Thank you, my lady."

She rode back out of the Man camp to where her own people were gathered. There she unsaddled her horse and set it loose to go wherever it would, to graze. She walked back though the line of sentries to the camp and found the tall man standing with his back to her. He was talking to the dark-haired slave she had seen earlier.

"Is that all you found in the ambassador's papers?"

"That is all that relates to the mission. If there were any unwritten instructions, they died with him."

As Ven came into the view of the slave, he flashed his eyes in her direction. The man turned toward her.

"Good evening, Troop Leader Ven. I hear you are responsible for our having fresh meat instead of beans tonight. For my men, I thank you."

"You should thank me later. When we reach the king's camp, the only thing to eat, other than meat and cheese, is what you bring. Elves don't plant crops, so there will be no beans, bread, or beer. After a month of nothing but meat and milk, you may be looking forward to a plate of beans."

"Then all the more thanks."

The man's Elvish was good but heavily accented with the broad vowels of the north. Seeing him off of his horse, he was taller than she had thought at first. His long hair was a match with her own and his round, blue eyes looked strange to her after the dark, almond eyes of the men she had seen before. They looked like the eyes that stared back at her out of her mother's mirror. His loose shirt of black silk could not hide the massive shoulders and arms under it. Thrust through a wide leather belt was a great axe. He turned and with his hand indicated the slave behind him.

"This is Ambassador Ni Kee. He will act in the place of the late ambassador."

The slave stepped forward and gave a bow. "Troop Leader Ven." As he bowed, the chain from his collar swung out to hang in front of him. He wore a short tunic of the same black silk as the man's shirt.

Looking at the chain, she wondered how her father would take to dealing with a slave as an ambassador. But that was his problem and not hers. She had other things to handle.

"May your mission prosper," she responded. "I have been told to find one in your camp called Fox and to offer him the welcome of Ked, our shaman."

The slave took a step forward. "I am called Little Fox. I am honored by the shaman's welcome."

Now this was even stranger. She was told to seek out two among the men. The man, Thord, matched what she expected of a warrior. But this slave was not what she expected when the shaman had told her to find a wizard. She had been too young to remember much of the last embassy from the west but it was certainly not like this. She would have to make sure no word of this reached her father before they arrived. She didn't want to miss seeing his face when both the ambassador and the wizard turned out to be a young slave.

*** 

154

Nikki had seen the hills to the northeast when they made camp last night, the dark green of pine trees and the gray of stone rising above the pale green-gold of the grass lands. Over all stretched a vast blue dome, now empty of clouds. With the sunset, riders had appeared on their line of march. Ven rode out to meet them. After a few moments, the riders turned and hastened back toward the hills. Now, as Thord's men approached those hills, the column moved among a vast herd of cattle. To the outside of the cattle were smaller herds of horses, each headed by a stallion. But where the cattle parted to let the column pass, the stallions trumpeted their challenges. Rearing and kicking the air, they passed back and forth between their harems and the approaching men. When that failed to turn the riders, the stallions drove the mares away from the column with nips and kicks.

Just inside a gap in the hills, they came upon the king's summer camp. Nikki had expected something very different. He had imagined either a city much like any other, of houses and shops, or a camp of tents and wagons. What lay in the shallow bowl in the hills was half a city, half a camp. Parts of it had the appearance of some of the ruined cities he had seen, with only the stumps of stone walls poking through the grass. But this was anything but a ruin. Brightly colored tents of hide were pitched over low, permanent walls of stone and turfs. The ridge poles of the tents ended in fanciful carvings of beasts and birds. Climbing up the hillsides to the edge of the trees were stone corrals, some empty and others dotted with horses and sheep.

Ven led them around the edge of the camp to some twenty plain looking tents.

"These booths are for you and your men." She pointed to paddocks and hayricks just beyond. "You can corral your horses in there. Either graze them or cut fodder in the plains. Save the hay for later. The ground is mostly free of snow here all year, but there may be times when the horses won't be able to find grass. Now, I have to speak with my father. I'll come back at sunset to see if you need anything. He will want to see you, but that will wait until tomorrow."

She turned her horse and cantered back into the main part of the camp.

Elves showed them to the booths. Thord and Nikki were shown to the largest, covered by a blue tent with yellow stripes of embroidery. When Thord balked at taking the largest, Nikki pointed out that as commander and ambassador, they were expected to show that status. "And we will need room to entertain guests. In the field, your duty is to

155

share hardships with your men. Here, your duty is to represent the emperor."

They followed an elf into the booth. Once inside, they were in a small foyer with a stone floor. The elf took off his light shoes and placed them on a shelf to the side. Only after Thord and Nikki had followed suit, did he pull aside the woven hanging that served as the inner door.

Though the outside of the structure had surprised Nikki, the inside was even more of a shock. Carved cedar poles supported a ceiling of heavy, cream colored felt. The sides were of woven tapestries with scenes of fanciful animals. Several of these tapestries were folded part way from the top to allow light into the room. Under his bare feet were thick rugs with a firmness that told of well-laid stone flags beneath. In the center of the room was a stone hearth surrounded by thick cushions. From near the hearth, a tall, thin pole ran to the roof to prop open one of several flaps, to let smoke out. Small lamps on chains were suspended from the rafters. The back was separated from the rest by a wall of tapestries. Doorways in that wall indicated two private rooms beyond.

\*\*\*

Ven stood in the doorway to the throne room. Looking down the steps, she watched the imperial party approach. She was acting as door warden for her father. Glancing back, she watched her father take his place on the carpet-draped stone that had been the throne of the Wagon People since they had taken this land, millennia ago. The stone was bathed in sunlight from one of the open flaps in the roof of the great tent that formed the core of the palace. As the men were reaching the top of the stair, Ven strode to the center of the room.

She raised her voice until it carried over the murmurs. "Your Majesty, the Imperial Ambassador Ni Kee and Imperial Captain Thord Thurgoodson."

She stood aside as the two approached the throne. She could see her father's gaze caught by the figure of the captain. The image of the man, with his helmet and its two long feathers, the bright yellow cloak, the ice blue coat of scale armor, and the great axe at his side, was sure to hold most of the king's attention. But when they bowed and the iron chain swung free from the brocaded breast of the ambassador's ill-fitting robe, she was pleased to see surprise, even shock, sweep across her father's face.

Straightening up, the ambassador began, "King of the Wagon People, I bring greetings and best wishes to you and your people from Emperor Wo."

Ven watched as her father began to get control of himself again. His slightly open lips closed and his eyebrows settled back down from his forehead.

"And... And my greetings to Emperor Wo."

This was better than Ven had hoped for. In her entire life, she had never seen her father at a loss for words. But the ambassador must have caught on to it as well because he stretched out the usual run of multiple exchanges of greetings until the her father had control of his emotions. Then he went to something that would not require any formal response from the king.

"Your majesty, as a token of the esteem Emperor Wo holds for you, let me present you with this small gift."

One of the accompanying men approached the king with a small casket. When he reached a patch where sunlight poured in from an open tent flap, the man opened the lid. The light falling onto the object under that lid was thrown back, dazzling the eyes. The inside looked to be filled with a fire of green and gold.

The king stepped down from the throne and looked closely. Motioning for the casket to be given to Ven, he turned to the ambassador.

"Tell the emperor that his gift is most welcome. Dwarf-worked stones are seldom found outside of the mountains and these are the best I have seen in a long age."

"Thank you, Majesty."

Ven thought there was more to the reply than acknowledging a gift well received. There was the sound of pride in it as well. Looking down at the open casket in her hands she understood the king's response. On a black silk background lay a brooch. A dragon disk! The dragon was made of emeralds set in gold, each stone perfect, the facets throwing their green light in countless directions. She looked at the gems and remembered watching The Little Fox dance for several nights in the moonlight outside the camp, on the road here. She had seen the eerie green glow when he danced and now thought she understood the pride in his response. The shaman had been right about finding a wizard among the men.

The king turned back to the men. "Ambassador, Captain, you must join me at dinner tonight. And I also invite the one in your mission called Fox."

At this the ambassador bowed. "I am the Little Fox, Majesty."

Ven's father didn't bother to hide his surprise at this. His brows rose and he cocked his head slightly as he looked at the Little Fox. "This is indeed the most interesting embassy to come to the Wagon People in all the years I remember. Yes. Do come and we can get to know each other better."

\*\*\*

"How is the treaty going?"

"Going? Master?" Nikki looked up from pouring the mildly intoxicating green elven tea into Thord's cup to look into his eyes. Such blue eyes. "We haven't started to talk about it."

"You've met with the king for the past three days and you haven't talked about the treaty?" There was a note of exasperation in Thord's voice.

"Master, remember in Dorisan, when you sold the ox cart and bought those donkeys? How long did you and the donkey trader sit and talk before either of you even said the word 'donkey'? If we start talking about the treaty in the next ten days I will be surprised. My father and the Owainian ambassador danced around a trade treaty for a month without bringing anything into the open."

Nikki's response was tinged with his own impatience at the pace. The only thing keeping that impatience in check was that he knew it had to be slow. Both sides needed time to get to know the other. Any faster and the king would think Nikki was desperate to conclude the treaty. The king would see this as an advantage and press for more concessions. While Nikki thought he had some leeway, he couldn't go beyond what was allowed in the instructions he had found when he went through the late ambassador's papers.

When he finished pouring the tea, Nikki moved to sit across from Thord on the thick carpet.

Now that the negotiations were his problem, Nikki was beginning to appreciate the months of study his father and the wizard Ganian had forced on him. What had seemed like mindless repetition of court protocol and politics was giving him insights into the dynamics of this king's court. The rules were all different, but Nikki could see similarities in how those rules applied to the players in this court and those in his father's. With that knowledge came the ability to manipulate those dynamics to his advantage.

"No, Master. This is going as fast as it can. And anyway, I can't bring the treaty up myself. I'll have to reach deeper into the gift chest before I can get one of the courtiers to bring it up for me. But even that will have to wait until I can make it seem not to be my idea."

Nikki looked up to see Thord, his head cocked, giving him an appraising look. "You're becoming less of a Little Fox and more of a big fox. And more, I am thinking, you enjoy this."

It was true. For the first time since the night he had left the palace and met Thord, Nikki was some place where he felt he fitted in with his surroundings. Here, he was aware of the similarities with his past and not the differences. In the elven king he saw much that reminded him of his father. There were differences that resulted from the nature of the two races, but their cares and hopes were universal to kings across races and nations. And he began to see something of his eldest brother in himself. After days of meeting people and talking about everything except what was important, he found he had begun to wear the bored and somewhat bemused face that had always distanced him a little from Crown Prince Danalo. Now, he was beginning to understand his brother, and in a way feel sorry for him. Because he was to be king, Danalo's whole life was spent keeping back from things. He had never been able to just enjoy some simple pleasure. Unlike his oldest brother, Nikki had the ability to fall back into the role of the Little Fox, where he could laugh and joke and take life as it was given. But as the ambassador of a powerful monarch, he was constrained to all of the posing that had consumed Danalo's life. When he danced, he balanced on a knife edge between a power beyond his grasp and joy beyond his dreams. In the role of the slave of a barbarian warrior, he was expected to take his fun where he could find it. At last he better understood, and felt sorry for, Danalo.

"Yes, master. I am enjoying this." The grin on his face was all from the Little Fox.

\*\*\*

"Ven, how did you come to be among the Wagon People?"

She looked over the brim of her tea cup. In the days since the embassy had arrived in her father's winter camp, she had come to know something of the man who led them. One trait she had found in him was the uncompromising forwardness of a soldier. This last question was an example of just that. She looked across the carpet at the man, Thord, and tried to answer with the same candor.

"I'm a changeling. Mother and Father won't say much about it. Twenty years ago, they took me from a crib someplace to the west. They say I'm the daughter of a noble but they won't say whose daughter or from what country. A rabbit was left in my place." She sometimes wondered what had become of that rabbit when the illusion spell had worn off. Hope said it was released. Fear whispered of some other fate. The thought of that woman's grief, when she had learned of the loss of her daughter, occasionally came to trouble her, on lonely nights under the stars, when she was away from her parents. But that was a lifetime ago and there was nothing that could be done now.

"With your hair and eyes, you could be from my country, but we don't have anyone who could be called a noble. But, I am thinking, you must be from around the Home Sea some place." With that, Thord put his cup to his lips. When he brought it down, she watched him wipe the drops of tea from his thick mustache with the back of a broad hand.

She looked past him toward the plains. The autumn weather was fine and they were having tea on cushions in front of the booth Thord and Nikki shared. "Tell me about your homeland. Is it far west?"

She listened as he described black and green islands set in the dark blue ocean and the people who lived there. As he spoke, she realized that this land of his was like her own. Both were made up of stony islands set in almost endless seas, the one of water and the other of grass. The peoples were alike as well, independent and proud. Warrior peoples, who traveled those seas where they would and who gave their allegiance, not for the chances of birth, but for courage and honor. Traits she saw in the man seated, cross-legged, before her.

He was looking west. "Someday, we will return to the Home Sea. There are things there that need to be set right." She heard an edge to his voice that came to her as a surprise. It left her thinking she didn't want to be on the wrong end of that setting things right.

Return to the Home Sea!

She sipped her tea and gazed out across the plains to the west. She had heard of the lands beyond the plains and the distant mountains, but had never traveled past the edge of the grass. What was it that called to her from those lands? What held her here? The only parents she had ever known were here. But they were becoming more and more distant. She knew they had taken her because they wanted a child, and it might have been centuries before they had another one of their own. But now that she was no longer a child, their interest was waning. She tried hard to be what was expected of their daughter. She practiced with bow and sword until she was a match for the best of the Wagon People. Her riding was the equal of any in the camp. But she knew that, in the end, she was not an elf. Someday, she would have to leave and live among others of her own kind. Since she had become a woman, the call of her own people had grown stronger as the months passed. Someday, she too would have to return to lands around the Home Sea and maybe set some things of her own right.

*** 

When the shaman, Ked, invited the Little Fox to attend a ritual, it was no surprise to him that the young man jumped at it. During the past half moon, they had spent as much time together as the Little Fox could spare from the duties of an ambassador. Ked had found him a quick student, just what he expected from the message the bard, Bel, had passed on to him. What he could teach would take longer to learn than several lifetimes of man, but in the time they had, the Fox had drunk knowledge in like a man parched from wandering the desert.

Now they sat cross-legged on the grass in the center of a circle made up of all the shamans of the Grass Elves. Beyond the circle stood a ring of great standing stones, the relics of a people who had vanished before even the elves arrived in this land. As the king's own shaman, Ked sat directly across from Nikki. From here, he looked into eyes dark but full of sparks reflected from the fire. *What would he find behind those eyes?* He asked himself. *Who was this slave, ambassador, prince, wizard?* Tonight they would find out.

The scent of the cedar smoke from the fire was overpowered by the smell of tension that filled the cold air flowing across the hilltop. The stars moved silently overhead. Ked saw Nikki's right arm shift slightly, the hand hidden by a hollow gourd. The left hand was still. A long strip of white silk stretched from inside the gourd, along the arm and across the shoulders and down the left hand. Trailing across the ground beside him, it moved in the slight breeze with a life of its own. But what kind of life?

When the full moon reached its zenith, the drummers began a slow, simple rhythm. The sound flowed out into the night to be echoed back from the weathered stones of the surrounding hills. Rattles joined the drums. The chant began.

Ked watched in the firelight. The chant rolled over the young man before him. For an hour it called into the dark for an answer. It sought inside for an answer. The answer came.

Nikki rose to his feet and began to step into the chant, his feet finding a path among the beats and the words. The hand holding the gourd swung low to the earth; the silk trailing from the other hand moved back and forth over the ground. Ked sensed the man was looking around the circle, not with the dark eyes that glittered in the firelight, but with other

161

eyes. The red light of the fire began to settle on the gourd and silk. A face appeared, long-nosed with pointed ears. The Fox.

*It was true then.* *There was a bond between this man and the demigod Luck.* Ked could no longer doubt what the western wizard had whispered on the Wind. Things were moving.

The vision took shape and became more solid. Now there was no gourd, no silk, no man. There was only the Man/Fox, merged into one, hunting for something. It raised its nose to the breeze. What it sought was far from here, yet known to the Wind.

The Man/Fox and the chant called out into the night and there came an answer. The dance merged with the chant and washed over the shaman with the force of a flood. Ked felt the call and didn't resist. He rose to his feet and joined in the dance. His own totem joined into the dance. Fox and Lion moved in an ever growing dance. By ones and twos, the other shamans joined in. Wolf, Deer, Bear all joined the shadows of the Fox and Lion that were thrown by the fire against the old stones. When dawn came, the hilltop was empty of all but the distant echoes of power.

\*\*\*

Over a thousand horse rode out of the hills in two columns. The right followed the White Bull standard of the king. The left was led by a pennant with an ice-blue dragon on a yellow field. Under the king's banner were six hundred elven archers on the fastest horses in the world. Under the Ice Dragon's banner were a hundred and twenty men with long lances and twice that number of elves with sabers. Between the columns rode ten shamans and one slave. Two days' ride in front of them, an army of sixteen hundred ghouls marched across the cold, windswept plain.

When word first came of the invading army, it was derided as nonsense. Why would the ghouls send so many into the plain? They would have to know that mounted elves could keep out of reach of an army on foot. The elves would lead them on until the ghouls tired of the game and returned to the mountains of the south. And why would they march out with winter fast approaching?

The king had called a council of the clan leaders and shamans. Thord and Nikki had been invited as well.

"They must be mad. To raid this time of year with an army of almost two thousand and pulling heavy carts, they are either mad or desperate." The speaker was Til, the head of the Bear Clan. It was a scout from the Bear Clan who had spotted the ghouls entering the plain. Til had delivered the news and now sat back down on a cushion.

Nikki watched and thought as Ked the shaman spoke up. "Mad? That may be. But why should they be desperate? This year, they have raided far and wide. Other than a few times," at this he waved his hand in Thord's direction, "they were successful. No, they are not desperate."

"Then they are mad." The dismissive tone in Til's voice made it sound as if he thought the question was answered.

Nikki wasn't convinced and it must have shown. The king turned to him and asked, "Ambassador Nikki, what do you think about this?"

Nikki got slowly to his feet, more to have a few more moments to think than for any other reason.

"When we fought the ghouls, there were only a few hundred. If they had carts, they must have left them in the hills and didn't risk them in the open. The scout said 'heavy carts.' If they were starting on a raid, the carts would be empty. This isn't a raid. Your Majesty, how many warriors can you put in the field?"

"Eight hundred now. Four times that in the spring."

"Right now, you have half the number that is marching this way. They can't expect you to fight. I don't see this as a raid. No, I think it is the first wave of an invasion, a move to drive you from your winter camp and occupy it themselves. If they can seize these hills, they will be in the heart of your country and can strike out in any direction. Once they have had time to fortify a camp, you will never be able to drive them out." As he spoke, Nikki looked from face to face around the circle. The idea sank in slowly. Some turned to each other with questioning looks. Others had the faces of those far away, seeing what they didn't like but had no way to change.

The king sighed. "Our eight hundred isn't enough to stop them, and we can't defend against them. If their plan is to come here, we will have to pull back and try to gather more forces before they get reinforcements."

Beside Nikki, Thord spoke for the first time. "Maybe not, I am thinking. You have eight hundred. I have a hundred and twenty. I've spent the last weeks drilling my men to act as heavy cavalry. If you will back us with several hundred of your strongest riders and use the rest as archers as we did, I think we have hope of stopping them."

They argued for hours, but in the end, no one had a better plan.

So now they were riding out to do battle. The columns rode in a circle of fog. Above them the sun moved in a dome of blue, resting on walls of billowy grey. Around him, Nikki could hear and see the shamans chanting the fog to life. He felt the gentle pull of that song as it tugged at the water in the grass and the earth. The chant brought the mist from the ground and shielded the army from the eyes of spies.

\*\*\*

Nikki sat on his horse alongside Ked. Behind them, the other shamans drummed and chanted. Nikki could feel the power flow across him on its way to the line of ghouls. From in front of him came the sound of gongs. Gongs clanging in harmony and in discord. Gongs ringing power. The force of it bent the grass in waves out from the center of the ghoul line. The waves met the power of the chant and broke in the field between the two armies.

"Their magic is strong, Little Fox. It would suck the life out of you if we didn't oppose it." Ked sat still on his horse. "You were lucky there were no wizards when you fought them before. Yes, their magic is strong, but it is limited also. Each gong you hear was cast for a single part of a spell. They can combine them to vary the spell but only in certain ways. That's where we can match them. The chant is infinite, filling all the space of this world. Mountains die but the chant remains."

Nikki could feel the tension between the two, the forces canceling each other. Neither one was able to overcome the other. But it was a balance that spelled doom to their plan. To break the ghoul's line, Thord's men had to attack within the area where the ghoul's magic held sway. As long as the banging of the gongs kept them at bay, they could do nothing.

The clanging of the gongs went on and on. Nikki could hear the waves roll across grass. As he listened, he began to pick up the notes and he started to understand the patterns they made. The patterns would shift and, at each shift, the force riding on them would swell or recede against the chant. The chant changed to work against the gongs, sometimes gaining ground and at other times losing it, never conquering it.

Now he listened to the note struck by a single gong. He followed it back across the plain to the source and tried to learn how it was made. The sound was not a pure note but was harsh, distorted in ways he could only guess at. The gong had been cast with glyphs worked into the bronze that made up its heart, glyphs that twisted the waves that left the gong until they were totally evil. He could feel that evil where it lived, inside the bronze.

He swung down from his horse and stepped forward, toward the sound of the gong. His feet began to stamp the earth, starting a beat, then changing it and starting again. He varied the rhythm until he found what he needed. He began to dance. In his dance, he rode back on the sound from the gong he had picked. He rode it back to the gong's heart. His spirit shook as the hammer struck the side of the gong, but didn't retreat. He felt the metal give under the hammer blow and felt it swirl around the edges to meet on the other side and then race back. The path of the blow flowed around the glyphs to bend the note to the will of the ghoul who had cast it hundreds of years in the past. Nikki forced his way into the bronze. He began to use the force that flowed around the gong to loosen the bonds between the copper and the tin. He began to deform the surface of the glyph, to change the flow of force through the gong. Instead of letting the force out through the rim, he channeled it back into the heart of the gong. The gong went silent. The hammer struck again and again, each time the force within the gong grew until it could no longer be contained. A clap like thunder marked the end of the gong and the ghoul beating it.

The magic shifted, faltered, was restored. The ghouls overcame the loss by shifting the pattern and increasing the pace.

Nikki moved to the next gong. He flowed into it, surer of himself. He set the bronze flowing until it too went silent. The magic faltered as the gong burst in a rain of molten bronze.

The next gong was flawed, the glyphs in it imperfect. The ghouls beat faster and harder, the forces building without his help. It cracked as Nikki was turning to another gong.

But there was no need. The music was failing, the magic broken. The spell surrounding the ghoul army collapsed. The chant rose triumphant. The ghouls, so confident in their magic, began to panic.

The king's archers rode in close. Where To'a's men had shot their arrows from the right or left, the elves rode in groups of fifty, weaving a pattern around their enemy. Their arrows came from all sides. Nikki watched as the ghouls pulled in tight and formed a square shield wall. They were forced to pull their spears inside to close up the gaps between their shields. That's when Thord charged.

He led half of his men straight for the center of the square. But just before he reached the ghoul line, his charge bent to the right and hit the corner of the square – instead of smashing into the heart of the enemy, losing his momentum, and being trapped. Their charge crushed the square's corner and rode down its side, where his men could pass on out of the ghouls, before they became bogged in a morass of enemy soldiers. Arrows poured into the disorder left by Thord's charge. The ghouls couldn't regain their shield wall before Lii's men hit them. Their magic gone, their shield wall crumbling under the force of Thord's lances, fear took over. The king had left one side with only fifty elves. Seeing this weakness, some of the ghouls broke in that direction. That's when the slaughter started.

The enemy fled by the dozen and by the hundred. But this time, there would be no escape. They had come seventy leagues into the plain and the king would let none return to the black mountains of the south. Thord's lancers ran down the larger groups of fugitives while the smaller ones were hounded by archers. The last ghouls died by the cold light of the full moon.

\*\*\*

The image of battle, spread out before Vorkki, faded. The air around him darkened and became cold. Around him distant thunder rumbled. He turned.

"Greetings, son."

The storm god glared at him, grey robe billowing and night black hair streaming behind him. "Don't call me son after you've interfered with my plans. And don't say you didn't. I know the feel of your work and it is all over this."

"Did I? I saw you writing in the sky to your priests among the ghouls. But why tell them to attack the elves? Wasn't it because the mortal, Taulgir, gave offerings you couldn't refuse?"

"I allowed a mortal to make offerings and I chose to grant his request. But you are responsible for the wizard and warrior being there to kill my people. Don't deny it."

"They were there under my guidance. But that is all. If they had not been there, would Taulgir have asked you to send the ghoul host north? I doubt it. That so many were killed wasn't my doing."

"You are interested in the two mortals. So it is your doing. Just tread lightly, Father." Storm turned and strode off, the cold and darkness following him.

\*\*\*

After the ghouls were destroyed, Nikki and the king quickly settled the remaining issues in the treaty. There was give and take on both sides, but it was done with more trust than had existed at the beginning. In the end, the emperor would get much of what he wanted without giving up more than he was willing. The king fared similarly. Nikki was prouder of the treaty than he ever imagined he could be. He was feeling good. The treaty, his treaty, was sealed.

Nikki was sitting on a cushion when Thord limped into their booth. He jumped up, but Thord waved him back down. Thord eased himself on to another cushion, with his leg stretched out.

"Can I get you something, Master?"

"No, Little Fox. I am fine. The bandage is more trouble now than the spear was."

Nikki settled back down beside Thord. His face must have shown what he thought of the world just then, because Thord gave him an appraising look.

"So my Little Fox is pleased with himself."

"Yes, I am. When this started, I didn't think I could be a diplomat, let alone negotiate a treaty. But I did. Yes, I am pleased."

With that out of his mouth, he found himself jerked off the cushion and on top of Thord. A hand gripped the chain where it met the iron collar and pulled his face up to those blue eyes. Thord rolled with him until Nikki was under Thord, the hand still tight around the chain.

Later, Thord rolled off of him.

"There, Little Fox. That's better. There are few things worse than a slave who doesn't know his place."

"And where is that, Master?"

"Right now, it is on your back. Sometimes it is in the throne room and sometimes it is making magic on a hilltop. But right now this is where you belong. Perhaps it is making a different magic."

"Well then, master, would you care to make some more magic?"

The guards Lii posted at the door to the commander's quarters knew to move further from the door when certain sounds came from inside. They did so.

\*\*\*

The weather had warmed as they left the plains and returned to Golden Empire. They had ridden from the king's camp with an escort of a hundred elves riding under Ven. Now outside of the first city on the border, Thord stopped the column. He rose in his stirrups and looked around at his men. Nikki sat his horse, tied to his saddle was the box holding the treaty. Lii and To'a were at the heads of their men. Ven sat her horse in front of the elves, the elf next to her holding aloft the Ice Dragon banner the elves had made when they rode out to meet the ghouls.

"Ven, my thanks to you and your troop for making the ride with us. When you return, give my thanks also to your king for his hospitality."

"Return? They follow you as your honor guard. They aren't going back yet. They are yours and will be yours for as long as you draw breath."

Thord was shocked. "You can't mean that! That could be years. Tens of years."

"There are bets. Some are saying less than five years, some twenty and others as many as fifty. But what is that to an elf? No, they choose to honor you, and that is the end of it. I too will stay with you for a time. Later, I have something to do in the west. But for the next few years, I will stay. Maybe we'll go west together."

# Chance's Children

## *Chapter 11*

They had been in the capital for the better part of a month since returning from the east with the new treaty. During that time Thord had been assigned comfortable quaters near the palace. Thord's company, and the honor guard of elven horse archers that returned with them, were given a campsite on an open field outside the city walls.

Upon turning the treaty documents over to the Minister of Barbarians, they were told they would be called to an audience where they would officially present the treaty to the emperor. In the meantime, all they could do was wait.

Thord spent the time drilling his troops alongside the elves. He was having a chance to practice some of the movements that he had used in the east. In a martial field before the city walls, his cavalry charged imaginary infantry over and over as he tried to work through the details of using horse archers to disrupt the front of a body of infantry and hold the flanks off guard, while the lances of his heavy cavalry smashed through the defending line. Each time, he shifted the pattern slightly, until he felt he had found the right combination. After that, the drills became more intense as Thord worked his troops through variations on those basic moves.

After more days of drilling, Thord began to see the gold and silver of officers silhouetted on the top of the city wall, watching. He was feeling confident of the maneuvers, when three of the officers on the wall came down and presented themselves.

"Captain To Waa Da, I am Major Lu and this is Captain Jo and Captain Kee," began the leader of the three. "We have been watching you work your men and are most interested in what you are doing." The three sat on their horses in front of Thord as his men reformed after a charge.

In their mid twenties, they were all roughly the same age as Thord. From the range of their armor, Thord could tell that while Lu and Kee were regular soldiers, Jo was an aristocrat who could afford the best. It was Jo who continued, "We have not seen anyone use both light and heavy cavalry working together before. If you would permit us, we would like to join your men and make some of the charges."

Lu broke in, "We would consider it an honor to accept your orders in this."

Thord looked them over for a moment. "I would be honored to have you. Major Lu and Captain Kee, if you would get a couple of lances you can join the main line. Captain Jo, your horse has the best chance of keeping up with the elves. Ask for Ven. She will tell you what you need to do. If you will join them we will begin."

At the end of the day, when Thord called a halt to the drills, the three officers broke from the ranks and approached Thord.

"Our thanks for an enlightening afternoon." This came from a dust and sweat covered Captain Jo.

"Yes," said Kee. "The Ice Dragon has both claws," he continued, pointing first to the archers and then to the lancers, "and teeth."

"If you are free this evening," put forward Major Lu, " we would have you join us and some friends at the Inn of the Western Clouds on the West Plaza. Bring a companion. And perhaps we can get some more recruits for your ranks."

\*\*\*

After the sunset bell had rung, Thord and Nikki walked up the steps of the Inn of the Western Clouds. The man at the door must have been told to expect them, for he immediately approached Thord.

"Good sir, are you looking for Major Lu's party?"

His deep bow and deferential manner left Thord feeling nonplussed. "Yes. Can you direct us to them?"

"Good sir, I would be doing you less than the honor you require if I did less than show you the way myself."

They followed their guide through a wide entry hall and into the main room of the inn. Coming to the center dining room, they were engulfed by the clamor of scraping chairs, rattling plates, and boisterous customers. They were led through the middle of the main hall to a flight of steps. As they ascended the stairs to the gallery of the second floor, Thord caught Nikki's hand signal. *Careful. Watchers.*

Thord looked casually around the room. *I see six.*

They were shown into a private room. Sitting at a large table were Lu, Kee and Jo. There were three other officers whom Thord had not met at the table as well.

Lu stood and greeted Thord as they entered.

"It is good of you to come to our small gathering. And I see you have brought your companion. Most excellent." Turning to the rest of the company, Lu made the introductions. "You already know Captain Kee and Captain Jo."

Pointing to a thick-set man with short grizzled hair and beard, he went on, "This is Colonel Lii."

Lii stood and gave a slight bow. "I am pleased to meet you, Captain To. I have already heard much about you from my son, Lieutenant Lii."

"Colonel, your son is a fine soldier and I am happy to have him in my troop." Thord bowed back.

Lu went on to introduce a tall man with a long drooping moustache as Major Ni. Lastly, he motioned toward a man whom he introduced as Major Wo.

Major Wo stood and gave a bow. "It is good to meet you. I have been hearing a great deal from Lu, Kee, and Jo about your practices, and it is good to have a face where I can hang what I hear."

"Sir, it is an honor to be here."

Wo held up his hand. "Please, now that the introductions are over, within this room there is no rank. And if it is acceptable to you, that includes your companion as well." Wo nodded towards Nikki. "Your name is?"

"Ni Kee," Nikki responded with a bow.

"That won't do. There can't be two of us" Ni interrupted. "Is there something else we can call you?"

"His name in my homeland is The Little Fox," put in Thord.

"Little Fox? That will do," Wo continued. "Little Fox it is. In this room we need neither commanding officers nor servants, only good companions. I'm sure we all know how to pour our own wine."

At that, Ni took a pitcher from the table and looked at it as though he had never seen one before. "This? What? Do I hold it over my mouth? Ah, a goblet." With that he started refilling the glasses near him and passed the pitcher on to Lii.

There were eight chairs around the table. Thord was directed to an empty chair next to Wo, and Nikki to a chair across from Thord, between Lu and Kee. The officers had hung their swords on the backs of their chairs and Thord slipped the axe from his belt and leaned it, head down, against the back of his chair.

When they were all seated, Lii stood and took up his glass and turned to Nikki. "It is our custom that the youngest offer the first toast. Though in all truth, we had started before you arrived."

Nikki stood and raised his glass. "To the Emperor!"

When the glasses were drunk, Ni stood. "At last, we can start dinner. I, for one, could eat my horse." He walked to the door and gave a signal to someone outside.

Looking over his glass at Thord, Lu said. "To, we have all told our stories until it isn't certain who remembers them best, the tellers or the listeners. So expect to be forced to do much of the talking tonight."

When the waiters with the food had arrived and left, Lii turned to Thord. "To, my son has told me about your axe. Could you tell us how it came to you?"

Thord had been feeling self-conscious about being in this group. Now, as he started to tell the tale of Vorkki and the axe, he felt he was on more familiar ground. And as dinner progressed from course to course, and the wine and stories flowed, he began to feel more comfortable. Still, there was something nagging at the back of his mind, something important he was missing.

The meal was at the middle stage with the table cleared of everything but soup. Wo was holding a full spoon in the air to cool and asked, "To, I am told your men call you the Ice Dragon. And from what I've heard of your fighting and now looking at your armor, I see how they would call you that. But doesn't it worry you that the emperor is called the Western Dragon and holds the word dragon as an emblem of his rule?"

Thord thought for a moment before answering. "My men started calling me that after we were ambushed by the ghouls. The Little Fox warned me that being called dragon would not be seen well in the capital. But if my men were ever to get back to their homes, they needed someone larger than a lieutenant of irregulars to lead them more than the emperor needed to be the only dragon. If he is worried, I will tell the men to stop. But for now, it makes them feel special and no commander wants to lose that."

At that, Lii raised an eyebrow and nodded to Wo. "True enough. No commander would willingly give up something that gave his men that feeling."

Later as Wo and Lii were talking about a skirmish in the west, the feeling of something out of place hit Thord. He looked at Wo and over at Nikki. Nikki caught Thord's eye and returned a look that said *I know.*

At that point, Wo pointed to Nikki with a half eaten pheasant leg. "So, Little Fox, I have heard the new treaty was all your work. Tell me about how you got the elves to agree to it."

"Should that be told here? Or shouldn't it be told in the palace where it can be more private?"

Across the table, Thord caught the crafty look in Nikki's eyes.

Wo must have seen it also, for he broke the sudden silence that filled the room. "Little Fox indeed. Fan Go warned me you were clever. How long have you known?"

"Not long, Wo. But I could tell you are too good a soldier to be only a major. And your sword is too old and used to be carried off-duty. Lii carries a sword of honor. You would surely have one, and not to carry it means that you have no need or perhaps no desire to show your status. That, and the watchers in the inn, told me someone important was dining here. When I put it all together it was clear you were the emperor."

Wo turned to Ni. "Well? Your men were spotted."

"You surprise me, Little Fox. I put my four best men on watch."

Thord turned and interrupted Ni. "Four? We saw six. Four downstairs and two more on this level."

Ni shot Thord a look and turned to Wo. "If you will excuse me, I have something to attend to." With that he got to his feet, took his sword from the back of his chair and left.

Wo watched him leave. "I doubt it is serious. But yes, Little Fox, you may be right about not discussing the treaty here. We will talk tomorrow in the palace." He reached behind him, over his shoulder, and eased the sword in its scabbard. The action was followed by the others. Thord moved his axe from behind his chair to lean against the table.

When the pheasant was taken away, Ni returned. "Pardon my absence. Everything is taken care of now. Unfortunately, we won't be able to ask the two others about their employer. But a search may turn that up later. Now, have I missed anything?"

Later, as dinner was breaking up, Wo turned to Thord. "About the name Ice Dragon, keep it. I think I will start an order of honor and call them my Dragons. That way, I can give honor where it is due and still keep the name dragon tied to me. As it is now, the only way I can recognize someone is to promote them in to the nobility, and that is not always possible. Now I will be able to give a title that will not officially offend my nobles. Wait in your quarters tomorrow, and I will send someone to bring you to the audience hall. Bring Ambassador Ni Kee too. Good night, Ice Dragon."

***

On the following morning, Thord and Nikki dressed for the audience. Nikki put out the best uniform for Thord and had, himself, put on the best-fitting of the robes he possessed. When their summons came, in the form of an official in the emperor's household, they followed to the Hall of the August Dragon.

Arriving at the palace, they entered through the iron-sheathed gate and found themselves in the gatehouse to the inner courtyard of the palace.

Nikki was not surprised to be searched for hidden weapons, but he was surprised by the guard's reaction to Thord. When the captain of the guards came to Thord, he made an overly elaborate show of searching Thord and removing his dagger. But he did not touch or mention the axe thrust through Thord's belt. This was all done with the scowl of a professional obeying an order outside of ordinary practice, one that he in no way liked.

When he was finished, the captain grunted something and Thord and Nikki were led into the courtyard. This was unlike the courtyard in front of Nikki's father's throne room. Instead of a flower-lined path, flanked by twin fountains, the central courtyard of the Dragon Palace was a vast paved plaza. The outer wall was bare of windows looking on to the courtyard. The massive block that was the Hall of the August Dragon stood in the center, its lower floor a blank stone wall. A single broad stair led from the plaza to the massive doors above.

They were halted at the top of the stairs. A bent man with a long beard held out a hand, blocking their way.

"Who is it that wishes an audience with the August Dragon?"

Nikki had expected something like this from the protocol of his father's court and was ready with an answer. "My master, To Waa Da Tu Goo's son, officer in the emperor's service, has come at the command of the August Dragon." He handed over the summons.

The old man disappeared inside the hall. A short time later, he returned and motioned for them to follow him.

Inside was a great hall, the ceiling supported on thick yellow columns. The air was warm and heavy with the scent of the throng of officials, partially covered by the smell of rose perfume that emanated for each person they passed. As he walked behind Thord, Nikki was forced to wonder if rose was always the perfume of the courtiers or if there was a notice posted each day giving a specified perfume.

When they crossed the gallery, the ceiling opened up. The inside was lit from above. What had appeared to be a second story was an open area surrounded by windows. The columns lining the central space tapered to split into the branching braces and trusses holding the roof, eight fathoms above. Passing the line of pillars, they were led onto an raised pathway, the floor on either side sunken one step. On both sides stood the court of the August Dragon. As they walked, Nikki noted the type and position of each group in the court. Though he had thought such things behind him, he found his ability to quickly recognize court factions remained. In the back on the left stood small groups of men with the look of prosperous merchants. On the right were clusters of soldiers, the feathers on their helmets proclaiming them to be colonels or generals. On the left, to the front, were the civilian officials. The shape and color of their hats declared their rank and function. Across from them were the nobles, dressed in rich brocades. Yellow stripes in the robes spoke of their position. Those with the widest bands of yellow stood in the front ranks. Out of the corner of his eye, Nikki watched as each group they passed eyed Thord and himself. All wore smiles, but on some, the eyes told something different. On some of the nobles, the lids drooped slightly in disdain of outland upstarts. Some of the merchants and officials looked with eyes partially closed, hiding the calculations that went on behind. The more practiced showed nothing at all. Now and then, a courtier would lose the façade for a moment and stare openly at the axe thrust through the belt of Thord's uniform, hands straying to where their own dagger or sword would have hung.

In front of them was a closed curtain. On its surface coiled a great dragon embroidered in gold thread. When they halted at the front of the audience hall, the curtain opened to the sides to reveal a second curtain. This one was of sheer cloth of gold. Through it, the figure of a man seated on a throne could vaguely be seen. In front of this last curtain stood a man in yellow robes holding a red fan in front of his face. The murmuring voices stopped, replaced by the rustle of dozens of heavy brocaded robes as their owners bowed towards the emperor. When the hall was silent, a voice rang out from behind the fan.

"The August Emperor recognizes his loyal officer To Waa Da and his slave the ambassador Ni Kee. Further, it is the Emperor's intent that a new rank be created for those of his servants who have given true service to the Emperor. This honor is to be called the Order of the Imperial Dragons. The Emperor grants the following privileges to those chosen for this honor: they are allowed to bear weapons in the presence of the Emperor, they are allowed to fly a banner with the image of a dragon, they are directly under the command of the Emperor, and they are allowed a personal guard of one hundred soldiers. The Emperor shows his trust in his officer To Waa Da by raising him to the rank of Major and Dragon and by naming him Ice Dragon"

The voice stopped. The Dragon Curtain closed. The room filled with the low buzz of dozens of voices whispering all at once. As they walked back through the hall, Nikki was aware of a change in the faces on either side. Now there were only two kinds of eyes, those few that openly stared in shock and the greater number that hinted at more complex levels of calculation.

When Thord and Nikki finally reached the gate to the outer courtyard, they were met by a youth of about thirteen in the uniform of the palace. His black hair was cut short and he wore a headband of yellow ribbon. When the boy looked at Nikki, there was something familiar in the eyes that looked directly at him.

"Ice Dragon, you and your slave are to come with me."

They followed him around the walls to a small, closed postern. Four guards stood in front. When their guide approached, one of the guards turned and knocked three times on the heavy panels of the door. Entering, they were led by a twisting route, past more guards, deeper into the palace. Finally, they halted in front of a richly carved door flanked by two guards. The guide opened the door and preceded them inside. The door closed behind them with a solid thump.

They stood in a covered walkway surrounding a small courtyard. Small trees and flowering shrubs were scattered around the edges of the flagstone court. The air was pleasant and smelled of flowers and roast meat. The dark polished wood of the pillars and overhead beams stood out against white plaster. Four chairs stood around a table cluttered with plates and goblets in the center of the courtyard. Standing beside the table was the emperor.

"Please come and sit down." He let his arm sweep around the table. When the youth reached him, the emperor gripped the boy by the shoulders and turned him around to face Thord and Nikki. "To Waa Da and Ni Kee, this is my son Bo'a."

Looking at the two standing together, Nikki understood why the boy had looked familiar. Set in the broad face of all the people in the empire, he shared the same piercing dark eyes that made his father so distinctive.

After they were all seated, the emperor went on, "I hope you don't mind me talking while we eat, but I have two more audiences this afternoon and that leaves too little time to be formal. To Waa Da, I watched you put away the honey roast duck last night. I had the cook make his so you could compare them. Sit. Eat."

Once they were all sitting down with full plates, the emperor gave a heavy sigh. "It feels good to sit and just eat with someone. When I am the on the throne, I am too sacred to even be seen. The voice of the emperor is too powerful for the ears of lesser men." Wo turned to Nikki. "What did you think of the court? It's not like your father's."

Nikki almost choked on a mouthful of duck. The only other sound was the scraping of Thord's chair on the stone. But Nikki's attention was fixed only on the emperor.

"Don't worry, Ni Kee. Your secret is safe with me and my son. Fan Go told me about you when he returned to the capital. He asked me to help you. After meeting you, I agree that you are someone who deserves what help I can give."

As the emperor spoke, Nikki tried to read his face, but failed. He turned to the one face he could read. Thord was settling back in his chair, his hand moving from where the haft of his axe rested against the table, back to the teacup beside his plate. Thord trusted the emperor and, since Nikki came to know the Floelander, he had learned that Thord's own honor gave him a gift for seeing it in other people. He let out a breath and turned back to the emperor. "But how did Fan Go know?"

The emperor smiled and raised his eyebrows. "You should understand by now that Fan is a person who sees more than what's shown and hears more than what's told."

When Nikki eased back in his chair, the emperor pushed a dish of spiced eggs toward him. "Now Ni Kee, we need to talk about just what I can do to help you. As I said, it isn't much. I can't send an army against this uncle of yours. I can't make you king. What Fan has asked me to do is prepare you for your role as king. I believe I have the skill to do that much. I want to take you into my civil service and give you experience in how to rule. I can't do much to protect you without drawing unwanted attention to you. So I can't give you more guards than those To Waa Da already has. There is something I can do, though. If there is a rumor about you being more than what you claim, Ni and his security men will hear it and bring it to my attention. If that happens, I'll give you the warning. It's the best I can do."

"Sire, that is more than I could hope."

"No sire here. Camp rules only, so call me Wo. I've found a small district for you on the edge of the city. It has a barracks where To Waa Da's men can stay next to a small mansion. You'll start as a fourth level magistrate. The sub-prefect in charge of that area is a good man and will help you get started."

Nikki looked from the emperor to Thord, who mumbled something around a mouth full of duck and nodded. Nikki turning back, lifted the chain from his chest. "Will there be a problem getting people to obey a slave?"

Bo'a answered for his father. "No. There are precedents for civil positions being held by slaves. The only difference is instead of buying you, the empire will be renting."

The emperor looked at his son and back to Nikki. "Not the way I would have said it, but that is accurate."

"When do I start?"

"The papers are waiting for you at the door. As of tomorrow morning, the city has one more magistrate. Now pass that duck back before To Waa Da leaves us nothing but bones."

\*\*\*

King Marcalo sat on the throne in the private council room. The coffered ceiling and wood-paneled walls made the room less grand than the Great Hall, with its gilt and marble, and more personal. It was a place to meet privately, without the need for officials and scribes. Here things could be done quickly and done quietly. It wouldn't do to have the men who now stood before the throne be seen with the king too publicly, nor could the details of this audience be allowed to become common knowledge.

"Sire, we are making progress in tracking Nicolio. Demons reported that he was in an elven land far to the east. He has since left there and has now traveled back to the Golden Empire. We believe he is in the capital but have not ascertained more information about what he is doing."

The black-robed speaker was Morik, the head of Marcalo's wizards. The king was becoming less patient with Morik's failure to deal with Nicolio. In the time since Marcalo had murdered his brother and usurped the throne, the wizards had only found his nephew's whereabouts twice and had failed at their one attempt to kill him. It made no difference that the assassins that he had dispatched on Morik's information had also failed to remove the prince and had not returned. Morik had still failed.

"I want him! I want him found and I want him dead!" The king's eyes bore into Morik. "Do I make myself clear?"

"Most clear, Majesty."

"Then you may all leave, except Taulgir."

When the other wizards were out of the room, the king watched Taulgir for a moment. The wizard stood with his head slightly lowered, the embodiment of deference. But the king was well aware that the man before him was as much a viper as anything that slithered across the ground. But he was a useful viper.

As always, Taulgir was dressed in a simple robe. But now the robe was of yellow silk instead of the brown linen he had affected when he first came to the king's notice.

Running his hand over the scabbard of the sword resting on his knees, the king continued. "What progress have you made in creating a shield to match my sword?"

"I am getting close, sire. One or two more sacrifices and I will have the knowledge I need. After that, it will take some time to prepare the ritual."

"If you need something, send word. You may go."

"Your Majesty." Taulgir bowed low and backed to the door.

***

Taulgir was inwardly smiling as he climbed into the litter for the return to his villa. Yes, a few more sacrifices would give him the power to make the shield the king wanted. It would also be enough to bind the king closer to him. He never doubted that the king distrusted him. A king who would murder his own brother for the throne distrusted everyone. But that wouldn't matter much longer. Just as he bound the war god to his will when he made the king's sword, so too the king was bound, when he wore it. The binding was by no means complete, but the sword had been a first try. As he grew stronger and his knowledge deeper, the level of control he could exert would grow.

As the litter carried him through the streets of the capital, he peered through the sheer curtains at the people. The same scene was enacted, over and over, as he passed. The litter would approach a group of people; one would look and quickly lower his head or look away. Some sign or word would be passed and the group would fall silent until the litter was gone. They knew him and what he was, and they feared him. Good, let them. For now it was the fear based on rumors of prisoners, dragged from cells in the night to never be seen again, the fear of the unknown. But soon, they would know him for what he was. Then they would have something real to fear.

Once in his tower chamber, surrounded by the instruments of his art and immersed in the familiar smells of working that art, he began to lay out the design of his next experiment. Over the past six months he had studied the old books of rituals and spells. For the last two months, he had been reconstructing some of the more arcane rituals and sacrifices only hinted at in the oldest books. Now he was close to his goal.

There was some resistance to his experiments. Someone was attempting to block him. The counter-spells bore the mark of a wizard of true power. It wasn't any of the king's other wizards. Of that, he was sure. No, this was someone else, maybe the late king's wizard, Ganian. It didn't matter. Whoever he was, he couldn't stop Taulgir's own spells. He smiled grimly. It was almost funny to know that someone was trying to block supplications to the gods. What would the priests say to that?

He had worked back from the rituals now practiced in the Earth

181

Goddess' temple and was close to discovering the older, darker rituals and the blood sacrifices of the past. But as with any of those elder calls to the gods, he needed to go beyond the knowledge held by the ancients, to succeed where they had failed. It wasn't enough to beg the gods for favors or cajole them into giving their blessing; he needed to command them. One by one, he would bring the gods under him, until only two were left. He had been told that there could be no influencing Chance and Fate. But he would put an end to Chance and supplant Fate with his Will.

\*\*\*

The chamber was dimly lit by four tall candles; their bronze holders stood on the floor forming a square. Between each pair of candles was a high-backed chair. A shallow iron brazier squatted on the floor in the center, its coals glowing red and giving off the smell of incense and something else. At its side was a large copper bowl with a copper ladle. In the dim light, its contents looked almost black, no longer the usual red of blood. In one corner was a heap of carpet; from under one edge jutted a small motionless foot.

Taulgir sat examining at the other wizards in the room as Morik droned on about the spell they were to cast. He had called up enough demons that he didn't need to hear an old man's advice and warnings. Particularly as a success was not what he wanted. This plan to use a demon to kill the king's nephew was not to his advantage. As long as the king felt threatened, he needed Taulgir to give him weapons from the gods. Taulgir's control of the king was not complete. He needed to be able to manipulate the king's insecurities. He preferred the prince alive. But at this stage, he was not going to be able to overtly interfere with the spell. Morik was suspicious of him and would detect any moves he made to block or deflect the demon. His position with the king was not strong enough that it could withstand being exposed by Morik. In another few weeks, when the shield was finished and in the king's hands, he would be able to eliminate the other wizards in this room, but not yet.

He would need to find another means of manipulating the king because tonight, Prince Nicolio had to die.

The spell was common enough, the setting of wards to protect the participants, followed by spilling blood to draw the attention of those in the other planes. Finally, the demon would be named and the gate between the two worlds would be opened. At that point, it became dangerous. The demon would have to be convinced to kill the prince and afterwards to leave this plane.

Taulgir had been asked to name a demon that could be controlled but was still powerful enough to act as an assassin. He could have picked any of a dozen demons he had used in the past. But the tasks they had performed for him were the kind that needed to remain secret. In the end he named a demon that was known as having a taste for young blood.

***

Thord lay, unable to sleep, looking out the open window into the night. Life had been peaceful for over a year now. But the daily rounds of the duties of an imperial officer and a magistrate couldn't hide the knowledge that someday, Nikki's uncle would find them.

All day something had brooded in the back of his mind. Something was wrong and he knew it. Something was coming.

The feeling of dread had been growing on him. He knew Nikki felt it. Thord had watched as all day, Nikki fidgeted with his collar, turning it and raising on his neck. Something was there in the background as if some small animal was gnawing at Thord's stomach. It grew strongest whenever he set his axe down. Now he lay in bed with his left hand on Nikki's arm and his right resting on the haft of the axe, beside their bed.

Thord gently lifted his left hand and turned to set his feet on the cool wood of the floor. The crescent moon gave him enough light to find his way to the door leading from their bedroom to the gallery surrounding the inner courtyard of their house. He allowed the night sounds to fill him. The guard on the front door scuffed his feet. He heard the sound of soft boots from above as one of the elves kept watch on the roof. Dawn would soon be lightening the east, bringing to life the city around them. But for now there was silence.

But there was something else in the night, something getting closer with each heartbeat, something that came from nowhere and from everywhere, some threat.

There! He heard a sound that was not part of the night, a distant snapping sound coming from the north-west night sky. The sound waxed and waned but always it came closer.

The guard on the roof heard it. "A demon! A demon on wings!"

Thord looked up and saw the elf silhouetted against the night. Even as he shouted the warning, he had an arrow notched and his bow bent. Thord could see the black form that moved in front of the stars, blotting them out for a moment as it passed across the sky. The snapping of leather wings came ahead of that shadow. As Thord watched, the

183

blackness of that form faded until the stars behind became faintly visible through it and, as it faded, so too did the sound. But just as Thord thought the demon had vanished, it strengthened again with the growing sound of its progress, always closer.

Thord heard the slap of bare feet on the floor behind him. Just as Nikki stepped onto the gallery, beside him, the night sky was filled with a screech of hate, of lust.

The alarm brought the sound of rushing feet and the light of torches, as elves and men rushed from the wings of the house. The thrum of an elven bowstring marked the flight of an arrow, but there was no sign that it hit its target.

The creature was descending now, directly over the house. Another arrow flew from the roof, only to bounce back onto the flagstones of the courtyard. Now just above the roof top, the demon began to fade again. In the light from the torches, Thord saw the next arrow pass through the demon's dim outline to disappear into the darkness beyond.

Thord turned back to where Nikki stood, his eyes fixed on the creature above them. "Stay back!" he shouted to Nikki and turned to look up at the horror that descended toward them. Two red eyes burned under a horned brow. Its great wings stretched out to either side as it slowed its flight. The monster's legs ended in talons like some giant hawk, its arms in three fingered claws, the middle claw a curved dagger. As it came closer, it began to fade again. But as the beast dimmed, a star above it burned brighter, a star as red as the demon's eyes. As Thord watched, the monster disappeared leaving only the blood-red star burning brighter than all the other stars. Then the star began to wane, and as it dimmed, the demon took form again, now just thirty feet above the courtyard.

Thord heard the slow beating of wings, the sound of bowstrings, and of bare feet behind him. The feet were not running but were stamping out a beat of their own on the broad wood planks of the floor.

The monster paused for a moment, then stooped on one of the archers on the roof across from Thord. The elf threw himself back but not in time. Blood sprayed into the moonlight as the demon's claw raked his chest. Thord could only watch as the creature faded, then see it reappear again in the sky, just above the roofline.

By now, a thin fog was rising from the fountain in the center of the courtyard. Thord could see more coming from the trees and drifting up from beyond the walls of the mansion. The beating wings sent it in swirls but still the fog rose. The sound of Nikki's feet grew louder.

The demon began to fade as it descended into the courtyard. Above, the red star glowed brighter, surrounded by a faint halo in the thickening fog, a red eye glaring down on the scene below. But this time, the demon didn't fade completely from sight. It dimmed and blurred but he could still see it. The wings beating stirred up the fallen leaves, sending them swirling into the fog.

As the beast's claws touched the stone flags, Thord jumped into the courtyard and rushed the monster. With his momentum behind him, he swung at the thing, only to have the axe pass through it. He leapt back from a raking claw only just in time; the claw passing close enough for him to feel the wind on his bare chest. Ven rushed out carrying a sword and shield. Now the monster was more solid, the thickening pall reducing the red star to a point surrounded by a faint red glow. Ven came from the side and struck a wing close to the shoulder. Her blade rang against the skin but left no wound. The demon turned and swung a taloned claw. It caught her on the shield and hurled her against the railing behind her.

The demon was now solid, the red star lost in the mist that blotted out the sky. In the dim light coming from a lamp in one of the windows, Thord watched the creature take halting steps on its clawed feet. He leapt forward again. A clawed arm came sweeping for his head, but he ducked below it and swung his axe at the monster's knee.

The blade bit. Skin parted and the flesh beneath.

With a scream of pain the demon toppled to the side, landing on one of its folded wings and rolling onto its back. Thord struck again, this time at a raised arm. The claw came off to fly across the courtyard and land beside the fountain. As Thord raised his axe again he was knocked off his feet by a clap like thunder. Lying on his back with his head raised he could see nothing of the demon. It was gone. The only signs of the struggle were Ven and himself lying on the ground and a few overturned potted plants. Behind him he heard the sound of Nikki's feet, no longer dancing, but running toward him.

"Thord! You killed it!."

He looked up at Nikki. Now the light was growing again. Nikki's eyes were full of concern as he looked down at him. But when Thord grunted and began to rise, Nikki smiled and, turning, ran to where Ven was just sitting up and slipping the dented shield from her arm.

"That was your fog?" She was rubbing her arm as she got to her feet.

"Yes, when I saw the red star fade, I thought the demon must be tied to the star, drawing its power from it. I hoped that if I could block the light, the thing would be wholly in this plane and maybe it could be killed. I didn't know if it would work but it was the only thing I could do that might help."

Thord came up to them. "Will it come back? Maybe with friends?"

"I doubt it. It must have cost my uncle's wizards quite a lot to bring a demon here and control it at such a distance." He looked up at the sky, now full of white stars. "He won't send another one, not for a while anyway."

Thord saw Nikki's eyes turn to the west and harden. "But it's time we left here."

\*\*\*

There was an audible snap when the first piece of the spell gave way. The room was flooded with the metallic stench of burned blood as the fire that fed the summoning released its smoke back into the closed room. For a moment, Taulgir was stunned. The demon spell had been broken; his control gone in an instant. The room was full of the aura of magic but now without the command needed to govern it.

Something was wrong beyond the broken spell. *Fool!* He thought. He had trusted the old wizard, Kirr, to call the demon, and the idiot was too stupid to realize the governing spell was gone. He was still summoning the demon. When the control was broken, the demon had been yanked back to its own plane. But Kirr's call was dragging the monster back, not to where the king's nephew was but back to them. Before Taulgir could intervene, the air in front of Kirr shimmered and the demon coalesced in the center of the room. The air reeked with the sulfurous stench of the other-world. The room filled with a dissonance formed by the monster's screech of rage and Kirr's own wail of despair as a great claw reached for him. The rage persisted after the sound of despair was cut short in a spray of blood.

Taulgir pulled himself together. The demon reached out toward the blood and dying life force that formed a cloud over Kirr's chair. Taulgir took that instant to push with his mind. He put all of his strength into the shove and toppled the demon through the aura of the dying Kirr and back into its own plane. The force of that push nearly sent him following after the creature. As he pulled back, he felt the force of a push of force from this plane. Morik had tried to help *him* over the edge as he had helped others. But Taulgir was too strong to fall prey to such a simple ploy. "Not yet, old man." He whispered. He saw Morik glaring at him through the smoke from across the room.

Taulgir looked around the room. Filee had fled. Her chair was empty. She had never been easy with the plan to use a demon. Taulgir

186

guessed that when the king's guards searched for her, they would come up empty-handed. He thought she had sensed what had passed between him and Morik and that she would not be fool enough to throw in with either side. He needn't factor her in his calculations.

Morik was another problem. The older wizard was now openly against him. But unlike Filee, Morik would not run so easily. Taulgir could only guess at the power that Morik could wield if pressed to the limit. But by the same token, Morik didn't know the power behind Taulgir's own magic. For the moment there was a balance of ignorance. Neither would press the attack until they were sure of victory. The attempt to kill him was only an overt move in the game the two had played for over a year now. It would come to a head, but not now. What was more important was why the demon had failed. Why was this prince still alive? Until now, Taulgir had considered Prince Nicolio to be a useful tool in his plans. The anxiety that Marcalo felt toward Nicolio provided a means to manipulate the king. Now it was clear the prince was more than just a tool. He was a threat. Taulgir had laid the spell with great care. Every aspect had been calculated to a hair's breadth. Even with the distance involved, to have the spell broken was a shock. Taulgir would have to move his plans forward or risk having the prince show up before he fully grasped the power he wanted, he needed.

## *Chapter 12*

Mu Bao, with his fellow junior scribe Lwo Gong, stood in the group of minor officials at the end of the reception hall. At the other end of the hall two men sat at a side table drinking wine. One of the men was well known to Mu. He was not a tall man, but his scarred cheek and polished armor gave him a stature that impressed young Mu. Major Dwoon had been military governor of Lo Nai for the last five years and, in that time, Mu had come to respect him.

The other man at the table was Major Dwoon's replacement, Colonel To Waa Da. And while he wore the badge of an imperial colonel, neither he nor the blue-white scale armor over his uniform were from any province in the empire. Mu couldn't be sure of his age, as all foreigners appeared to be the same age until they suddenly looked old. But Mu was certain that he couldn't have been born when Major Dwoon joined the imperial army.

Colonel To Waa Da said something to the young slave kneeling beside his chair. The slave stood and walked over to where Mu and Lwo stood. Like his master, the slave was outlandishly dressed. He looked like an eastern barbarian with a short vest of black fur coming down only as far as the top of his stomach. White silk trousers were tucked into black boots. The trousers were laced up the sides and pulled tight until they fit like a second skin. His bare arms were well muscled, but not overly so. A heavy iron collar ringed his neck.

Bowing in front of Mu and Lwo, the slave said, "Sirs, my master wishes to speak with you. Please be so kind as to follow me."

The slave turned and led Mu and Lwo across the hall to where the two soldiers were seated. As they approached, Mu adjusted his robe and reached back to straighten the long black hair flowing from his top-knot down his back.

Major Dwoon introduced the young men to To Waa Da. "Colonel, these are the two scribes who will serve Magistrate Ni Kee when he arrives. This is Scribe Lwo and this is Scribe Mu."

The colonel looked over the two scribes with his bright blue eyes.

"I need to know more about the city and want someone to show my slave around. Which of you knows the city best?" the colonel asked. Mu was not surprised by the thick accent, but was surprised by the soft voice that came from the man's huge chest.

"Oh, Mu knows the city very well," Lwo volunteered.

The blue eyes looked at Lwo for a moment and then at the slave who had knelt beside the colonel's chair. Mu could see some unvoiced message pass between the two before the eyes swept back to Mu.

"Good. Mu, I want you to show my slave around. He knows to look for what I need. Take him wherever he wants. Keep him out of trouble and be sure he is back before the feast this evening."

\*\*\*

As Mu and the slave entered the courtyard of the fortress, they were met by the captain of the garrison replacements. Mu had seen him earlier and heard him called Captain Lii.

"Good day, Sir." The captain bowed to Mu then turned to the slave. "Little Fox, where are you going?"

"Scribe Mu is taking me to tour the city."

"Do you want an escort? A couple of my men would be happy to go with you."

"No. What my master needs to see may be seen best without appearing in the company of soldiers. That would draw too much attention."

Turning to Mu, the captain said. "Well, don't let him get too close to a wine shop. He winds up under the table more often than sitting at it."

"You and my master were happy for me to serve the wine from under the table two nights ago," the Little Fox replied with a broad grin.

"We had no choice. You were there and wouldn't pass the wine jug up to us. We had to get under the table or go without."

"Ah," said the Little Fox. "But if you hadn't joined me, I would never have told you of the girl's name written on the underside of the table."

At this the captain's face turned red. "You imp! You nearly got me murdered. When I asked the innkeeper to introduce me to the girl, she was the man's mother."

"Oh. That would explain why the staff was burning some of the tables in the courtyard when we left that morning," The Little Fox looked thoughtful as he spoke.

\*\*\*

Mu and the Little Fox left the gate of the citadel and walked down into the city. Lo Nai seemed like most cities on the edges of the empire. Its main streets were of cobbled stone and were lined with two- and three-story masonry buildings. The shops and houses had heavy wooden bars on the lower windows; the thick doors leading into the shops and inns stood open. Everywhere the streets were kept clean of the filth that was the common burden of city life. In the poorer areas, the houses and shops were, for the most part, of wood with a few stone and brick buildings. There the streets were prone to twist more and showed the signs of less care.

Within the walls, Lo Nai was like many cities. What set it apart was what lay beyond those walls. Wherever there was a gap in the houses and shops, or down any straight street, loomed a mountain. The city was at the bottom of a large valley surrounded by vast, snow-covered peaks. Where there was a view of the lower slopes, the mountains were covered with trees, but these ended partway up revealing great cliffs of bare rock and ice. The sunlight coming through the thin mountain air was amplified by the light bouncing off the ice-covered crags that rose over the city. Mu felt his own joy of the city grow as he watched his charge draw in a deep breath of delight in the clean air, and saw him turn in slow circles gazing up at the grand views presented by the surrounding mountains.

When they had crossed the city and come to the north wall, the Little Fox climbed to the top and looked out over the valley.

Pointing to the fields that filled the valley, he asked Mu, "That is barley out there. How soon before it is ready to harvest?"

"Three weeks, or maybe four down at this end," Mu replied. "It will be a week or more later, further up the valley."

"Four weeks isn't much time." Now, pointing to the northwest where an arm of the valley disappeared behind a great shoulder of mountain, he asked, "Is that the Jade Gate?"

"Yes. Beyond there the empire ends and the wild lands begin. But the tribes of goblins have been quiet for the last twenty years. They're too busy with their own petty wars to do more than small raids in our direction. Major Dwoon has been able to halt even those since he took charge here. The only travelers through the Jade Gate now are the merchants that the pass is named after."

"How many people live in the villages outside the walls?"

Mu had to think for a moment. "The three villages have some one hundred families. Counting the old and the young, there may be some eight hundred people."

"Eight hundred," repeated the Fox. He turned his back on the valley and looked into the city. "Eight hundred. And ten times that in the city already," he went on softly.

They wandered the city for a hour and were on one of the cobbled back streets. The surface was rough and undulating, its worn granite stones pushed up or down by weather and years of cart traffic. In front of them, the stones had been pried up and lay next to a pile of sand and gravel. The road beyond was level and new-laid. Scattered about were shovels, rakes, and wooden mallets. To the right the street opened into a small plaza, empty now, but Mu knew it held a small market every five days. On one side of the market, the counter of a food shop enticed passersby with the smells of roast fowl and barley and onion soup. Near the shop were a few tables and chairs for customers. On the other side of the plaza, the dusty street workers sat eating lunch.

The Little Fox suggested they stop in the open market for some food and drink. "If you will sit, sir, I will get something and bring it to you."

Mu had lived too long on a junior scribe's salary to argue with a free meal, so he found an unoccupied table under a tree and waited until the slave returned with a tray of food and a small bottle of barley wine.

"When you have finished eating, sir, it would help me if you would pretend to doze for half an hour while I talk to the local laborers."

The suggestion and accompanying wink intrigued Mu so much he agreed, if only to find out what the slave had in mind. The Little Fox took a bun and ate it off to the side as Mu finished his meal and a better bottle of wine than he had tasted in some while. When he finished he hunched his shoulders and leaned his chin onto his chest and feigned sleep.

After a few minutes, the slave quietly got to his feet and returned to the wine vendor. When he came back he was carrying a large flask of the cheap wine that Mu was used to drinking. He walked some ways off to sit near a group of workmen. After taking a drink from the bottle, he started speaking with the men. Speaking may not be the closest description, thought Mu. Flirting might be a better term. The bottle was passed around and, though he couldn't hear what was said, what Mu could see through half-closed eyes convinced him that they were talking about more than the weather. When the bottle was clearly empty, the Little Fox kept talking with them for some time. Finally, the workmen returned to their tools and the Little Fox came back to sit near Mu.

"I'm done," he whispered. "We can go on now, sir."

Mu made a production of yawning and getting to his feet and they left the market.

"What did you learn that could not be found out by just asking?" asked Mu as they walked down a side street.

"I learned much more from them than they would have told a government scribe," he replied. "They told me the names of several merchants who are trustworthy and of some who have dealings that are less so. I learned that there is less work than workers, and that wages are low and the price of barley is high. And I learned that Wa Gee, whoever he is, has warts in a place that makes sitting hard."

At this last revelation, Mu doubled over laughing and almost tripped. "Wa Gee? Wa is in charge of maintaining the streets and city walls. That would explain quite a lot about his occasional unpleasant manners."

As Mu and The Little Fox were walking on the street that ran beneath the walls, they came to where a small house had been built against the walls. In front was a small garden where an old man in a blue robe and a straw hat stood with his back to the street, pruning a rose bush.

The Little Fox turned to Mu and remarked, "A beautiful garden. It reminds me of gardens in the capital."

"Oh, that is Prefect Fan Go's garden. He moved into the house at the foot of the wall when he retired here."

Mu hadn't even finished speaking before the Little Fox was running up to the old man.

"Wait! Come back," Mu cried. "You can't disturb the prefect." But the Little Fox had already ran up to him and bowed.

"Prefect Fan Go. I trust you are well."

"Ah," said the prefect. "Little Fox. I have been expecting you."

The hand that was about to drag the Little Fox away froze on the end of Mu's arm.

The Little Fox stood in front of the prefect. "Lord, I have a message from Wo Fa Gee."

"From Wo?"

"Yes lord. He hoped that coming from him you would accept it as a request from an old friend. He hopes you will return to the capital soon. He misses your company."

"And Wo sent this by you? Little Fox?"

"Yes lord. He told me he was afraid that if he sent it with my master or Magistrate Ni Kee you would see it as an official request and he doesn't want you to come because feel you must."

"Well, I will think about it."

"Please do sir. I think he feels very alone and needs to have someone around as a friend."

Official request? Wo Fa Gee was the birth name of the emperor! With a shock, Mu realized that the emperor had entrusted a private message to this slave. Maybe Lwo had misjudged the value of acting as a guide to a young slave.

\*\*\*

Mu and The Little Fox returned to the citadel just before dusk. Once inside, they were led by a guard to the residential area. At a wooden door guarded by a pair of soldiers from the new garrison, The Little Fox turned to Mu.

"Please come in. We have some matters to discuss while I get ready for tonight's feast."

One of the guards opened the door and The Fox entered. Mu couldn't think what else he could do and followed. When he was inside and the guard had closed door behind him, he was surprised when a eunuch rushed out of another room.

"There you are! There is barely enough time to get you ready for dinner. You can't go looking like that. Come along."

"But I have some business with Scribe Mu!" protested The Fox.

"It will have to wait." Turning to Mu he continued, "Please, there are wine and cakes on the side table. Please take some, and I will have him back out in no time." With that, he dragged his charge into the back and closed the door behind them.

Mu thought to himself that if Lwo was spending his time getting into the graces of Colonel To Waa Da, at least he, himself, would be well fed. He poured himself some wine. Very well fed indeed, he thought, after tasting the wine.

As he waited he looked around and was surprised by the contents of the room. He had expected the room of the Little Fox's soldier master, a barbarian soldier at that, to be simpler or garish. But the thick rug under his feet, with its phoenix and cloud pattern, would not have been out of place on the floor of a palace. The same was true for many of the smaller objects that had been placed on the tables and shelves around the room. He found none of the weapons or other trophies of old wars that Major Dwoon kept.

After something more than a quarter hour, Mu was getting restless. He really should try to find and present himself to the new magistrate. And that would be harder to do if he had any more of the wine he had been offered. He had just put down his goblet and was turning towards the door he had entered when he heard the door at his back open and the eunuch saying, "Magistrate, you haven't much time before you must go down to dinner. You mustn't stay long."

Mu froze. He turned and bowed at the same time. Keeping his eyes low, he could see the blue and silver embroidered bottom of the magistrate's robes.

"You're still here, Mu. Good. We need to talk," came the voice of the Little Fox. "I need a head scribe, and I think you may be just the man I want."

Mu looked up. There in the blue robe with the tall blue and silver cylindrical hat of a second degree magistrate was the Little Fox. Within the robe's high silk collar was the iron collar with the chain hanging down to rest on the embroidered emblem of the imperial civil service. Mu remembered to close his mouth as the magistrate turned to the eunuch and continued, "Kio, I want a chair behind my place at the table for Mu here. Make sure it's close enough that I can get his opinion when I need it."

He pointed to a small cushion on a window seat. "Also take that cushion and have it put on the chair of Wa Gee with my compliments."

"Yes, Magistrate. But don't delay long." Taking the cushion, the eunuch was gone.

With that Ni Kee turned back to Mu. "Now, you must think that you have been ill used. But I wanted to get to know the city. I said people would tell a slave more than they would tell a government scribe. How much less would the magistrate hear?"

"Yes, sir, your disguise was most effective."

"Disguise? There was no disguise," Ni Kee said, lifting the chain from his breast. "This is very real. As the Little Fox, I belong to Colonel To Waa Da. As Magistrate Ni Kee, the emperor has also chosen to make me magistrate of Lo Nai. There isn't any conflict between being a magistrate and being a slave. A wise man once told me a king was the slave to his people. But since then, I have learned that any free man who wants to govern well must also be a slave to the needs of the people."

Pointing to the side table, he went on, "We haven't much time, but have another glass of wine and put some cakes in your pocket. I doubt you will get to eat much at dinner this evening and I plan on working you hard."

Lowering his cup from a last drink, Mu saw the magistrate standing before the window, looking out over the city below. Ni Kee turned back to Mu. "I think you should know what I'm asking of you before you agree to work for me. The city will be attacked soon. The emperor's agents have learned that the goblins in the mountains are going to launch an attack as soon as the barley fields are harvested."

Ni Kee turned back to the window and paused to look out before continuing. "They plan to march on the city and take it by storm. The empire can't move enough men, in time, to defend it. To Waa Da's men are the best that could be sent here ahead of the attack and they are too few to hold the city for long. The current garrison was never much more than a night watch. It's being sent down to the next town where there is no garrison."

The magistrate turned back to face Mu. "It will be up to us to defend the city. If you don't want to stay, I will understand. If you do stay, the all I can offer is a hard work and the risk of death."

Mu stood, trying to take in all that he had heard. Before him stood a man younger than himself, wearing both the silken brocade of an imperial magistrate and the iron collar of a slave, an outlander, who had calmly taken on the job of defending a city foreign to him. Mu thought about the city. He had always wanted to get away from here and make his life in the capital. But now, given the choice, he found it wasn't as easy to leave as he'd imagined. Beyond the reluctance to leave was the understanding that deep within the offer was the hope he would stay, the faith that he would stay. Magistrate Ni Kee needed Scribe Mu to stay and Ni Kee wanted Mu to stay.

Mu sat the empty cup on the table. "Magistrate, I will stay."

"Mu, you honor me with your trust."

\*\*\*

As the formal dinner progressed, Mu was delighted to find that the cakes in his pockets were unnecessary. He was able to eat from a small table placed next to the chair he was given behind the magistrate. From there he was able to look out over the crowded hall and observe the faces when Ni Kee took his seat beside To Waa Da. The look of shock on Lwo's face when he recognized Magistrate Ni Kee as the slave of this morning was mirrored in several other faces.

Magistrate Ni Kee or Colonel To Waa Da would turn to Mu from time to time and ask a question, but for the most part he was left to watch and listen. On one side, the colonel spent most of the evening talking to Major Dwoon about old wars and past adventures. On the other side, Ni Kee was talking to Prefect Fan Go. Mu found himself surrounded by war and blood and by music and dance, wondering which was harder to follow. While he knew little of war, from what he heard passing between the magistrate and the prefect, he came to realize he understood even less about dance.

"There was never any doubt," Fan Go was saying. "I knew you would be able to dance beyond yourself. Do you feel ready now to try and move back into yourself?"

"Into myself?" The edge on Ni Kee's voice sounded anxious. "I have to say that I've thought of trying it. But I'm not sure what I should look for and not sure what I would find."

"What you find, Little Fox, will remain hidden if you don't look. You have the strength. Will you have the time?"

At that, Ni Kee gave a chuckle. "Time? I have a three month backlog in the courts left by my late predecessor and a city and countryside to prepare for an invasion, with only four weeks to do it. If I go without sleep entirely, it can't be done. Can we start tomorrow after lunch?"

Sitting behind Ni Kee's chair, Mu looked around him. Lined up against the wall behind him were five of the elves who accompanied the magistrate and Colonel To Waa Da. They stood in their light blue cloaks, their hands resting on the pommels of their thin, curved swords. With their long golden hair and smooth skin, they were almost indistinguishable, one from another. It was only after some time that he realized the middle one was not an elf but a woman, and a striking woman. She was dressed like the elves on either side of her, in loose trousers, with a short tunic under a brown leather cuirass. Having seen her, he found it hard to keep his attention on his duty to Magistrate Ni Kee. During one of the duller speeches, by the head of the cooper's guild, he stole a glance behind him. She was looking straight at him. She smiled. Caught, he quickly turned back to the speaker, not as much to hear as to hide the color he felt rising in his face.

When the feast was over and Mu was following the magistrate and the colonel to their quarters, the guard fell in behind them. Reaching the door of the colonel's suite, Mu was released for the night and told to return an hour after sunrise. When the door closed, two of the elves took positions on either side. Mu had turned to leave when a hand gripped his shoulder. Turning, he found himself looking into the clear blue eyes of the woman in the elven guard.

"You are Ni Kee's new scribe." Her command of the language was good. Though even without the golden hair and blue eyes, there were clearly, signs in the accent that said she was not from the empire.

"We will be working together, so I thought we should meet. I'm Ven, the leader of the elves that follow To Waa Da."

Mu was very conscious of the hand that gripped his shoulder and the nearness of the face in front of him. "I am Mu," he managed to stammer.

"Good. We will have a chance to talk later, but not tonight. You will need to rest for tomorrow. Magistrate Ni Kee has worn out more than one scribe in the past and you will find yourself very busy in the next days." She must have misunderstood his reaction to her as relating to the prospect of working for the magistrate.

She went on to say, "Don't worry, he's not the magistrate all the time. He's good company, when the Little Fox is out. Good night."

She released his shoulder, turned, and walked away. His eyes followed her as she strode down the hall, past the guards at the door. The grins on their faces told him more than he wanted to admit about the look on his own face. He found his hand massaging his shoulder where she had gripped him. He turned and hurried out of the citadel to the familiar safety of the cold room he rented above the bookseller's shop.

Once in his room, he threw himself on his cot and stared up at the ceiling, his thoughts whirling. A slave who was an imperial magistrate. Head scribe to a man who knew the emperor. Long golden hair. Head scribe. A warm, strong hand on his shoulder. The sun was just creeping over the mountains when he woke.

\*\*\*

When Ven came into the main hall of the citadel, she had already been awake for several hours talking to the sentries and checking the horses. When she entered the hall, she found Thord and the Little Fox having a breakfast of barley porridge and apples.

"Sit. Have you eaten?" The Little Fox pointed a spoon covered with gummy porridge at an empty chair across from him.

"I've eaten, but I'll take one of those apples." She pulled the chair back, reached for an apple and sat down.

The Little Fox was in a good mood, she thought. Then, he always seemed happiest when he had something to do and there was plenty here that needed to be done. As she sat, paring the apple with her dirk, Mu the scribe came in and bowed to the Little Fox.

"Not yet, Mu save the bows for the court. I'm not a magistrate while I'm eating breakfast. For now, I'm just the Little Fox. Sit and have something to eat. We have a long day ahead."

Ven watched as Mu, clearly ill at ease, took a chair across from her. Nikki waved to the kitchen and a servant brought out another bowl of porridge.

Ven was amused by Mu. She had listened as he spoke to Nikki at the banquet and was intrigued by the knowledge he possessed. But when he had spoken to her, it was like listening to a child, the way he stumbled over simple things. His long black hair was so different from her people. His eyes were like the elven eyes she knew, but dark, not blue grey. She was also fascinated by his hands. When he wasn't doing something with them, the fingers lay flat, almost open. The other men she knew all had hands that, even in rest, curled to match the memory of the hilt of a sword. She looked down at her own fingers and saw the curve of that same fixed grip. Looking at her hand, she was also aware of the row of calluses that marched from the base of her little finger to the first joint of her first finger; a line that matched the worn spots on the grip of her sword. She could almost envy a life where the pen or brush was more important than the sword or bow. Almost, but not yet.

Soon, there were two competing conversations going. One was between Nikki and Mu, about the state of the courts, and the other was between Thord and herself, about the chances of defending the outer wall of the city. Occasionally, someone would cross the boundary between and offer some thought about the other conversation. This broke down while Mu was explaining to Nikki that a local farmer had brought a suit against his neighbor's goat. Thord was talking about defending the bridge outside the east gate.

Nikki asked, "It's nonsense. How would a goat defend itself?"

Thord looked over and replied, "With a tower and archers."

They both looked at each other and broke out laughing.

When he gained some control of himself, Nikki stood and turned to Mu. "Enough. Let's get out of here before we become as crazy as they are."

Mu rose and followed the Little Fox out the door. Ven watched him as he walked. She noticed that for a man who spent his days at a desk, he still had a sense of grace to his movements. Under the light linen robe, she could see the lines of his body moving as he walked, the soft cloth gliding over the muscles underneath. And his hair, flowing down his back, caught her attention. She was used to elven hair, so fine it looked like a golden mist. But his was black as night, glossy and thick. Even at ten feet, she could see where single strands broke free of the long tail falling from his head. When she turned back to the table, she saw Thord giving her an appraising look.

"And what are you staring at?" her question came sharp, driven by an intensity that surprised her.

"Nothing." This was said with a grin that she found made things even worse. "Let's ride out and look at the walls." He stood up and strode out of the room.

\*\*\*

Mu saw the sun falling below the tops of the mountains. They

199

were in the magistrate's private office on the second floor of the court. The windows looking out to the west and south were open, letting in the afternoon light. The magistrate and he had spent all day at the carved rosewood desk, stopping only for two hours when Ni Kee had left to visit Prefect Fan Go. Turning, he saw Magistrate Ni Kee push the stack of unread papers to the side.

"Mu, I think it's time for dinner. These can wait until tomorrow; they've waited until now. While I get loose of these robes, send everyone home and then come to the dining hall."

"Certainly, Magistrate."

As Mu put the stack of unanswered petitions in the cupboard, he thought on the changes that had hit his life. From the second scribe of a fourth level magistrate, he was now the head scribe to a second level magistrate. He would be able to move out of his tiny room and into an apartment or even a house. He could even hope to marry.

When he finished, he walked across the courtyard of the citadel to the dining hall where the garrison ate its meals. On the way, he tried hard to not stare at the soldiers. The imperial troops were a mix of the previous garrison and the replacements. It was easy to tell the difference, though. The old garrison wore the yellow uniforms he had known his whole life. The soldiers that accompanied Colonel To Waa Da were dressed in yellow too, but with light blue cloaks. There was something else about them that separated the two groups. That difference was harder to place. The new troops seemed more intense about every thing they did. In Mu's imagination, their swagger said, "we have looked death in the eye and laughed." He envied them that, even while he knew it was not something he wanted for himself.

The rest of the troops were something new to Mu: elves. Of course he knew of them, and had read accounts of the different embassies that had journeyed to the lands to the east. But he had never seen any of them. Now there were a hundred in the city. A hundred elves and the woman, Ven.

Ven was something that troubled him more than all the changes that had hit him in the last two days. She was not like any woman he had ever known. She was forceful, far beyond the women he had met.

He had always thought of his mother as such. She had been able to control her household to an extent that belied her quiet voice and downcast eyes. First Mu's father and later, after his father's death, Mu himself had given way to her. The only time he had stood his ground was in the matter of a marriage. But a marriage could only be arranged by the head of the house, and as such Mu had refused to approach the father of the docile young woman his mother had chosen. Even now, Mu feared that if his mother had lived longer, he would have given into her. But that was an old story.

Ven was different. She was neither the pliant woman that was the poet's ideal nor a tigress in disguise. She looked him in the eye when she spoke and said what she thought. Nor did she hide her body in the long gown proper for a woman. He still was thinking of her when he bumped into the half-open door of the dining hall.

Entering the hall, Mu found Ni Kee sitting next to Colonel To Waa Da. At one end of the table was Lieutenant Lii. Across from the colonel was Ven. Mu was not happy when he saw the only other chair at the table was next to Ven. Any hope of moving the chair or pulling up another was crushed when the magistrate pointed to the empty chair.

Ni Kee pushed back from the table and stood up. "Sit, I'll get you some of this pork."

"Sir! You can't!" Mu's protest was cut short by a wave of a hand.

"No trouble. Tonight, I am tired of being a magistrate. It feels good to do something that doesn't require passing a judgment on what's right or wrong or what is best for the empire. I've served wine to kings and cabbage to goblin farmers. Tonight, I'm serving roast pork to a scribe. I'll get you some wine as well."

When he sat down, Mu was very aware of the woman beside him. When she reached across in front of him to take a piece of barley bread, he couldn't but take notice. As she came closer, the scent of her golden hair washed the smells of food from his mind.

The arm reaching in front of him held his attention. The pale lines of scars were drawn across the sun-browned skin. She must have seen him staring.

"That long scar came from a javelin on our northern border. We rode against goblins raiding cattle. I've forgotten where most of the others are from."

Ni Kee came back with a plate piled with meat; in his other hand was a goblet.

"Ven, your wine is low."

Mu saw her place a long-fingered hand over the cup. "Don't bother. It's my watch tonight."

Dinner was pleasant, or it would have been if Mu could have relaxed. But the presence of Ven beside him was constantly on his mind. Whenever he knew she was looking his way, he felt awkward. When he had to speak to her, the words were hard to find.

When the pork was gone, another round of wine was poured.

Mu halted Ni Kee in mid-pour. "Not too much, I have to walk back to my room."

"I've been thinking about that," came the response. "It would be better if you were closer. We will be putting in late nights over the next few weeks and having you nearby may save us both time. But where can we put you?"

Ven spoke up. "There will be an empty room across from mine in the east hall, as soon as the old garrison leaves."

Mu was horrified.

Captain Lii spoke up. "It's next to my room. I like the idea of quiet scribe as a neighbor much better than a loud sergeant. Tomorrow, I'll send some men to move your belongings in the afternoon."

Ni Kee finished filling Mu's glass. "Excellent. It will be good to have you close to the court, Mu."

It was done. He had no choice. "Thank you, Sir," was all that was left to him. Looking at the faces around him, he saw a strange, compressed smile on Ven's face.

***

Mu was at his desk, finishing the final copy of a court decision. Through the door behind him came the sounds of music, played softly, and the thumps of bare feet on the polished wood floor. He was comparing the copy against the rough draft, when pale blue filled the edge of his vision. He raised his eyes to see Ven standing in front of his desk. Her fists were resting on her hips and her eyes scanning the room. She looked down at him.

"He's inside, alone, with the prefect?" Framed as a question, it was more of an accusation.

Mu nodded.

"No guards in the building at all. Anyone could get in here."

She was correct. But Mu had to wonder why anyone would want to enter a building most people tried to avoid, and what she was worried about. He felt her eyes boring into him as if he could correct the lack of guards. But Ni Kee had been adamant. There were to be no extra soldiers in the court. The people had to feel free to talk about problems without the presence of swords.

"You've never carried a sword." Again what could have been a question was not.

Her eyes locked on his hand. He looked down to see his pen rolling from finger to finger. He slipped the pen under his hand.

"Something I do to keep my fingers warm." He didn't mention that he did it when he was nervous and he was always nervous when she was present.

"It doesn't seem cold in here."

What a strange woman! First questions that are statements, and now a statement that's a question. He was still wondering about her when she turned and left.

The next morning, Mu found Ven again in front of him again, this time holding a small bundle. When she laid it on the table, it made a muffled clinking sound.

"If you haven't learned by now, I have to tell you that your magistrate has enemies. He will not take the steps needed to protect himself, so it is up to the rest of us to protect him."

Mu was aware of the way the soldiers all watched Ni Kee. The only time Mu saw him alone, without a soldier nearby, was in the court. Even then he was aware of the guards that stood in front of the building and the guards that lounged in the shadows behind. Mu nodded.

"Good. But I need you to help." As she talked, she began to open the rolled cloth on the desk. When she was finished, she laid out two bundles. One was a very fine yellow brocade sash with two pouches sewn to it. The other was a pile of large carpenter's spikes tied together with a yellow ribbon.

"It's too much to expect you to learn to use a sword, and a knife in untrained hands is more a threat to the holder than anyone else. But you know how to move a pen, so I tried to find something that was close to what you already understood."

Mu's bafflement at the combination of a sash and spikes turned into alarm. The vision of him trying to stab a burly, dagger-wielding assassin with a nail, barely as long as his hand, left him speechless. Ven must have caught the look on his face.

"Don't worry. I can teach you how to throw them in a few days. We will start this afternoon. Now, stand up." She walked around the table and gestured for him to rise. She took the sash and placed the spikes in one of the pouches. She bent at the knees until he found himself looking at the top of her golden head. She began to unfasten his sash. He quickly tried to stop her, but she just batted his hands away and continued. When she had pulled off his old, brown sash, Ven took the new one and reached around his waist to tie it on.

Standing, she stepped back and looked him up and down. If she noticed the color of his face, she didn't mention it. "There, you look good. That old sash was too dull anyway. Now remember to always keep them on the side across from your right hand. When you pull the first one out, your arm will already be in a position to throw. After you've thrown it, your left hand can be holding the rest ready. I'll be back at lunch and we'll see what you can do with them." She gave his sash one more tug to settle it and left him staring at the door as she closed it behind her.

He was still standing, looking at the door when Ni Kee came out of the back room.

"Mu, I need to know more about this case the barley merchants are bringing against the Millers' Guild."

When Mu turned, the magistrate's eyes widened. "That's a new sash. It looks very good on you. You have good taste." With that, it was back to business. But for the rest of the morning, Mu was left thinking about golden hair and arms around him. And he wondered what this afternoon would bring.

When Prefect Fan arrived, Ni Kee told Mu to have lunch. No sooner had the door to the inner office closed than Ven was standing again in front of him. She had a small basket under her arm that smelled of duck and hot barley bread.

"Let's go. If we get an early start, we can have some food as well."

Stepping out the back door of the courts, they were in a small, walled yard. In one corner was one of Lii's men, sitting on a stool. His head was down but Mu clearly saw the bright eyes looking out from the shadow of his helmet. Against a wall leaned a wide plank as tall as a man. Ven placed the basket on a bench, twenty feet from the plank.

"Let's give it a try." She pulled a dirk from where it had been hidden in her boot and, with a flick of her wrist, sent it to stick in the center of the plank. "That's the idea. Now take one of the spikes and try to stick it about chest high."

Mu stood in front of the plank and pulled one of the spikes from his sash. He felt its weight. He rolled it in his fingers as he would his pen and found it heavy but not unfamiliar. Trying to mimic Ven's throw, he sent it at the plank only to find himself jumping sideways to avoid the spike as it bounced back, spinning wildly.

Ven stooped down to pull the spike from where it had embedded itself in the earth. She walked to the wall and began to beat the stones with the tip. Coming back, she held it in front of Mu. He could see the blunted end where there had been a sharp point.

"Now let's try that again."

Later, they sat down to lunch. They shared the duck and talked. He listened to her stories of the elves and told her what he knew of the mountains that surrounded the city. As they ate, he passed her a piece of bread. When she reached for it, their fingers met. He let his hand hold the bread for a moment and felt her fingers against his, delaying just a moment before taking the piece. Maybe these lessons weren't going to be as bad as he thought.

\*\*\*

Prefect Fan picked up his cup and walked to the window. The Fox was staring out and munching on a small cake. Fan came up to stand next to him. Below was the back garden attached to the court building. Not so much a garden as an abandoned garden, overgrown with vines and holding scattered pieces of broken furniture. In it were the scribe Mu and the golden-haired woman, Ven. She was holding Mu's wrist in one hand and had the other hand under his elbow, straightening his arm position. Fan could hear her explaining something about "snapping" his wrist.

The Fox continued to gaze down. "When Ven wants something, she is persistent."

"She is that. The woman is determined to teach Mu how to defend himself, and you."

"Ah, that too."

\*\*\*

Mu came into the magistrate's office to find Ni Kee sitting at the carved desk putting his seal on a letter.

"Here Mu, this may interest you. It is a recommendation to the Capital that Lwo Gong be promoted to scribe, second degree, and transferred to the central administration."

"But Magistrate, I thought you believed Lwo was … was less than ideal as a scribe." Mu found it hard to voice his own thoughts about Lwo.

"Oh, I do. Read the letter and tell me what you think."

Mu read through the letter. It was filled with flowing, round statements expressing how the "good governance of the empire" would be "best served" by a suitable position being found in the capital. As Mu read, he was struck by how little the letter actually said about the qualifications of Lwo. On a second reading, he found that there was no mention of any quality that belonged to Scribe Lwo.

"I think, Magistrate, that if I were to receive this letter I would find some harmless position for this person, where there would be no chance of further promotion. You get rid of a problem and Lwo is happy

205

at being promoted and sent to the capital. I will remember this if ever I'm in the same position. And now, sir, to today's business." With that he began the list of cases before the weekly session of the court.

***

"I need those troops."

The sharp edge in Nikki's voice jolted Thord. They were sitting around a table in the small council chamber with Ven, Mu, Lii and To'a.

"We don't know what the goblins will do when they see we've pulled back into the city. If they try a siege, we will need every sack of barley we can get just to hold out." Nikki's eyes were boring into Thord. "You've explained the risks of a small force being surprised by the full goblin army, far from the city. But how much more is the risk to a hundred unarmed farmers being attacked by a small scouting party?"

Thord had heard Nikki use that tone before, but only aimed at subordinates that were not following through on an order. It came as a surprise that Nikki was using it on him. It was even more of a shock to realize that Nikki, as the district magistrate, was his superior. Magistrate Ni Kee was ordering Colonel To Waa Da to move men away from the walls and that was the end of it.

"As you will, Magistrate. How many men do you want?"

"That's up to you Colonel. Whatever you feel is enough for a rear guard action if the goblins show up in force."

"Fifty should be enough." Thord couldn't keep all of his emotions out of his voice. But he could make his own withdrawal. "You will excuse me. I have to make the arrangements."

He rose and stalked out of the room. He was in the open courtyard before he realized he was holding his breath. He barked at a soldier who approached him and turned up a stair leading to the top of the wall. He charged up the stairs, two steps at a time. At the top, he gave the sentry a look that sent the man scurrying to the far end of the wall. Alone, he stopped and looked out from the battlements. He drew in a deep breath. He needed to get control of himself. What had happened? Magistrate Ni Kee had given him an order. Orders were nothing new; he had taken them for the past two years. But an order from Nikki was new and it brought up something that had lain in the back of his mind for a long time. Thord was afraid. He was afraid of losing Nikki.

From the first time Thord realized he could have Prince Nicolio, he knew it was only in passing. Thord knew he would have to return him. At the time, it hadn't seemed like a great loss. But now things were different. He loved Nikki.

Thord thought back to the first night on their flight from the assassins sent by Nikki's uncle. He had urged Nikki to trust him and Nikki had. He also thought back to the night in the dwarf mountain, when Nikki promised him he would always belong to him. Now it was Thord's turn to trust Nikki.

Thord looked out beyond the walls. Below, the flat fields of mown barley near the city were a reminder of what had just happened. He turned to look inside the citadel. There, his men were drilling, polishing their armor or any of the hundred things soldiers did to fill the time waiting for battle. It was so different from what was outside the walls that he paused. He drew in another breath. The air was clean and crisp. The same mountain air passed over the fields and the courtyard.

Thord always laughed when he saw the confusion in Mu's face as the Little Fox turned into Magistrate Ni Kee. Now he was the one who was feeling the bite of the Little Fox. He smiled. It was funny. The smile turned to a laugh. He was still laughing when he came down from the wall to see about a guard for the farmers up the valley.

***

"Little Fox, bring me more wine!"

Thord's voice jolted Nikki back to the here. In a room where the only sounds were the occasional grunts from Thord and Lii, and the clicking of ivory pieces on the King's Men game board, the words were deafening. With a start, he realized some time had passed since he sat down to read the report before him and he'd not the slightest idea what it said. He rose from his chair, grateful to be freed from the thoughts that were plaguing him, grateful for something to do. But walking to the table he couldn't help picking up where his thoughts had been when Thord broke in on them.

Nikki was upset. Today, he and Thord had fought. It was simple enough. Thord wanted to burn the last few fields of barley instead of harvesting them. He didn't want to stretch his troops out by using them to protect the men and women in the fields. Nikki needed the grain from the upper end of the valley to fill the granaries. Thord was right in saying that dead men didn't need barley, but Nikki knew he was right that, without the grain, the old, the young, and the sick would die, even if spared from the spears of the goblins.

As magistrate for the district, Nikki had no choice but to overrule

Thord in the council chamber. Thord's cold "As you will, Magistrate." had come as a jolt. Nikki couldn't remember ever making a decision against Thord's wishes. In some ways, it frightened him. He found himself moving out from under Thord and the protection he offered. It would have been so easy to accept Thord's will and burn the fields, but Nikki knew he was right. He knew there were risks involved in his choice. If the goblins attacked while the farmers were still in the field, many could die, both the farmers and the soldiers guarding them, soldiers that would be needed on the wall. Nikki knew as well, the loss of the first encounter with the goblins would be a blow to the morale of the men defending the city. But the risk had to be taken; there wasn't enough grain for both the people and the garrison.

Nikki brought the wine pitcher to where Thord and Lii were sitting, and refilled their cups. When he finished putting the pitcher back, he didn't return to his report. He looked at the pile of papers. They reminded him how lonely he felt. Calling for more wine was the first thing Thord had said to him since the council. The first thing he'd said since Nikki had overruled him.

Instead of going back to the desk, Nikki turned and walked back to where Thord sat. He knelt down, resting back on his heels, and leaned his head against Thord's thigh. He could feel the warmth where his cheek pressed the heavy cloth of Thord's tunic. Thord's fingers slid into his hair. Nikki raised his head into that touch. The fingers tightened, pulling back on Nikki's head, raising his face toward Thord. With his other hand, Thord held the goblet to Nikki's lips for him to drink. The taste of the wine was sweet on his tongue.

"It's all right, Little Fox," Thord said when he took the goblet away. "Magistrate Ni Kee has to do what he thinks is best for the people in his charge. It's all right."

The hand eased Nikki's head back on to Thord's thigh.

Nikki relaxed. On the table above him, the game continued. Nikki was aware of it only through the clicking of the tiles and the shuffling of Lii's feet. He watched.

A click was followed by Lii stretching and crossing his feet in front of him, leaning back in his chair. Thord shifted slightly against him, followed by another click of a tile being moved. For a moment, Lii was still. Then, his feet were pulled back to rest on their toes as he leaned forward. Nikki could see his agitation as the toes tapped the floor. Finally, Lii's feet came to rest, flat-footed, under him.

"How can I play a man who refuses to be rational?" Lii said. "I should have had your tower with my bowman. Then you do that. It's that damn luck of yours."

The fingers played with Nikki's hair.

"Yes, it is my Luck."

***

Thord paced down the line of men, Lii walking at his side. The men were lined up, fifty men in a row and four rows deep. They were dressed like soldiers but Thord knew differently. They were militia, not soldiers. Each man held a crossbow and carried a pouch with a dozen bolts sticking out of the top. A round iron helmet and a short sword finished their gear. For the past twenty days, Lii had drilled them with their crossbows. Thord insisted that they be given some training with swords, but that was not because he had any hope they would learn it. Instead, he hoped it would give them enough courage to stand their ground when the battle came. Men who believed they could fight were less likely to run when an enemy came at them. The regular troops would do the fighting. The militia only had to stand back and pour crossbow bolts into the enemy, stand and not run.

Twenty days ago, Thord had walked down this line scowling and berating the men. He had picked several men from the ranks, ordered them to shoot at the targets across the field and insulted them and their mothers when they missed. This time, he praised them on their progress. When he pulled men from the line, he took men who he knew would shoot well. This time, he meant to bolster the men's confidence. There wasn't enough time left to push their training. These men would soon be fighting for their lives and the lives of their families.

***

Only the Dance remained. The ninety-seven hand gestures had vanished, along with the seventeen postures and the twenty-three steps. Now there was only the Dance.

Nikki allowed his focus to open. But this time, he allowed the Dance to open inward. The Dance had burned away the anxiety he had voiced to Fan when they started. He no longer feared what he might find within himself. He danced.

Inside, he found nothing.

He found everything. The void contained the memories of a lifetime.

There were the worries of Magistrate Ni Kee for the people in his charge stretching beyond the Dance in all directions. So too, did the joys of Nikki, the slave. But flowing through all, he found the thread that ran back through time and was the Dance. He saw back through the Dance to the first dance, long ago in the great hall of his father. Again he danced with the unknown juggler. From that dance, he could see a line that stretched forward. A line that was made up of power and love, braided together to form a bond that joined all the rest. Boy, prince, slave, and wizard. All were different and all were the same.

He opened the Dance to the outside to find he no longer danced. The Dance was within him and he had no need to move. He was free to tap into the prince and the slave and the wizard. He could reach the love and the power deep inside and find the boy.

***

It was hot in her room and Ven couldn't sleep. She had thrown open the window, but the narrow slit was better at keeping out arrows than letting in a breeze. Putting on a long robe of light silk, she slipped out, barefoot, to find fresh air and maybe the sleep her body said she needed. She had climbed the steps to the south wall of the fortress and was walking along the parapet. Here the wind off the mountains was cool and sweet, smelling of pine. Above, the sky was clear. The stars stood hard and bright in the mountain air. By the starlight, she could just make out the silhouette of the guard in the tower at the end of the wall.

She stood for a moment, leaning between two merlons, thinking. In the past few weeks she had surprised herself more than once by her reactions to the people around her, especially Mu. The easy relationships between her and the elves she had grown up with didn't apply to him. Even what she felt toward Thord and Nikki didn't explain it. What had started as an amusing flirtation had changed somehow. It had changed in ways she was having a harder time explaining to herself.

The scrape of a shoe on stone brought her around sharply. There, in the faint light, she saw a figure stepping from the deep shadow under the tower.

"Pardon me, Ven," came Mu's voice. "I was too tired to sleep and came up here to walk off some of the fatigue." He started to pass her, moving toward the steps. "I'll leave you alone."

"No need to go. There's enough room on the wall for two sleepless people." Her response came quicker than she had intended. Though often preferring to be alone, she really didn't want him to leave. Now speaking a little slower, she went on, "Please stay."

210

He stopped in front of her on the narrow parapet, his back to the courtyard below. "I want to thank you for taking time to teach me to use the spikes."

In the faint light, she thought she could see a smile. "Oh, it's no problem. You learn quicker than I expected."

"Thank you anyway. I know you do it to help guard the magistrate." Now he was looking down, not meeting her eyes.

"That is why I started, but now I am enjoying working with you." Why had she said that? That wasn't what she meant to say, though it was true. She did find it fun. In the few weeks she had known him, she felt closer to him sometimes than to any of the others. As much as she liked Thord, there was always something about him that kept him distant from her. She liked the Little Fox but the parts of him that were prince and magistrate were always distant. She never could be certain which one she was talking with at any moment. Mu was different. He was always what he seemed to be and never something strange or remote

With a start, she realized she had been woolgathering. Mu was still in front of her, his eyes looking into hers.

"What were you thinking, just now?"

His question shook her. She was surprised by his candor. What could she say? All she could think of was the truth. "I was thinking about you." Now she had said it. What to say next? She could see him looking at her, could see the glint of starlight off his eyes. He was so close she could feel his breath on her cheeks. The smell of the pine slopes was now buried by his scent.

He stepped to her and took her in his arms. His kiss was quick and not very accurate. Letting go, he stepped back. But he missed his footing on the narrow walkway. Arms flailing, he began to fall backwards. Ven grabbed his robe with both hands and pulled him back from the edge. When he at last had firm footing, she could feel his ragged breath as she held him against her breasts.

"I'm sorry. I shouldn't have done that." His eyes were turned away from her.

"You're right. You could have gotten killed."

"That's not what I meant."

She didn't let go her grip on his robe or let him pull away. "Oh. Is this what you meant?" She pulled him even closer and kissed him. Her kiss was slower and far better placed. At some point, she was aware that his arms were around her. When they pulled apart, she saw the silhouette of the tower guard over Mu's shoulder. She couldn't tell if he was facing away or looking straight at them, though she was sure she would know come morning.

\*\*\*

The alarm broke from the lookout posts overlooking the northern arm of the valley. In the still air, the black smoke rose from the ridge to spread in a wide band across the Jade Gate. The attack was beginning.

\*\*\*

In the past weeks, Mu had spent the midday with Ven, practicing with the iron spikes. Ven had been right. The spikes were close enough to the pens that had become part of his life that they quickly became an extension of his hand. As his skill went from missing the plank most throws to leaving the spike embedded in the wood every try, his confidence followed along. Once he could stick a spike in the chalked circle, she had slowly reduced the circle from a hand span to the size of an apple, to smaller than a coin. "A man's eye," she had said.

They were eating in the garden behind the court, no longer overgrown since Ni Kee had had it weeded and replanted. Mu watched as Ven turned her head, taking in the trees and flowers. She inhaled and let out a slow sigh. Mu inhaled as well. The scents of the flowers were mixed with the smell of her leather cuirass and of her hair.

She smiled and turned to him. "This is the time I love the best, the day before going into battle. Knowing it may be the last good time in your life makes it more beautiful, makes it almost sacred. The flowers never smell the same; the food never tastes better, the sky never as blue."

He looked at her. "I can't share your feelings. I understand, but that's all. I only know tomorrow will come and this may all be gone. This garden, you, all could be gone. I wish tomorrow never had to come."

"You're right, of course." She looked at him. "But it will come. We don't have the power to stop it. All we can do is try to do what we can and hope to live through it." She took a sip of the wine beside her.

"I understand, but this is new to me. I don't have your courage. I'm not as sure of myself as you are."

"You have the courage you need. You've just never looked for it." She rose and walked across the garden to the wooden target. She reached down and took a piece of chalk from the ground.

Mu watched as she drew a circle on the chewed wood. This time the circle was again as large as an outspread hand.

She stayed beside the target. "I want to see four spikes in the

212

circle."

Mu stood and reached into his sash. But as he took the spike out, he stopped and stared. Ven still stood next to the target, but she held her left hand, palm out and fingers spread, over the circle. "No. You can't. I won't do it. What if I miss?" His mind balked at the thought of a spike driven through her hand into the wood.

"You won't miss. Four spikes, one between each pair of fingers. You can do it. You need to know you can. Ni Kee will need you tomorrow. I will need you tomorrow." She paused to take a breath. "Now do it."

He had hit smaller targets. He knew that. His right hand trembled as he held the first spike. He forced himself to still his mind. Only the spike. Only the gap between her thumb and first finger. He threw.

He willed his eyes to stay open, to followed the tumbling passage. His breath came out in a deep sigh when he saw the spike jutting from the wood, exactly where he had meant it to go. Looking over, he saw the smile on Ven's face. She didn't say a word as he took up the next spike. This time, his mind cleared more easily. He threw again, to see the iron stuck between her first and second finger.

He looked at the next gap. It was smaller, the second and third fingers unable to open as wide. He felt the weight in his hand. Again he threw. Again the spike stood out between the two fingers.

He looked at the hand on the wood. What he saw left him afraid. The third spike stuck out just above where the last one would need to go. He had not only to hit the narrow wedge formed by her third and small fingers but to not have the turning spike foul the one just above. He would need to change his throw to spin it slower and change angle to make it spin from the side. He felt the weight of the iron and looked again at the distance. He threw.

The sound of the heavy spike sinking into the wood was followed by a shout from Ven. "You did it! I knew you could." She took her hand from between the four spikes and tugged them from where they were buried, deep in the plank. "I never doubted you." She came up and hugged him to her. When his arms went around her, she pulled back just enough to look into his eyes. "I knew you could." Any response from him was smothered by her lips.

She pulled back and released him. "I have to go to the walls. We'll meet at dinner." She laid the spikes on the table and left.

Mu picked up the spikes. He put three of them back into his sash. He sat down looking at the fourth, staring at the streak of blood near the tip.

\*\*\*

Nikki stood on a terrace gazing over the city. Below, the street ran down to the main gate, the shops and houses on either side, shuttered, locked. The only signs of life were the tiny figures of soldiers on the wall above the distant gate. But they were not what drew Nikki's attention. In the far distance, a dark red line snaked out of the gorge. An army of goblins marched on the city. The morning sun sparked from the tips of steel spears. At this distance, the forms of the individual warriors were lost, along with the sounds of stamping feet. What came across the valley was the thunder of beaten bronze. A break in the line held a darker knot of goblins; from it the sound of *power* flowed across the valley to hammer against the cities' walls and defenders. Nikki sought over the fields for the source of that pounding magic. His mind pushed through the waves of power until he could come no closer.

Sixty goblins, dressed in red and bearing poles on their shoulders, carried a platform supporting a great bronze drum. It squatted on four legs: a hoof, a wing, a fin, and a dragon's claw. Around its base marched a frieze of figues, two by two, of the races and beasts of the world. Sacrifices forever going to the furnace where it was cast. Four demon faces watched from the bronze, faces that were more than just bronze. Four priests struck the drum with mallets. Power jumped from the surface with each blow, driving Nikki back.

\*\*\*

Ven turned from the street to where the distant figure of Mu stood on a low terrace beside Nikki. In front of the gate, the road looked like a giant writhing serpent, its scales flashing in the morning sun. But the scales were the shields of hundreds of goblins, forming a roof and walls as their line approached the wall. Jutting from the head was not a dark, forked tongue but the head of a battering ram. Ven watched its approach from the battlement.

On either side, her archers could do little more than watch. Occasionally, an arrow would streak from the walls to find an exposed ankle. When that happened, the shield above would bob as the snake crept forward. Then a gap would appear, to be filled with arrows. A goblin, either dead or wounded, would be pushed out of the body of the snake, and the scales would close in again. The snake kept crawling closer.

Beyond, out of bow shot, a square of goblins stood guard around a platform. On it stood four goblins. Between them was a drum. Each goblin struck the drum in turn.

Boom.

Boom.

Boom.

The sound rolled across the field like thunder. Where Ven stood, she could hear it echoing back from the surrounding mountains. With each crash, the world around her seemed to weaken.

Boom.

Boom.

The stones beneath her feet shook to the pounding. Mixed with the thunder of the drum she could hear the hinges of the gate groaning.

Thord turned to her.

Boom.

"The gate will never" Boom. "hold. Do what" Boom. "you can to slow them." Boom. "I will go down to the" Boom. "men behind the gate." Boom. "We will let" Boom. "them in far enough" Boom. "for you to shoot them" Boom. "from behind." He leapt down the stairs at the back of the gate tower.

Boom.

A townsman took his place beside Ven. She watched as the man heaved a head-sized stone out over the wall. He was already reaching for another when the block struck the back of the serpent. A shiver went through the goblins but the ram kept moving to the gate.

The tongue of the serpent drew back. With a shout, it came forward to strike the wood and iron of the gate.

Boom.

The ram beat against the gate the same instant as the drum beat against the walls. Ven could feel the shudder that came through the stones. The gate couldn't hold long.

From behind her she heard Thord's bellow. "Open the gate!"

Below, the ram swung forward. But instead of the thunder of the beam striking the gate, the ram kept moving. The head of the snake broke apart as the ram's momentum carried it forward into the open gateway.

The solid wall of goblin shields failed as those swinging the ram tripped over each other, carried along with the heavy beam. From both sides and from through the gate, a hail of arrows flew into the ragged line of shields.

Dozens fell. But the rest rushed into the open gate. More fell to archers on the walls as they turned their shields to the open gateway. But they didn't stop.

Ven turned to see the battle in the courtyard behind the gate. There Thord had formed a shield wall ten paces from the gate. Between his men and the gate was a disorganized mob of goblins trying to break through Thord's men.

Ven ordered her archers around to send their arrows into the goblins massed below. Here the goblins were too tightly packed to bring their shields over their heads. Soon goblins were treading on their own dead to get at the line of defenders.

Blood and bodies filling the space before him, Thord held the center of the line. A ripple in the mass of goblins moved straight to Thord. Out of the swarm of goblins came a black-tipped spear. It came at Thord and struck his shield.

Ven saw him go down.

Goblins surged forward at the same time the men on either side of Thord turned to press around him. In the confusion, half a dozen goblins broke through and started to run up the street toward where Ven could see Nikki and Mu with only a couple of guards.

She had to decide. If she turned her archers on the goblins running up the street, Thord might be killed and the battle lost. If she didn't, Mu might be killed. She chose the battle before the gate. If it was lost, all was lost. She bit her lip and sent an arrow into a goblin's back.


*** 


Thord was jolted by the pain in his left hand. The agony ran up his arm, a cold, sharp point cutting through flesh, tendons, and bone. Its black tip, now covered in blood, stood out from where his fingers tried to grasp his shield.

He stepped back from the pain, to slip on blood-soaked cobblestones. His foot came out from under him and he fell.

His jaw clamped shut as a wave of wrenching pain shot through him. His fall pulled the shield and his hand from the tip of the black blade.

Biting his lip against the pain, he gripped his shield with his thumb and one finger as his shield again sprouted a span of sharp-edged black, this time grazing his arm.

Another spear darted past his head. Back up the shaft was the grinning face of a goblin. The face went slack, the barbed and bloody head of an arrow jutting from below its chin.

Thord twisted his shield to the left, exposing his body but clearing the way for his axe. A sideways swing brought the axe head down on the spear shaft.  Half laying on the stones, his swing was short and weak, but the blow broke the shaft.  The spear head shattered like glass, a black splinter cutting Thord's jaw.

The press was gone.  Using the axe handle, Thord levered himself to his feet to stand in a ring of his own men.  Three fingers on his left hand refused to grip his shield.  But the other two held firmly to a handle now covered with blood, his blood.

He crowded forward to take his place in the shield wall.  He was greeted by a blur of goblin spears, goblin shields, goblin faces.  And he was greeted by a cheer from the men around him.

Before him, the goblin attack was faltering.  More and more, the dead were piling up in the space between him and the gate, the work of the swords and spears of the men beside him and of the rain of arrows that still poured down from the elves above the gate.

But the thunder of the great drum still roared, beating back on his men and goading the goblins forward.

*** 

Nikki felt helpless.  He had failed to stop the drum from coming close to the city and now the gate was breeched.  Part of his mind was aware of the men that now fought, replacing wood and iron with flesh and steel.  The rest of him was probing the drum and the power that radiated out from it.

With each blow of the hammers, power poured from the demons held in the bronze, demons trapped in the drum.  Nikki felt the aura of the great magic worked when the drum was cast, capturing the demons in the metal.  He could see them staring out at him from the surface, held inside rings of braided bronze, cast in relief on the sides of the drum.  Each braid was joined by a knot at the bottom.  If he could bring his power on the knot, he could break the spell that held the demons.  He could free them and the destroy the power of the drum.  If he could only bring his own power to the bronze!

Whether the goblins knew what he wanted to do or not, they blocked him.  Each time he drew near, the hammer blows and the power they stirred would drive him back.  As long as the power was focused toward the city, he was helpless to stop them.

Nikki rose above the scene of the battle.  He let himself drift up, looking for something he could use to slip past the drummers.  Up here, he felt the backwash of power.  The waves of force coming out from the drum, and their echoes, produced eddies that were sucked back toward the drum.

From on high, he saw something else, something that moved behind the goblins. Banners! Banners that flowed in the wind. The yellow banners of the emperor's army.

Nikki wasn't the only one to see gold and crimson silk held aloft. A drummer with his back to the city saw it too. His hammer hung over the drumhead for an instant. In that instant, Nikki rode down the wave of sound returning to the drum.

Careful not to become trapped himself, he worked into the bronze knot below the first demon. He felt the bronze soften and yield to his mind. The demon pressed hard against the knot, almost undoing his work. The knot gave.

Eyes full of hate, the demon shot past Nikki to the nearest drummer. The goblin ripped his own flesh trying to pry the demon from his face. Nikki was already weakening the knot of the next demon when the goblin's strangled scream was cut short.

The second goblin drummer fled as the bronze knot bent. Another demon free and a second scream of horror, of pain, of despair. The third demon followed.

With the fourth demon free, Nikki returned to his body, passing over the goblins fleeing from the gate, over the crowd of men dragging the goblin ram inside and pushing the weakened valves of the gate closed.

The sobs of hard-taken breaths filled his ears. His breaths. Another sound was there as well. He looked around him. The first thing he saw were bodies. At the edge of the terrace lay the bodies of his two guards. On the bloody street around them were the crumpled shapes of four goblins.

Halfway between the guards and where he stood, Nikki saw the body of a fifth goblin. At his feet sprawled the body of a sixth, arms wide, one hand still clutching a blood-covered sword. The goblin's face lay on the stones, a black iron spike stuck up from the base of his neck.

Nikki turned to a sound from his left. Kneeling in the dusty stone flags, his head bowed and his hands gripping his thighs, was Mu. The sound was of air pulled through clenched teeth. Nikki ran to crouch in front of him. As he took Mu's shoulders in his hands, Mu's face came up, his eyes meeting Nikki's.

Mu sucked in a deep breath. "Are you all right, Magistrate? Is it over?"

"Yes. It's over."

Pounding of boots on the cobblestones brought Nikki up on his feet. Mu stepped in front of him, a long spike in one hand. But the feet belonged to Ven and a handful of elves, carrying bows with notched arrows. She stopped when she saw them. Her eyes scanned the scene and she lowered her sword until the tip hovered over the ground. With one more look at the bodies strewn on the pavement, she walked to where Nikki stood, with Mu now behind him.

"Is everything well, Magistrate?" She faced Nikki, but he could see her eyes were focused on Mu.

"Yes, Mu killed two goblins who would have killed me."

"Three."

"Three?" Nikki turned back to Mu.

"Three." Ven repeated. Hooking her thumb over her shoulder to the bodies at the edge of the terrace, she went on. "One of those has a spike in his eye."

"Three." Mu whispered.

Ven's eyes locked on Nikki. "Nikki, he's going to be all right but Thord's been hurt. He took a spear in his hand."

Hurt! All right! He's hurt. Nikki's feet began to move without his thinking. He'll be all right. Nikki stopped before the second step.

He had responsibilities. He had thousands in his charge. He couldn't abandon the city for one man.

"I will need to see what harm's been done to the city." Nikki was interrupted by Mu.

"I will do that, Magistrate. You go to him. I'll report to you." There was a force behind Mu's voice that was new to Nikki. Mu was standing straighter than Nikki remembered. "This is as much my job as yours. Go to him, Little Fox."

The Little Fox gave Mu a smile and ran for the city gate, a pair of elves pounding behind him trying to keep up.

***

Mu stood on the edge of the terrace, his arm around Ven's waist, her sword scabbard hanging between them, pressing into his hip. Beyond the walls he could see the emperor's army driving the goblins back toward the mountain gap. The road and the fields were littered with the dark specks marking the dead.

Ven was finishing telling him about the battle at the gate. "I knew you could protect him."

Mu could feel Ven's breath as she spoke.

"I was barely able to protect Magistrate Ni Kee. But you saved the Little Fox. If To Waa Da had died…"

219

"Don't worry. I've never seen anyone with that kind of Luck."

"I think their luck must rub off." He pulled her closer.

***

"The dance is contained within you. Reach inside for the dance. Reach into yourself."

Nikki heard Fan's voice. A voice so far away it could have been an echo of a lesson weeks old. A voice so close, it came more from inside his head than from his ears.

"Move into yourself, then down your arms to your hands. Only there can you bridge the gap."

It was not Nikki's own hands, but the blood-soaked hand resting on them, that gripped his attention. The torn flesh. The splintered bones jutting out.

He reached into himself and found his own blood and followed it down to his fingertips. There he was able to jump across to the blood that covered his hands, Thord's blood.

Nikki looked up into blue eyes. Pain shot through him. The pain that lined those eyes.

"Accept the pain. But don't stop for it. You have to work through it."

Nikki's breath came back, sucked in through clenched teeth.

"Carefully, work the ends of the bones back together. Help the blood wash out the wound. Find any dirt and bring it to the surface."

The pain was almost unbearable. But Nikki bore it. Thord bore it. In his mind Nikki found the grains of sand, the bits of leather, and the splinters of wood. He gently nudged them to the surface, where the blood carried them down onto his own hands and away from the wound.

The bones fit back together like the shards of a broken cup. As each one was complete, he wrapped it in some of his own power. They would heal themselves now.

"Good. Good. Now the tendons. Stretch them back, but gently."

Yes, four of them had been severed. The goblin blade had made clean cuts. He found he had to fray the ends to merge them back. He let the bonds that held them together weaken enough that they would join again. They bulged a little at the join but would stay together.

Then came the veins. They were the easiest. He pushed them into place and they sealed. He gently washed the blood from both their hands.

"Don't close the wound. It will need to drain. Just wrap it in cloth and tie it firmly."

220

Nikki looked back up into Thord's eyes. Much of the pain that had lined them was gone.

"So this is what my Little Fox has been doing these past weeks with Fan." Though strained, Thord's voice came through a faint smile. "You have been forgetting how to dance."

"I always dance for you, Master."

\*\*\*

The hall was crowded and noisy. The food and wine flowed alongside the voices. In one corner, four musicians had given up trying to play over the din and were joining in the feast.

Nikki sat on the emperor's right at the head table. On his own right sat Thord, looking uncomfortable in full dress uniform, his bandaged hand resting on the arm of his chair. On the other side of the emperor sat Colonel Lii.

At their backs hung three banners. In the center was the banner of the emperor. To either side were the banners of Lii and of Thord. Three dragons: the central dragon, the gold of the western sun, clutching a ball in one claw and a sickle in the other. Lii's banner bore a grey dragon holding a wide-bladed spear. Thord's ice blue dragon reared up holding an axe and a plumed helmet. The faces that turned up to those banners glowed with a fire that Nikki shared. Victory.

One face in the throng below caught Nikki's attention: a familiar face sitting at the table set aside for the scribes. Among the scribes in the emperor's retinue was a face he knew. Next to Mu was Bo'a, the emperor's son.

"Your Majesty, I see you brought your own scribes with you."

"Yes, Magistrate Ni Kee. I find it useful for those in positions of authority to have wide experience. Don't you agree?" There was no missing the emperor's smile. "I have another diplomatic mission that I want you to take and I would like to send some scribes to help."

Lii leaned over. "Sire, are you sure you want to do this? They are in retreat, but will they listen to us?"

"Ni's agents are quite sure that certain factions in the goblin lands opposed the attack. They will listen." He turned to look Nikki in the eye. "They will listen to the right voice. Will you do it?"

"Majesty, I have to tell you that I mean to resign. It's time I went home."

"I guessed as much. When I talked to Fan this afternoon, he warned me of the possibility. But in my heart I knew you would be leaving before I set out from the capital." The emperor frowned slightly. "But do this. The main goblin city lies to the north and west. It must be south of your homeland. Even if you stop and get me my treaty, it will be faster than going east and then north the way you came. Besides, Bo'a would be disappointed."

***

For the past ten days, they had passed through a land of high peaks and narrow gorges. Thord shielded his eyes with his hand as he scanned the upper slopes. The column was moving in the shadows of the great mountains at his back, but the snow- and ice-covered peaks stood in the bright sun, throwing the light down onto the trail at his feet. Here the road passed beside a mountain stream. Like the streams that flowed from the glaciers of his homeland, it was milky white with its load of crushed stone.

His men had met no goblins as they moved through the mountains toward the heart of the goblin lands. Whether this was because of the captured goblins he had released to carry word of the embassy, or the emptying of the land during the attack, he didn't know. What he did know was he felt vulnerable this far from support. If the goblins planned treachery, there was little the five hundred men under his command could do but attempt to fight their way back out of the mountains. He could only hope the emperor's contacts in the goblin lands knew what they were saying.

Thord turned in his saddle to see Nikki riding behind him. Beside Nikki rode the emperor's son. Mu was behind them, looking past them and Thord to something in front. Thord turned to see Ven riding fast with two of the elves who had gone ahead to scout. She reined her horse beside Thord. A smile passed between her and Mu before she turned to face Thord.

"You need to ride ahead and see this." To his questioning look, she continued. "There are no troops in front or up any of the side canyons. But you should see what is ahead."

She put her heels into the flanks of her horse and rode ahead. Thord had little choice but to follow. He caught up with her when she stopped at a crest in the trail. What lay beyond took his breath away.

Below them was a valley dotted with lakes and covered with farms. The burnt brown of drought-stricken fields made a sharp contrast to the snow-capped mountains towering around them. In the center stood the chief city of the goblins. Its high stone walls and blue tile roofs echoing the rugged mountains and the azure dome of the sky. Half a dozen towers rose from different places, to loom over the city. The road they were on wound its way down the slope in front of them to cross through the fields and enter a great gate that gleamed in the sun with the same blue as the roofs.

On the road, a party of goblins hurried toward them.

Thord halted the column just before it crossed the ridge. He saw no reason to give away how many, or few, his men were if the goblins didn't already know. With Ven and a dozen men, he rode a little way down the slope to wait for the goblins.

*** 

The air flowing under the tent flaps was cool, even at midday. Nicolio sat on a cushion facing a low table. Across from him a dwarf from a nearby mountain kingdom fidgeted on a similar cushion, trying to find a comfortable position for his short legs. Nicolio pushed a pitcher of the local brew across the table toward the dwarf.

"Thank you, but no," the dwarf said, holding his hand up, palm out. "I'll come to the point. I have word from my kinsmen to the east. They said I would find you here and that I should offer you what help I can."

This brought a slightly raised eyebrow from Nicolio.

With a soft snort, the dwarf went on. "Oh we hear many things. I knew something of you even before Kronnar's message. I also hear a great deal out of Tronmar and none of it is good. The king rules with a bloody fist and his two chief wizards are openly at odds. In the name of crushing treason, lands are seized along with the owners. Everywhere there is talk of rebellion, and where there is such talk, more people disappear. There are rumors of priests being locked out of their temples and of dark things that no one will speak about happening behind those bolted doors."

Turning to look out to the mountains framed by the tent door, he continued. "It's even started to affect the lands this far south. The weather began to change last winter and now the sudden drying or flooding of the streams has destroyed the crops all through the mountains. The goblins are a proud people. They choose war over begging. Something else to lay at the feet of your kinsman."

The dwarf turned back to look hard into Nicolio's eyes. The look was returned.

"To take the throne, you'll have to fight. There is little enough I can do to help you. But I can guide you through the tunnels under the mountain to the southern border of Tronmar. And I can leave you with enough gold to hire a thousand men."

At "a thousand men" Nicolio's jaw started to drop before he caught it. "That is beyond generous, sir."

"No, it is little enough if it can restore peace to the north. I would offer more but it will take more time to raise than I think you will have to spend it." The dwarf rolled to his feet with Nicolio following. "I will take my leave if I may, lord. I will come to you again when you are ready to journey north."

"I don't know how I can repay you for your generosity."

"Win." The dwarf turned and stumped out of the tent.

***

Mu worked the cramps out of his hand while they walked. Being beside Ni Kee during the treaty negotiations was exciting but writing out the notes was hard work. Of course the Prince Bo'a was there, but Mu wanted to be sure everything was written down, and better to write it all twice than to miss something. He glanced back over his shoulder to see the prince, trudging behind him, carrying the heavy wooden writing box on his shoulder. Ahead of him Ni Kee and Grey Dragon Lii walked side by side. Mu was able to catch some of the low conversation that was exchanged. Most of it had to do with how to improve the road between the goblin lands and the empire without compromising security for either side.

Coming to the edge of their camp, they were met by To Waa Da. This produced a round of "Magistrate," "Colonel," and "Colonel." Here in sight of the city, they were quite formal.

Waving a hand toward the tent he shared with To Waa Da, Ni Kee asked Lii if he would like to have dinner with them.

"No, Magistrate. This may be one of the last chances I will have to eat alone with my son. I thank you for the offer, but must decline."

"I understand, Colonel. We will not keep you any longer. We will meet again in the morning, then." As Lii departed, Ni Kee turned back to Mu and the prince. "We can get you to join us, I hope. There is a lot to discuss before tomorrow."

The magistrate turned to Colonel To Waa Da. "Colonel, will your men be ready to move in two days?"

"They will, Magistrate."

"Good. We may have the treaty signed late tomorrow and I would like to leave as soon as possible after that."

"My men can do it."

Standing before the tent door was Ven, speaking to the two elves guarding either side. She reached across and pulled the brocaded tent flap open and held it for To Waa Da and Ni Kee to enter. As Mu walked past her she gave him a private smile, and closed the tent flap once the prince was inside.

In front of him, Ni Kee lifted the red cylindrical hat of a first level magistrate. Mu could hear the sigh as he placed it beside To Waa Da's helmet.

"Finally done. I thought the heads of the two merchant guilds would never decide on whether rock salt would be traded in baskets or bags. But it's done." Ni Kee turned to Mu and Bo'a. "Sit, please. Give me a moment to get out of these robes and I'll see about dinner."

Mu waited for Bo'a to sit before he settled onto a cushion. Behind him, he could hear a sound like leaves in the wind as To Waa Da took off his armor. But his eyes followed Magistrate Ni Kee, as he passed through an opening to disappear into the back of the tent. Mu knew that when he came back, he would be the Little Fox, and not Magistrate Ni Kee. For the hundredth time, he wondered what went on when Ni Kee changed from one to the other. Sometimes, like now, it would happen where Mu wouldn't see it. Other times, it happened before his eyes. In a heart beat, the one was replaced by the other. That was the most jarring.

And then there were the times Ni Kee became the wizard.

Mu turned back to find Prince Bo'a watching him.

"Your Highness." He barely got the last word out of his mouth before a raised hand stopped him.

"Not in this tent. As guests, we need to follow the rules of our hosts. In here there are no ranks or titles." Bo'a tilted his head slightly, still looking at Mu. "You're going to follow him, aren't you."

It wasn't a question. Mu knew he was right. It wasn't a question for either of them.

"Yes."

"Father told me you would. You know that if you stay, you will rise to great rank. The Empire needs men like you." Bo'a turned to look at the empty doorway where Ni Kee had disappeared. "But father says that you are needed elsewhere, as much or even more."

A breath of cool night air at his back told Mu the tent door was opened. He didn't need to turn. The familiar tread of soft elven boots told him that Ven was walking toward him. He turned to look up at her as she stopped beside him. Some part of him knew that To Waa Da took a seat opposite him. But his eyes were locked on the blue eyes in the face leaning over him, now framed by the long golden hair the flowed down on either side. Their smiles met.

The voice of the Little Fox broke in on him. "Ah Ven, you're here, good. Can I pour wine for anyone?" Mu knew this last question was only courtesy. The Little Fox was picking up the ewer from the side table as he asked.

Again Mu felt cool air at his back. But this time it carried the smells of roasted meat and hot barley bread.

The food was laid out and the Little Fox finished pouring wine and knelt beside his master. To Waa Da raised his goblet. "To good friends, always."

When they finished the toast, To Waa Da and Bo'a reached across to the platter full of duck.

For the most part, they talked about trivial things. The Little Fox kept the wine flowing. The table reached the stage of bones and empty plates; the Little Fox was pouring another round of wine. Thord reached across the table to put his hand over Bo'a's goblet.

"No, Nikki. That is enough for a young scribe."

The Little Fox looked at Bo'a and shrugged.

"To Waa Da is right, Little Fox. Father would agree." Bo'a sighed and reached for his water goblet.

The Little Fox continued to pour wine around the table.

The plates were cleared and replaced with a dish of figs when To Waa Da set his goblet down and lightly slapped the table.

Slap slap-slap slap slap. Slap slap-slap slap slap. "Dance, Nikki." Slap slap-slap slap slap.

The Little Fox lifted his head from To Waa Da's shoulder. In a single fluid motion, he came off his knees to stand behind To Waa Da. He stood unsteady for a moment, then drew in a deep breath.

Slap slap-slap slap slap. To Waa Da's hand on the table was echoed now by the Little Fox's hand on his own thigh. He moved to the open side of the table, his back toward Mu and the others. When he turned slowly around, his eyes were half-lidded and he bore a faint smile.

Slap slap-slap slap slap. Mu looked down to see his hand beating out the rhythm on its own, along with three other hands. His eyes were drawn up to where the Little Fox danced. The brown eyes, the smile and the dance engulfed him.

Hands coming together formed the peaks of mountains–the mountains standing to the north.

A hand broke free in a trailing cloud.

An upright arm became a broken cliff with the other hand pulling a waterfall down its stony face.

A spiraling hand rose up the side of the mountain on finger-feathered wings, wheeling on the wind pushing against the rock. The hand floated higher and higher to air that was thin and bitterly cold.

Snow and ice under the sun dazzled the eye until everything turned dim and red.

Wings became a cloud that looked down on hidden valleys and frozen lakes. Drifting north on the wind. One cloud among many.

Pain! Gasping for breath. Mu's eyes saw the Little Fox topple over, his head in his hands. Before he hit the carpet, To Waa Da was there to catch him.

Bo'a snatched the goblet from where To Waa Da had been sitting and sprang up to kneel beside them, spilling a trail of dark red wine in his haste.

Ven stood too, blocking Mu's sight, a dagger in one hand, looking around the tent for the source of the threat.

Mu found himself kneeling, looking into brown eyes, unfocused, distant.

To Waa Da's voice broke the silence. It came soft but compelling. "Little Fox, come back to me. Come back. You are safe." The Little Fox stirred in the great arms that wrapped around him. The eyes drifted back.

"I'm all right, I think." The voice was low and came from some distance.

"Yes, I'm all right." He looked up at To Waa Da with a wan smile. His eye turned toward Ven, where she stood clutching her dagger. "You don't need that. There are no enemies nearby."

Ven lowered her dagger but didn't put it back in its sheath.

Bo'a knelt, holding out the wine cup. "What happened? We were in the mountains. You were in the mountains. Then... What?"

"He's waiting for me." The hand that took the goblet from Bo'a trembled. "I knew he would be but I didn't..." He twisted in To Waa Da's arms and sat up. "Master, can Bo'a have that wine now?"

To Waa Da's shoulders shook with a chuckle that seemed as much relief as anything else. "Yes. He can have his wine. One last round I am thinking."

When the Little Fox climbed to his feet, Mu looked into his eyes.

"I'm all right, Mu." He took a breath. "Yes, all right. You need a glass of wine and I need to pour one."

When they were seated, Nikki came to Mu first, with the wine pitcher. Mu could see the trembling in Nikki's hands as he began to pour. The stream of red wine was broken and wavering. The wine splashed over the side of the cup. Mu raised his hand but Nikki kept pouring.

227

"I'm all right. Just let me pour."

Nikki's hands steadied as he poured. By the time he filled To Waa Da's cup, Nikki was in control again. He sat the pitcher on the table and knelt beside Thord.

Seated and his goblet empty once more, Mu looked across to see the Little Fox leaning his head against To Waa Da's shoulder. He was aware of the long hand that rested on his own thigh. He placed his over hers. When he turned to Ven, he was met by a pair of blue eyes and a slightly crooked smile.

A chuckle came from Bo'a. "Well, that's the sign that I should go to my cold, lonely bed." He rose and bowed to them. "Good night." He laughed again and walked through the tent flap into the night beyond.

Ven squeezed Mu's hand. "Yes, we should go too."

To Waa Da stopped running his fingers through the dark locks laying on his shoulder. "Good night to you." He stood up easing the Little Fox down to the cushion.

Mu and Ven said their final good nights to To Waa Da at the tent door. Looking back, the last thing Mu saw before the tent flap fell back across the doorway, was To Waa Da lifting the sleeping Fox into his arms.

As they walked back to their tent, Mu reached out and pulled Ven closer to his side. The night was colder than he remembered.

*** 

Taulgir sprang to his feet, knocking over the small table with its silver platter and severed tongue. Prince Nicolio had brushed the barrier. He was in the mountains to the south. Taulgir would have to put off seeking the name of the wizard who opposed him from inside Tronmar, at least until later. Now he was focused solely on the prince.

Taulgir rushed out of the room and down the empty hallway to the shrine of the Earth Mother. He stopped in the center of the spiral of black volcanic sand traced out on the floor. From here he sent his mind out on the lines of power that radiated from beneath his feet. He rode the power south but found the wall of his spell blank, empty. Nicolio must have touched it with his power about him. The wall was not strong enough to catch and hold him. Taulgir's chance to take the prince unaware was lost. Now there was no chance of an easy kill.

Taulgir spent some time reinforcing the wall. He wouldn't be able to trap the prince, but he would make sure he knew if the prince crossed over the mountains. He would be ready.

\*\*\*

Ganian put his pen down and rubbed his temples. The characters were already fading from the parchment in front of him.

It was getting harder and harder to move against Taulgir. The man's power was growing with each moon while his own slipped away. But, while he could no longer match Taulgir force against force, he still remained free and was able to interfere with some of his spells. Taulgir was a young man and lacked experience. Ganian might lack the power to meet him head on, but the centuries had given him the subtlety to deflect Taulgir's spells without being caught. That would have to do, until Nicolio arrived. Then let Taulgir beware.

\*\*\*

Vorkki passed under the stone arch leading into the mountain. The golden light that followed him dimmed as he entered the central chamber. Seated on her granite throne, the Earth Mother slept.

He had hoped to find her awake and alert to the danger but hadn't expected it. An age ago, when the Elder People called the gods to this place, it had been to watch over the Children below. Of all the gods, she carried the will of the Elder People closest to her heart. But even she was unable to block the works of the wizard.

Vorkki didn't bother to try and rouse her. She was sated by offerings. He felt her power sinking into the throne and through the stone floor beneath his feet. Most of that power was taking the paths it always took, into rivers and mountains, and flowing through the soil. But he sensed the fraction that was out of place, that part that was being drawn by the mortal wizard. He knew of the blighted crops, the infertile soil that was the result of this shifting of power. Turning, he left. There was nothing he could do. In the domain of the Earth Mother, Chance held no power.

## *Chapter 13*

Captain Borodo twisted his body away from the tree root that was jabbing his side. I'm too old for this, he thought. But with Tronmar ready to ignite in rebellion at the first spark, every possible source for that spark had to be checked. When word had reached his ears that something was happening in the mountains on the southern border, he sent one of his scouts. Eight days passed and the scout had failed to return. Unwilling to send someone else, he came himself. Leaving the mercenary company he commanded four leagues to the north, he had ridden alone to scout the area.

Now he was lying on a ridge, thinly covered with pines, looking down at a village less than half a league away. From this distance, he could see the picketed horses and stacked lances that meant cavalry. By the number of horse, there could be no less than two hundred soldiers. And these were soldiers and not brigands. The order below showed a level of discipline that did not come with bandits. He didn't recognize the pale blue of their cloaks as the uniform of any of country on the Home Sea. Nor could he make out the device on the banner, flying over a building he guessed to be the village inn. He would have known if a troop this large had passed across the Killar border, so they must have crossed the mountains from the south or moved in from western Tronmar.

As he watched, Borodo saw three figures enter the inn. Two were soldiers, the other was clearly a prisoner. Borodo couldn't be sure at this distance, but he thought it could be his missing scout. A few minutes later the prisoner was escorted from the inn to a small building at the edge of the village.

He continued to watch as the sun dipped towards the mountain tops to the west. He was studying the land between him and the village for the best approach route when a twig snapped behind him. He spun to the side, reaching for the hilt of his sword, when he froze. Behind him stood three elves, two with notched arrows pointed at him and the third holding the end of a broken twig in either hand. All three were grinning.

"We are sorry to frighten you, but we couldn't stand here all evening waiting for you to turn around." The elf with the twig spoke the language of Tronmar with the same archaic accent that was found in some of the more remote villages Borodo had visited.

When Borodo glanced back down the hill behind the elves, one of the elves holding a bow said, "Don't worry about your horse. She is already pastured with ours on the east end of the town. Now remove your sword belt."

The first elf dropped the two ends of the broken stick and took Borodo's sword and dagger. As they marched him down to the village below, Borodo was conscious of the stiffness in his right boot that was his dirk.

When they reached the inn, Borodo was able to see the banner clearly. It bore a dragon in the same pale blue as the cloaks of the soldiers. And he was able to see the soldiers. They were not all elves. Half appeared to be men, but with hair as black as the elves' hair was gold. He was led past two men guarding the inn door and into the common room. There he was pushed into a chair at one of the tables. Two elves stood behind him while the third disappeared into a back room. After a few moments, he returned with someone Borodo first took to be another elf. When the fourth person came closer, he realized that it was a young human woman of about twenty. She was dressed much like the elves he had seen, in the same pale blue with a brown cuirass. Rising over her shoulder was the hilt of a long, slender saber, the tip of its scabbard visible, angling out from behind the opposite hip. She took the chair across from him, turned it around and sat astride it with her hands on the chair back. She looked him over with eyes that seemed to miss nothing.

"Why were you spying on us?" Her voice was firm and her manner direct. "We don't like spies."

"What makes you think I was spying?"

"Come now, we caught your scout days ago. Now you come with two hundred men a day's march behind you. We know you are in the pay of the king of Killar and that your company is made of men from Tronmar. What do you plan to do?"

Borodo sat silent. It was clear to him that the woman knew more about him and his movements than he liked. But just how much did she know and what was a company of elves and outlanders doing here at the edge of both Tronmar and Killar?

He decided to play for time–and to play for information. "What our plans are depends on you. The king of Killar is always interested in the movements of armed men on his borders. But he is also interested in hiring mercenaries. If you're looking for work, he will pay well."

"We are not hired swords!" She spat out the words.

The force of the reply caught Borodo off guard. Even brigands would have played along with such an offer, if only to find out if there was a pay chest near at hand. If they were not brigands or mercenaries, what were they doing here?

She rose and nodded to the guards behind him. "Lock him up until the Dragon has time to speak with him." Hands on his shoulders pulled him to his feet and he was taken outside.

Stepping into the street, Borodo's two guards guided him towards the edge of the village. There, among the timber-frame houses and barns, they took him toward a small outbuilding against one of the corrals used to picket the cavalry mounts. Through the wooden fence, he saw a group on the other side of the corral walking in the opposite direction. His heart almost stopped when he saw them. The first was one of the dark haired soldiers. It was the other two who affected him. In front was a tall man with long, blonde hair. Behind him walked a smaller young man in an iron collar. It had been years since he had seen the taller of the two, and then only for a couple of hours. But not a day had passed without Borodo remembering the Floelander, Thord Vorkki's Child. The other he would have known in any crowd -- Nicolio! He covered his shock by pretending to stumble. He didn't want his guards to know that he recognized someone in their camp. All thoughts of why this troop was on the border were pushed from him by the need to reach Nicolio to rescue him from the hands of the Floelander.

One of the elves drew a leather cord from his belt. Borodo was pushed face first against the wall and his hands tied behind his back. A door was opened and Borodo, unceremoniously shoved inside. Before he could get his balance, the door closed, blotting out most of the light. He heard the creak of a hasp and the click of a lock. He rushed to a crack between the door and the frame in time to catch sight of Nicolio and Thord coming into view. They stopped at the end of the corral, just out of earshot. Thord spoke to the third man, who turned, and disappeared behind the fence again. Then the two of them walked down the road to the inn. Borodo watched as the guard at the inn door made a gesture that could only be a salute and the two of them passed into the inn.

Borodo's two guards started to walk away.

Borodo leaned his shoulder against the door, testing the lock. The door shook slightly but held. He expected it to be solid and it was. The testing was for the benefit of the elves, who were still in earshot. He wanted them to know he couldn't get out by forcing the door. Sure enough, one of the elves called back that the door was stouter than he was, and they both walked on.

In the dark interior, Borodo worked to come up with a plan. He had a secret knife. That was to his advantage. Though one knife against two hundred with swords and bows meant that if he was caught, bluff would be of more use than steel. He was locked in a small building on the edge of town. Nicolio was somewhere in the inn, a hundred paces away, an inn with guards on the front door. He would need to break free and then enter the inn unseen. When he was led here, he noticed the houses between the corral and the inn had low walls or fences facing the street. So there was no way he could approach the inn from that side. But, he remembered seeing similar walls and low outbuildings behind the houses, with kitchen gardens beyond. Any sentries would be in the fields, outside the town, to prevent someone entering the village, not to block movement inside the village. His few minutes inside the inn were enough to assure him that the layout inside was going to be similar to any of a hundred inns he had seen in the past. Whether he could find Nicolio once inside was a different matter. This and more raced through his head as the light failed and the shadows merged into blackness.

Borodo sat on the floor and kicked of his boot. He twisted around until he could get his bound hands on the boot and pull out the knife. He cut his own wrist twice before he managed to saw through the leather cords. Once free, he looked around his prison. There was a three-legged stool in one corner. He also found a short piece of firewood beside the door, probably meant as a doorstop. He hefted the wood. Not the best club but better than nothing. Peering out the door, he waited.

Through the crack in the door, he saw one of his guards returning with an earthenware pitcher and a cup. Borodo hurried and sat on the stool with his hands behind his back, holding his club.

Borodo heard the click of the lock and the door opened.

"After Ven's questions, you must be thirsty. I can't untie you but I can give you something to drink." The elf poured something from the pitcher into the cup and turned to set the pitcher on the floor.

Borodo whipped the club from behind his back and struck the elf on the back of the head. A hard smacking sound was followed by a dull thud as the elf toppled to the floor.

The elf was breathing but would be unconscious for a long time. Borodo took the elf's dagger and went to the door. He peered around the door to find the street empty.

Slipping out the door and over the corral fence, he was greeted by the whicker of two horses, two saddled horses. Fast horses ready for dispatch riders. Fortune was with him. Crossing the corral, he was over the other fence and among the beanpoles.

He was able to move fairly easily for the first half of the distance. Then he had to dive behind a chicken coop as a farmer and his son came out and sat behind one of the houses. Both had tankards and they talked in low voices as they sat.

"Papa, I want to do it. I want to join the army and fight for the king. Caelo can handle the farm. There isn't enough land for both of us anyway."

"Son, I don't doubt your courage. But I do doubt your sense. You've not trained for war. You see the men around us. They know their swords like your mother knows her favorite spoon."

"I know I'd have a lot to learn, but I can do it. You talk about the men here, but none of them was born knowing how to fight. Maybe the elves, but not the men."

"Well, we'll talk more tomorrow. But for now, not a word to your mother. She'd get so upset she'd be throwing pans and who knows what."

With that, they both went in and left Borodo with the chickens. *Fight for the king.* He thought. Then these were allies of Marcalo. Nicolio must have kept up the disguise but for how much longer could that hold? If Marcalo saw him, his life would be over. Now it was even more important that he rescue the prince, the true king.

Free to move again, Borodo was soon at the side of the inn. A thick vine leading past an open second floor window was enough to let him inside. There, in a room with a table strewn with papers, he listened at the door. He could hear voices from below. They were climbing the stairs, four of them.

"You say you caught a spy? Do you know whose?" The Floelander!

"Killar is what he claims. But he's from Tronmar." That was the woman who had questioned him.

The footsteps were getting louder. They were coming up the hall! Borodo desperately looked around and found a door leading to a small room with a bathtub. He had only just pulled the door closed, when the squeaking of a door hinge and a crack of candlelight beneath the door to his hiding place announced their arrival.

"I don't like it. There are too many people who know what we're here for. Someone will tell the wrong person and it will be out." This last voice was new. Though the accent was heavier, the voice was quiet and thoughtful.

The grating of chairs being pulled to the table and the rustle of papers being moved was followed by the sound of a platter being placed on the table.

"What does the Little Fox think of this?" Thord again.

"I think the duck will get cold if we keep this up, master." Nicolio's voice!

"Whenever we get too serious, the Little Fox can always bring things back to reality." This was the stranger's voice and it was said with a hint of laughter.

The rattle of plates was followed by a bump and a clang of something hitting the table.

"There goes your wine, Mu." Again Nicolio.

"I'll get a towel." The voice came with the quick tread of feet towards the door to where Borodo was hiding! It was now or never.

Just as the feet reached the door, Borodo shoved it open with all the force he could muster. It hit a body on the other side. He burst into the room to find the stranger, called Mu, sprawling on the floor, Nicolio on the far side of the table, the woman was at the end of the table closest to the door, and the Floelander sitting between Borodo and the table, with his back half turned, looking over his shoulder. Borodo leapt across the room and, grabbing Thord by the tunic, pressed the point of his stolen dagger against Thord's throat. For a moment everything held still. Then...

"Borodo!" Nicolio shouted.

"Release him!" The woman's voice was a strong counter point to the soft hiss as her sword cleared its scabbard.

Scraping sounds from behind him.

"Mu! Don't!" This was constricted by the knife at Thord's windpipe.

"Nobody move or I slit his throat."

"Borodo!" again Nicolio, but with pleading mixed with the surprise.

"Nikki. Wait." Thord held still. "Borodo, you know you can't get clear of here. If you kill me, the elves will hunt you down. There is another way to do this. Do you still play bones?"

Borodo wished the Floelander didn't make perfect sense. He knew he was trapped. His only chance of getting Nicolio away was to do it in secrecy. That being gone, so was any hope. He nodded. "I still have the dice you left me with."

"Then a bet. You win, you take Nikki and are free to leave. I win, and we have a drink and remember another time, but Nikki stays with me. Either way, nobody has to die."

Borodo pulled back the dagger. "A bet." He turned and stepped to the open side of the table. The woman still had her sword drawn and now Borodo could see the man he had knocked to the floor, standing and holding something long and grey in his hand. A heavy nail? Thord stayed seated but turned his chair to face Borodo, the scraping of the chair legs loud in the silence. He could see the end of Thord's axe haft jutting above the table beside Thord's elbow.

"Nikki, make some room to play."

As Nicolio moved the plates and used a napkin on the spilled wine, Borodo fished two worn dice from his pouch. When he set them on the table, he was surprised to see Nicolio and Thord look at them and exchange smiles.

Nicolio grabbed the jug. "This needs more wine."

"It was my roll that won before. You roll first this time." Thord's voice was full and sure.

Borodo took the chair across the table from Thord. As he sat down, Nicolio slid a goblet toward him. He placed another in front of Thord, who took it and held it up.

"Luck."

As he echoed the toast, Borodo heard Nicolio, standing beside the table, whisper, "Luck."

Borodo rolled a nine -- a three and a six. "Three nines, twenty-seven."

The game began.

The dice passed back and forth. At each roll their counts rose. Within three rolls each, they were in range of twenty-seven, with Borodo at twenty-two and Thord at twenty-three.

Borodo held the dice. From behind him, he heard the woman say, "Three coppers he goes over."

The man behind Thord had put away the nail and stood with his arms crossed on his chest. He nodded. "Done."

Borodo rolled a double six for 34, seven over but an easy road back.

The man behind Thord grimaced.

Thord took up the dice and looked at Nicolio standing beside the table.

"Little Fox, give me your Luck."

Borodo wanted to shout, "No, don't do it." But the prince leaned over the table, the chain hanging from his iron collar almost touching the polished wood. He took the hand that held the dice in his own two hands and blew on it. Thord rolled.

Double twos, Lover's Eyes. Twenty-seven.

Borodo's growing sense of loss was all but knocked out of him when he saw Nicolio grab Thord by the head with both hands and kiss him. Then, as his mind reeled at seeing this response from the prince, he was struck a second blow when the prince leapt around the table and

237

hauled him to his feet. The fierce hug he got would have squeezed the breath from him, if he had any breath left.

"Borodo! I knew we would find you. Now this calls for a celebration. I'll get more wine." Borodo was released but the prince was stopped by an upraised hand. The woman blocked his way.

"You stay and talk. I'll see to the wine and another plate as well. I'll have them sent up while I have a word with the guards." This last was said with a voice that could have been Borodo's own if someone had passed his sentries. She walked out and closed the door behind her.

"Oh, that was Ven. But you met earlier." Nicolio turned and wrapped his arms around Borodo again. Nicolio turned to Thord, pulling Borodo with him. "You've met Thord. The man standing behind him is Scribe Mu."

"Don't squeeze the life out him. Let him sit, Nikki. Mu, you too."

Borodo found himself pushed into a chair and the prince topping his goblet from the wine jug. Watching Nicolio move about the table, pouring wine, his mind raced over what to do about the prince. Bet or no bet, he had to get Nicolio away before King Marcalo found him. How he was to do that, given what he had seen pass between the prince and Thord, was far from clear.

When Nicolio was seated, Thord held up his cup. "To Chance meetings."

They drank. Borodo found the prince's eyes were fixed on him. "You look no worse for wear, Borodo." Leaving his eyes on Borodo, the prince turned his head slightly toward Thord. "I told you we would meet him again, Master."

"You did." With a hand rubbing his neck where the tip of Borodo's knife had left a red mark, he went on, "But I didn't expect it to be so pointed a meeting."

There were footsteps, followed by a knock on the door behind Nicolio. Borodo took another sip of wine as Nicolio jumped up and opened the door. Though the door Borodo could see a large balding man in an apron, holding a tray. The man's eyes moved around the room until he looked straight at Borodo, then turned back to Nicolio.

"I brought more wine and a plate for your guest. I also took the liberty of bringing more of the lamb pie, Your Majesty."

Borodo choked on his wine.

Thord pushed a napkin across the table to Borodo. "I am thinking, we have a lot to talk about."

# Chance's Children

## *Chapter 14*

Thord looked down at the map spread on the table. "Four hundred trained men with a hundred leagues and the army of Tronmar between us and the capital. Marcalo will soon know we're here. We can't stay and wait for them to move first. And if we retreat, no one will follow us the next time. We have to move ahead, and soon."

Ven was seated across from him, looking at the map and paring a thumbnail with her dirk. "Not just four hundred. There are ten more recruits, joined from this village."

Thord frowned.

Ven put the dirk on the table. "Give them the honor they deserve. They may not have the training of soldiers yet, but they have the heart."

Thord had seen men with more heart than skill. He'd killed no few of them. "I don't want to lead young boys to their death. Nor do I want to set farmer against farmer."

"If you don't lead them, they'll follow anyway. They hate Marcalo and they love Nikki. Ten men may not be much, but they will grow from every village we pass. Those ten will be a hundred and then a thousand. Nikki?" She turned to where Nikki stood.

"Thord, they have to come. Tronmar is theirs as much as mine. If the people won't join me, then I'm wrong in returning."

He was right and Thord knew it. "They will come. But I don't have to like it."

Borodo spoke up. "There won't be any farmers standing against us. Marcalo can't call up the peasant levies. He won't dare arm them. And there are more than farmer's sons who'll join you." Borodo leaned across the map and tapped his finger near the center. Under his finger was the small drawing of a tower. "There are several garrisons that will come over to you. They may march out under Marcalo's orders, but if we can get word to them that you're alive, Nicki, they'll come over to your side. They're good men and hate the usurper."

This caught Thord's attention. "How many men?"

"Three garrisons I'm sure of, maybe fifteen hundred men. There are another four garrisons that may not join but will find an excuse to stay where they are when Marcalo calls them. I only know of four that will come to stop us. Of those, only one stands between us and the capital. They won't risk a fight alone. They'll fall back to the city and wait for us."

Lii asked, "Can these troops be trusted?"

"The three I know, you can count on. How much trust you can put in any others will depend on how they see our chance of winning."

Ven looked at Borodo. "Your men will be here by tomorrow night." Turning to Thord, she asked, "When do we march?"

Thord looked around at the faces of the group. Ven's was eager to be on the move. The lines of Lii's face showed nothing, but Thord caught the glint in his eyes. Not a warrior, Mu bore the resignation of a man faced with an evil that could not be avoided. Borodo's face was turned toward Nikki, waiting. But Nikki's eyes were focused on something beyond the walls of the room. Thord watched him for a moment before speaking. "We should leave the day after Borodo's company arrives. The sooner we're on the move the better. Nikki?"

Thord saw Nikki's slight frown as he answered. "Maybe. We may wait another day beyond that."

Thord knew Nikki was expecting something to happen. He'd asked what it was, but Nikki would only say he didn't want to spread what might be a vain hope.

Thord leaned his weight on the table. "Then in three days, at the latest, we march north."

\*\*\*

At noon the next day, Borodo's men marched into the town. A table had been set in front of the inn and covered with the best rug the town elders could find. On it, Nicolio stood wearing a yellow tunic and a soldier's blue cloak. He was acutely aware of the weight of the circlet of gold on his brow and of the iron chain hanging from his collar. One step behind him and on his right towered Thord, his armor sparkling like ice in the sunlight. His hands clasped the head of his axe, its haft grounded on the table, between his boots. On Nicolio's left stood Mu in the position of Chief Councilor. He could feel the table move as Mu shifted his weight from foot to foot.

To the left and right of the table stood the ranks of elves and men. Nicolio could make out the figures of Lii and Ven in front of their troops. But of all his 'army,' he was proudest of the ten young men arrayed in front of him. Though their uniforms were hastily thrown together and didn't always fit, he knew all he needed from the way they stood with their backs straight and their heads held high.

The other side of the street was lined with all the men, women, and children from the village and from much of the surrounding countryside. Their mood was festive with gleaming eyes set in smiling faces. Some of the eyes directly across from Nicolio held tears as they looked at the young men standing at attention. But those eyes also shown with pride.

A cheer started at the edge of the village. To his left, Nicolio could see Borodo's cavalry entering the street, two abreast. As they approached the inn, he became aware that they were not leading the column. In front of them marched two small boys with a dog dancing around them. These earned some claps, a few tossed flowers, and a woman's shout from the crowd threatening dire consequences at some future time.

Fifty horse and three times that of foot paraded past Nicolio. As they passed, he studied the faces they wore under iron and leather helmets. Some were the faces of hard-bitten men, regular mercenaries. These came for the pay. There were younger faces among them. The eyes that looked out of those faces were full of hope, eyes burning with the desire to free their homeland. But there were some faces showing a darkness that took Nicolio aback. When these men looked at him, they didn't see a king or a pay master. They saw a path to vengeance for horrible wrongs done to them or to their loved ones. When he looked in their eyes, he was afraid—but not for himself. He feared for what he would find in his country that could have driven these men to such hate.

The last soldier had marched past and the last flower had been thrown. Lii and Ven were dismissing their troops when Nicolio looked up to see the last of the forces of Tronmar enter the town. This was no company of mailed infantry nor squadron of cavalry, but a lone man on a tired horse. Nicolio knew who it was before the face became visible. He leapt from the table into the startled group of recruits and their gathered families. He raced toward the rider with his feet flying over the ground. Behind him he heard the shouts of "Sire" and the pounding of feet, as the recruits tried in vain to catch up to him.

By the time he reached the rider, man and horse were surrounded by a dozen elves. Two were holding the horse's bridle. As Nicolio broke into the circle, one of the elves was asking, "Your name, sir?"

Nicolio answered the question with a shout of joy. "Ganian! You came!"

"Of course I came. You've been expecting me, haven't you?"

"I hoped more than expected. But what is important is you're alive and here." Looking up, Nicolio could see the face he remembered from what seemed a lifetime ago. The eyes still sparkled and the brows still jutted out from above those eyes. The mouth bore the same small smile of a joke just shared but never told. But there was more, the worn look of long struggles.

*\*\*\**

With one hand, Marcalo clutched the arm of the throne. With the other, he gripped the hilt of his sword. "What do you mean, Nicolio is here? Tell me, and your life depends on what you say." He glared down at his former chief wizard.

"Nicolio is here in Tronmar. He is in the south of the country with a force of some five hundred soldiers, and he has started to march north."

"How do you know this?"

"Unlike others, I make it my business to know what happens in your kingdom, Sire."

Marcalo knew Morik meant Taulgir by this "others." He also knew that Morik brought him this information only to strengthen his own position. But all of that was secondary to the news of his nephew. "Tell all you know."

Morik gave a detailed account of Nicolio's recent movements. Marcalo recognized the hints sprinkled throughout of the treachery of Taulgir in allowing Nicolio to enter the kingdom. He knew better than to take those hints at face value. But he also knew that like Morik, Taulgir played his own game for his own reasons. Marcalo leaned the sword against the arm of the throne and took his hand off the hilt as he listened.

"Peasants and townspeople are joining him?"

"Yes, Sire. Your nephew's army grows every day. There are rumors among the garrisons that some of them will go over to him as well."

Yes, Marcalo thought. There are always malcontents willing to jump at the first sign of change. For the past two years he had been forced to deal ruthlessly with such. He would need to be easier on those whose loyalty was less sure. After this crisis was over, he could weed out the traitors. Yes, once Nicolio was dead he would be able to show what came of treason.

Looking up, Marcalo caught sight of Taulgir being let into the throne room unannounced. Marcalo marked the face of the guard that held the door open for the wizard. Another face to watch.

"Majesty, I came as soon as word reached me of your nephew's presence in the country."

Watching the guard pull the door closed behind Taulgir, Marcalo wondered whose ears and tongue brought him the news. "Yes, Taulgir. Morik here was just telling me the news. How did he slip into the country, Taulgir?" Marcalo became aware of the pained look on Morik's face. Sweat was beginning to bead the wizard's forehead.

"He had help from the dwarves in the southern mountains, Majesty."

The strain on Morik became clearer. He filled the pause that followed Taulgir's sentence to say, "I will leave you now if I may, to see what else there is to learn."

"Yes, go now. We will talk later." Marcalo's head ached.

As the older wizard turned and left the room, Marcalo felt the fingers of his right hand itching. He also noticed that Taulgir's right hand was slowing moving where it hung at his side.

"Majesty, I feel we should lure Nicolio closer to the capital. It will be easier to deal with him before the gates of the city than at a distance."

Marcalo didn't need to hear Taulgir to think the same thing. He knew the temper of the army units between here and the south, and knew he would be lucky if they didn't desert to a man. There were loyal troops in the capital and to the north, but he had moved the suspect units south to distance them from him.

"Yes, let him come north." The itch in his hand was gone. Marcalo looked down to see his fingers wrapped around the hilt of the sword. It felt warm with the power that flowed from it into his arm. "Yes, let him come."

\*\*\*

The villa had been beautiful in its day. The main hall was large, with a high, coffered ceiling and tall doors opening onto the veranda. The gardens below showed the signs of thoughtful plantings. But now it had fallen into decay. Weeds grew between the roses, and dust lay thick on the floor and mantelpiece. The smell of mold filled the place. Nicolio remembered the last time he had been here, what seemed like, and may have been, a lifetime ago. Then it had been the country home of Baron Gelo. He had visited it with his father on his twelfth birthday when they came here to pick out a horse for Nicolio. Now the mansion was an empty shell. The remaining servants told him the baron had crossed the new king and his lands were confiscated. They couldn't tell him where the baron and his family were. All the steward could say was they had ridden out hours before Marcalo's soldiers had arrived to arrest them. The man hoped they had escaped.

Looking out, beyond the garden, Nicolio could see his army, Tronmar's army. Their tents were pitched in what had been the horse pasture. They dotted the grass like hundreds of brightly-colored mushrooms. Over a thousand men and nearly a hundred elves walked or rode on that field. Companies of infantry drilled. Even at this distance, he knew which were the regular garrison troops and which were made up of the peasants and tradesmen who had flocked to the dragon banner. The uneven lines of the recruits were a sharp contrast to the hard edges of the regular units.

In the distance horses grazed. The smoke from cook fires rose to scent the air with the smell of sausages and onions, not quite masking the other smells that followed an army. Ten leagues beyond, behind the trees that bordered the field, waited the city of Tronmar.

He had fled and for years lived on the run. Now he was back and loath to go the final distance, to the walls of the city. When he looked out over those who followed him, he saw not just an army but his people. Many of them would die if he made the wrong decisions, and some would die even if he made all the right ones. But traveling the road here, he had seen the consequences of doing nothing.

He listened to the sounds of footsteps behind him. He didn't need to turn to know it was Ganian. The wizard gave off an aura that Nicolio couldn't mistake. "Have the scouts returned?"

"No, Sire, not yet. Even those sent to this side of the city won't be back for some hours, and the ones going north of the city can't possibly make it back until sometime tomorrow. You don't have to give the order to advance today."

"Am I that transparent?"

"Just to those who know you."

Nicolio turned to see the old man smiling at him. He had that smile that is only seen on the old, the smile that is reserved for teachers and grandparents. *I have stood where you stand, feeling alone, and I know now that others were with me then as we are with you now.* Nicolio could only smile back and hope.

The corners of Ganian's smile turned down into a frown. "You know I won't be able to help you much in the coming battle. My time is almost over."

Now it was Nicolio's turn to frown. "Yes, Great Uncle, I guessed as much."

"You guessed that as well, I see."

"It wasn't hard." Nicolio looked into the old man's eyes. "You always reminded me of Father. When I thought about why there were no records of the last third-born prince, I knew someone must have removed them from the palace library. And since you came back, I've felt something that draws us together."

Ganian moved to the window and looked out. "Then you know that my power is passing to you. Soon, most of it will be gone. I can't say I am glad to see it go, but it's not for me to decide. I'm just grateful it's you."

"Will it be enough?" Nicolio stood looking at the old man. "Marcalo's wizards are powerful."

"We won't know that until you confront them. Don't give up hope, just know you won't be alone."

Nicolio turned back to the window. In the distance he could see the tiny figure of Thord standing under the Dragon Banner with a group of officers, watching a group of former farmers standing in open ranks while Lii's heavy cavalry charged at full speed between them from behind to gallop at imaginary enemies. The line didn't waver. Maybe there was hope.

***

The grand dining room had been turned into a council room. The dust had been swept out, and the long table turned and pushed to one end to look down the length of the room. Thord sat with Borodo and Lii on the right and Mu and Ven sat on the left. Nikki sat in the center. Thord looked out at his captains in front of them. Before the table stood the first of the scouts to return. This one had been sent to the fishing villages just south of the city.

"Majesty, there is a fleet drawn up on the shore near the city. I counted fifteen Floelander ships pulled onto the beach. There is a guarded camp in a meadow near to the ships. Sergeant Tomo sent me back to report. He believes the Floelanders are not there as mercenaries for the usurper. Nor are they raiders. There are people moving freely between the camp and the village. Tomo stayed to make contact with them. I watched him enter the camp from a distance. He was stopped at the perimeter by guards. A white-haired man in a blue robe met him and they both went into the center of the camp."

"A white haired man wearing blue? A Law Speaker!" Thord turned to Nikki. "After the butchery in the palace, no one from the Floelands would fight for Marcalo. Fifteen ships is at least six hundred men. That is too many for a raid, and raiders would not travel with a Law

247

Speaker. No, they are here for some other purpose." He looked to the end of the table where the wizard Ganian sat. "Do you know something of this?"

"No more than you. There must be something behind this, but it is not my doing."

Thord turned to see Nikki's half-lidded eyes peering at something beyond the ceiling. His gaze returned to the soldier. "You had a hard ride. Get something to eat and drink, but don't go far in case we need to ask you something again."

"Thank you, Your Majesty." The man bowed and, turning, walked out. At the door, he passed an elf hurrying into the hall.

Nikki turned to face Thord. "We have to know what your countrymen are doing here. Someone must be sent to their camp."

The elf strode straight across to where Nikki sat and stopped in front of the table. "Sire, that won't be needed. Six Floelanders and one of our scouts just entered the villa, riding hard. They are waiting at the door."

Nikki gestured to the guards to let the Floelanders pass. The first man to enter was the scout Tomo. "Sire, I have brought men from the Floelands who would speak with you." He stepped aside and six men strode through the door. Two tall men came in first. One was middle aged and wore a hauberk. He carried a long sword at his side. The other was older and unarmed. Four younger men with hands on sword hilts followed them. They stopped in the center of the room.

The older man took one step forward. Gesturing toward his red-haired companion, he spoke. "I bring you Grimwald Spearbreaker. I am Fellbrand Law Speaker." He looked directly at Nicolio.

"War on the wind, we are come.

"Sword and shield we offer now.

"Fallen guard's kin seek the Fox King."

Fellbrand stopped. In the pause, Nikki stood. "I am the Fox King."

***

Spread on the scarred wooden table was a map of the city. Nicolio studied the thick black line that marked the city wall.

Ven looked at him. "We either have to lay siege and starve the city, or storm the walls."

"I do not like those choices, Fox King." Grimwald looked up from the map. Leaning forward on scarred fists, with his long red braid hanging from his shoulder to brush the map, he went on. "Fifteen years ago, I fought at the siege of Kelwood. More died from the plague, inside and out, than if the city had been stormed and burned. But we don't have enough men to take the walls in a rush." He stood up from the table. His head was a finger's width under the heavy beams of the farmhouse kitchen. "Even were we to take the walls, Marcalo Mad Dog would just pull back into the citadel. We would have the city but still not have him."

Nicolio knew he didn't have the men to invest the city. With the arrival of the Floelanders, he had more men than his uncle, but to close all the roads would thin his men to where an attack at any one point would break them. Borodo had been right when he suggested leaving the north and west roads open. By threes and tens, soldiers had been deserting Marcalo for the past two nights. Not enough to weaken him but enough that the subsequent executions reduced morale inside the city.

"Can we bribe a gate, Sire?" Mu said from behind him.

Thord gave Nicolio's answer before Nicolio could open his mouth. "I would not trust anyone in the city. It would be an easy trap to lay."

"We can't wait them out and we can't force the walls." Ven's frustration was clear in her voice. "Are there no secret passages? No ways into the palace that you learned as a child?"

Nicolio looked across the table at Ven. "There are a few. But my uncle is the one who showed them to me."

Nicolio chanced to look up. On the top of a cupboard, among earthenware pitchers and copper pots, a dried starfish leaned against the wall, a child's trophy from a day at the sea. He smiled, remembering peaceful times playing in the sea below the palace. He had once found a starfish just like this one. It disappeared and he had always blamed one of the maids.

The smile froze on his face. The memory came to him of where he found that starfish. It was hot and he was swimming in the basin behind the palace water gate. The guards wouldn't let him pass through the water gate to play in the bay and he was swimming near the culvert at the other end. Diving, he found that one of the bronze bars that blocked the culvert was bent and broken, damage from some storm. The gap was large enough for him to easily pass through. Beyond the mouth of the culvert was the perfect starfish, waiting for him to pick it from the rocks. No one else swam there. If there was a secret way into the palace, it was between those bars.

## *Chapter 15*

Borodo stood watching the walls. His feet were sinking in the rain-soaked field. Around him hundreds of men were busy moving ladders and setting up mantelets. They were in bow shot of the wall, but the defenders did little to hamper his men's efforts. The noise was impossible to hide, nor did he want it hidden.

Through the early morning rain and drizzle, he was watching for a sign.

Above the walls, occasional flashes of light appeared. They came and went faster than he could turn his eyes to see them, but they were there, like the flashes on the margins of sight when the mind was wandering–only these were real. They were comforting. They meant that in the tent behind him, the wizard Ganian was still holding the usurper's wizard at bay.

"I wish I could be with them."

Borodo didn't turn at the sound of Mu's voice. "We are needed where we are." He understood Mu's complaint. He, too, wished to be with the king. But someone was needed to draw the enemy to the outer wall. And that someone was him. And if the plan worked, someone would be needed to take charge of the city behind them, and that someone was Mu. They were stuck. His jaw twitched as he forced his teeth to stop grinding.

He still waited for a sign. A sign to attack.

*** 

After the cold rain, the sea water was warm. Ven swam in short quiet strokes, pushing the bundle of reeds tied around her sword scabbard in front of her. The throwing knives in her belt pulled down on her. To either side and behind her swam two elves and three Floelanders. In front of her the seawall of the palace loomed, behind them the long ships were already lost in the misty rain.

There was no alarm from above.

She reached the opening in the wall. In the shadow beneath it, the green of the bronze bars looked almost black. Handing her sword to an elf, she pulled herself down along the third of the thick bars. There, well down, two of the bars were broken. They bent inward, beaten in by some storm-driven log. She slipped through the opening to surface on the inside. One by one, the others followed her through the grate.

Ven stopped at the far end of the culvert. From here she could look back down the quay to the main gate. She could barely make out the figure of a guard, huddled under the gate's overhanging arch. On the far side of the gate, yellow light streamed out from the open door of the gate tower.

She motioned the others to swim along the sides to the low landing below the gate tower. She pulled herself out of the water and hugged the wall to keep out of sight of the guard. Creeping closer, she could hear the guard talking to someone.

"Come on, Sergeant, how about giving me a break? It's cold out here."

The answer came from inside the door. "What are you complaining about, Mendo? Would you rather be on the walls waiting for an elven arrow in your gut? Shut up and keep watch out the gate."

When Ven came to the edge of the gate, she saw the guard peering out through the heavy bars of the portcullis toward the harbor. His spear leaned against the wall, his helmet beside it. She waited until the first of the elves was crouched on the landing below a flight of stone stairs leading up to the tower.

Hefting one of the knives from her belt, she waited until the guard turned further away from her. With a snap, she sent the dagger spinning across the gap. It sank to the cross piece in the guard's throat. He spun around toward her and clutched at the hilt. With a gurgling sound, he fell to his knees and toppled to the flagstones.

The first elf was against the wall behind the tower door and the others were dragging themselves from the water when a voice came from the tower.

"Mendo, quit the racket. Mendo?" A head appeared poking out from the door, turned toward the gate. Before the man had time to see the slumped body of the guard, from behind, an elven dagger cut his throat.

Ven raced to the gate and drew back the heavy bar that locked it in place. She swung out onto the bars of the gate and began climbing across its face to the far side. There one of the Floelanders was pulling back the other bar.

They raced to the tower. Inside, two of the Floelanders were already standing beside the windlass. When the third joined them, Ven nodded and they began turning the drum, taking up the slack on the chain. With a screech, the portcullis began to move up, into the wall.

A voice called down from the wall. "What's going on? Nobody told me about opening the gate. Sergeant?"

With her head out the door, Ven could see the silhouette of a man looking down from the parapet.

"Sergeant?" The head pulled back. From the wall a voice shouted. "Attack! Spies at the water gate! Guards!"

Now that the alarm was raised, the elf beside Ven raised a small hunting horn. Two short notes followed by a long blast. Over the groaning of the gate as it inched its way up, and the creaking of the windlass and the chain, she heard answering horns coming out of the mist.

Ven slammed the door shut. Throwing the bolt, she drew her sword and waited.

\*\*\*

Thord stood in the prow of the lead ship, one foot on the rail and his left hand bracing himself on the carved dragon figurehead. Water ran off his helmet and down his face. In front of him, the grey rain blotted out all sight.

A horn! The signal!

Turning back to the men behind him, he shouted, "Row!" From a dozen ships, horns rang out in answer to the lone horn before them. Oars struck the sea, followed by a sucking, gurgling sound as they tore through the water.

Ahead now he began to see the dark mass of the wall.

Closer. He could make out the gate. It was half drawn, a dozen men clung to it, weighting it down, keeping it from being opened more.

"Archers." Thord's order was late. As it came from his throat, arrows were flying past his ears. Cries and splashes told of the falling men. The gate rose further.

The ship's prow pushed into the open gate. The mast fouled with the wall. Thord and the first of his men were on the quay and charging into the knoy of Marcalo's soldiers beating against the tower door.

Thord's axe came down on the shield of the first of the guards. When it came up again, an arc of blood streamed out from its edge.

A heavy broad sword came out of the melee to bury its edge deep in the rim of Thord's shield. Flinging the shield away, Thord took the axe in both hands and killed the swordsman. When the second man went down, the door of the tower burst open and Ven's long blade lashed out to kill the man before it.

The guards turned to flee, only to be dropped by arrows before they could make the foot of the long stair leading up to the palace above.

Behind him, Thord heard Nikki's voice. "Up the stairs! We have to get on top before more men show up."

The rumble of feet running on wood. More men were pouring through the gate now, emptying the ships tying up to the one wedged in the gate.

Once above the quay, Thord stood with Nikki, Ven, and fifty picked men. Grimwald set off with four hundred Floelanders to secure the palace gates before troops could be called back from the outer walls. Thord saw some of the men raise their swords in salute as they passed piles of fire blackened stone, all that marked the ruins of the Floelander barracks.

"Now, let us hunt." He turned toward the palace. "Which way, Little Fox?"

"They are waiting in the throne room."

"I am thinking, they should not have to wait long."

A half dozen Floelanders, all former guards who knew the palace, ran in front of them.

***

Taulgir stood on the dais. At his feet knelt the blank-eyed guard who had brought the news of the attack. Taulgir's left hand gripped the man's curly brown hair. In his right hand, he clutched the ivory handle of a dagger. The grey surface of the flint blade already carried pockets of fresh blood.

He looked down at the knife. Taulgir regretted breaking off the ceremony he had been performing. It was incomplete. He had had to leave the bound sacrifice still flopping on the dungeon floor. No matter, it was better this way. Once he dealt with Nicolio and this lot, he could take his time with finding and killing Morik.

Taulgir looked past the man at his feet, to where the king stood on the lowest step of the dais. Looking at Marcalo's back, Taulgir wondered again just how much control he had over the king. Marcalo had a strong will. But with the war god's sword in his hand and the earth goddess' shield on his arm, Marcalo was bound to Taulgir's will enough for the moment. After the battle, it might be time to dispose of the king. His usefulness as king at an end, it would be time to work some of the spells that called for royal blood.

Now, Marcalo was needed here.

The sound of shouts and the ring of steel beyond the closed doors of the throne room heralded the arrival of the prince and his men. Taulgir waited. Who knows, he thought. One of the buffoons might get lucky and kill the prince without his interfering.

The door burst open. Four long-haired barbarians charged through the doorway carrying bloodied swords.

One elder Word. The flint knife plowed a bloody furrow down the arm of the guard at his feet. The scream of his victim was echoed from the front of the hall. Four lifeless bodies struck the polished stone floor.

Two more figures ran into the room. One was another barbarian. The other was the prince.

Jabbing the blade into the helpless guard's arm, a second Word slammed the doors shut behind them. The only sound now was the faint hammering of sword pommels on the thick panels of the door.

A thrust deep into the man's shoulder sent a red wave of power across the throne room. It was met by a warding gesture and a stamped foot. The wave broke around the two men.

"Good." Taulgir looked down to the prince. "You put up a fight. But you can't win. I have the power of the gods to draw from. In the end, your life is mine."

The big barbarian beside the prince took a step further into the room. The ice blue scales of his armor sparkled in the torch light. "If you had that power, I am thinking, we would not be here." He gripped an axe in his two hands. Taulgir could feel the power boiling off the steel head and washing through the hall.

"Kill the barbarian!" he screamed at the king. "What are you waiting for? Kill him!"

The edges of the sword and the axe picked up the torch light and threw it back into to room as red sparks. Taulgir didn't need to waste his power to know the axe was god forged. Once he had it in his possession he would study it. Now he had to deal with the prince. He stooped to plunge the knife into the slumping guard's left arm, sending a twisting line of fire across the room, only to have it extinguished before it reached the prince.

A god's axe. If he wanted help from Marcalo with Nicolio, he would need to push the odds in the king's favor.

With the hand locked in the guard's hair, he twisted the man's face in the direction where the barbarian stood. A Word. A quick slash on the face. An eye, across the nose to the other eye. A black mist formed around the barbarian's face. Now let the barbarian fight what he can't see.

Taulgir turned back just in time to beat off an attack that would have splintered the bones in his arms.

\*\*\*

Blind! He couldn't see. Thord stopped, trying to remember where Marcalo was, where Nikki was. He turned his head from side to side, but there was nothing. Was everyone blind?

"What? Barbarian. Can't see me?" Marcalo's voice came out of the blackness, in front and to the left. The voice stopped, but the sound of boots on the stone told of Marcalo moving directly towards him.

On his right he could hear the sound of Nikki's feet and the rustle of his tunic. He moved further to the left to give himself more room. The sound of the boots shifted direction.

"Don't worry about the blackness. Where you're going you'll get used to it."

Thord pushed away the other sounds in the hall -- the wizard, Nikki. He drew in the sound in front of him. The voice, the tread of boots, the rustle of cloth, and the creak of the leather grip on the shield. He listened for the sound of a long blade passing through the air.

He was afraid. Fear lay on him as heavily as it ever had. He could feel death in the air. He took the fear into himself and let it heighten his senses. He could hear Marcalo move toward him.

Thord grinned. Moving in front of Marcalo came the smell of perfume. At least he would always know how close Marcalo was to him.

Just in front of him now, Thord heard the sound of the left boot twisting on its heel. The creak of the leather shield grip moved from in front of Marcalo to his left, and the sound of the sword cutting the air, sweeping in high, towards Thord's head.

Thord stepped back with his left foot. Sliding his right hand up the haft of his axe, he blocked the descending blade. The edge cut into the wood, but it stopped.

He heaved against the pressure of the blade and pushed Marcalo back.

Feeling the blade withdrawn, Thord thrust the axe head in the direction of a sharp breath. The tip of the axe head penetrated something and fouled for an instant before breaking free again.

Thord stepped back as the sword whistled through the air where he had stood.

"Wizard! You lied to me!" The bellow came from ten feet in front of him now. "You told me your magic would protect me."

From further in front of him came a strained answer. "Kill him, you fool! I don't have time to help someone who can't even kill a blind man."

Footsteps coming at him. There was no sound from the sword. A thrust.

Thord stepped forward to the right and swung with all his might. He felt pain lance up his left side at the same time he felt the axe head strike hard against Marcalo's shield. The room echoed with the sound of rent steel, splintered wood, and a muffled snap. Thord clamped his teeth against the pain.

"Gods!" Marcalo's feet staggered back. Now there was pain in the voice, pain laced with fear.

Thord heard the clatter of the shield as it hit the floor.

The blackness was giving way to a grey haze. In it Thord could see the outline of Marcalo on one knee, supporting himself with his sword tip down on the polished stone floor. Blood pulsed from his severed left arm.

***

The iron collar burned at Nikki's throat. Each time he blocked the wizard's attack, it grew hotter. Taulgir was powerful. Nikki couldn't deny it. His attacks were swift and subtle. It was all Nikki could do to fend of the thrusts of power that crashed over him. He waited for a chance to strike back.

He had tried several times to beat down the wizard. But each time, he wasn't fast enough or powerful enough.

But time was on his side now. The life force was leaking out of Taulgir's victim. Soon, the man would die and there would be an end to the blood magic.

Nikki knew it. So did the wizard. That made him all the more dangerous.

Nikki danced inside and out now. The outer dance was working a wall between him and Taulgir, the inner dance probing.

There was a hint of something outside of the struggle with the wizard. There was some other power at work. Weaker, wounded but there.

A cry of pain brought Nikki's mind to where Thord fought. Marcalo was down; Thord stood over him with the axe raised.

A Word. Nikki knew at once his mistake. He turned to see Taulgir draw the knife across the throat of the man at his feet. Red blood welled up from the slash.

A wave of power engulfed him. Nikki felt himself falling to his knees. Live! he willed himself.

But there was more going on. On the dais, Taulgir was staring down at the man, now gripping the wizard's legs.

There it was again, the other force.

"How dare you interfere with me, Morik!" Taulgir plunged the flint knife into the guard's chest. Again and again. "Die, you fool. You can't stop me."

Nikki began to rise.

A Word. Taulgir threw the dagger. Not at Nikki but at Marcalo.

The blade turned over and over in the air. A black wave followed it out from Taulgir. A wave of death.

Inches from Marcalo's back, the blade was blocked by a swing of Thord's axe. The stone blade shattered.

Without the blood needed to complete the spell, the wave stopped. Nikki could feel it ebb back toward the dais.

"No!" Not a command but rather a wail of fear and despair came from Taulgir as the blackness coalesced around him.

Blood magic called for blood, if not the blood of a king, then the blood of the wizard who called it forth. Taulgir collapsed on to the stone, his body twisted and distorted.

Looking at Thord, Nikki saw Marcalo topple over into a wide pool of red. There was nothing to be done. The last drops of his uncle's life left through the severed shield arm. The crown on his head rolled off to lie in the center of a sea of red.

Thord stepped away from the body and, pressing a hand to the wound in his side, reached down for the crown.

"No. Leave it." Nikki straightened up. "It has been part of too much evil." He brought his mind to the flagstone beneath the crown and softened it. The crown sank into the floor leaving a ring in the blood where it had lain.

A sound that had grown in Nikki's mind now broke in, along with the door. Three men holding a heavy bench burst into the hall. Ven and her drawn sword were right behind them.

She stopped and looked around at the bodies and at Thord and Nikki.

Turning to the men with the bench, she berated them. "I told you to hurry or we'd miss the fun, and now it's over."

At the word "over" a cheer rang from the men in the hall. It was taken up by other voices outside. A cheer that would spread.

***

"Are you happy with the outcome?"

Chance turned from the balcony to face War. "It ended well. And you? Your warrior king is dead."

Red hair blown back by the wind, Arjel leaned over the balustrade. "He was no loss. When he chose to attack a blind man, he proved he had no honor. I withdrew from him then." War turned to look at Chance. "But you did well. Your young wizard was strong enough and I am growing fond of the warrior. He shows more honor than is usual among mortals."

"Yes, he is an interesting man. Do you regret the loss of the other wizard?"

War turned back to look down on the palace below. "It was good to feel the old rituals again. But it wasn't the same."

Chance looked out over the clouds, into the blue distance. "Yes, it wasn't the same. When the last of the Elder People called us to this place it was different. They brought us to watch over the Children when they knew their own end was coming. They called on us not for themselves but for others."

"It did feel good, though, to hear the old words. It was too bad that the wizard got the most important word wrong." War continued to watch the Children below. "He mistook sacrifice for offering. The Elder People sacrificed themselves. All he did was offer others."

"He read what he wanted to read." Chance turned away from the scene below. "Are you interested in a new game?"

"The same dice?"

"Maybe."

## *Epilogue*

King Nicolio and High Marshal Thord Thurgoodson were riding through the hills west of the capital, they and fifty guards, grooms, and assorted lackeys. They were passing through a stand of dark dense pines, the road little more than a rutted track. The sunlight broke through the pine boughs to throw irregular patches of gold on the forest floor. The air between the trees barely moved; the only sounds were those of hooves on hard earth and the creak of saddle leather. Nicolio pulled in a long breath full of the smell of pine needles.

After months trapped in the palace, putting back together the pieces of a kingdom nearly destroyed by misrule, Nicolio had jumped at the chance when Thord suggested a ride outside of the city. Despite protests from members of his council that the kingdom would collapse if he was gone for more than an hour, they had been riding all morning and not found rebellion in the villages nor seen a column of smoke rising from the capital behind them. Now, with the city hidden by the trees, he felt some of the weight of kingship falling from his shoulders. He looked across at Thord, riding beside him, and smiled. They hadn't spoken since passing through the Gate of the Vineyards. At first they were riding too hard, putting distance behind them, and later there had been no need to speak; they each knew what was passing through the other's mind. They had been through so much together. They had survived attacks by wizards and assassins, by demons and ogres but yesterday they came face to face with the threat of a royal marriage, and there was no escape in sight.

The council was adamant. "The king must produce heirs."

What made the problem worse was knowing they were right. Nicolio knew it. Thord knew it. There was no way around the fact that the throne of Tronmar had to have an heir and there was no one close enough to the royal line to produce one. King Nicolio had to marry, whatever Nikki thought about it.

Ahead of them, the four elves in the vanguard sat their horses in the light at the edge of a glade. They were all looking to the right waiting for Nicolio and Thord to reach them. When Nicolio came out of the trees, he could see against the forest a smithy with smoke rising from its chimney, and two figures standing in front of the broad, open doors. One of the elves had dismounted as Thord and Nicolio rode up, and took the reins of their horses. He looked up at Nicolio and nodded his head in the direction of the smith.

Thord gave an short laugh. When Nicolio looked across at him,

Thord turned back to him and said, "Little Fox, I am thinking someone wants to see us. We wouldn't want to keep him waiting." He swung a leg over his horse and slid to the ground. By the time Nicolio had dismounted, Thord had pulled his axe from its loop on his saddle and slipped it through his belt. "Come, Little Fox." He took Nicolio's hand and led him up the path toward the waiting pair.

As they approached, Nicolio studied the two who stood beside the anvil at the front of the smithy. One was a tall man, well built, with raven hair. He wore only a leather apron over black trousers and boots. His arms were crossed on his broad chest. He smiled through a thick black beard. The other was a youth in a short red tunic. His hair stuck out from his head like a brush dipped in red paint. Nicolio thought he knew him from some place but couldn't think where.

"Good day to you, Thord Thurgoodson. I see you found someone to fix that axe."

*Fix that axe!* Nicolio thought. Then it hit him where he had seen the youth before. "Red?" The name fell out of his mouth.

The young man cocked his head and grinned. "Nikki, I told you Luck rode with you."

Thord slid the axe from his belt and extended the haft toward the smith. "You've come for this?"

"Not really. I'll take it if you don't want it but you may have need of it still."

Thord pulled the axe back. "I'll keep it then. Though, I am thinking it won't be called for, the way things are now."

"Oh, that may change." The smith turned to Nicolio. "Nicolio, do you still find the collar weighs on you?" He pointed to the anvil beside him. Laying across the top was a heavy hammer. Beside it, its edge gleaming in the sunlight, waited a chisel. "If you want, I can remove it."

"No, Lord." Nicolio glanced over to Thord. "I'll keep the collar. I've found the crown to be much heavier. You could remove the collar but still I would not be free."

Vorkki raised his eyebrows, the corner of his mouth curled up. "Is it so hard to be a king? Is there no pleasure in ruling well?"

"Lord, it's not ruling that I find so hard. It's being ruled. As a slave, I had one master. Now I have thousands, all wanting to control some part of my life. My council has all but demanded that I marry and each member has a favorite candidate. As king, I have little say in *whom* I marry and none at all in *if* I marry. The kingdom needs heirs and I am the only one who can produce them." He felt the weight of Thord's arm on his shoulder and look up into the blue eyes. For a moment, he was lost again in the depths of those eyes. Vorkki's voice called him back.

"Yes, kingdoms must have heirs. It's too bad that there is no one close enough to you. The treachery of your uncle has left you without brothers to rule the kingdom. Only your uncle's daughter could take the burden from you if..." The god let the words trail away into a sigh.

The weight of Thord's arm was lifted from him. "Little Fox, what is this about your uncle having a daughter? I have never heard of any family of his in these last months."

Nicolio thought back to when he was five or six. As any child would, he had asked his uncle if he had a wife. The strange look in Marcalo's eyes had frightened him, and he had run to his father. He remembered the sad look on his father's face. He was told never to mention either his uncle's wife or daughter. Only later had he heard the story from his brother, Danalo.

"My uncle lost his only daughter a few years before I was born. His wife came into the nursery one morning to find a baby rabbit in the crib. She never recovered from the shock and died a few months later. None of the wizards my uncle hired could turn the rabbit back into his child."

Nicolio had always found the story sad, but he didn't expect Thord's response. The Floelander gave a little snort. This led to a chuckle and then to laughter, an uncontrollable laughter that rang in his head. But Thord wasn't laughing alone, Nicolio was almost deafened by the sound of Vorkki's laughter washing over him in great waves. He turned to find an open meadow. There was no sign of the gods beyond the laughter still ringing in his head. He looked back at Thord.

"I don't understand. What is happening?"

Thord pulled in a great gasp of air, tears ran down his cheeks. He grabbed Nicolio and pulled him to his chest. Thord finally managed to say the word "Ven." Nicolio looked up into his face. "Ven," Thord repeated. "Ven the Changeling was stolen from a noble house and a rabbit was left in her place. Ven is your cousin! She's already carrying Mu's child, an heir. You are free!"

www.ingramcontent.com/pod-product-compliance
Lightning Source LLC
Chambersburg PA
CBHW021520240626
47154CB00002B/712